THE BEES

Born into the lowest class of her society, Flora 717 is deemed fit only to clean her orchard hive. Yet Flora has talents that are not typical of her kin. And while mutant bees are usually instantly destroyed, Flora is reassigned to feed the newborns before becoming a forager, collecting nectar and pollen on the wing. Before long, she finds her way into the Queen's inner sanctum, learning secrets both sublime and ominous. Flora's ascent disturbs the natural hierarchy of the colony, incensing powerful enemies. But when she feels compelled to break the most sacred law of all, her instincts are overwhelmed by love, as all-consuming as it is forbidden.

THE BEES

LALINE PAULL

ISIS
LARGE
PRINT

First published in Great Britain 2014
by
Fourth Estate
an imprint of HarperCollins*Publishers*

First Isis Edition
published 2015
by arrangement with
HarperCollins*Publishers*

A catalogue record for this book is available
from the British Library.

ISBN 978–1–78541–124–3 (hb)
ISBN 978–1–78541–130–4 (pb)

Published by
F. A. Thorpe (Publishing)
Anstey, Leicestershire

Set by Words & Graphics Ltd.
Anstey, Leicestershire
Printed and bound in Great Britain by
T. J. International Ltd., Padstow, Cornwall

This book is printed on acid-free paper

For Adrian

Prologue

The old orchard stood besieged. To one side spread a vast arable plain, a dullard's patchwork of corn and soy reaching to the dark tree-line of the hills. To the other, a light-industrial estate stretched towards the town.

Between the dripping trees the remains of a path still showed. A man in early middle-age kicked at the tall nettles and docks to widen it. Neat in her navy business suit, a younger woman followed. She paused to take photographs with her phone.

"I hope you don't mind but we've put out some feelers, and we're already beating them off with sticks. Prime brown-field location."

The man stared through the trees, not listening.

"There — thought for a moment it had vanished."

An old wooden beehive stood camouflaged against the trees. The woman drew back.

"I won't come any closer," she said. "I'm a bit funny about insects."

"So's my father. He calls them his girls." The man looked up at the low grey sky. "Is that more rain? What happened to summer?"

The woman glanced up from her phone.

"I know! I've forgotten what blue sky looks like. Must be hard with the kids off school."

"They barely notice. They're always online."

He walked forward and peered closer at the hive.

A few bees emerged from a small hole at the bottom. They walked along a narrow wooden ledge and hummed their wings.

He watched them for a while then turned back to her.

"I'm sorry. Now is not the right time."

"Oh!" She put her phone away. "Have you changed your mind?"

He shook his head.

"No. I'll sell . . ." He cleared his throat. "But not yet. It feels wrong."

"Of course." She hesitated. "I suppose it's very hard to know approximately . . .?"

"Could be months. Could be tomorrow."

The woman allowed a respectful silence.

"Well, rest assured that when you *are* ready, it's a seller's market."

She began walking back along the path.

The man stood alone by the hive. On impulse he put his palm against the wood, as if feeling for a pulse. Then he turned and followed her.

Behind them, bees rose into the brightening air.

CHAPTER
ONE

The cell squeezed her and the air was hot and fetid. All the joints of her body burned from her frantic twisting against the walls, her head was pressed into her chest and her legs shot with cramp, but her struggles had worked — one wall felt weaker. She kicked out with all her strength and felt something crack and break. She forced and tore and bit until there was a jagged hole into fresher air beyond.

She dragged her body through and fell out onto the floor of an alien world. Static roared through her brain, thunderous vibration shook the ground and a thousand scents dazed her. All she could do was breathe until gradually the vibration and static subsided and the scent evaporated into the air. Her rigid body unlocked and she calmed as knowledge filled her mind.

This was the Arrivals Hall and she was a worker.

Her kin was Flora and her number was 717.

Certain of her first task, she set about cleaning out her cell. In her violent struggle to hatch she had broken the whole front wall, unlike her neater neighbours. She looked, then followed their example, piling her debris neatly by the ruins. The activity cleared her senses and she felt the vastness of the Arrivals Hall, and how the vibrations in the air changed in different areas.

Row upon row of cells like hers stretched into the distance, and there the cells were quiet but resonant as if the occupants still slept. Immediately around her was great activity with many recently broken and cleared-out chambers, and many more cracking and falling as new bees arrived. The differing scents of her neighbours also came into focus, some sweeter, some sharper, all of them pleasant to absorb.

With a hard erratic pulse in the ground, a young female came running down the corridor between the cells, her face frantic.

"*Halt!*" Harsh voices reverberated from both ends of the corridor and a strong astringent scent rose in the air. Every bee stopped moving but the young bee stumbled and fell across Flora's pile of debris. Then she clawed her way into the remains of the broken cell and huddled in the corner, her little hands up.

Cloaked in a bitter scent which hid their faces and made them identical, the dark figures strode down the corridor towards Flora. Pushing her aside, they dragged out the weeping young bee. At the sight of their spiked gauntlets, a spasm of fear in Flora's brain released more knowledge. They were police.

"*You fled inspection.*" One of them pulled at the girl's wings, while another examined the four still-wet membranes. The edge of one was shrivelled.

"Spare me," she cried. "I will not fly, I will serve in any other way —"

"*Deformity is evil. Deformity is not permitted.*"

4

Before the bee could speak the two officers pressed her head down until there was a sharp crack. She hung limp between them and they dropped her body in the corridor.

"*You.*" A peculiar rasping voice addressed Flora and she did not know which one spoke, but stared at the black hooks on the backs of their legs. "*Hold still.*" Long black callipers slid from their gauntlets and they measured her height. "*Excessive variation. Abnormal.*"

"That will be all, officers." At the kind voice and fragrant smell, the police released Flora. They bowed to a tall and well-groomed bee with a beautiful face.

"Sister Sage, this one is obscenely ugly."

"And excessively large."

"It would appear so. Thank you, officers, you may go."

Sister Sage waited for them to leave. She smiled at Flora. "To fear them is good. Be still while I read your kin —"

"I am Flora 717."

Sister Sage raised her antennae. "A sanitation worker who speaks. Most notable . . ."

Flora stared at her tawny and gold face with its huge dark eyes. "Am I to be killed?"

"Do not question a priestess." Sister Sage ran her hands down the sides of Flora's face. "Open your mouth." She looked inside. "Perhaps." Then she inclined her head over Flora's mouth and fed her one golden drop of honey.

The effect was immediate and astonishing. Clarity washed Flora's mind and her body filled with strength.

5

She understood that Sister Sage wished her to follow in silence, and that she must do whatever she asked.

As they walked down the corridor she noticed how every bee averted her eyes and busied herself, and how the dead body of the young worker was already far ahead of them, carried in the mouth of a dark hunched bee who walked in the gutter. There were many more of the same type, all moving on the edge of the corridor. Some carried bundles of soiled wax, others scrubbed at broken cells. None looked up.

"They are your kin-sisters." Sister Sage followed Flora's eyes. "All of them mute. Presently you will join them in Sanitation, and perform valuable service to our hive. But first, a private experiment." She smiled at Flora. "Come."

Flora followed gladly, all memory of the killing lost in her longing to taste more honey.

CHAPTER
TWO

The priestess walked swiftly through the pale corridors of the Arrivals Hall. Flora followed closely, her brain recording all the sounds and scents as different kin broke free of their emergence chambers. Many more dark sanitation workers moved along the gutters with bundles of soiled wax. Noting their sharp distinctive odour and how other bees avoided any contact with them, Flora drew closer to Sister Sage and her fragrant wake.

The priestess paused, antennae raised. They had come to the edge of the Arrivals Hall where the countless rows of emergence cells finished, and a large hexagonal doorway led into a smaller chamber. A burst of applause from within carried out a thrilling new odour. Flora looked up at Sister Sage.

"Unfortunate timing," said the priestess. "But I must pay my respects." Once inside, she put Flora to wait by the wall then went to the front of a crowd of bees. Flora watched as once again they burst out clapping, gathered before the entrance of a still-closed emergence cell.

Flora gazed around this beautiful room. It was obviously an Arrivals Hall for more favoured bees, for it was spaciously arranged around two rows of central cells, each one made up of six grand and beautifully carved individual compartments. Sister Sage stood in the welcoming committee before one of them, where many bees held platters of pastries and pitchers of nectared water. The delicious smells sharpened Flora's own hunger and thirst.

Muffled curses and thuds came from within the decorated walls of the compartment, as if the occupant was leaping and jumping. At the sound of breaking wax, the assembled sisters redoubled their applause and their kinscents flowed stronger with excitement. Flora detected a molecule of a different scent and her brain knew its pheromone signal: *A Male — A Male arrives!*

"Worship to His Maleness!" cried several feminine voices as a big carved piece of wax fell out, followed by screams of delight as through the hole came the plumed head of a brand-new drone.

"Worship to His Maleness!" the sisters cheered again, and they rushed to help him out, pulling the wax free themselves and making a staircase of their bodies.

"Quite high," he said as he walked down on top of them. "And quite tiring."

He puffed his dronely scent around himself, rousing more sighs and applause.

"Welcome and Worship to His Maleness." Sister Sage curtsied low. As all the other bees graciously did the same, Flora stared in admiration and tried to copy the movement. "Honour to our Hive," said Sister Sage as she rose.

"Too kind." But his smile had charm, and all the sisters returned it, gazing at him avidly. He was rumpled but elegant, and very concerned with the exact set of his neck-ruff. When he had finally arranged it to his liking, he bowed with a great flourish. Then, to the sisters' fervent applause, he showed himself off from many angles, stretching out his legs in pairs, puffing his plume and even treating them to a sudden roar of his engine. They screamed in delight and fanned each other, and some scrambled to offer him pastries and water.

Flora watched him eat and drink, her own mouth dry and her hunger keen.

"Greed is a sin, 717." Sister Sage was beside her again. "Take care."

She walked on, and before Flora could look back at the drone her antennae tugged sharply from the line of scent the priestess had attached without her knowledge. She ran to catch up.

As she followed, the vibrations in the comb floor became more insistent, stronger and stronger as if it were a living thing beneath her, energy running in all directions. With a buzzing sensation through all her six feet, a torrent of information rushed up through her body and into her brain. Overwhelmed, Flora stopped in the middle of a big lobby. Under her feet spread a vast mosaic of hexagonal floor tiles, the patterns scrolling across the lobby and down the corridors. Endless streams of bees criss-crossed around them and the air was thick with scent broadcasting.

Sister Sage came back to her.

"Well! You appear to have accessed every floor code at once. Stay very still." She lightly touched both Flora's antennae with her own.

A new fragrance cocooned them. Flora breathed it deep inside and the rushing confusion in her brain subsided. Her body calmed and her heart filled with joy, for the fragrance told her with utter certainty that she, Flora 717, was loved.

"Mother!" she cried out as she sank to her knees. "Holy Mother."

"Not quite." The priestess looked gratified. "Though I am of the same noble kin as Her Majesty, all praise to Her eggs. And as the Queen most graciously permitted me to attend Her today, I am richly blessed with Her scent. That which you feel is but a tiny fraction of the Queen's Love, 717."

Sister Sage's voice came from a great distance and Flora nodded. As the Queen's Love flowed through her body and brain, all the different frequencies and codes in the tiles slowed and clarified into a map of the hive, constantly running with information. Everything was fascinating, and beautiful, and she turned her gaze to the priestess.

"Yes. Very receptive." Sister Sage looked at her, then pointed to a new area of the mosaic. "Now stand over there."

Obediently Flora moved, feeling how the comb transmitted subtly different vibrations and frequencies. She adjusted her feet to receive the strongest signal, and the priestess watched with keen attention.

"You feel something — but do you comprehend it?"

Flora wanted to answer that she did, but her physical bliss prevented her speaking and she could only stare. At her silence, Sister Sage relaxed.

"Good. Knowledge only causes pain to your kin."

As they walked on, Flora's euphoria stabilised into a feeling of deep physical relaxation and heightened perception. Only now did she fully appreciate the beauty of Sister Sage's elegant form, how her pale gold fur lay in silky stripes against the thin brown gloss of her bands, themselves exactly matched by the shade of her six legs. Long translucent wings folded down her back and her antennae tapered to fine points.

They continued deeper into the hive, Flora entranced by its carved and frescoed walls of ancient scent and the beautiful blend of her living sisters. She did not feel how the golden tiles changed underfoot and the bare pale wax began, or how the priestess spread her cloak of scent over them both as they entered an empty corridor which held no vibration at all.

Only when they stopped before a small plain doorway did she feel how far they had travelled, and that she was still very hungry.

"Soon." Sister Sage answered her as if she had spoken. She touched a panel in the wall and the door opened.

CHAPTER
THREE

The little chamber was tranquil and bare, and a beautiful soft smell filtered through the walls. The pale hexagonal tiles showed a wide tread of past wear across the centre of the room and Flora set her feet wider in case there was any information to detect.

"All long gone." Sister Sage had her back turned but she still knew what Flora did. "And you will hold your tongue."

Then came the sound of running feet, and another bee burst into the room. She stopped in shock at the sight of the priestess standing before her.

"Sister Sage! We were not expecting you." By her hard shiny bands she was a senior, but her fur was yellow, her face coarse and her antennae blunt. She bowed deeply. Sister Sage inclined her head.

"Sister Teasel. Are you well?"

"Never doubt it; every Teasel as strong and willing as ever. You will not find sickness in this kin! Why? Has someone been found ailing?"

"No. Not at all." Sister Sage's attention rested for a moment on the far wall. Flora looked too. Where the worn tiles ended was the faintest outline of a third door.

Sister Teasel clutched her hands together.

"A visit from a priestess of the Melissae is always an honour — but did not Sister in her wisdom order this side of the Nursery closed off? Otherwise someone would surely have been stationed here to receive you —"

"I wished to avoid notice." Sister Sage gazed down the dim corridor from where Sister Teasel had come. Sister Teasel took the opportunity to stare at Flora. Alarmed at her tangible disapproval, Flora attempted a clumsy curtsy. Sister Teasel rapped her hard on the closest knee.

"Forward, never splayed!" She looked to Sister Sage. "Such boldness! But by her wet fur she is newly hatched — I do not understand."

"We were obliged to wait while a drone emerged. She saw such antics there."

"Oh, a new prince! Honour to our hive — was he very handsome straight away? Or does it come upon them as their fur rises? How I long —"

"Sister Teasel, how many nurses have you lost?"

"Since last inspection?" Sister Teasel stared in alarm. "Compared to other departments, hardly any. We are not like foragers, we keep ourselves safe from the outer world and its perils — but even our kin will sometimes suffer —" She cleared her throat. "Six, Sister, since last inspection. I move them on for the slightest sign of confusion or hint of ailing — we take no chances. And of course, we have only the purest kin here, and the most obedient." She coughed. "Six, Sister."

Sister Sage nodded. "And what do you hear, of other departments?"

"Oh! Mere canteen gossip, idle tittle-tattle, nothing I would repeat —"

"Please do." Sister Sage focused her attention on Sister Teasel, her scent flexing in the air. Flora looked down at the waxen tiles and did not move. Sister Teasel twisted her hands together.

"Sister Sage, we are very fortunate in the Nursery, plenty of food, everything brought to us — we do not feel the shortages, we face no dangers . . ." She faltered.

"Come, Sister. Unburden yourself." Sister Sage was calm and kind, and Sister Teasel dared look up.

"They say the season is deformed by rain, that the flowers shun us and fall unborn, that foragers are falling from the air and no one knows why!" She plucked at her fur convulsively. "They say we will starve and the babies will all die, and my little nurses are worrying so much I fear they will forget —" She shook her head. "Not that they do, Sister, ever, for they are most strictly supervised and the rotas are always guarded, so even if they *could* count — you may kill me if it is not so."

"You need not give permission."

Sister Teasel burst out laughing and reached for one of her hands.

"Oh, Sister Sage, it does me such good to jest with you — now I have shared the burden, I am no longer fearful!"

"That is the role of the Melissae: to carry all fears, so the hive is free." A calming scent flowed from Sister Sage and filled the chamber.

"*Amen*," said Sister Teasel. "But oh for the courage of the kin of Thistle."

"Why? What do they do?" Too late Flora remembered herself.

Sister Teasel glared at her in outrage, her own distress forgotten.

"She *speaks?* The impudence! Sister Sage, please, spare my curiosity and tell me the reason for her presence. If it is to clean, then I shall add her to the next detail — but I hope all Sanitation is not now possessed of tongues for we shall be in uproar!" She glared at Flora. "Obstreperous dirty creatures."

"Does Sister Teasel stand in judgement of our purpose?"

"No, Sister, never. Forgive me."

"Then kindly recall that variation is not the same as deformity."

"Sister graces me with her superior wisdom — though to my ignorant eyes those terms are one and the same." Sister Teasel stood back from Flora. "How monstrously large she is — and that fur when it dries will be thick as a drone's, and her shell as black as a crow's — not that I have ever seen one, thank Mother."

Sister Sage became very still.

"You are fatigued perhaps, by your long duty? Your loyal heart wishes to serve longer, yet your spirits tire?"

Sister Teasel shook her head in alarm. Sister Sage turned to Flora.

"Open your mouth, 717, let Sister Teasel look."

Flora obeyed and Sister Teasel promptly peered in. She looked to Sister Sage in surprise. Then she grasped

Flora's tongue and pulled it to its full length, before letting it snap back in her mouth.

"I see! It might indeed be possible, but with that tongue comes —"

"She will lose its use when it is time for her to rejoin her kin. And should it linger, I will personally wipe any knowledge from her mind. Test her, and if she does not produce anything, send her on immediately." Sister Sage looked kindly at Flora. "This experiment is a great privilege. What do you say?"

"*Accept, Obey and Serve.*" The words blurted from Flora's mouth unbidden.

Sister Teasel shuddered. "Let us hope she will. Such ugliness!"

Ashamed, Flora turned back to Sister Sage as her shield, but the priestess had vanished.

"They do that." Sister Teasel watched her. "Never know where you are with them, always surprising you. Come along then." She opened a door and Flora smelled the sweet pure fragrance beyond it. "If Sister Sage hadn't told me to do this herself, I'd call it sacrilege." She pushed Flora through the door with her foot. "Let's get this over with."

CHAPTER
FOUR

The enormous nursery was filled with row after row of glowing cribs, some with little rippling streams of light above them. Flora followed Sister Teasel deeper into the chamber. To her wonder, the light was in fact a luminous liquid, pouring in droplets from the mouths of the young nurses who leaned over the cribs. Many more of them moved silently about the ward, young and pretty with glowing chins.

"It is so beautiful!"

Despite her resentment, Sister Teasel smoothed her chest fur and nodded. She pointed to an unattended crib.

"What gender?"

Flora looked in. The larva was newly hatched, soft pearly tendrils of shell still clinging to the translucent white skin. Its tiny face was closed in sleep and a sweet milky smell drifted above it.

"A female. She is so perfect!"

"Just another worker. Now find a male." Sister Teasel indicated the whole vast nursery.

"Yes, Sister." Flora raised her antennae. On each row she drew in the smell of female babies, strong and constant.

"You can't do it from here, you silly girl."

Flora did not answer. She smelled the different kin of the young nurses, and all the thousand female children. There was no scent of male.

"I have searched and there are none. Why is that?"

Sister Teasel stared at her.

"Late in the season Holy Mother stops making them." She shook herself. "A good sense of smell is not enough to keep you out of Sanitation. Now hold your bold tongue and let us conclude this foolish experiment."

Sister Teasel pushed Flora to the first worker crib she had shown her, and tapped on its side so that the little creature woke. When it opened its mouth and began to cry, she folded her arms in satisfaction and looked at Flora. "And now?"

Flora leaned in to look, and the larva baby flexed and stretched towards her. Its warm scent rose more strongly, threaded with the delicate fragrance of the Queen's Love. Immediately, two pulses began flickering in Flora's cheeks, and her mouth began to fill with sweet liquid. She looked to Sister Teasel in alarm.

"Flow!" cried Sister Teasel. "Don't swallow, let it come!"

She guided Flora into the right position as the luminous drops spilled from her mouth. As they fell onto the larva baby it stopped crying and wriggled to lap them up. The drops thickened into a thin stream which pooled around the baby's body until it could drink no more.

18

The liquid ebbed and Flora's cheeks stopped flickering. Completely exhausted, she held the side of the crib for support. The baby grew as she watched, and the base of the crib glowed. Other nurses looked across.

"Well!" said Sister Teasel. "If I had not seen it for myself. A flora from Sanitation, able to make royal jelly — Flow." She corrected herself. "You must only ever call it Flow."

"Why, Sister?" Flora felt warm and sleepy.

Sister Teasel tutted.

"No more questions. All you need to remember is to feed as your supervisor instructs you. Not a drop more, no matter how the babies beg. And they will. Now I must find you a place to sleep — though I don't know what the other girls will say about it. You mustn't expect them to touch or groom you."

Sister Teasel led Flora to a rest area where young nurse bees lay talking quietly or sleeping, luminous traces fading round their mouths. She lay down at once.

"Flora 717 is here by Sister Sage's express wish." Sister Teasel's tone dared anyone to remonstrate. "Yes she makes Flow and yes it is most irregular for her kin, but we are in the season of irregularity, with the rain and the cold and the lack of food — so we will all be helpful. Is that clear?"

The nurses murmured assent and placed food and drink within Flora's reach, but she was too tired to move. Sister Teasel's voice continued above her and she knew that when the comb shivered, the divine fragrance that rose up from it was the Queen's Love, and that this was the sacrament of Devotion. She wanted to join the sweet harmony of nurses in prayer, but the room was warm and dark, and the bed was soft.

Like the other nurses, Flora's job was simple. She must give Flow to the babies as directed, rest when it stopped, then repeat. As Sister Teasel had stressed to Sister Sage, the feed timing was very strictly observed and marked with different bells that signalled one or other area of the nursery was due more, or must now stop feeding. These constantly chiming bells, and the shimmering energy of the fed larva, created an intense and dreamlike aura in the nursery, but one sound always alerted Flora's attention. It was the bright resonant tone of the sun bell, and its particular frequency told all the bees that beyond the safety of the hive walls, day had risen again.

Flora particularly enjoyed its vibration and listened out for its rare pleasure. Every three chimes, the supervising sisters came round and collected all the nurses whose fur had risen and whose Flow was dwindling, and replaced them with new ones, fresh from the Arrivals Hall, their fur still soft and damp.

Flora's fur had not changed, so she was kept on. By the sixth sun bell, every nurse around her had changed, but her own Flow continued as strongly as ever. Supervising sisters also changed, but there were always several Teasel in their number. As she watched them go about their business, Flora began to understand the workings of the Nursery.

20

The cribs were always being rotated. Each day the nurses who were soon to leave would clean out a thousand of them, then a small army of sanitation workers would arrive to remove the waste and scrub the floors. Surreptitiously, Flora watched them. Though they never made eye contact or said a word, their vigorous energy was tangible and all the nurses were relieved when they left, none more so than Flora, ashamed of her own kin. Then the nurses would prepare the empty cribs in the newly cleaned area and the supervising sisters would say prayers of purification, before veiling the whole section with the shimmering scent of discretion, ready for the Royal Progress when the Queen laid her eggs.

When the next sun bell sounded, the glorious fragrance of new life rose in the Nursery and a thousand new eggs lay pure and perfect in their cribs. Every bee in the Nursery joined in songs of praise for Immortal Mother's fertility. It took three more sun bells for the eggs to hatch into larva babies, and then it was time to feed them Flow.

Under strictly timed supervision from a senior sister, for the next three days Flora and other feeding nurses watched in amazement as the babies grew before their eyes. Their sweet scent rippled with changes in their bodies, and then came the stark moment when the supervising sisters piped a quick whistle to stop the feeding. No matter how hungry a baby might be, not a single drop more might be given, for it was time to wean them in the Category Two ward.

21

To Flora, this was a highly desirable place to work. Through the big double doors that separated the two nursery wards, she had often glimpsed older nurses playing and singing with the bigger children, even cuddling them in their arms.

Everything about the Ceremony of Transition was exciting to Flora, from the way the babies started wriggling and laughing in excitement at the delicious food smells coming from the double doors dividing the wards, to the first strains of the cheerful hymns sung by the nurses who came for them. With graceful curtsies to all in the Category One ward, even Flora, they scooped up the laughing babies and the doors closed soft behind them.

With their fully risen fur, elegant limbs and narrow curtsies, these sophisticated Category Two kins of Violet, Primrose and Vetch won Flora's particular admiration. Discreetly in the dim holy atmosphere of Category One, she practised her own curtsy to overcome her shameful splay — just in case Sister Sage should reappear and move her to Category Two.

This was such a wonderful thought that Flora began including it in her prayers at Devotion. She forgot it each time the enchanting fragrance of the Queen's Love rose up through the comb, but when the nurses changed again and her fur had still not risen, she gathered up her courage and sought out Sister Teasel.

"You want to *move*?" Sister Teasel stared at her in amazement. "From Category One, the holiest place in the hive and the closest you will ever come to Her Majesty? Why, She passes by us every day!"

"But I have never seen —"

Sister Teasel swiped Flora's antennae with a sharp claw.

"Impudent, ignorant girl! Do you think a flora, a *sanitation* worker, is ever likely to be in the true presence of Her Majesty? I knew it would come to this! I was against it from the start — why, pray, are you now so eager to move to Category Two?"

"It looks so bright and happy there. And the nurses play with the children."

"Yes, and as a result they are riddled with frivolity and attachment. I cannot believe it — move *away* from the Queen? Please, tell me: do you fantasise you are a forager, able to survive beyond Holy Mother's divine scent? For clearly it is not enough to be a nurse!"

"It is, Sister — forgive me for asking —"

But it was too late, for Sister Teasel's agitation spread through the whole ward. The babies grew fractious, distracted nurses looked up from their feeding and Flow splashed against the cribs. Sister Teasel waved her arms at them.

"Focus!" She turned back to Flora. "Now you listen to me. We deliver one outcome here: identical care for identical brood. There is no improvising, no requesting a transfer, and, until *you* were forced upon us, no exception to the immaculate kin of our nurses."

"I know, Sister, I'm very grateful, it's just that so many nurses have changed —"

"What business is that of yours? Have you been trying to count?" Sister Teasel came close to her. "717, have you been studying the rotas? Confess at once if you have, for it is a matter of hive security — what do you know about them?" Her scent became fragmented with anxiety, and the babies began crying again.

"Nothing, Sister! I just wanted to ask —"

"There, that is the seed of it: you *wanted!*" Sister Teasel groomed her antennae back from their trembling state, then glared at Flora again. "*Desire is sin, Vanity is sin* — it is all very well praying and splaying, 717 — and don't think I haven't seen you practising your ridiculous curtsy —"

"*Idleness is sin.*" Humiliated at her exposure, Flora continued the catechism. "*Discord is sin, Greed is sin —*"

"And as for your appetite — as bad as a drone's. No matter what the sainted Sage may think" — and here Sister Teasel threw a quick glance around the ward — "you are typical of your kin. Greedy, ugly, obstinate things! Girls, what is our first commandment?"

"*Accept, Obey and Serve,*" chanted the eavesdropping nurses, staring at Flora.

"*Accept, Obey and Serve.*" Flora knelt before Sister Teasel. "*A flora may not make Wax for she is impure, nor work with Propolis for she is clumsy, nor may she ever forage for she has no taste, but only may she clean, and all may command her labour.*"

"Exactly." Sister Teasel's antennae twitched. "Yet here you are, feeding the Queen's newborns. Summer is cold, floras speak: the world is upside down! Just be grateful for the honour, for it will soon be over. But I wish I knew when, for I have never seen the like of your Flow."

"What does it mean, for my knowledge to be wiped?"
Sister Teasel's expression softened. She sighed.

"You will find out soon enough. Now, spare us both — ask no more questions."

Flora returned to the main floor, her hope replaced with dread. She joined a group of nurses who stood waiting to hear which section next needed Flow, their mouths already brimming with the bright liquid. The chime sounded, and ahead of them a dark little sanitation worker ran to get out of their way. Walking at the back of the group, Flora saw her clearly, cowering with her pan and brush and holding her wings so that she would not touch a higher kin by accident. Their eyes met for a moment. The little worker grimaced in a smile. Flora looked away and hurried on.

The next baby was big and hungry. She gazed down at its open mouth, always the trigger for the pulses in her cheeks to begin the feeding trance. Nothing came. The twisted friendly grimace of the sanitation worker stuck in her mind and Flora shook herself. She adjusted her position and concentrated.

The baby yearned up towards her, open-mouthed. The pulses in her cheeks flickered, and a few drops of Flow seeped out. Flora shook her head so they fell onto the baby and it lapped them hungrily. It looked up and opened its mouth for more. She concentrated until the sides of her mouth were throbbing with the strain, but nothing came. The baby began to cry.

A new nurse appeared at Flora's side, her mouth and face glowing with fresh Flow. She was very young and deep in the feeding trance. She stood by Flora's side and leaned over. Immediately the luminous stream began to fall and the baby quieted as it fed. Confused, Flora stepped back.

"The miracle," said a kind, familiar voice, "was that you could feed at all."

Sister Sage stood by her, beautiful and frightening. She smiled.

"If your job bores you, 717, I will give you something more exciting to do. Consider it another test."

CHAPTER
FIVE

At the sight of Sister Sage all the Category Two nurses and nannies curtsied, though they looked warily at Flora walking with her. The priestess was not angry that her Flow had stopped, and seemed only to want to talk.

"I would have said the experiment was a success," she said to Flora. "And I am sure Sister Teasel impressed on you the privilege of such sacred service."

"Yes, Sister. I am very grateful."

"But you are very curious about Category Two — a rather prosaic place, to my mind. Why is that?"

The more she breathed of Sister Sage's strong scent, the more Flora grew calm, and felt an overpowering desire to tell the truth.

"In Category One everything is always the same."

Sister Sage laughed.

"The very point of identical care. Yet it bored you."

"Yes, Sister. Forgive me." Flora lowered her head, but Sister Sage raised it and held her long antennae over hers.

"We will forget the folly of the curtsies and your boldness in hoping to see Holy Mother, for I hear you are also very devout and hard-working."

"I hope so, Sister."

"And you love the Queen?"

"With my body and my soul." Flora's antennae trembled as she felt Sister Sage reaching deep into her mind.

Would you serve Her any way you can?

"With my whole life."

"Good." Sister Sage walked on. "In this time of scarce forage, you have been surprisingly useful in the Nursery. Sometimes it works to spare the deviants, and experiment a little." She smiled. "Is this place as you imagined?"

"Better, Sister! It is so lively, so full of wonderful things —"

"Then look your fill. I wish you to know it."

Flora could not take Category Two in at once, with its decorations and beautifully tiled play areas. Pretty nurses and nannies sat with their vigorous little charges, singing and playing games, or feeding them from shining platters. Healthy beautiful child-grubs were everywhere, their cheerful snubby little faces speckled with golden pollen dust. Gone was the heavy scent of Flow and the mumble of prayer, and in its place nursery rhymes, laughter and the bright aroma of fresh bread.

Sister Sage watched her. "What do you know of feeding patterns?"

"Nothing, Sister." Flora admired two fat child-grubs, chuckling as their nurses tickled them. "Sister Teasel asked me that. All I know is that timing is very important and there are a lot of bells." Her own arms tingled to hold one herself and she turned away lest the sin of Desire take hold. "And we must always stop at the right moment and never give a drop more."

"Because . . .?"

"I'm not sure, Sister."

Sister Sage touched one of Flora's antennae with her own, and Flora felt a piercing resonance in her mind. The sensation grew almost unbearable, then abruptly stopped as Sister Sage released her.

"Good. You are truthful." Her long antennae flexed. "Tell me, though, about my sisters Teasel: do they hold any meetings or gatherings in the Nursery?"

"I don't think so." Flora felt a strong urge to please the priestess with the right answer. "But I know only the one, my supervising sister."

"Ah yes. To you they are all the same. And so they very nearly are, though they must still use speech to know each other's thoughts. It is most quaint. But you will tell me if they hold private meetings, do you understand?"

"Yes, Sister."

They had come to the end of the Category Two ward where great panels of carving marked another set of doors. Flora could not decipher the markings but knew instinctively not to touch them. Sister Sage answered her unspoken question.

"They speak of Holy Time, when we have all slept in prayer." Her voice was soft and her face shone as if she experienced some great inner joy. "Each Devotion, we recall something of that state." She remained rapt in contemplation.

Flora felt it correct to stand in silence beside her. A movement caught her eyes. It was another of the wretched sanitation workers, working along the ward gutter with her pan and brush, and looking directly at Flora and the priestess. Flora pressed her knees together and drew herself up as thin and tall as she could, trying to emphasise their difference. Steadily sweeping, the worker passed on. Though nothing more than a look had occurred, Flora was angry and agitated.

"Do not blame yourself: no one may choose their kin — or all would be Sage." No longer in her enraptured state, the priestess smiled. "Because you lack botanical heritage, yours forms the base of our society. Or rather, you draw it from impure and promiscuous flowers, shunned by this hive."

"Sister Sage! Sister Sage!"

Sister Teasel's high, strained voice reached down the long corridor of Category Two. They smelled her streaming panic before they saw her, running towards them with antennae waving and wild fear on her face.

"Please — you must — both of you, I beg you —" Sister Teasel could hardly speak. "Everyone must report at once, the fertility police are here now on our ward!"

As Flora followed Sister Sage back through the Category Two ward, every nurse and nanny clutched her little charge tight to her, and stared at them in silence. Up ahead through the big double doors, the Category One ward was no longer dim and hushed but starkly illuminated and pulsing with a harsh bitter scent. Flora stumbled as her brain struggled to recall it. Sister Sage took her by the arm to quicken her pace and strengthened her own scent around both of them.

"You have nothing to fear."

They went into the ward. At first Flora thought the nurses had gone because all the cribs were unattended and the babies were already starting to cry, but then she saw them all standing in lines near the ward sisters' station. Some openly wept in fear, their antennae waving uncontrollably, while others stood rigid. Standing around the edges of the ward were the fertility police. Their kin-scents were hidden under their masking scent, their eyes were blank, and their fur was slicked dark against their bands — but Flora recognised them from the Arrivals Hall. Sister Sage curled a filament of her own scent around Flora's antennae and she felt her mouth clamp shut. The priestess joined her to the end of the first row then stepped forward and bowed to the police.

"Sister Inspector, Sister Officers. Welcome."

The Inspector saluted her, then turned to address the nurses.

"Another wing deformity has been found." The masking scent distorted her voice to a harsh buzz. Despite their fear, the nurses murmured in revulsion.

"Praise to the vigilant Thistle guard on the landing board." Her scent fired in jagged bursts as she surveyed the nurses. Sister Teasel began to weep.

"Not *here*, Madam Inspector, never in Category One, it is not possible — Holy Mother is here every day, Her scent so beautiful and strong — there can be no —"

"Silence!" the Inspector spat at her. "Do you think I mean the defect could come from *Her Majesty*? You fly close to treason yourself, Sister —"

"Holy Mother strike me dead before my next breath if so!" Sister Teasel fell to her knees, but Sister Inspector yanked her back on her feet.

"Measure her." She shoved Sister Teasel at two of her officers and they lashed their black callipers around her thick waist. Sister Teasel voided herself in fear and the smell mingled with the scent of the nurses' terror, rising from their breathing spiracles. Behind them all the babies began to cry. Sister Sage looked on calmly.

"Not her, at any rate." The Inspector released Sister Teasel then turned to the nurses. "Deformities mean evil roams our hive. Somewhere hides a desecrating heretic, who dares steal sacred Motherhood from the Queen. That is why sickness comes, that is why deformities rise. From her foul issue!" Her antennae twitched compulsively and Flora felt her longing for violence.

"Only the Queen may breed," responded Sister Sage, looking at the nurses.

"*Only the Queen may breed,*" some of them managed to reply, but others stared at Sister Teasel, her antennae bent in shame as she desperately cleaned herself. The Inspector held up a long sharp claw to the ward.

"We will search every crib, we will measure every nurse's belly until we find the culprit. And then we will tear her filthy body apart and cleanse our hive of sin."

32

"Do what you must, Sister Inspector." Sister Sage bowed again.

Sister Inspector signalled and some of her officers began moving systematically through the rows of cribs, while others used the black callipers on their arms to measure the bellies of the terrified nurses.

When it was her turn, Flora looked in distress at Sister Sage, convinced her greedy appetite would mark her as doomed, but the priestess ignored her. The callipers went round her belly but the police moved on, measuring each bee until all the nurses were cleared and none found guilty.

Those who dared turned to look at the cribs where the larva babies wailed as officers swept each one up. With the powerful scanners of their antennae, they sent sharp vibrations through the small tender bodies. The babies cried in fear and regurgitated their Flow, and the smell of it mixed with their infant defecation.

"*Our Mother, who art in labour.*" Sister Teasel's voice was faint, but her nurses joined their own in support.

"*Hallowed be Thy Womb,*" they sang to control their fear.

"*Thy Marriage done, Thy Queendom come.*"

Flora wanted to join in, but the scent from Sister Sage had bound her rigid.

"*From Death comes Life Eter —*" The beautiful voices stopped at the sharp squealing from one of the cribs.

Every nurse stared in horror as one of the officers bent over it. The squeal became an anguished shriek as the officer held up a larva baby, struggling to roll itself up. Another officer pulled it open with a sound of tearing skin.

Standing by Flora, Sister Inspector slid a claw from her gauntlet. "Bring it."

Muffling the baby's screams, she scanned it with slow-burning antennae until its pearly skin withered. "It is possible," she announced. "It has a foul strange scent."

"That is fear!" cried Sister Teasel.

Ignoring her, Sister Inspector held up the baby and pierced it with her hook. It shrieked and twisted in agony as she offered it to her officers.

"Destroy it."

"Wait." Sister Sage pointed to Flora. "Let her."

With a jolt, Flora felt herself released to move. Sister Inspector pulled her claw from the larva baby to drop it on the ground, but Flora caught it and clutched it to her, the first child she had ever held. Its warm blood soaked into her fur and she pressed the agonised little thing close to her, trying to staunch the bleeding.

Eat it alive. The voice spoke inside Flora's own mind. She clutched the baby tighter and a searing sound went through her antennae.

Do it NOW. Tear it apart.

Flora bowed her own head over the baby and shielded it with her arms. The voice roared louder in her mind.

DESTROY IT —

Her antennae felt like they had burst with the blow that struck her. She staggered and fell, the baby still clutched to her. Blows shook her body and her antennae became two pulsing rods of agony. The screaming baby was pulled from her grasp. She felt its warm blood splash her face and heard its tearing flesh and the grunts of the fertility police as they devoured it. As Flora screamed, her tongue twisted hard in her mouth and she choked on the sound.

"I asked too much . . ." Sister Sage's voice was close and gentle. "The experiment is over."

CHAPTER
SIX

Flora regained consciousness lying on dirty blank tiles. A low moaning came from nearby, but when she tried to locate the source a searing flash forked through her head and she cried out.

"Don't move . . ." A weak voice spoke. "The pain is less —"

Through the snarling odours of the small chamber Flora became aware of the faint scent of the kin of Clover.

"Was it you?" The voice was young and ragged. "For I swear it was not me."

Flora tried to answer, but to move her tongue was agony.

"Silence." Sister Sage entered, followed by a group of her identical doubles. All wore the ceremonial pollen marks of the Melissae priestesses, and a strong astringent scent flowed from them. Flora shrank in terror, but they paid her no attention. Instead, the first Sister Sage knelt down by the Clover and stroked her face.

"Your crime is behind you now, and you harm only yourself by maintaining your lie." She waited, but the Clover lay panting and did not speak. Sister Sage leaned closer. "How many eggs did you lay? Did you wish to be Queen?"

"Never!" The Clover struggled to rise on her broken limbs. Her wings were shrivelled and curled. "I beg you believe me, I have not profaned our holy law, *Only the Queen may breed* —"

One of the other priestesses stepped forward as if to strike the Clover, but Sister Sage held her back and soothed the Clover again.

"Why did you hide from the police? Was it to keep spreading your deformity through our hive with foul eggs? We have found the young sisters with your defect, your *issue*." Sister Sage hissed the word and the Clover began to weep.

"I swear again I have never laid —"

"Your wings show your true evil. And deformity creeps through our hive."

The Clover gave up trying to stand.

"Then maybe Holy Mother lays bad eggs."

The priestesses hissed and rasped their wings like knives. Sister Sage lifted the Clover off the ground with one hand.

"You blaspheme, at the moment of your death?"

The Clover raised her antennae to high shivering points.

"*From Death comes Life Eternal.* Holy Mother take me back."

The priestesses surrounded her and flexed their abdomens high. Flora saw the tips of their bodies draw in to a hard point, and as they sang the Holy Chord together their delicate barbed daggers slid out. The chamber filled with the scent of venom, the Holy Chord rose louder until the air reverberated — then the priestesses stung the Clover from all sides. She cried out once — and then the sweet scent of her kin burst bright upon the foul air and was gone.

The priestesses turned to Flora. She felt their probing attention work its way down her sore antennae, deep into her head. She curled herself up as small as she could, to brace for the searing chemical pain they would drive into her brain — but it did not come. Abruptly the intimate invasion withdrew. The priestesses talked together in low voices and despite her fear, Flora listened.

"Cornflower yield is poor. Even the buttercups are short —"

"The foragers speak of more green deserts —"

"When they fly at all, in this rain."

"We cannot fight the season." By the rich particular timbre of her voice, the speaker was the same Sister Sage Flora knew. "We cannot fight the rain, we can only provision ourselves as best we may. So unless she be heretic or deformed, in such a troubling season, every single worker is an asset — and I am loath to lose one more."

"Hardly an asset," said another voice. "She defied you over the baby. I vote to give her the Kindness — I would not waste my venom on her."

Flora lay very still.

"I will kill her myself when her use is over," said Sister Sage. "But the first fault was mine. I acted independently."

38

The air in the chamber contracted as the priestesses twined and flexed their scents together in consultation. Then one fragrance formed, no longer dominated by the harsh astringent top note, but smooth, warm and powerfully calming.

"Only the Queen is perfect. Amen."

Even in her pain, Flora heard the choral beauty of their voice when they spoke together, and breathed more deeply. When a foot nudged her she did not resist.

"It is true. Such size and strength makes her useful," one of them said.

"Provided she is docile," said another. "To have a rebel in that kin — and one who could have learned of feeding —"

"That will never happen." Sister Sage knelt down beside Flora, and looked up at her fellow priestesses. "More than one of us should do this, to be sure."

"Of course," said another. "Dirt and fear will be her only guides."

Three more priestesses knelt by Flora's head, so there were two at each antenna.

Then they all touched their own to hers.

The sensation was very strange. As the chemicals jolted into her brain her body shook, but she did not feel pain, only waves of numbness, stronger and stronger until her consciousness shrank to calm and blackness.

"717." The voice came from a great distance. "Get up."

The massive limbs beneath her lurched into life and Flora stood. Dimly she felt energy of other beings around her, then the comforting dull rhythm thudding through the comb under her feet. It went up into her body and her brain. Without conscious thought, Flora lifted the body of the dead Clover into her mouth. As she did so the rhythm in the ground grew stronger, pulsing with each forward step she took to lead her onto the coded tiles. Pulled by the frequency, she carried the dead Clover out of the detention chamber, into the huge traffic of bees.

To shield her antennae from the many bruising signals in the air she walked with her head low. Air currents and electrical pulses from thousands of bees rippled against her, but Flora ignored them all. The pulsing track alone held her focus, clear and simple across the perilously busy lobby where she had to slow down because of the tempest of data underfoot.

A rush of workers came through in a tumult of scent and Flora lifted her head — then the rhythm of the foot-current drew her on. She trudged past the doorway of a great hall from which came the cheering of many voices, and some vast foreign scent blew through the air, but the stimulation was too much and she shrank low to the ground to keep going.

She found herself walking in a group also carrying pungent loads, and realised one was speaking to her. Flora looked into the dark face of a sanitation worker, urgently trying to guide her through a doorway. Flora stepped in, and found a clear space on the floor. The simple scent tiles prompted her to lay down the dead Clover's body, and immediately another worker took it away. Hands pushed her back out into the corridor into another stream of sanitation workers. They marched in silence with their dark heads lowered, their aspect no longer dirty and vile, and their scent a comfort.

There were no chiming bells to mark time in Sanitation, only the differences in the smell of the dirt they cleaned, and the very basic food they ate. There was no chatter or gossip because none of the cleaners could speak, so they derived companionship from labouring together, and pressing close to share their scent.

Like the rest of her kin-sisters, Flora worked in a dull haze, interspersed with pauses for Devotion. When the fragrance of the Queen's Love rose through the vibrating comb, the sanitation workers stopped wherever they were and cried out in slurred reverence, and Flora felt a moment of blissful relief from the constant pain in her head. Then they all returned to work, and her consciousness shrank back down to whatever task was in hand.

Sisters of all kin were born and died by their hundreds every day, so collecting the dead was a common occupation for every sanitation worker. As she carried body after body, Flora grew familiar with the routes down from the top and mid-levels of the hive, to the morgue and waste depot on the lowest level. Certain routes were blocked by kin-sensitive scent-locks, which stopped the floras polluting holy areas of the hive, like the nurseries on the mid-level, or the Fanning Hall and Treasury on the top level. After being buffeted back once or twice by the powerful scents, even the slowest sanitation worker like Flora learned not to try that way again, but sometimes on the mid-level of the hive, drifting scents of the Nursery tugged at her brain. The longer she stood, the more they distressed her, until she blundered away groaning.

Despite their status as lowest of the low, even in the department of Sanitation there was a hierarchy of ability. Certain floras could leave the dull, thudding foot-tracks and collect waste from difficult areas, and these sisters were also used to make short waste-disposal flights with corpses or particularly foul-smelling loads, dropping them a hygienic distance from the hive. The second group, to which Flora belonged, experienced such agony in their antennae if they diverged but one step from their ordained track, that the outer limit of their roaming was down to the morgue, or the freight holding area, both on the lowest level of the hive and near to the landing board. Sometimes Flora would pause here, where the vast foreign scent of Air swirled so strong about her body that her wing-joints trembled with a strange sensation — but to dwell on it was to invite pain, and to return to her duties, a relief.

Each sanitation detail had a supervisor from a higher kin, for they were not to be trusted on their own. Today, Flora's supervisor was a Sister Bindweed, a long narrow bee with sparse fur and a brusque absent manner. She had them working in a vacant area of the Drones' Arrivals Hall, cleaning out recently used incubation chambers in preparation for repair with consecrated wax.

Each bee had her own set of chambers to work on. Though none of them could speak, they grunted and scraped away with the same rhythm, apparently enjoying their work. Some scrutinised their neighbour's labour, mutely pointing out the tiniest particle of remaining dirt, while others checked the soiled wax was efficiently compacted for removal. There were no guiding foot-tracks between the drone chambers, so to block painful confusion Flora clenched down on her scarred antennae to focus on the smallest possible area. It made her obsessive, but her work was immaculate, and Sister Bindweed had to shout and throw a piece of wax at her when it was time for Devotion.

From their place in the Drones' Arrivals Hall, all the sanitation workers could hear the massed choirs of the hive singing through the carved walls. As the vocal vibrations sent the fragrance of the Queen's Love shimmering through the membrane of the honeycomb and deep into their bodies, some of the floras made incoherent sounds of happiness, while others made rhythmic movements as if they were trying to dance. Flora was one of the many who stood transfixed by the blissful sense of being loved — until the divine surge began to ebb away.

A strange sensation rose inside her, strong as hunger but not for food or water. It was as if her abdomen dragged heavy behind her, and her rigid twisted tongue swelled in her mouth. As her detail returned to work, the sensations grew more insistent. Trying to rid herself of them, Flora shook herself from side to side.

"Stop that, you stupid creature!" Sister Bindweed took out her thin rod of propolis resin that she used to poke the sanitation workers without incurring dirty contact and waved it at Flora. "Get into that cell and clean it, unless you want me to send you for the Kindness."

Obediently Flora climbed into the next vacated drone cell. The air was pungent and fetid, the walls and floor crusted with faecal waste. Even through Flora's deadened senses, her brain thundered with the chemical onslaught from the waste of this drone. As the foul smell destroyed the last fragrant vestige of the Queen's Love, a sudden rage rose up inside Flora. She attacked the wall with her jaws, furious at the sexual odour of the filth. The tightness in her mouth ignited in two points of pain on either side of her face, but she worked on in a frenzy, tearing out great soiled chunks of wax and hurling them into the corridor. Then all her sound and vision cut out and she was left in a chaos of odours.

Terror-stricken, Flora threw herself out of the drone's chamber and onto the ground. Somewhere nearby the thinnest filament of the Queen's Love lingered on the ground where it had come through the comb, and she threw her body down against it, breathing it in to counter the flashing black pain in her head.

"717! You are behaving like a demented bluebottle — stop that!"

44

Sister Bindweed tried to kick Flora back to her feet, but with her massive strength Flora clung to the wax until she drew the last molecules of the Queen's Love into her body. Sister Bindweed's puny kicks did not hurt, because something far more powerful was taking place in her mind and body.

Her tongue, so long hard and twisted, was warming and softening, and the disgusting taste of the drone waste was fading. Strength was coursing through her body, and her antennae throbbed as their inner channels opened up, restoring her vision and hearing. Most amazing of all was her sense of smell. She could discern all the different waxes used to make the floor tiles on which she lay, and the propolis inlay of the drone cells; she could smell the warm dirty odour of the sanitation workers' bodies toiling around her —

"Enough!" Too angry to use her propolis rod, Sister Bindweed grabbed Flora by the edge of a wing and started pulling her towards the doors. To resist was to tear the membrane, and Flora was forced to hurry with her.

"If you cannot perform the simplest task" — Sister Bindweed pushed Flora out into the busy corridor — "then good for nothing is what you are, and no more use to this hive!" Sister Bindweed shouted so vehemently that Flora smelled the half-digested pollen bread on her breath, and the slow taint of old age moving in her belly.

"You stand there until the police patrol comes by — they'll know what to do with you, make no mistake." Sister Bindweed shuddered at the smell of her own hands where she had grabbed Flora, and went back inside.

The Drones' Arrivals Hall opened onto a main lobby filled with thousands of bees moving in all directions, never colliding. For a few moments Flora stood motionless, absorbing the tides of scent information that surged through the air and the vibrations in the coded tiles.

Rose Teasel Malus Clover came the rapid knowledge as different sisters passed her by, *Clover Plantain Burdock SAGE* —

At that last and fast-approaching kin-scent, a jolt of fear propelled Flora into the great moving mass of bees in the lobby. Instinctively she wanted to hide, and though a thousand floor codes pulsed their messages at her, one overrode them all, and it came from her heart: *Beware the Sage*.

CHAPTER
SEVEN

The scent of the priestesses faded as Flora went deeper into the warm aromatic criss-crossing of her sisters, their body heat blending their kin-scents together in fragrance and gossip. To listen to their bright voices and understand all they said was a wonderful thing, and she was soon caught up in the major news of the moment, coming through the floor codes and the excited antennae all around her: the rain had stopped, the clouds had parted, the foragers were returning.

"Nectar comes!" shouted some bees. "The flowers love us!"

The comb shimmered and every bee felt joy running through her feet at the sweet smell coming up from the lower level. The bees pushed back to make a passageway through their numbers, and Flora found herself crammed wing to wing at the front of one cheering group, making space for those who were to come.

The bees redoubled their cheers as a forager ran between their cordon, her throat distended with the precious burden of nectar she carried. Filaments of golden scent drifted on the air behind her, telling of the flower that had yielded its sweetness. Flora stared enraptured as more and more of them came through —

sisters of all ages and kin, some with ragged wings, some young and perfect, all with the golden fragrance of nectar streaming behind them.

As the molecular structure of the flowers went into Flora's brain, a strange sound startled her. Sisters either side of her looked at her with compassion — and Flora realised it was her own voice, moaning incoherently as she tried to join in the cheering. The last forager ran past, the golden filaments of nectar scent trailing behind her, calling for Flora to follow.

The golden fragrance drew Flora on, until to her shock she realised she had passed unscathed through the scent-gates on the staircase to the highest level of the hive. There was no time to wonder at that, for now the party of nectar-bearers were passing down a long corridor whose immaculate pale tiles were inlaid with details of flowers. They were prayer tiles, preparing those who walked on them for the sacred mysteries beyond, and each step triggered chemical verses to unscroll.

At the back of the procession, Flora waited for an alarm to sound at her profane presence on this highest and restricted level of the hive — but a cloud of incense rose up beneath her feet just as from those ahead and joined her to the procession. And then, as the two tall double doors in the middle of the passageway swung open to admit them, her soul filled with joy. Waves of raw floral fragrance billowed out on warm air and as Flora entered the sacred refinery of the Fanning Hall, she beheld the genius of her people.

★　★　★

A golden mist and soft harmonic chord shimmered from the centre of the great atrium, whose six towering walls were made of interlocking chalices of honey, all capped and consecrated with the Queen's seal, and curved in to make a domed ceiling. Far below stood hundreds of sisters in concentric circles, all fanning their silver wings. Their faces were joyous and blank and before each was a large chalice of raw nectar. From these vessels the mist and music spiralled into the air as the water evaporated from the nectar, thickening it to honey.

Only now did Flora realise that every forager and receiver of the procession was busy decanting their precious load into open wax chalices, and that she alone had no function there. She knew she should leave — the very presence of a sanitation worker in this holy place must surely warrant punishment — yet it was so wondrous that she could not bear to. From the scented shadows she watched the foragers and their attendants emptying their loads, then straightening their wings and walking out. One of the last young receivers was clumsy and spilled some nectar down the side of a wax chalice, but in her hurry to remain in procession she just glanced down guiltily, then ran to leave with the others.

The tall doors swung closed and the rings of sisters resumed their silver shimmer. The Holy Chord rose up and their wing-beats stirred fragrance through the warm air. To hide in the shadows felt disrespectful so Flora stepped out. Some instinct impelled her to bow to the centre of the atrium, but no sooner had she touched her antennae to the wax floor than her wing-latches clicked open, her virgin wings trembled as her engine fired, and she was lifted off her feet.

Some sisters glanced up, searching for the sound. Flora clamped her thoracic muscles together and dropped down to the wax before they could locate her. She latched her wings tight against her back and looked around in alarm. Bad enough for a sanitation worker to be trespassing here, but to have used her wings —

The extraordinary sensation subsided into her body. To calm her racing brain, Flora looked for any dirt to clean, but the Fanning Hall was immaculate. The only minute element of disorder was where the young receiver had spilled some nectar, now drying down the side of the wax chalice, and the tiles on which it stood.

At the scent, Flora's belly clutched in hunger.

Desire is sin, Greed is sin —

But surely cleaning it would not be sin?

Careful not to let her profane body touch the chalice, Flora knelt down beside the spill and was overcome with the fragrance of honeysuckle. The living spirit of the crimson-gold blooms warmed her body with energy, and she was licking up the last molecules from the tiles when she heard the commotion outside.

The massed vibration of many agitated sisters came closer down the passageway, voices raised in protest.

"Honey!" boomed a deep male voice. "Now!"

"Please Your Malenesses," cried a female voice. "Stop!"

Flora leapt back in alarm as a party of drones barged in and swaggered down the centre aisle towards her. They

50

were huge and pungent with big handsome faces, sun visors over their eyes, and their thick fur was styled with pomade. The shimmering circles of sisters slowed their wings and turned their faces towards the intruders. No one noticed Flora.

"Sir Poplar, Sir Rowan, Sir Linden, all noble sirs," cried another sister running after them, "let us send to Patisserie or —"

"We said we want honey!" shouted another drone.

"A proper deep suck of it," called one more, "none of your dainty little sips."

They began stamping their great armoured feet on the comb, chanting for honey and nectar. The mist from the chalices evaporated, revealing the sisters' distressed faces.

"Keep fanning, pretty sisters," called one of the drones. "We do not linger, we are on a mission of Love! And you, old girl by the door with the long face — good cheer from you too, for we fly for the honour of our hive!"

"Worship to Your Malenesses." A senior Sister Prunus dropped him a deep curtsy. Flora joined in as all around the other sisters copied the obeisance. As she went low she stared at the drones' armoured feet, their powerful tendons and thighs, and the underside of their huge thoraxes. Their smell was high but not unpleasant, and her breathing spiracles dilated to inhale more deeply.

"Might we most respectfully suggest, Your Malenesses" — and Sister Prunus rose to her feet — "that because of the constant rains, and this time of austerity, you might confine yourselves to our recently gathered nectars? For instance —"

"Honey is our want, so honey we must have." The drone threw a big muscular arm around Sister Prunus and his scent drifted across her face. "Think now of those foreign princesses, waiting for us. How fatigued, how impatient for love must they be? Would you bind them in chastity a single moment longer? Or shall we fill our bellies with the strength of this hive, then free them with our swords?"

Sister Prunus gasped at his lewd gesture, her antennae waving wildly. The big drone laughed and released her, and all the sisters laughed too, avid for more of his scent. Sister Prunus quickly groomed herself to hide her shining face. Then she stepped forward and clapped all her hands.

"Their Malenesses will take their Right of Access."

Trapped between the disapproving sisters at the doors and the gluttonous drones, Flora remained where she was. The drones made very free in the Fanning Hall and, like every other sister, Flora watched in astonishment as they tasted different honeys, slurped from effervescing pails of raw nectar and whirled fanning sisters out from their sacred circles to dance with them. The one who pawed Sister Prunus was boldest, and his kin was Quercus.

"Linden!" His shout echoed around the holy chamber. "Come here, you fine little runt, and taste your namesake — lime-blossom is good eating!"

"Only the best for me." A small drone straightened his neck-ruff and crossed to where Sir Quercus stood gorging. When he bent to taste it, the other pushed his face in it, then grabbed him by the fur and pulled him out, laughing at his jest.

"A king's share, to console you for your certain failure."

Sir Linden wiped his face of honey and forced a grim smile.

"You are too sure, my brother. For I hear of queens who will favour wit over strength." He pulled his ruff straight. "Such a one will be mine."

"Ha!" Sir Quercus patted him so hard he staggered. "My wit is all pent in my prick, so I shall triumph with her as well."

"Unless a crow choose you first and snap you in its great blue beak!"

The sisters gasped at the mention of the bird.

"More likely take you," said Sir Quercus, "who can barely keep up with a butterfly. Though you'd not make much of a feast."

Sir Linden continuing his grooming. "Unlike you, so large and magnificent."

"You speak truly." Sir Quercus turned to the sisters. "Fortune favours me, does she not, ladies?" And he swelled his sturdy thorax, raised his fur in three tall crests on his head, and pumped his male aroma so it rose up around him in a cloud. Some sisters swooned, and some, like Sister Prunus, spontaneously applauded.

"Who will groom me?"

Several sisters rushed forward and other drones unlatched their wings in invitation and they too were attended. Flora began edging to the doors.

"You there — wait!" Sister Prunus came towards her. "We have not called for Sanitation — what in the air is a dirty flora doing here? Did housekeeping leave the scent-gate down again?"

Flora was about to answer, then held her tongue. She nodded and grunted.

"Oh, these shortages are becoming abominable. The wrong kin everywhere — and yours so stupid and slow you cannot follow the simplest track." Sister Prunus looked at Flora suspiciously. "Unless you were stealing!"

Flora urgently shook her head and put her antennae low. Her kin behaved cravenly, she had seen and hated it so many times — but now she did the same, backing away as if in terror. She bumped into someone behind her, and Sister Prunus smacked her on the head between the antennae.

"Your Maleness, allow me to apologise." Sister Prunus smiled sweetly. "Please forgive the soiling contact. I will call a higher kin to groom you clean."

"From Sanitation, is she?" It was Sir Linden, the only drone unattended. "Are they all so hairy? Do not trouble yourself, Sister Primrose, today I have a mind for something different. This one may groom me."

"Your Maleness — a *flora*?"

"Do not question His Maleness's particular preference." He looked at Flora, and she saw how honey was still caught in his fur. "Bring me some spurge nectar."

"*Spurge?* Your Maleness jests!" Sister Prunus laughed hysterically. "He knows that we would never serve it, corrupt as it is from the Myriad's feet." She folded her hands. "You will not find it in this hive."

"Oh. A pity, for I heard it was good, with a cricket's kick."

"Your Maleness, nobody here would say that, for no forager —"

"It was no forager, Sister Plantain —"

"Prunus, Your Maleness."

"As you wish, madam. But it was a fine dark fellow at Congregation who stank of it, and he said it made his dronewood hard as the twig we stood on."

"Stop, please! Your Maleness speaks too boldly —"

"At least, I think that's what he said, in his thick and foreign tongue."

"Foreign?" Sister Prunus recovered herself. "From what direction? I only ask because the Sage like to be informed of all immigrants in our neighbourhood." She lowered her voice. "In case of disease, you see. Also, they take our nectar."

"Calm yourself, Sister, this Congregation was further than you could fly."

"Oh, I am just a house-bee, I did not presume! But — Your Maleness is not thinking of inviting any guests? Our pantries are emptier than we would like —"

"Do you not think I have enough competition as it is?" Sir Linden looked gloomily at the other drones being groomed. "In any case, the dark fellow was last seen leading the field in pursuit of a very fine princess, and is probably now king in some sumptuous palace. Run and tell your dreary priestesses that."

"Fresh news, I shall!" Sister Prunus bobbed a curtsy, rejuvenated with excitement. "News is always of value to Sister Sage — thank you, Your most generous Maleness." She ran off.

Flora started after her, anxious to be gone.

"You're not going anywhere." Sir Linden pointed to his crotch. "You have to groom me. I can't be the only one without someone."

At his strong smell, another pheromone lock burst open inside Flora's antennae. Her mind flooded with disordered images —

— *larva babies in their cradles* — *a shrivelled wing pulled taut* —

She felt him trying to push her down.

"Are you deaf? Groom me when I tell you — it's the Law."

A baby on a hook —

Flora shoved him away and ran out into the prayer-filled corridor. He followed.

"I am a Prince of the realm! You *will* obey me!"

Trapped between the drone and a phalanx of identical Sage priestesses marching towards the Fanning Hall in a cloud of incense, Flora hunched herself down like the lowliest sanitation worker.

"How dare you —" Sir Linden lunged for her and slipped in the path of the Sage priestesses. Unable to pass a male without obeisances, they were forced to stop while he got to his feet, cursing wildly.

Flora did not look back but ran as fast as she could. She almost missed the small dark doorway, but as she dashed in to hide, the ground fell away under her feet and she tumbled, for it was not a room, but a staircase.

The steps were deep and steep and she kept her wings tight against her body as she struggled to right herself. Falling against an old wax wall, she clung and listened for pursuit from above.

There was neither scent nor sound, only the pumping of her own blood and the thirsty pull of air into her breathing spiracles. Flora forced her panic down. Her newly functioning antennae told her she was on the lowest level of the hive, and the final flight of steps levelled out into a narrow corridor that led to a door. She crept forward to scan what was beyond.

Through the old wax she first detected the distinctive odour of her own kin, and then the long inert forms of bees. It was a worker dormitory, and a cleaning detail. Deeply relieved, Flora opened the door — and stepped into the morgue.

Several of her kin-sisters stared back in equal surprise, then emitted a strange sound, that might have been laughter. One signalled her to close the door, then they continued taking bodies down from the racks. For the first time, Flora became conscious of a definite intelligence behind their strange faces. With a start of excitement, she understood that these floras were from the top echelon of Sanitation, taking the cadavers to the landing board, to fly them out of the hive.

Flora bit hold of the biggest, heaviest corpse she could see, a bald old sister from Patisserie with hidden pollen in her pockets. Then she followed her kin-sisters out of the morgue towards the sun-warmed wood of the landing board, and the vault of sky beyond.

CHAPTER
EIGHT

A great crowd blocked the lobby to the landing board and the sanitation corpse-bearers were forced to wait. Eddies of warm dry wind swirled towards them, then came cheers and applause as bees pressed back to make a corridor of space, and the foragers came rushing through. Awestruck, Flora stared at the dishevelled sisters with their blazing faces and radiant ragged wings, who smelled of no kin but the wild high air. They ran into an imposing atrium that opened off the lobby, from where there was more stamping and cheering, and the crowd poured in behind them.

The sanitation workers moved on towards the landing board, into a cordoned-off area, to prevent contamination of higher kin passing to and fro on hive business. The sun's warmth created a festive atmosphere, and Flora thrilled at the sound of her sisters' flight engines humming through their registers. She watched water-gatherers returning with bulging throats, their faces sculpted sleek from their work, then chains of receivers passed in exotic loads of raw pollen, never dropping a single grain. More wind-blown foragers came and went and Flora admired them with all her heart.

"Corpse-bearers next!" It was the stentorian voice of a Thistle, traditional guards of the landing board.

Flora walked out of the dark, closed hive into a dazzling world of light and space, and a floor made of wood. It was completely blank of any codes except the bright scent beacons laid along the edge to guide the foragers home, and the only other marker was the sun.

"It's busy, so stay low and be quick." The Thistle guard spoke loud and slow. "You know where to go — don't linger, and return on the left."

Flora shook her head.

"Your cleansing flight — even your kin can remember that one place." The Thistle called to the bees jostling behind Flora. "Patience, sisters!"

Flora raised her antennae, searching for information. It made her head hurt and she looked down. Below the landing board in the tangle of grass and nettle and dock and trefoil that locked to the dense wet earth, disturbing scents wove strong and strange, telling of other creatures that lived there. The green began to seethe.

"Stop that — no one looks down." The Thistle pulled Flora away. Both of them turned at the huge rumble of thoracic engines. The pungent smell of drones billowed out onto the landing board and led by Sir Quercus the drones marched out. Plumes high, visors down and their massive chests expanded, they turned to the Thistle sentries and showed their best aspects. The Thistle guards dropped nominal curtsies.

"Worship to Your Malenesses." Their tone was respectful, if not fervent.

60

"And honour to our hive!" roared Sir Quercus, and all his brothers cheered as they crowded out onto the landing board. The smell of honey percolated through their thick aroma. As one, the sisters looked down. Their precious golden wealth clogged the drones' feet, was trodden across the landing board and trailed back into the hive. Shocked faces of other sisters crowded in the doorway behind them and the Thistle guards' antennae flickered rapidly at each other. No one said a word.

With a mighty bang the drones unlatched their wings, fired their engines for flight and tuned their roars to a rousing thunder. Flora saw Sir Linden at the rear, his fur still sticky as he struggled to stabilise his own slightly higher pitch. Too late she shrank behind a Thistle guard.

"You there!" he shouted into the noise. "How dare you disobey me? Come and lick my feet clean —"

He jumped back as a forager landed on the board in front of him.

"Make way, Your Maleness." She pushed past to where Flora stood with Sister Thistle. "Lily 500 returning." Her nectar-scented voice was hoarse, her bright ragged wings told her age, but she radiated energy like a tiny sun.

"Madam Forager, we know you well." Sister Thistle bowed deeply to her.

Lily 500 was about to go into the hive, then turned to the drones.

"No sister shall lick *our sacred honey* from your feet. Would you draw the Myriad to watch and mock us?"

"What Myriad, noble crone?" Sir Quercus barged forward. "There are none today, so wish us Queenspeed and be out of our way!"

The old forager glanced at Flora, but spoke only to the Thistle.

"You are charged to keep the board clear, yet a corpse-bearer lingers."

"Forgive us, Madam Forager, you are right, but they have sent out an ignorant one! What am I supposed to do? I cannot send a corpse back in, and she certainly cannot drop it from the board —"

"As if I would suggest that. Shortages and incompetence —" Lily 500 pulled out one of Flora's wings. "Nothing the matter with them!" She scanned Flora's antennae with her own. Flora winced, and the forager looked to the guard. "They have wrecked her brain so badly it is a wonder she can see or hear."

"Good madams!" interrupted Sir Quercus. "Gossip elsewhere: you delay our squadron. We like to leave with a good show, not all raggle-taggle like you ancient independents. So now if you would kindly move."

Lily 500 held her ground. She flicked an antenna and a young Clover receiver ran out from the hive, knelt before her and opened her mouth. Lily 500 arched her body, triggering a stream of golden nectar from her own crop into the Clover's mouth. When there was no more, the Clover bobbed a curtsy and ran back inside.

"Crone vomit?" Sir Quercus was appalled. "Is that what we're drinking?"

"Nectar, Sir. How did you think we carried it?" Lily 500 turned to Flora. "Hold your burden tight, and follow."

She pushed her off the board.

Blades of grass slashed towards Flora's face, the rough wooden slats of the hive grazed past her antennae and the sun spun as she tumbled through the air. She flailed for balance and then, with a thunderous vibration, her flight engine fired her up in a great jet of speed and she was aloft, mounting the air behind the silver trace of Lily 500's wings. Behind her came the massive blast of the drone squadron lifting off, and faint cheering from the hive far below, but she did not look down.

They rose up over the orchard, cool wind streaming down Flora's sides and fluttering the dried edges of the dead sister's wings, still held tight in her mouth. The sun warmed her wings and a thrilling power surge took her higher so that the world spread wide in all directions, the grid of green and brown below, the dark rise of the hills, the rough odour of the sprawling town —

It seemed to Flora that she heard the Holy Chord, though that was impossible for they were far beyond the hive. Its source was Lily 500, her wings two humming arcs of light around her. Flora sped forward to her side. The old forager veered away and Flora followed through trails and tunnels of scent, sweet and bitter threads of odour, focusing into the strong clear scent of resin and propolis as the conifers came into range. Lily 500 made a tight agile loop around Flora, forcing her down so she saw where to make her drop.

With the release of the burden Flora shot up into the sunshine and flew loops of pure joy and relief. Her vision sharpened so that far below she could see two raucous bluebottles chase each other, and below them, male mosquitoes whined their song over a pond, their blue streamers fluttering from their antennae. Even lower the dark blood-filled females cruised at the water's edge and Flora stored every minute detail before she surged higher. For the first time in her life she was utterly free, with no walls or rules to curb her, and she dived and soared for joy. The more the sun warmed her, the greater grew her strength and skill and she looked for Lily 500 to thank her — but the old forager was already a speck in the distance.

She was alone in the bright vastness. In an instant, a ravenous hunger seized Flora's body and homesickness hit her soul so hard that she cried out in surprise. She could not smell the Queen, nor any sisters, nor the hive, the orchard, nor one familiar thing.

The more she searched, the more the void of sky pressed her body to a speck, until she felt so small and alone that without a sister to cling to she thought she was dying. When her body lifted on a wave of acrid air, Flora soared crazily and saw that it came from a great black bird high above her — *a crow!* Her alarm glands fired and she sped away from it in blind panic.

Devotion Devotion Devotion — Flora searched the air for any scent trace of Holy Mother and scanned the foreign shapes and colours below her in an effort to reorient herself. Massive green and beige fields dulled the air with their monotonous scent and she veered away to glean any clue for home. With a surge of relief she picked up the scent of the orchard and then of her sisters — never more beautiful. Their mingled scent grew stronger as Flora entered the air corridor back to the hive, and her joy in flight was nothing compared to her gratitude in homecoming. The little green ruffle of the orchard came into view, and then the tiny grey square of the beehive. Not until this moment had Flora known how much she loved it and all who lived there. She could not wait to fold her wings and run into its warm depths, and press wing to wing with her sisters in the sacrament of Devotion.

At the thought of the Queen, Flora scented the precious molecules of her divine fragrance, poised and spinning like jewels where the air currents converged. Her heart filled with passion and confidence, but as the hive came nearer and the earth and trees raced past below, she saw foragers streaming back through the orchard, racing for the landing board. A new scent mixed with the homecoming scent, and as Flora began her descent her venom sac swelled hard in her belly and her dagger unsheathed.

The code was alarm: the hive was under attack.

CHAPTER
NINE

Laid at close intervals along the length of the landing board, the alarm pheromone flashed its message across the orchard air. The last foragers rushed to get in as a foul alien scent mingled with it, sweet and corrupt like rotting fruit. It came from the lurid straggle of wasps hovering near the hive, drunk and jeering. Flora could hear her sisters yelling at her to hurry, but as she descended through the smeary marker trails the wasps littered in their wake, they turned their black gazes on her and sizzled their stings in welcome.

Flora curved up again on a blade of air and the wasps shrieked with laughter at her cowardice — before she hurtled at one of them and knocked the vile creature out of the air into the apple leaves. The touch of the wasp's body against hers enraged her and she drove herself up higher, looking for another. But the wasps were already above her, buzzing high and furious as they swayed on their points of air, not to be taken like that again.

"Dirty fiends!" shouted one of the Thistle guards to the wasps. "Infidel!" But her trembling antennae gave lie to her brave words.

Flora dropped down onto the landing board between the sentries. She smelled their flaring war-glands and knew her own streamed as strong, but a wave of fear came from within the hive.

"What did we expect," muttered another guard in a low voice, "leaving honey on the board? Advertising our wealth to the Myriad, no one to clean it, everyone rushing out crazed as soon as the sun shines —"

She sprayed a great jet of her war scent into the air and the wasps laughed shrilly. They flung back the challenge with a hard gust of their own harsh smell and its oily particles settled on the landing board.

"Closer!" yelled the first Thistle who had spoken, her antennae rigid with rage. "I cannot smell you until I stick my dagger between your filthy plates." She too buzzed a blast of her war-gland at them.

"Oh, you fat and useless creature," called back one of the wasps, pirouetting to show her tiny waist. "What pale squirt was that? I doubt you can even fly." Her friends reeled in the air, hissing with laughter.

"Stay!" A new Thistle held back her colleague. "They try to draw us." She motioned to Flora. "You're big and brave — get inside and hold the line."

Sisters stood densely packed and silent, their battle glands flaring and weapons at the ready. The smell of fear trickled up here and there, but every sister pointed her antennae forward and none gave way to it. Flora waited in the vanguard as the Thistle pumped out wave after wave of war scent, but the orchard was silent.

The bees waited. Murmurs began. Perhaps the wasps had gone. Wings crushed, the heat was rising, and a tide of irritation seeped through the crowd. And then — a wave of acid air rushed in and every sister's feet felt the heavy alien vibration as a great wasp settled on the landing board. There was the sound of a hard scuffle and then a cracking sound. A Thistle guard screamed, then another. Standing right at the front, Flora saw it all.

The wasp was a huge female with bands of acid yellow and glossy black. Her head was as large as three sisters' and she used her slashing claws to catch the guards one by one, killing each one with a snap of her heavy jaws. Then she flattened her long antennae, crouched down and peered inside the hive.

Spasms of fear shot through all the bees at the sight of her glittering malevolent eyes, but not one of them moved. Flora stared back at the wasp and felt her dagger slide out. The wasp smiled at her.

"Pretty pretty . . ." She drove a whip of her acid scent down the passageway, wrapping round the antennae of dozens of bees so that they yelped in anger and disgust. She pushed her huge face closer, blocking the light.

"Greetings," she hissed softly, "my sweet, juicy cousins." Her claw flashed into the hive, close enough for Flora to see the entrails on its tip and smell the Thistle's blood. To stop herself running, she dug her claws harder into the comb. Deep within the hive, a faint vibration pulsed towards her. It spoke in her mind.

Keep still. Hold firm and wait.

Flora gripped harder into the wax and held the wasp's stare. The wasp gazed softly into her eyes, willing her closer. The scent of its malice rose stronger.

Draw her in, spoke the thought in Flora's mind. *Lure her, lure her . . .*

Flora stepped backwards and all her sisters moved with her. The vibration in the comb came stronger and they felt it too. She kept her gaze locked with the wasp's.

Lure her. Draw her.

Flora let her antennae tremble and the wasp pushed in closer.

"Are you the one, shall it be you?" Her voice had a soft sing-song cadence, but her gaze was hard and calculating. "What a fat feast you will make, little cousin . . ." The wasp eased herself deeper into the hive entrance, and Flora could not hold in her fear, for with her sisters so dense behind her there was no retreat from mortal combat.

The wasp's body rasped on the hive floor. Four of her six elbows were in, the only light the yellow striping of her face. Flora dug down into the wax again, but the voice in her mind had stopped. She would be the first to die, but she would fight for her sisters' lives, for Holy Mother's life.

She unlatched her wings and heard the sound of every sister doing the same.

"No," the wasp crooned, pulling her last pair of legs into the hive. "We should not fight: all I want is to take you to meet the chil . . . dren, all the hungry . . . little

... *children* —" A claw slashed out and she laughed. "Forgive me, you're too delicious."

DRAW HER . . .

The voice was clear and strong in Flora's mind. She whimpered and backed away and the wasp crawled in after her. The smell was suffocating and her soft hissing struck terror into Flora's body. She felt that all her sisters had crept around the edges and their numbers had filled from the back. There was no more room to move. The monster gathered herself to spring.

NOW!

Flora roared it as the wasp lunged — and sprang upon the monster's back, her claws scrabbling for purchase on the slippery armour.

The wasp hissed and writhed in a frenzy of rage, one sister after another shrieking as she snapped their heads in her jaws and ripped their bellies with her claws. Flora fought her way up to the wasp's head and the lashing black whips of the creature's antennae. She caught one in her mouth and bit down.

The wasp cried out and hurled herself against the walls, trying to crush her attacker against them. Flora clung on and spat the foul blood as below her sisters threw themselves at the thrashing foe. Then Flora lunged for the other antenna, cracking it off the wasp's head so that the hole jetted pulses of green blood. Screaming in agony and rage, the blinded wasp killed sister after sister, but she was one against many and the tide of bees kept coming until the stinging biting weight of their bodies covered her and held her down unable to move.

70

Then they beat their wings, fast and tight with fury so that the air heated until they themselves could barely breathe. The wasp was strong and kept struggling, but she grew weaker, and then she stopped. Only when her smell changed and the bees heard the dull cracking of her shell from the heat did they cease their fanning.

The great wasp lay dead, and so did hundreds of brave sisters closest to her, killed by the colossal heat. Many others were maimed in the fight, and outside on the landing board, fallen Thistle sisters lay dead or mutilated in the sun. The air was thick with the foul scent of the wasps and the blood of bees, but the hive was saved.

The dead wasp was a horrific sight. The huge glittering black eyes were cooked white, and two green blebs of blood marked the roots of her antennae. Herself unhurt, Flora began to help her wounded sisters. More bees came running from all areas of the hive with vials of holy propolis to bind up the broken shells of any who might live, but the casualties were countless.

Flora carried fallen sisters out to the sunny landing board and laid them down gently, knowing they would not return. Many lay in agony with their limbs crushed. Flora stopped to comfort one, a sturdy little Plantain whose face was half gone. Sage priestesses moved among the dying to bless them with the Queen's Love and ease their passing. One in particular caught Flora's attention, the sun bright in her pale fur. The priestess turned to look, and by the power of her gaze, Flora knew they had met before. Quickly she walked back into the hive, to the group of sanitation workers gathered at the wasp's body.

They were wild-eyed and terrified of the huge carcass, until Flora spat out a mouthful of its blood and grabbed one of its legs. It broke away from the body as she pulled it, and the sanitation workers roared in approval. No longer afraid, they fell upon the wasp, tearing what was left of her to pieces, and carrying them out. Then, because the scent of the battle was broadcast on the air far and wide, the remaining Thistle guards let them hurl the pieces over the edge of the board.

Bees of all kin scrubbed away at the landing board to rid it of the wasp's foul smell, and as each section was cleared the priestesses passed along the edge and laid new markers to cleanse and re-consecrate the hive. Sisters looked for dead of their own kin, then the priestesses stood wing to wing and sang the Holy Chord as even the timid house-bees came forward to fly the dead to the burial area. Flora searched too, but no sanitation worker had fallen.

"Your kin does not fight." It was Sister Sage, the pale priestess who had taken Flora first to the Nursery, and then the detention cell. "Though you did, and bravely. Why did you not run back inside?"

"The voice in my head." Flora felt no fear. "It told me what to do."

Sister Sage looked at her for a long time.

"That was the Hive Mind. It has also restored your tongue." The priestess touched her antennae to Flora's, and once again the divine fragrance of the Queen's Love filled her soul. "You are indeed unusual."

"Is my Holy Mother safe?"

"More questions . . . Yes, she is. And it is our ancient law that no matter what her kin, any sister who channels the Hive Mind in times of crisis may be taken to meet Her. If, of course, she survives. It appears you have." She clapped her hands together, and six beautiful young bees arrived at her side. All wore fresh veils of the Queen's Love, which made their faces iridescent.

"Behold the Queen's ladies-in-waiting. Go with them, attend them well."

CHAPTER
TEN

The ladies spoke very prettily to Flora as they led her through the hive, in accents so refined it was hard to understand them. Outside the silent Dance Hall the lobby was busy with sisters rushing to help the wounded. From there the ladies escorted Flora up an unfamiliar staircase whose steps chimed softly in welcome. They emerged in a small hall in the mid-level of the hive, near to the hallowed Chapel of Wax.

The soothing warm smell of the Nursery drifted in the corridor and Flora hoped they should pass through it so that she might see the babies again — and so that Sister Teasel and the other nurses might see how she was honoured for her service to the hive. But the ladies took another route, down the long passageway between the worker dormitories and the Arrivals Hall, and beyond Flora's knowledge of the hive. They stopped at elegant doors made of many different shades of gold, cream and white wax and exquisitely carved with flowers. Lady Burnet held them open.

They entered a small vaulted chamber made of immaculately plain cream wax. Three silver and three green pitchers stood on an old hexagonal table, but otherwise the room was empty. The air was so full of the Queen's Love that it sparkled, and Flora laughed in joy as she breathed it.

"Holy Mother is near! Am I really to meet Her?"

Lady Burnet smiled and took up one of the pitchers from the table.

"Yes, my dear, but you are unclean, and first must be prepared."

Then each of the ladies took a pitcher and stood around Flora, pouring ceremonially in turns, pure water then healing infusions in case of injury or disease. Flora shivered as the wasp's blood mingled with that of her fallen sisters and ran down her legs and drained into a channel in the ground. Then the ladies encircled her and fanned her as if she were a chalice of nectar. Only when Flora's thick russet fur stood high and dry were they satisfied she was clean. While Lady Primrose and Lady Violet each used a lump of golden propolis to fill in the many scratches on Flora's legs, they all sang softly in another language, lilting and beautiful.

"What does that mean?" Flora felt ashamed at the care they lavished on her.

"It tells of Her Majesty's marriage flights." Lady Primrose giggled.

"Shh! Not for her ears!" Lady Violet smiled at Flora. "Though you shine so clean you're barely a flora at all now."

"Thank you." Flora tried to curtsy. At this all the ladies came forward to demonstrate the correct way, guiding her limbs with delicate hands.

"It is not your fault." Lady Burnet was so kind. "You cannot help your kin."

"Yet she was so brave" — Lady Meadowsweet also smiled at Flora — "and seems so willing and humble — could we not do a little more with her?"

"We could!" Lady Primrose took hold of Flora's fur. "Make it softer."

"Shine her whole cuticle, not just the legs — make her colour seem lighter."

"Do something about her breath —"

Flora swallowed hard. "I am very sorry, my ladies. It is the wasp's blood."

"So shocking." Lady Burnet offered her water to drink. "But how wonderfully you speak; I can understand nearly every word. Not like a flora at all. Now if only you did not look it! Ladies, it would be a fitting tribute, would it not, for her bravery? Would you like that, my dear?"

"To change my kin?"

"And lose your wonderful heritage of service?" Lady Burnet laughed. "Goodness me, no! But we might disguise it, a little."

When they had exhausted their skills with grooming, pomade and propolis, the ladies trained Flora how to sit and rise, but were forced to let her splaying curtsy go uncorrected, for there was nothing to be done with that. When the comb trembled through the hive the ladies did not move to attend the service of Devotion, for here the Queen's Love filled the chamber so strongly that anyone who entered became euphoric as they breathed.

76

Flora's joy increased when she saw the food. Patisserie and nectar finer and more fragrant than she could ever have imagined were served to them by pretty sisters from Rosa and Bryony, but on observing Flora's manners, the ladies all agreed she was still too uncouth to meet Her Majesty. They made her demonstrate the correct way to eat and drink so often that for the first time in her life, Flora's hunger was satisfied and she could leave food uneaten. Then they bid her keep her hands still to let set the fashionable shapes they had twisted into her fur, so she rested in great contentment, listening to their bright bubbling conversation — and, despite the vanity, surreptitiously admired the sheen of her newly polished legs.

After supper they took Flora with them to fulfil the daily duty of visiting the Queen's Library. When they closed all the doors of the hexagonal chamber, one continuous mosaic of coded scent tiles ran round the walls, and featured on each was one small central panel. Flora sniffed in fascination, detecting the bouquet of home amidst the many unfamiliar smells.

"Instead of Devotion," whispered Lady Primrose, "we maintain the Stories of Scent. Not nearly as pleasant, but just follow along and we shall soon be out. We'll only do the first three, so don't worry."

The ladies formed a line and put Flora at the end. They walked in a circle around the chamber repeating the Our Mother, and then Lady Burnet stopped in front of a panel.

"The first story is called *The Honeyflow*." She smiled at Flora. "The lightest touch, then move back." She dipped her antennae and touched the panel to demonstrate. Immediately the scent of flowers rose up from it, developing and blending as each of the ladies took their turn. Flora marvelled to recognise the ancient kin-scents: the Sage and the Teasel, the Rosebay Willowherb, the Clover, Violet, Celandine, Burnet, Thistle, Malus, Bindweed and all of them. Of the floras, there was no reference.

"Quickly, my dear." Lady Burnet's voice had the slightest tremor. "We must move along."

As Flora touched her antennae to the first panel, all the blossom of spring burst into life and the air was filled with orchard sweetness and the scent of lush grass. But before she could fully enjoy it, a pressure wave went through the air in the chamber. She heard the harsh caw of birds and smelled the sharp tang of a wasp.

As she leapt back in shock, all the ladies laughed nervously.

"A common reaction," said Lady Burnet, "but it is only a story; it cannot hurt you. Fresh as dew, yet made in the Time before Time. Is it not a marvel? And better that we learn of the Myriad — though you of course have met one already."

The ladies clapped politely. Flora felt embarrassed.

"There are others — of the Myriad? Not just wasps?"

"Oh, they are legion. It means all those who would hurt us, or steal from us, or who pollute and destroy

78

our rightful food. Like flies, for instance." Lady Burnet put a hand to her head. "Take great care in here, lest all the stories stir at once — our antennae would split with shock." She turned to her ladies. "I think we may conclude for this evening."

"But there are five more." Flora gazed at the other walls, from which intricate and unknown scents coiled then curled back in, without diffusing into the air. She looked to the ladies for explanation and saw all of their antennae quivering with stress, and that Lady Primrose was on the edge of panic. Lady Burnet forced a smile.

"To tend these panels is to strengthen the Hive Mind with the ancient scent-stories of our faith. The priestesses do not expect us to read each one." She looked down. "The first and second panels are enough. The rest . . . hold terrors."

"I am not afraid," said Flora. "I long to serve my hive."

"My dear — please recall your kin. Do not presume —"

Lady Meadowsweet coughed and looked at Lady Burnet, a world of meaning in her gaze. "Does it matter who reads them, if the duty is done?"

"Yes," added Lady Violet, "I have heard her kin have less nerves."

"And would be less affected," agreed pretty Lady Primrose.

Flora stepped forward.

"Please, my ladies, if I may do any duty, to the hive or the Queen — I am strong and willing" — pressing her knees tight, she knelt before them — "and I long to serve!"

The ladies clapped again. Lady Burnet raised her up.

"Very well. The second story is called *The Kindness*."

Flora saw how the ladies flinched at the name. She stood up stronger.

"I have heard that word before. I will do it."

She walked to the next panel. As she touched her antennae to it, the voices and hubbub of the hive rose up all around them, and the wonderful comforting smell of sisters rustling their wings for sleep. She was overwhelmed by love for all her sisters, and the beauty of the hive. Then her feet tingled as if walking on coded tiles, and in her mind she saw herself walking down a long corridor, with a Thistle guard. She saw herself kneel, her knees still splayed, then bend her head low to the wax as the guard braced her feet and raised a great sharp claw above her.

Forgive me, sister —

Pain streaked through the join of Flora's head and thorax. She cried out and staggered back from the panel.

She was in the Queen's Library, and the ladies stood watching. She felt her body — unharmed — but the shock of the blow reverberated.

"I — I don't understand."

Lady Primrose giggled nervously.

"Every sister sees her own end. Though we never go as far as you just did — it is enough to walk the corridor and know what is coming!"

"The Kindness means death?"

"*Amen*," chorused the ladies. "No use to the hive, no use for life!"

At their hysterical laughter Flora laughed too, excited by the terrible vision.

"Let me do another! Now I understand —"

"You understand nothing — you are merely brave." Lady Burnet leavened her words with a smile. "But if you *would* take one more, then half are done, and our duty is amply fulfilled." She followed Flora's eyes around the last three. "No. Those are too strong, only the priestesses tend those stories."

"Then one more." Flora drew herself up, proud of her courage and the awe in the eyes of these fine ladies. "And with all my heart."

The other bees stood near the door as Lady Burnet positioned Flora at the third panel.

"Keep your wings latched," she told her, "and stop at any time."

Flora stepped forward and touched her antennae to the wax mosaic. It was plainer than the second, its scent held close to the wax as if to shield its secret, but as she focused, its peculiar fragrance structure began to part.

First came the intense bouquet of the hive, strong and welcoming and laced with the wealth of a million different flowers' nectar. It smelled of sunshine and sisters, and Flora drew it in more deeply, searching for the strange accent note she had first registered. It darted at the edge of her consciousness, just out of reach.

"Good, that is enough," murmured Lady Burnet from the door. "Let us go."

But the olfactory loop held Flora's attention: the hive, the sun, the honey — then without warning came a blast of wild cold air and choking smoke. Flora staggered. Her body was in the room but her senses flooded with the panic of ten thousand sisters roaring their engines, the dazing sun and the overpowering smell of honey.

"That story is called *The Visitation*."

The voice was sweet and thrilling, and the hand that touched Flora took away her fear.

"It tells of robbery and terror, and the survival of our people." The scent mirage was gone, and in its place an intense pure wave of Devotion filled the chamber. Flora dropped to her six knees, at last in the presence of the Queen. She laid her antennae along the ground in reverence.

"Brave daughter."

Flora looked up. At first all she could see was the golden aura, but then Her Majesty's beautiful eyes shone through, lit with kindness and love. She was magnificently large, with long shapely legs and a graceful tapering abdomen, full and buoyant under the golden tracery of her folded wings.

"Mother," Flora whispered.

"Child," said the Queen. "Do not be ashamed." She raised Flora to her feet and smiled at all her ladies. "Come, my daughters, let us be more comfortable in my chamber, that I may hear about my ancient cousin Vespa's wicked venture."

CHAPTER
ELEVEN

Flora 717, low of kin and sweeper of filth, now sat with the Queen and her ladies in Her Majesty's own private sitting room, eating jewelled lily-cakes and drinking fresh nectar, while she told her story of the wasp and the heat ball. Without warning the Queen scanned her, then to Flora's shame the smell of the wasp rose from her body again. The ladies started in fright and protested they had washed her.

"Hush, daughters." The Queen smiled. "I only wished to make sure that even in its last traces, the scent of the Vespa had not changed. Her ancient envy still beats strong; that is why they want to steal from us, as if our honey or our children will give them our power. In the Time before Time they chose blood above nectar, and we became foes."

Lady Burnet clasped her hands. "Immortal Mother protects Her children."

"*Hallowed be Thy Womb,*" all the ladies responded, Flora too, as the words rose unbidden from her tongue.

"Leave me, daughters."

Then the Queen lay down on her couch of petals, folded herself in a haze of scented sleep and vanished from their view.

The ladies showed Flora her bed, and it was soft and sweetly scented, almost as fragrant as the cribs in Category One.

"Because the Nursery is just beyond that door," said Lady Violet from her neighbouring couch. "Perhaps you shall see it tomorrow when we attend Holy Mother at Her Laying Progress. With all the eggs and glowing cribs — it is a sacred marvel beyond words." She coughed. "Do not be offended if we cannot take you."

"I will not."

"Your humble attitude is honour to your kin." Then Lady Violet wrapped herself in a thin scented veil of sleep and spoke no more. Flora lay in the darkness, breathing in the divine nurturing perfume that held them like a tender embrace. She drew it deep into her body until she felt her abdomen soften and glow.

The next morning the sun bell rang and the Queen's fragrance rose strong and sweet as the ladies opened the doors to the Nursery. They called Flora to come with them and they entered the great chamber of Category One behind a dense veil of seclusion. They were now in the most sacred area of the hive, the Laying Rooms, row upon row of immaculate cribs empty and waiting for the Queen.

The Queen's scent rose high as she went into her birth trance. Her face shone brighter, her scent pulsed, then with a fast graceful rhythm she began swinging her magnificent long abdomen from side to side, each time sliding the tip deep within a crib. At the back of the

Progress, carrying the water and cooling cloths, Flora saw the faint point of light remaining in the wax, where a tiny new egg adhered to the bottom. Each one glowed with soft gold light then faded down as the Queen moved on, her birth dance so hypnotically beautiful that Flora wanted to swing her own body in joy, but seeing that none of the other ladies danced but followed most demurely, she held her urge in check and did as they did.

Six times she returned to the Queen's chambers for fresh water and pollen cakes before all the cribs were filled. The Laying Room was soft and bright with new life, the Queen stood proud and exhausted, and her ladies wept in delight.

Back in the Queen's chambers, Lady Burnet directed Flora to clean and make ready the common parts while she and the other ladies took Her Majesty into her private sanctum to prepare her for rest. As Lady Violet closed the doors, Flora curtsied and gazed her last on Holy Mother, her heart filled with love and a tearing sadness that this day of beauty and wonder was over. With scrupulous attention she swept and cleaned, knowing that when the doors opened again, she must leave.

The ladies-in-waiting filed back out. Determined to show that a sanitation worker had manners, Flora pressed her knees straight and curtsied to Lady Burnet.

"Thank you for all your —"

"Oh, do not be so craven." Lady Burnet had a strange look on her face. "Holy Mother has requested you attend her again."

"Me?" Flora looked around at the ladies. None smiled.

"You." Lady Burnet spoke neutrally. "Do not linger, go at once."

The Queen parted her golden aura when Flora entered and bade her sit beside her. Then she drew it close again, so that Flora was wrapped in it with her.

"I have not left the hive since my marriage flight. Now I only taste the world through food and drink, and the stories of my Library." The Queen gazed through her golden veil, as if out upon the open sky. "Did they frighten you?"

"Yes, Holy Mother, at first. Then I wanted to know more."

"They tell of our religion, and must be fed with attention. After my labours I have not strength to scent them myself, though my ladies do their best. The priestesses read them when they can, but in these strange times they are so busy with matters of governance that it is not their priority." The Queen smiled. "Tales of the world, my daughter, of beauty and terror."

"Holy Mother, I will read them gladly — after the wasp, I fear nothing."

The Queen's laugh sent ripples of delight through Flora's body, though she did not know how she had so amused her.

"Let us see," said the Queen. "The first three will be enough for you."

And so Flora kept her position as attendant to the ladies-in-waiting for another day, fetching water and refreshments for them until the Queen had laid her thousand eggs and returned to her chamber — and then her second job began.

While the ladies groomed each other, ate their supper and the Queen rested, Flora went to the Library. Without the anxiety of the other ladies around her, she was calm and could focus, and the intense energy of the chamber no longer overwhelmed her. In the still air she detected wisps and trails of the story fragrances as their living energy drew her attention and sought release — but this time she was determined not to lose control.

Very carefully, Flora scented the first story panel. There it was, *The Honeyflow* in all its blossoming glory, the foragers calling to each other in the Old Tongue — and there were the terrors of the Myriad lurking in wait.

Beside that was *The Kindness*, where a sister saw her own death by the hand of another. Then came the third, that honey-scented door to chaos — *The Visitation*, from whence a filament of smoke curled out its invitation. Flora stepped back, and the smoke retreated. The Queen had said three panels were enough, but excitement coursed through her body. If the priestesses were too busy to read the last three panels, then surely it would be of benefit to the hive if she could perform that service.

She looked at the last three panels. No tremors went through her antennae, nor did her feet drag forward without intention. The lilting singing of the ladies in the rest area beyond came through the walls, sweetly reassuring. Flora stepped up to the fourth panel, and the singing grew louder. A beautiful choral sound filled the chamber, the sound of ten thousand sisters singing one word that ebbed and flowed around the Library, as if they moved just beyond its walls. Flora could not quite decipher it, and as she concentrated the Library filled with the bright busy smell of the Dance Hall — and a great pressure wave rolled through the chamber.

Expiation! The choral blast of the word made Flora stagger. It echoed and died away, and the scent of the Dance Hall faded down.

Flora shook herself, her blood racing. Though she did not understand the strange word or the scents, and the feeling in her body challenged her to flee, the Queen wanted her to know the stories, and she would not fail her.

Flora moved on to the fifth and penultimate panel. At first glance it was very simple — just one carved leaf. As she looked more closely, it took on a golden hue and its fili-greed veins pulsed energy that grew into a stalk, then a stem which stretched down the length of the panel and into the floor, its golden roots spreading all through the chamber and back up the walls until they met overhead. The heavenly smell of Holy Mother rose up strongly, mingled with the rich aromatic scent of pollen. Flora looked up and saw the roots had joined into a knot at the centre point of the vaulted Library ceiling that swelled into a crown-shaped fruit. It grew larger and larger, then burst apart in a shower of golden dust.

The Library returned to normal — but a blow of sadness struck Flora in her heart as the name of the panel spoke in her mind. *The Golden Leaf.* Suddenly the beauty of the strange story was loathsome and Flora felt a terrible grief — but nothing had happened, nor was she hurt in any way. She stepped back from the fifth panel. It was deeply disturbing — and yet even as Flora recoiled from the dark and twisting feeling that had risen in her heart, a little part of her mind whispered praise for her own endurance — she had read five stories! How pleased the Queen would be with her, and how wonderful to be able to help the busy priestesses!

There was one last story. The sixth panel smelled inert, yet held a powerful stillness. Cautiously, Flora focused on it. Nothing happened; no scent, no image, no sound came forth, but the air in the Library grew warm and close. From the centre of the little panel blew a faint trace of fresh air. Feeling as if she was suffocating, Flora could not help drawing nearer.

The Library vanished and she smelled the Nursery. One crib pulled her closer, huge and dark. Deep within it a baby cried in pain, and a cold wind howled. As Flora ran towards it, the crib began to rattle and break apart. The baby cried louder and as she leaned over the crib to see it, a twisting black comet screamed out of its depths and into her brain.

Flora came to her senses back in the ladies' quarters, lying on a bed. She heard Lady Burnet and the others talking quietly — until they heard her sit up.

"Such vanity," Lady Burnet said, "such folly."

Flora stood up. Her body trembled, and she looked around in fear, but all was quiet.

"Crawling out of there raving and ranting," continued Lady Burnet. "Comets and cribs — I am sure Holy Mother said nothing about touching those panels —"

"She did." Flora's voice was thin. "She wanted to know —"

"Tales of terror and madness? You surely misunderstood Her Majesty, for only the priestesses may touch the Sacred Mysteries — why would She ever ask *you*, a sanitation worker? I think the wasp cost you your senses."

"Yes, my lady." Flora's heart filled with shame at her mistake. She had misunderstood the Queen, and been foolish and vain.

"Despite that," said Lady Burnet, "Holy Mother is ever-loving and forgiving, and has asked that you attend her." She stood back, her face rigid with resentment. "Do not keep Her Majesty waiting."

The Queen was resting on her couch in a shimmering golden aura, but she opened it to admit Flora, then closed it about them. Flora wanted to talk, to tell Holy Mother about her experiences in the Library, but each time she tried to speak, a strange weariness took her tongue, and she felt tears rising.

"Hush, little daughter," the Queen said softly. "I heard that you read them all. I too once knew them, but it was many eggs ago, and I have forgotten." She smiled and stroked Flora's face. "You will recover."

Flora nestled against her wise and beautiful mother, breathing the healing fragrance of Her Love deep into her body. It had changed — in a most subtle but distinct way. Something was new in its molecular structure, but just as Flora sniffed it deeper, the Queen twisted and gasped in pain.

"Mother!" Flora leapt up. "What is it? Shall I call one of the ladies?"

"No —" She gripped Flora's arm and pulled her back. "No — stay with me." Pressed against the Queen, Flora felt another shudder pass through both their bodies.

"Holy Mother, let me call them —"

"No!" Pain clamped the Queen's voice. "We need no assistance."

Then whatever seized her relaxed its hold, and she let go of Flora. She flexed her long abdomen and settled herself again.

"Our Progress was normal today, We filled every crib with life, did We not?"

Flora could not speak, for the reverberation of the Queen's pain was still ebbing from her own body.

"If We had missed one, Our ladies would say — that is their job, but they did not, so all must be well." Her Majesty took a deep breath. "It must be the cold — has Our hive been cold, daughter?"

"Not to me, Holy Mother," said Flora, "but they say our fur is so coarse my kin feel nothing."

The Queen smiled, and her scent flowed strong again.

"All is well. But do not speak of this to anyone, do you understand?" She wrapped her fragrance around Flora's antennae. "Promise me," she whispered.

Enraptured, Flora nodded. "I promise . . ."

The Queen kissed Flora's head. "Go."

None of the ladies looked up as Flora emerged from the Queen's sanctum. As she sat down with them, those closest got up and moved. Lady Burnet stabbed her embroidery hoop with her golden needle.

"Lady Burnet — forgive me if I have offended you —"

"Me? Oh no." Lady Burnet smiled but her eyes were cold. "Your boldness does credit to a drone — but is simply out of place here." All the ladies heard footsteps in the passageway outside, then came a timid knock on the door.

"Ah! Enter." Lady Burnet rose.

A very young sister also from Burnet entered, her fur already teased and styled like a lady-in-waiting. She curtsied perfectly to them all, antennae demure and downcast.

"Flora 717," announced Lady Burnet, "your time with the Queen has ended, and with it, all privilege of access. Leave now."

"Now? But Holy Mother will wonder —"

"You flatter yourself. She will not. Now back to Sanitation where you belong."

★ ★ ★

Flora went blindly. The pain of Lady Burnet's words, the humiliation of her sudden expulsion, and most of all, the folly of imagining she had a permanent place serving the Queen in her chambers.

She could not feel one pulsing foot-track, one scented code — all she was conscious of was the thinning of the scent of the Queen's Love, weaker with every step she took away from her presence, and the dull ache in her belly that had started when the Queen gasped. It was stronger now, concentrating itself deep within her abdomen.

Flora stopped. Holy Mother needed her. She needed to be cared for. She, Flora 717, should not have listened to Lady . . . Lady . . . All the names of the ladies-in-waiting slid from her mind. She tried to place them all, sitting on their chairs . . . but the memory blurred as she summoned it. The Library — the panels — the scent-stories Holy Mother had asked her to learn . . . everything faded to nothing, except the disturbing new sensation in her belly.

Flora looked down at her body. Her legs were still striped with propolis, her fur still pomaded with curls and patterns. She had not imagined it, she *had* been taken there. She *had* met the Queen and been wrapped in Her Love. Flora searched her body for any trace of that sweet scent, but it had completely vanished.

She started to shiver. Sisters passed all around her, their antennae streaming with nonsense and gossip and instructions. Everything they said was meaningless and angered her, because all she craved was the Queen's Love. Desperately Flora began to groom herself, searching for some filament, any remnant of the blissful scent, but all she tasted was folly and vanity. To her relief she heard the bell, and then felt the faint vibration running through the ground.

It signalled Devotion, the service she had not needed to attend for as long as she served the Queen. Flora spread her feet wide to locate the nearest place of worship. It came from directly beneath her, in the Dance Hall on the lowest level of the hive, where the power of a thousand sisters was already gathered. A crowd of workers poured past to get there in time. Empty and heartbroken from her expulsion, Flora ran to join them.

CHAPTER
TWELVE

The mood of the sisters in the Dance Hall was agitated. Crowded wing to wing with sisters of every kin, Flora's mind and body clawed with the need for the Queen's Love. Other bees were also anxious, and she heard many complaining of hunger.

Still they waited. A few bees began to emit jerky little buzzes of fear as the divine pheromone level dropped, but others with more in their bodies touched them and hummed reassurance as they shared what traces they had left. Then with a jolt the floor trembled, the vibration surged, and the scent of the Queen's Love began to rise. Those sisters with room to move knelt down on the comb and wept in relief, while others lifted their heads to hum the Holy Chord. At the vibration in the comb and change in the air Flora pressed her six feet down into the wax, opened her spiracles and drew the fragrance deep into her body.

It had no effect.

All around her sisters were enraptured in a blissful state of union with the Queen, but Flora remained trapped in her own consciousness. She scanned the crowd. To her surprise she noticed several other sisters who, though they stood very still, were alert to everything around them. Their bearing was calm, with an air of detachment. Flora stared a moment, then recognised them. They were foragers.

The vibration began to subside. All around the Dance Hall bees smiled for joy, antennae high and quivering in clouds of the Queen's Love. Longing for the reassurance of some humble labour, Flora looked for other sanitation workers — but before she could find one, a rowdy cheering broke out, the crowd rippled apart and a nectar-scented forager ran in.

Finding space by Flora, she began to dance. Slow and clear she stamped out a simple phrase, over and over until the bees understood it and the rhythm caught. Then she clicked her wing-latches open, pulsed her thoracic engine and shimmered and stopped her wings to the same rhythm. Other bees applauded and began to follow as back and forth she ran, into one section of the crowd then another, trailing the lure of raw nectar behind her. She stopped at another forager and fed her a drop from her own mouth. The sparkle of fresh nectar lit the air and the bees cheered again, and more ran to learn the dance.

Flora ran too, thrilled by the mixed scent of nectar and the cold fresh air clinging to the forager's wings. Her mind grew sharp with excitement as her feet picked up the choreography — and suddenly she understood the language of the dance.

Go South! sang the bee's steps. *For this long!*

There were fields — she described the pattern of the crops — the heavy waving heads of grain, the great west current of air that always blew through them — more fields, the stream, *count two fences* . . .

Then East! And the forager ran again, swirling and buzzing her abdomen to urge more sisters to follow. Many bees shouted in excitement and ran to leap into the air themselves, but Flora followed close behind this wonderful bee, copying her steps.

And turn and go on.

"Turn and go on," sang Flora behind her.

And then Here, the flowers, the nectar, the sweetness!

"The flowers, the nectar, the sweetness!" shouted the bees, dancing their map to the treasure.

The bright-winged forager came to a halt. So joyful and precise was her dancing that Flora had thought her young, but now she saw the ragged wing-tips, thinning fur, and scrapes on her armour. It was Lily 500, who had pushed her off the landing board. With a pulse of her antennae, Flora remembered the first panel of the Queen's Library.

"Praise end your days, Sister," she said, in the Old Speech.

Lily 500 looked at her intently. She straightened her wings but did not latch them.

"What do you want?" Her face was cross-hatched with tiny scratches and both antennae were cracked at the base, as if they had borne great stress. "Speak," she said, "or my flowers will close their mouths while I wait for yours to open. I must return, they wait for me. Some will not open for the touch of any other. Pride is a sin, but that is the truth." She looked at Flora. "You suck in my scent as if I were the Queen."

"Forgive me, Sister — I mean Madam — the wild air smells so good."

"Today. Yesterday it was befouled, and the day before that and the one before that, which is why everyone has empty bellies. But better go hungry than eat tainted bread." She sniffed Flora. "Where have you been, to eat so richly? Your kin are not kitchen bees."

"I was taken to the Queen, as reward for facing the wasp."

"Ah yes. I heard Lady Vespa was well cooked. Yet you survived."

"By the courage of our sisters Thistle, who perished."

"The destiny of their kin." Lily 500 stepped around Flora. "You will excuse me; I have lost the knack of polite conversation."

"Wait, please!" Flora ran after her. "Madam Forager, do you have any work for me? I will serve in any way —"

"If you followed the dance, then you know where to go." The forager walked more briskly. Shocked, Flora hurried alongside her.

"But my kin may never forage, it is written!"

"I read flowers, not scriptures. But I know our hive is in grievous need of food and that you have wings and courage and a brain. Do not annoy me by asking permission." Lily 500 pushed her way out into the lobby.

Flora stood for a moment, unsure of her invitation. The forager glanced back at her — and she ran to follow.

98

Lily 500 was fast and deft through the crowd. In her struggle to keep up, Flora crashed into another bee. Pollen cakes slid across the floor and a young Willow scrambled to retrieve them.

"Oh, they will punish me, I have broken so many — please, sister, I beg you, do not tell them or they will say I am too weak to work and send me for the Kindness —"

"Tell who?" Flora quickly helped her gather them up, keeping one eye on Lily who stood waiting on the far side of the lobby.

"The police! They came on a health inspection to Pollen & Patisserie, and asked who was tired — and all those who raised their hands were taken for the Kindness!" The little Willow wept again and grabbed Flora's hand. "I have committed the sin of Waste — please, sister, it is not much further — will you help me?"

Across the lobby, Flora saw Lily's bright wings disappearing down the passageway to the landing board. It was too late. She nodded.

The grateful Willow admired Flora's propolis-striped legs as they walked together, carrying the heavy tray. "I am sure they will appreciate it," she said. "They like us to be adorned."

"Who will?" But Flora needed no answer, for now she heard the booming of roistering male voices, and smelled the high scent of the Drones' Hall.

There were two such masculine salons in the hive, both situated for Their Maleness's convenience. One was on the top level adjoining the Treasury and

Fanning Hall, the other, on this lowest level near to the landing board. They were places of rest, refreshment and rowdy behaviour, constantly staffed by a willing rota of young sisters and supervised by the most diplomatic of older ones.

As Flora and the Willow approached the double doors they could hear the clamour within for food and nectar, which became a roar of approval as they entered with their tray of treats. Before they could set their burden down they were surrounded by brawny hands grabbing the cakes and pollen loaves, and it was all they could do to withstand the rush until only crumbs were left.

"They went to a far-distant Congregation today," whispered supervising Sister Cowslip. "And one was chosen. Now all the rest gorge to restore their spirits."

"Nectar!" shouted a drone from his banquette.

"Bread! Hot and sweet like the bud of the next princess!"

"Oh, Your Malenesses, please!" Sister Cowslip fluttered four hands. "What will these simple house-bees make of such language?" She turned to Flora and the Willow. "Quickly: some unguents for Their Malenesses. We must relax them, or they will eat us out of our hive."

Flora and the Willow went into the food service area, littered with the remnants of pastries and dregs of litter. The Willow gobbled leftovers but Flora stood very still. A tremor ran through her belly, and she bit back a gasp.

"They say the foragers grow lazy," the Willow said thickly, "that's why we're always hungry."

"Indeed they do not." In her indignation Flora forgot her pain. "I saw many dance directions today, and you would not speak so if you saw the rips and tears on their bodies. Yet still they fly."

The Willow shrugged. "It is just what people are saying." She went out with her bowl of massage ointment. As soon as she had gone, Flora curled her body over and breathed deeply until the strange sensation passed. Then she peered out into the hall. To her dismay she saw the dandified little figure of Sir Linden standing talking to Sister Cowslip. Too late, she ducked back.

"You there," Sister Cowslip called her. "Who do you attend? His glorious Maleness here requires grooming."

Praying her striped legs and pomaded fur concealed the truth, Flora took a bowl and went out.

Sister Cowslip sniffed her immediately. "You have a most peculiar odour, almost like a cleaner —"

"Sir Linden!" Flora dropped a narrow curtsy. "Forgive my past mistakes, I beg to now attend you!"

Drones nearby burst out laughing.

"Ugly but keen, Linden. Better than nothing."

He sniffed at Flora. "Oh, it's you! The disobedient one!"

Sister Cowslip looked from one to the other.

"I'm sorry to hear that — I am sure we can find one better, Your Maleness —"

"No no, this exact one will do. Begone." He waved Sister Cowslip away, then spread his legs and puffed his chest at Flora. "My masculinity no longer scares you?"

"I must bear it, Sir." Flora kept her antennae downcast.

"Indeed! Well then, up with you and do my bidding — or it's the Kindness!" Sir Linden beckoned she follow, strutted through the other drones then threw himself down on a banquette. "I am ready. Begin."

Flora looked at the other sisters and their drones. Reluctantly, she began anointing Sir Linden's legs. The hooks on the third pair were so small as to almost be like a sister's.

"You may say pleasant things to me." Sir Linden shifted more comfortably.

Unable to think of anything, Flora began humming a melody the ladies had sung in the Queen's chambers. Sir Linden looked up.

"That is a bawdy tune; you should not know it. Continue, but no words or Sister Cowpat will evict you. Then I shall have no one, not even a fright like you." He stared morosely round the chamber. "Quercus was chosen today. I suppose you heard."

"Glory to our hive."

"Oh, spare me — he was just a great flying wad of sperm. The thought of that boorish idiot in a golden palace, drowning in honey and mounting his royal beauty at will —" Sir Linden shuddered in irritation. "And as for that fat oaf —" he gestured at Sir Poplar. "It's a miracle he's still alive, for he is so loud every bird in the sky must hear him taking off, and so slow a flower might bloom and die before he rises."

"Then it is a race?"

"A race and a chase."

102

At his words a nearby drone leaned forward.

"Until every princess is mated!" he cried.

"And every brother, king of his own palace!" called another.

Many drones stamped and cheered, and Sister Cowslip glowed in delight and sent her girls scurrying around to replenish empty goblets and plates.

"You see?" Sir Linden threw himself down again. "That's the essence of it. Congregation is all about shouting, shoving and bragging — then barging ahead."

"Is it . . . a ceremony?"

"Stupid girl — a *place*. A subtle place in the highest reaches of the air, at a sweet convergence of the winds. A place where all the noble males of different hives come to gather, and princesses visit to make their choice." He pulled his ruff straight. "Of course, the more fellows the better the atmosphere — but the more competition."

"There is not a princess for each?"

Sir Linden laughed and turned again to the Drones' Hall. "Brothers!" he called out. "My loyal retainer knows nothing of our magnificent work — shall we speak to them of Love?"

"Yes! Love!" cried out all the sisters in the Drones' Hall, even Sister Cowslip. "Tell us of Love, please!" They clustered around their drones, and all faces turned to Sir Linden. He cleared his throat, puffed his ruff, and began.

"Hear you that our noble brother Quercus is taken up to glory, by a princess fairer than any sister of hive or heaven, with limbs of gold and fur of brightest light.

103

Recall how she roared upon us at Congregation, faster than a swooping jay, and swept us with her ray of lust, so that the leaves themselves shone gold!"

At this all the drones roared and cheered and some grabbed their crotches, shouting crude praise for the erotic perfection of this foreign princess. The sisters nudged and whispered to each other, envious and enraptured.

"Congregation, you simple sisters of the hive," Sir Linden continued for the general benefit, and the pleasure of being the centre of attention for once, "means the place of Air, near trees of such particular majesty they are gods in their own right, and only drones may dare ascend their heights, defying the birds to breathe our lust on all the winds." He looked around to gather all attention. "It is the place where princesses come to find the sacrament of Love, delivered by Our Maleness." At this all the sisters applauded and cheered, and their excitement drew forth more scent from the drones.

"Fine talk, Linden," called one.

"Now my sword longs for action!" shouted another.

Urging each other on, the drones began revving their thoraxes. Streaming pheromones, they jumped up one by one, and there before the eyes of every sister, they grew strong and noble, their faces rugged and handsome. Even Sir Linden no longer looked petulant and slightly feminine, but elegant and finely formed, his face intelligent with mischief.

The drones stamped and shook their armour straight and Sir Linden motioned Flora to stand behind him.

No longer spoilt and indolent but gleaming with grooming and bursting with testosterone, the drones formed their martial phalanx. Their scent rose and the sound of their armour reverberated as they began to stamp in unison.

"*Congregation, Copulation, Coronation!*" they chanted again and again, and the sisters cheered them on. Flora stood too but Sir Linden pushed her back down.

"Oh no — you will not leave this Hall until they bring word of my triumph with a discerning princess. Believe me, hairy girl, it shall take place." He looked at her. "Until then, you will stay here, by my explicit instruction."

Furious at herself for choosing to help the Willow above following Lily 500, Flora forced herself to nod.

"Excellent." Sir Linden banged his armour plates together like his brothers and marched out with them, plume held high.

Flora longed for Sir Linden's success for it would free her from servitude in the Drones' Hall, but by the afternoon every single one of them was back, cursing and swearing that the rains had returned. Flora silently cursed as well, for confinement with the high hormonal smell of the drones made both her head and belly ache.

Sanitation workers had more freedom than drone-maids — and Sister Cowslip would be only too glad to evict her when she knew the truth of her base kin. Flora waited until Sir Linden lay sated and snoring, and then went to confess her trespass.

Sister Cowslip did not react, even when Flora repeated it, but stood motionless at her reception station near the doors. Flora sniffed her. She was a bee of late spring and her time had come.

Flora let her natural kin-scent rise up from her own body, then pulled in her antennae like the humblest of her kin. Making sure Sister Cowslip's wing-latches were secure, she lifted her in her mouth and slipped out into the corridor.

Swirls of warm fresh air came in from the landing board, and by the chains of sisters passing aromatic bales of pollen back into the hive, Flora knew the rain had stopped. She edged forward in the slow lane, her heart thrumming with excitement as she heard the sound of forager engines taking off and landing, so close outside. She felt her wings long and strong down her back, and the elastic tension of their membranes. Lily 500 said there was hunger, and that she was fit and able. If she found food, and the hive was hungry, how could that be wrong?

"Sanitation to exit."

At the gruff call of the Thistle guards, Flora and a few others of her kin stepped out onto the board.

Sister after sister hummed her engines and fired herself into the dazzling blue sky. Flora unlatched her wings, adrenaline pumping through her body. She started her engine.

"Stop at once!" voices shouted, and several Thistle guards ran out onto the board. "All flight is cancelled by order of the Sage, effective immediately!"

106

Foragers waiting to leave shouted their disappointment, but more guards ran out and pushed all the bees back from the edge. Others began laying homecoming flares, and another pulled Sister Cowslip from Flora's grasp and threw her over the edge.

"We should not do that!" Flora's engine thrummed inside her chest, the filigree of blood vessels in her wings was tight with power and her feet were light on the wood. To be so long in darkness and servitude, and then at the very lip of freedom to be turned back —

"They come — stand aside!" The guards pushed all the bees back as returning foragers approached in the flight corridor to the hive. Some of them swerved wildly and Flora held her antennae aloft, but there was no trace of wasp attack, only the soil and the plants and incoming sisters —

The first bee crashed onto the board at her feet. She was a forager from the kin of Poppy, but her scent was overlaid with something alien and ugly, and a grey film covered her whole body. She crawled towards Flora.

"Help me, sister. I beg you."

Some instinct made Flora jump back from the forager's desperate lunge, and all the bees stared in bewildered horror as the Poppy stopped and was violently sick. Other bees came crashing down onto the board around her, their eyes wild and their bodies speckled with the film of sickness.

CHAPTER
THIRTEEN

Her body tense from thwarted flight, Flora went back into the hive. Pausing in the crowded corridor to re-latch her wings, she heard the weak raised voices of the Poppy and other sisters coming from an antechamber near the morgue. Before she could hear what they said the Thistle guards hurried everyone back inside, pushing them towards the Dance Hall.

Jittery bursts of buzzing came from the large assembly of bees. The pulses in the comb had called them there but it was not time for Devotion, nor, despite the definite trace of fear drifting in from the landing board, was there any smell of wasp. There was, however, an unpleasant odour somewhere close and Flora instinctively drew away. The whole crowd rippled and flexed as one, and when the movement stopped, certain bees stood isolated in pools of space. Each was a forager, standing with her head down and her sides heaving for breath, and each showed the same grey film on her body as had the Poppy who crashed to the landing board.

A Sage priestess rustled her long elegant wings for attention. Her antennae scanned the large hall.

"Sisters in One Mother, we give thanks for the sacrifices and valour of our noble foragers, *Amen*."

"*Amen*," murmured the bees, currents of alarm passing between them.

"Behold our sister foragers, whose work is honour and whose precision, zeal and stamina give life, health and wealth to our hive. But whose mistakes, and hubris, bring disease, disgrace, and death. Many sisters have fallen sick and died today, and now we are certain of the cause." Sister Sage pointed and two Thistle guards brought forward an old forager. Those bees nearest gasped in shock.

"Madam Lily 500," intoned Sister Sage, "what do you wish to say to your sisters and to Holy Mother, whose life you have brought into danger with your error?"

Lily 500 raised her head. Her voice was hoarse but calm.

"I do not make errors. The field was clean when I was there."

"No. It was poisoned. *And in your error* you sent countless sisters to their deaths. See the wounded now, the venomous mist burning holes in their bodies? And we have found tainted pollen in the stores, no doubt also gathered in error after your directions. Your prestige has made you careless —"

"I danced the truth!" Lily 500 raised her voice. "If the pollen was tainted I would not gather it — if the field was poisoned I would die rather than return — I swear on every royal egg —"

"And now Blasphemy!" called out Sister Sage. "Blasphemy, pride and error."

"— and I swear on my love for the Queen that when I went to the flowers the mist was not there, nor have I ever gathered unclean pollen!"

Sister Sage spoke quietly. "Brave sisters who suffer, come forward."

Those isolated bees whose bodies were covered in the tiny grey specks and bore the strange scent walked or were guided forward to the centre to join Lily 500. Some of them still scraped away at their bodies, trying to remove the grey film. Lily 500 stared at them, then bowed her head.

"Forgive me, my sisters. I should have died, than brought this home."

No one spoke. Then a squad of identical bees parted the crowd, their fur slicked dark and their kin-scent veiled under a thick masking odour. They stood by Sister Sage.

"Madam Forager, Lily 500, you have endangered our hive by your error. For the protection of Her Majesty the Queen, Source of Life and Immortal Mother, we must cleanse our hive of sickness." Sister Sage looked around the silent hall. "If any sister ails, let her prove her love for Holy Mother and come forward."

No one moved. In the silence Flora ran her consciousness round her body. On the landing board she had forgotten everything in her excitement at flight — but now she could feel the strange sensation in her belly again. It had more pressure, and as she focused on it, strange prickles of energy ran through her. It was no

110

longer pain, nor did she feel sick in any way. She decided not to speak of it.

Sister Sage looked at Lily 500.

"We will remember the wealth you brought. Praise end your days."

Before the old forager could respond, the police dragged her away. At this humiliation of one of their greatest, all the sisters stared in shock.

Sister Sage's face shone bright and tremors flew up her antennae as if she were at Devotion. "The Kindness is only for the diligent. Those whose carelessness endangers the hive may not receive it. We fearlessly protect Holy Mother for we know *from Death comes Life Eternal.*"

"*From Death comes Life Eternal,*" responded all the bees. Then in one shared impulse, every affected forager unlatched her wings and stepped forward. Together they faced the police.

"Death flies close on every mission," said one, her body also speckled with the grey film. "We need no escort now." The foragers bowed to their sisters. "*Accept, Obey and Serve.*"

"*Praise end your days,*" said all the bees. The foragers walked out, the police guard behind them. The bees waited in silence, the comb underfoot completely still. They heard the weak engines of their sisters start up on the landing board, and the power surge as they leapt the air. Every bee in the Dance Hall strained to hear their engines fading as the sick foragers flew far from the hive, never to return.

"Get back to work," Sister Sage announced. "Prepare for health inspection."

The atrium emptied at great speed. Sisters rushed to get away from the police and Flora attached herself to a large detail of sanitation workers. They were going to the morgue where the day's dead bodies must be removed, and their supervising sister was another Bindweed.

"Because of poisoned pollen you will drop the bodies far beyond the orchard," she told them. "And you will not return."

The workers looked at each other in alarm, but Sister Bindweed smiled.

"It is to the honour of your kin! You are so numerous that we can easily spare a few to ensure good hygiene. It is your privilege: *Accept, Obey and Serve!*"

As the sanitation workers mumbled their incoherent response, Flora heard a cry of pain. She smelled Lily 500 close by, mixed with the harsh scent of the police.

"Let me die with honour," came the forager's hoarse old voice. "Let me go with my forager sisters — I promise I will not return —" She cried out as if she had received a blow. The sound came from the waste depot near the morgue.

"I beg you," came Lily 500's agonised voice again, "at least kill me before you throw me to the Myriad — oh, my sisters have left me! I want my sisters!"

Flora left her sisters going into the morgue and ran to find Lily.

★   ★   ★

The old forager's legs dragged on the wax tiles behind her and her wings were broken at both latches. Carrying her by the thorax, two on each side, the police turned down the approach to the landing board. Even outside in the bright air their powerful scent hurt Flora's antennae as she ran towards them.

"Please," she said, "may I attend my sister?"

"Lily 500 is sentenced to death. Do you seek to share her end?"

"No, Officer, only to pray with her. I heard her call."

Flora dropped to her knees. The officers' feet had huge black hooks and smelled of different kin, hideously mixed.

"The forager is unclean."

"Yes, Officer, but I carry every kind of waste and do not fear disease. *Accept, Obey and Serve.*"

The police were silent, though their antennae radiated together. They stood back.

"Quickly," said one. "She is sentenced to die in exile."

Flora went to Lily's side. Every joint of the old forager's body was broken.

"To stop me returning," whispered Lily. "As if I wished to live, after my mistake." She gazed at Flora. "I know you . . ."

"I saw you dance. You were so strong and beautiful and I wanted to follow but —" Flora could not finish. Twelve black hooked feet walked closer.

"Please, Officers, we must pray —" Lily 500 pressed her antennae tight against Flora's. "Open!" she whispered. "Do not waste it —"

A huge rushing sensation poured down Flora's antennae and a torrent of sound and scent and image filled her brain. She did not feel the kicks that separated them.

When Flora could see again, Lily was gone and only one police bee stood on the board with her, looking up into the blinding blue. High beyond the orchard, a tiny black speck separated into two. One fell towards the earth, and the other turned and headed back to the hive.

Flora got to her feet, flashes of flowers and petals and fragrance filling her senses. The sky was wide open. But before she could unlatch her wings, the second police bee had landed beside her.

"Number and kin." Her voice was ugly and abrasive and Flora could see Lily's blood still wet on her jaws. If she flew now they would knock her out of the air. She bowed her antennae subserviently.

"Flora 717. Sanitation."

"Then get there."

Flora ran back into the hive, Lily's voice and chemical memories still flashing in her mind, long after she had rejoined her kin.

CHAPTER
FOURTEEN

Flora joined the first sanitation detail she found —
scrubbing out the Dance Hall. They worked in sombre
silence, for nowhere in the hive was the comb more
sensitive to the chemical signals of the colony, and it
transmitted flashes of fear and pain as the health
inspection continued in the hive. Outside in the lobby
more floras carried newly dead bodies of ailing
house-bees to the morgue, all with the sickly smell of
tainted pollen on their mouths, and their heads hanging
limp after the Kindness.

Flora turned away and focused on minute particles
of dust trodden into the worn wax tiles where the
foragers danced. She hoped Lily 500 had died in
the air, not fallen into the grass still conscious,
helplessly waiting for the Myriad. The bell rang for shift
change and she went up with the other floras to the
mid-level canteen — but for once the smell of food did
not move her. All she wanted was dark seclusion.

In a worker dormitory she found the segregated kin
area and threw herself down in a corner bunk. Her soul
hurt from the violent loss of so many sisters.

"*From Death comes Life Eternal*," she repeated in
her mind, but the words gave no comfort. She curled

her body tight in grief — to feel the pressure in her belly push back, stronger. As Flora shifted to ease the sensation, a wave of energy rolled through her.

The image of a purple foxglove shone in her mind, its ultraviolet runway glowing in welcome. She felt the cool soft press of its petal tunnel, then a shiver of delight as its pollen brushed against her fur. A bead of nectar pulsed sweetness and she stretched out her tongue —

Flora jolted awake. It was completely dark, the air had cooled, and every berth held a sleeping sister. She breathed in their heat-exhausted bodies and their kin-scents — many floras around her, and then the Dandelion, the Bindweed, the Plantain nearer the front and the better ventilation. From the stale pollen on their breath she guessed that the latest fresh loads had been destroyed in case of contamination, along with the brave sisters who brought them.

The pressure in her belly was worse, and the more Flora tried to settle herself, the more insistent it became until she was forced to get up. Swaying her abdomen relieved the sensation — but also made her scent rise more strongly, disturbing her sleeping neighbours. Flora could not help thinking of Lily 500's sickness, and how closely they had touched. Perhaps she had caught something — perhaps she was at this moment transmitting it to every sister around her.

As she tiptoed out of the dormitory her belly pulsed as if forcing her forward, and the pain eased a little. Walking in the dark corridors of the hive, without the day's tumult of scent and sound, its sweet bouquet rose through the comb on all sides until every sister's kin-scent blended in its beauty. For the first time, Flora smelled its separate elements. The essence of a million flowers combined with the purity of the new wax cribs, the rich aroma of pollen wrapped around a piquant note of propolis, and beneath it all, the hive's deep gold core of honey.

A spasm of pain made Flora drop to her knees. Her belly was her only consciousness, pushing tauter and harder so that she felt she must burst and die.

The agony faded in ripples. Flora lay in shock, her face pressed to the comb floor of a corridor on the mid-level. It was still night, and it was quiet and dark. She felt the tip of her abdomen throbbing, and something warm pressing against it.

A single pulse came through the comb under her body, its fine thin energy stronger as she felt it, running through her body until her mind connected to it, and she smelt its beautiful fragrance.

Flora pulled herself round and gasped in shock. The thing that touched her was small, warm and glowing. It was slightly pointed at one end, and as she stared its scent rose more strongly, activated by her attention. Flora looked up and down the empty corridor, then back at the egg.

Her egg.

"No." Flora did not know if she spoke aloud or not. It was impossible: *Only the Queen may breed.* That was the first law of life, so holy it needed no place in prayer for it was a rule literally incarnate in every sister's body.

Flora raised her antennae, searching for the fertility police. They were all powerful, they would know and be here any moment and when they came she would not ask for mercy for her unspeakable act. It did not matter that she had not meant it, that the crime had come without warning. She stared at it.

The egg was glowing brighter and its fragrance was the sweetest thing she had ever smelled, sweeter even than Devotion. But that very thought was evil.

Flora looked around, waiting for deliverance. They must come, and if they did not she must call them. *Only the Queen may breed. Only the Queen —*

Repeating the words, Flora lay down and curled herself around her egg. Its fragrance filled her senses like her first Devotion and its touch infused her with a fierce joy. Flora looked in desperation for anyone to come and save her from her sin, but the hive slept on. Then a thought occurred to her. The Nursery was close by, and Sister Teasel would know what to do. Very gently, Flora picked up her egg.

She could not help it — her arms cradled it softly, her antennae bent to feather it with loving touches, and her heart swelled with love.

The child they tore apart — twisting in agony on Sister Inspector's hook —

Her antennae seared and she clutched her egg closer, drawing her own scent around it like a shield. The egg responded, tender and fragile and pressing strong against her. Flora's cheeks began to tingle with the sweetness of Flow, but she swallowed it down. She must go to the Nursery before her courage failed. Holding

118

her beloved egg for the last precious moments, Flora forced herself to walk through the doors of Category One.

Sister Teasel sat snoring at her station. Flora went closer, until she stood in front of her. She held up her glowing egg. Sister Teasel did not wake. One antenna sagged sideways, the other trembled as if she dreamed. All around them the long rows of Category One cribs were quiet, faintly glowing from the last feed of the evening. The nurses' rest area was still.

"Sister Teasel." Flora spoke loud enough for her to hear. The old bee did not stir. Flora looked around. At the far end of the ward was the start of Category One, and beyond that, the veil of scent that hid the Laying Rooms from view. That was where the newest eggs would be found in the morning. Flora's egg shimmered in her arms. Soft and quick, she walked down the rows of cribs towards the laying area. She was almost there when a sound stopped her.

"Who's there?" Sister Teasel's voice was thick with sleep. "Lady Speedwell?"

Flora did not move, the egg bright in her arms. Sister Teasel tidied her antennae and brushed herself off.

"Forgive me for not greeting you," she said. "It has been such a trying day for all of us." She leaned forward to whisper. "I hope it is not blasphemy to ask, but did you come to say Her Majesty has laid in Her privy chamber again? Oh, and to think that you found me sleeping — what is our hive coming to?" She laughed nervously. "It is the scant rations you know, one needs energy to stay awake." She peered at Flora. "You will not mention I slept, will you?"

Flora forced her knees together and curtsied. Sister Teasel sat down in relief.

"Good girl. You know where to put it."

Flora went to the most secluded part of Category One, where the pure new cribs held the latest eggs. She placed her own deep inside one, and watched it roll with its own inner life to secure itself to the wax by its pointed end. Flora leaned over, inhaling its precious scent as deeply as she could. She stroked it one last time.

If she were Lady Speedwell she would return to the Queen's chambers through the Laying Rooms, and Sister Teasel would think it odd if she did not. Praying nothing had changed, Flora slipped through the veil of scent. The Laying Rooms were empty and prepared for Her Majesty's next Progress. Through one door was the rich beauty of the Queen's chambers — and certain discovery, for the ladies-in-waiting would raise the alarm at her trespass. But when she had attended the Royal Progress and been sent to and fro for water, she had used the little door that opened near Patisserie. Very carefully, she tried the handle. It was unlocked.

The scent of the hive began to change as dawn rose but the comb was quiet and no one stirred as Flora returned to her dormitory. Her bunk was completely cooled of body warmth as she lay down and curled her abdomen in for sleep. The tip still throbbed, yet she felt oddly calm. All she wanted was to draw the last of that beautiful scent into her mind, and feel that warm tender shimmer of life against her body again. She had committed a crime yet felt no guilt, only love for her egg.

Flora listened to her sisters' sleep and the birdsong start in the orchard, and waited for retribution.

CHAPTER
FIFTEEN

"Wake up." The voice was brusque. "717, wake up and follow me at once!"

Flora jerked awake and looked into the eyes of a senior Sister Ilex, the kin immediately below the Teasel. Other bees still slept, but the air smelled of early morning. Flora stood, aware of the soreness at the tip of her body. They had found her out, and Sister Ilex was here to take her to her death. Flora bent her antennae low.

"Holy Mother forgive my sins. I am ready."

Sister Ilex sniffed at her.

"How strange, they told me you smelled quite rank, but to me you smell sweet as the Nursery. Ready for what?"

"The Kindness."

"What on earth for?"

Flora held her antennae from trembling. Sister Ilex did not know her crime, nor smell the egg. She had come for a different purpose, and looked at her keenly.

"I should have carried the dead yesterday," said Flora. "Instead I prayed with Lily 500."

"Which is precisely why you have been chosen. Now come quickly."

Sister Ilex led her down the corridor past the Dance Hall and the freight waste depot, to the empty receiving area near the landing board. Then she signalled and, instead of the fertility police that Flora expected, a young sister appeared with a fresh honey-cake. Sister Ilex held it up and the smell made Flora ravenous.

"Before Lily 500's sentence was carried out, you engaged in a reckless and sentimental exchange with the deceased forager, did you not? And she imparted you her knowledge?"

Flora nodded, her attention riveted by the sweet dense cake.

"It may still have value. If you can access it, then you are suspended from sanitation duties today, and may instead try to redeem yourself and serve your hive."

"With all my heart."

Sister Ilex gave Flora the cake, and never had food been so delicious.

"Rains have blighted our season of plenty and yesterday's health purge was a drastic protective measure — but if we lose any more foragers to the poison we will not be able to gather sufficient food for the winter. Therefore it has been decided to send out scouts to try to locate all tainted sources. Obviously because of the risk of death, the lower the kin the better. With Lily 500's knowledge and your brute strength, you might have some success."

Flora finished the cake and the honey brightened her mind.

"I am a scout? I can forage?"

"717, restrain your ego. Your kin may never fly, except to carry waste or in sacrifice for the good of the hive." Sister Ilex led her out onto the dazzling landing board. Thistle sentries saluted.

"Do not tax your brain, but fly about as chaotically as you will. Just go as far as Lily 500's data permits. If you get lost, so be it. If you draw the Myriad, you face them alone. And if you do manage to return but carry sickness, you will be denied entry — though someone will come out to hear any news you bring."

"But if I return healthy and with knowledge, I should go to the Dance Hall."

Sister Ilex laughed.

"A positive attitude is just what we need, 717. Very good!"

"Azimuth: the exact degree of the sun. Radius: a section of the perimeter of a circle. North, South, East, West. Distance measured in leagues —" Flora stopped because the sun's warmth sent her blood pumping into the veins and capillaries of her wings. Her latches sprang open, the four gossamer membranes stretched wide and flight-tight, triggering her thoracic engine. A power surge filled Flora's body, her chest spread broad and her wings hummed brightness.

"You will wait for permission!" shouted Sister Ilex above Flora's thoracic roar. "You will —"

Flora did not hear the rest. With the slightest press of intention, the air rushed beneath her wings and the apple trees fell away below. She took a strong high course and as her antennae automatically adjusted to flight position, she felt a channel open deep within them through which streamed Lily's knowledge and aerial skills. The hive was a tiny grey square, the orchard a thin green ruffle between the fields and the grey industrial estate — *Birds*, Lily's caution came to her mind. *Storms. Windows.* But the scent of nectar carried on the warm dry air currents rolling high above the land and Flora joined with them and rode them.

"Fly about chaotically," Sister Ilex had said, but Flora 717, lowest kin of the hive, needed no instruction. Far beyond the dull fields of wheat and soy, a vast golden plain of rapeseed radiated in the distance, the oily-sweet smell of its nectar rising warm and seductive on the air. Flora locked onto it and as she flew nearer saw and smelled enough nectar and pollen to fill every chalice in the Fanning Hall, stack the walls of the Treasury with honey, and make bread to fill the hungriest mouths.

"*A flora may not make Wax for she is impure, nor work with Propolis for she is clumsy, nor may she ever forage for she has no taste, but only may she clean, and all may command her labour.*"

Determined to prove her worth, Flora began her descent towards a million tiny golden mouths. Each showed a faint ultraviolet line pointing to its well of sweetness, and those florets stirred by her wing-beats murmured in pleasurable anticipation. Countless foragers worked the huge golden field and for the first time in her life, Flora lowered herself onto a willing flower-head.

The stalk held a number of little florets, some of them shy and not quite ready, so Flora climbed around

125

to make her choice. Transparent filaments on the stem caressed her legs, the plant bobbed under her movements as if urging her on — and then she found her first bloom, just that instant perfectly ready.

As Flora's tongue unrolled towards the bead of nectar, tiny particles of orange pollen tingled against her fur. The taste of the nectar was so bright and the energy release so sudden that she almost fell off the flower-head — and then the after-taste developed, a deeper musk changing the first sweetness. Flora's flight had used half the fuel from the honey-cake and she was hungry again, so she drank from floret after floret, from stem to stem until she felt her strength return and a satisfying weight of nectar in her crop.

Flora imagined the faces of the Thistle guards as she returned radiating the sweetness of her forage, and then it occurred to her she could bring pollen as well. If she let the florets brush against her, she could comb the orange dust straight into her baskets, but she saw that a forager from another hive had a better way. This more sophisticated sister rolled her pollen into balls and then packed it down into her leg panniers, and soon her last set of legs bulged with orange badges of industry and she flew away.

Flora thought to copy her effortless style, but found it was very skilled work. She grew frustrated at dropping packages down through the leaves, but only when she decided to fly down to retrieve one did she see the horror beneath them.

The earth was littered with bodies. Covered in black ants, a bloated mouse stared up with white eyes. Dead

126

sparrows lay between the plant stalks, their beaks open and their tiny tongues dried grey. Between them were dead bees, countless numbers of them, and wasps, and flies, their bodies speckled with the pale grey film that had condemned those foragers in her own hive.

Flora lurched up into the air through the plant stalks. The golden field tilted and swung as she struggled for balance and the earth pulled as if her crop of nectar was tied to a corpse on the ground. Flora's venom sac swelled tight in her belly and she whirled in the air firing her alarm glands in all directions, searching for the giant wasp or horde of the Myriad that had killed so many. But she was alone with the sun and the sky and the field of poisoned gold.

Movement caught her eye. Deep between the flower stalks, there toiled on the ground a glittering black army of ants, dragging the body of a red-tailed Bombini, one of those solitary bumblebees that cruised the orchard and exchanged pleasantries with the sisters of the hive. By the look of her fur she was freshly dead. Flora hovered as low as she could and called out in clumsy Hymenopteraese, the old shared tongue.

"Speech, sister?"

The largest of the ants paused from directing the column's labour. Her mandibles shone black and strong.

"Speech, sister," she replied in her strange accent.

Flora struggled to remember the coded tongue from the Queen's Library.

"The dead," she said, "befell?"

"Sick rain."

"When?"

The big ant pulsed her antennae. "Two . . . sun."

"Two days ago?"

The ant nodded, then returned to her column as it dragged the bumblebee away. Nearby, the black tide rose up over a fallen sparrow.

Flora had seen enough. If the sick rain was two days ago, then Lily 500 had made no mistake when she danced her coordinates, and the flowers were clean. But now they were poisoned, and she herself had eaten and drunk from them.

As Flora fired her engine and launched herself into the sky, she felt the effects start in her body. She gained altitude but lost balance, and as her wings began to numb she keeled wildly from side to side. Her body compass swung in all directions, her antennae hissed with static and then she lost all scent. She fought her way higher to the guiding warmth of the sun, fear pounding in her mind as the nectar in her crop began burning her from within. She searched the air but all markers for home were gone.

The golden field shrank down beneath her and her wild blind ascent threw her into a cold and twisting current that hurled her half a league in what direction she did not know. A brown crop spread out below and was gone — and then she glimpsed a mass of churning green treetops approaching. Choking and whirling, Flora struggled to the edge of the fast current and flung herself out. She tumbled down through the leaves, struggling to grab anything she could.

128

The leaves were dense and she managed to cling to one. She dragged herself to the node with its twig, feeling poison burning through her crop and beating her antennae with toxins. The trees were sycamores and their sticky simple odour had something of the high sexual odour of drone in it. A spasm rose in Flora's body but she clung to her leaf-stem until it rose to her mouth. She spat repeatedly — but because she had drunk so much in order to return fully loaded to the hive, she knew it would now take time to empty herself.

Flora cursed her greed as she clawed the poisoned pollen from her panniers and hurled it as far as she could. Her intestines burned and her limbs shook as the toxic nectar seeped through her body, weakening her by the second. From longing to forage and leave the hive far behind, now all Flora wanted was the sweet bouquet of home and the warm press of her family around her. Now more sisters would die because she would not be able to get back and warn them of the danger of the field of gold — all her sisters, the babies in the Nursery —

My egg! She had not thought of it since leaping from the landing board, but now she felt it as strongly as if she held it in her arms, its shimmering beauty and radiant force against her body. And feeling such love must surely compound her crime against Holy Mother and her hive. Flora groaned — even when she had the chance to redeem herself, her pride had led her into folly. Better to die cleaning drone cells than bring this on her hive.

Cleaning drone cells. Those filthy fetid cubicles — Flora's gut convulsed at the memory. Suddenly she knew what she must do. Securing her grip on the twig, she incited the full taste and feel of that oily faecal waste on her tongue, with its pungent odour of male genitals —

With a violent spasm of her intestine, a jet of poisoned nectar gushed through the air.

"Holy Mother's cunt, what was that?!"

Flora had not imagined the smell of drones. With a roar of anger a battalion of them rose up through the leaves in front of her. One of them cursed and spun round, wiping the poisoned effluvia from his helmet.

"What reeking princess is this?" he yelled. "Brothers, I leave her to you, for she is the foulest-looking thing I ever saw!"

"That is no princess," cried another. "What pestilent sister dares climb up to Congregation — smite her, someone!"

"Careful — she makes to spray again!"

Flora let the last jet of poison fly from her body and the drones exclaimed in disgust and reared back in the bright air.

"Forgive me, Your Malenesses." Flora wiped her mouth. "I was sent out to bring news but I swallowed poison in the field of gold, so do not go there."

"Do not come here either!" It was the large pale drone whose plume she had defiled. "If there is an uglier sister then I have never seen one. Linden, by her livery, is she not from your hive? What a poor ill-favoured place it must be!"

130

"Then pray do not visit! And forgive the sabotage of your fine looks, but it gives the rest of us a chance."

Flora saw that Sir Linden hovered a safe distance from her, and hundreds of drones in different livery hung in the air all around, idly curious of the female intruder. Some of them teased the large pale drone, and he flew away in anger.

The breezes stirred the sycamore boughs and music shimmered from its leaves. Flora looked around in wonder. With her body cleared of the poisoned nectar, she could now draw in the deep earthy fragrance rising through the bark and feel the life-force of the tree, and see how all around it drones from different hives hung in the air, competing to rev their engines louder, or tried to outdo each other with displays of aerial prowess.

"Yes, I think you will live." Sir Linden settled nearby. "Why are you here? Please tell me you did not follow me. I would be so ashamed."

"No! I was sent as a scout —"

"Yes, well, go back and report that Congregation is exceptionally crowded with large and stupid fellows from better hives than ours, who clearly eat better food, surely served by more comely and well-tempered sisters. You have not been a good advertisement —" Linden stopped short, his attention caught.

All the drones turned to face the same direction and began roaring and cheering, their chests revving like thunder and lifting them up into the air. A thick sexual scent billowed from their abdomens and flowed across

Flora's antennae, and with it another scent, strong and intimately female.

"Today! My princess comes!"

Sir Linden pumped his scent glands furiously as he threw himself up to the height of his comrades and Flora heard the slightly higher timbre of his roar as he joined in their growling chord of lust.

The air churned and the leaves trembled at the approach of the virgin princess. She scythed past the treetops on a blade of air, too fast for capture but slow enough to flaunt her gleaming tawny bands and the lustre of her golden fur, a cloud of musky perfume swirling in her wake. The drones threw themselves into a frenzy of aerobatic displays, roaring and posturing and thundering to and fro to draw her attention, and in response she spiralled and plunged, the better to show her long shapely legs folded under her elegant body, her tiny waist, and her full regal abdomen that tapered to a pouting golden bud.

The drones cheered and bellowed out her praise and again the princess shot past them, this time letting her wings murmur of her pleasure in sex, and her command that the drones provide it. Flora caught a glimpse of her beautiful face before a powerful wave of her royal scent stirred music from the leaves and the drones roared off after her in a rage of lust. The air echoed and Flora felt the reverberations through her body as she watched them disappear into the bright air.

When the winds dispersed the vivid erotic odour of Congregation, Flora raised her antennae and searched for the hive. The faint thread of the orchard came

132

across the vast monotonous fields — a long flight into the wind on an empty crop — but Flora knew the lives of her sisters depended on her hard-won knowledge. She increased her wing-power and sped for home.

Far below her on the dun-brown field, black shapes rose cawing into the air. By the blue-black flash of their wings, Flora knew they were crows — and that they blocked her path to the hive. If she kept her course they would catch her; if she fled too far her fuel strength would give out. Either way, without her warning, more sisters would die in the field of gold.

The cawing rose to a higher pitch and Flora knew they saw her.

CHAPTER
SIXTEEN

Burning with adrenaline from emptying her fuel reserves, Flora flew higher and faster into the headwind. The smell of the crows hit her antennae and her brain screeched as Lily 500's hoarse voice cut in.

Low! she shouted in Flora's mind. *Drop lower!*

As she saw the red eyes and black beaks, Flora swerved low and hard beneath the crows, dropping through the air currents towards the smell of the earth and corn. The strobing shadows of the flock passed over her. All except one.

A sudden down draught bounced Flora's body higher in the air as the crow dived for her and snapped its massive beak. It whirled around looking for her, cursing in vexation. Flora rolled and tumbled in the swell from its huge stinking wings and sped low above the spiking corn stalks. The crow flapped and cawed in excitement as it searched for her, and she did not dare stop.

Shelter by the edge! came Lily's data, but there was no edge; the field was vast as the sky and all Flora could see were the racing spears of grain that would beat her from the air if she misjudged her level. The wind threw a carrion-footed scent over her like a net and Flora knew the crow was close and low behind her.

The edge! The edge! There it was — a low line of green hedging hidden in the moist division of the crops. She fled towards it, not knowing what good it would do — and then she saw the bright flutter of other insects above the flowering weeds — flies and gnats and white butterflies spiralling in the sun —

Use them!

Flora sped towards them, the crow hard behind her. She had one glimpse of the butterflies' surprised faces and the beautiful bronze tips of their wings before she burst through the crowd of insects, sending them into a whirring panic in the path of the crow. She heard its flapping wings as it thrashed along, snapping up as many as it could catch.

Flora drove herself high above the hedgerow and spun until she locked onto the scent of the hive. Beneath her, the crow cawed in triumph. She did not need to look to know the butterflies were gone.

The orchard was a sweet-scented sight, the little grey square of the hive even dearer as she descended from the turbulent heights down to the landing board.

"Halt, sister." Two Thistle guards came forward as soon as her feet touched the wood. When they had scanned her and could find no trace of the grey film they escorted her to the Dance Hall, where a crowd stood behind a sickle of identical Sage priestesses. She felt their keen attention rove her body and draw deeply on her scent.

"Your smell has changed."

"I had to void myself," Flora said, "in the field." As another Sage priestess walked behind her, she felt her antennae begin to throb. It was so unexpected and intimate that for a second Flora did not react. The priestess began pushing the probe of her will into Flora's mind.

My egg!

Flora's war-gland flared at the threat. Without knowing how she did it, she felt her antennae lock so hard that the priestess instantly withdrew her attention.

You will not hurt my egg!

Anger shining in her beautiful eyes, the priestess came round to face Flora.

"What strange sister is this, who can hide her thoughts?"

Another priestess joined the first, and Flora felt their combined will focusing on breaking into her mind. They probed her antennae with their powerful scent, trying to force their chemicals into her brain — but despite the burning pain, Flora maintained her lock. She concentrated on speaking calmly.

"Forgive me, Sisters," she said. "When I knew I had drunk poison, I locked my channels lest I signal falsely and draw others into danger. Now I cannot open them."

"Very . . . prudent," said one. "And how did you know to do such a thing?"

"Lily 500 gave me her knowledge." Flora did not react as they released her, but she could feel the glands

136

in her mouth moistening. She longed to hold her egg again and the smell of the Sage made her want to flee.

"You are agitated, Flora 717." A third priestess came to study her. "Good communication is even more vital in these difficult times — let us help you open your channels again." Her scent was far more powerful than the others, and Flora knew this was the priestess who had chosen her in the Arrivals Hall.

"*Accept, Obey and Serve,*" she said loudly, to cover her fear. "Forgive me, Sister Sage, but I saw much harm and I must dance without delay, to spare our hive." She ran onto the dance floor where the tiles were scuffed by the feet of a thousand foragers past. The scent of flowers rose up from the wax, and Flora began to dance.

To begin with she copied the style of Lily 500 as her steps told of the huge full fields she had travelled, bare of forage but stained by the low dank vapour of the road that cut between them. Then she danced the scanty hedgerows and then the great golden field of poison, with all the creatures dead upon the earth and the ants that ate them. There were murmurs of horror and cries of disappointment at the waste of pollen and nectar when Flora danced its vastness, but all the Sage watched in silence. Then she danced the field of corn and the crows, and the sunken hedgerow at its edge giving sanctuary against the avian Myriad — though at the price of other lives. At this, some foragers gave solemn applause.

"The hive comes first," called out one, "else how could we return?"

"You did what any of us would," called another, and the applause grew.

"Silence!" Sister Sage signalled to stop her dancing. Flora stood with her sides heaving and the electrifying choreography still running through her body as the priestess addressed the assembled sisters.

"The true passage of bud to bloom to fruit to seed is coded in the walls of Her Majesty's Library — but this new season of flood is not inscribed. Every sister knows our forager losses, but coarse wings may endure more than those of high-born kin — and so for reason of these extraordinary times we announce an exception to the ancient order of our hive. Flora 717 is permitted to forage."

At first there was total silence. Then one forager began to clap. Then another, and another, until every sister in the Dance Hall was applauding and humming her approval. Joy and gratitude ran through Flora's body as she felt their blessing and saw their shining faces — and also fear, at the sight of every priestess staring at her.

Flora's longing to be close to her egg was now a physical ache, but she stood in the lobby accepting congratulations from sisters who had never before spoken to her. It would now be much harder to visit the Nursery, for though Sanitation were regularly called in to clean, foragers famously had no interest in eggs or children — whereas the kin of Teasel lived for nothing else. As Flora smiled and thanked the passing sisters, a daring thought occurred to her. She would publicly

138

visit Sister Teasel for old times' sake, and take a nostalgic and admiring tour of the Nursery.

But that plan would have to wait, for the next cadre of foragers due to depart came out of the Dance Hall and smelled her low fuel supplies. Now she was one of them, they insisted on taking her with them to the canteen, even the most taciturn of them stressing the importance of proper energy supplies before a mission. All the other bees gave them precedence, and after they had received their food — one tongue of honey on a thick slab of pollen bread — they ate without speaking, for every atom of fuel was precious and gossip squandered strength.

Flora was grateful for their silent camaraderie, for in the privacy of her own mind she needed to calculate how long she had to visit before her egg would hatch, grow, and leave the Nursery. Her time in Category One felt very distant — but she remembered the sun bell rang three times before an egg hatched to a larva baby.

She ate her bread and concentrated. Yes — then three more sun bells while the babies were fed Flow, then they were big and healthy and moved to Category Two. She knew nothing after that, except the children were at some point taken off and sealed for Holy Time, that mysterious interval before a bee was born. Flora could not think where in the hive it happened. Every single bee had passed through that sacred phase, but she had no memory, and her own emergence was now a blank.

Flora returned to her immediate concern — the need to visit Category One before six days had passed. If she did not, it might be impossible to find her child amid thousands. The very thought of her egg made her mouth moisten with sweetness.

The closest forager looked up and sniffed her. Flora stood up.

"I am ready."

When the foragers smiled, their beauty shone past their cracked and weathered faces. They stood and bowed to her, then unlatched their wings all together with the sound that so long had thrilled her. Flora pressed down her secret and let her wings unlatch too, proud and grateful to be one of their elite and honourable number. Before six days passed she would visit Sister Teasel and find a way to see her child. But first, and with all her strength and passion, she would serve her hive.

CHAPTER
SEVENTEEN

To secretly atone for her egg, Flora gathered more pollen and nectar than any other sister. Because of the threatening skies, the foragers each made hundreds of flights while they were able, but later in the day when the clouds darkened and the wind gusted, Flora alone stayed out, fighting her way towards the sweet distant flower-wealth she could still smell.

Through watching other sisters she quickly learned the pleasantries some blooms demanded before they would release their nectar, but she studied the bumblebees as well, and their cruder ways, until she could also barge at mallow flowers and pump her tongue, forcing them to give up every drop of nectar. Lily 500's data was immaculate at factoring the imminence of rain, distance to the hive and fuel remaining, and Flora used it to pack her panniers so full of pollen that only a bee of her strength could carry it. When she landed back on the board just as the first raindrops began to fall, even the Thistle guards cheered at her daring and profit.

When the shower passed and the sun shone bright, the foragers went out again and the increased warmth brought new pollen and nectar to the flowers' lips. This time Flora took pleasure in the delicacy of her approach, and studied the ways of the smallest sweetest blooms she could find, tiny pimpernels and forget-me-nots hiding in the pockets of the fields. The energy of the sun on her body, and the joy of foraging filled her soul, and when she thought of her egg, it was as a bright bud she had not yet visited, glowing as it grew. She flew the fields and gathered until the light began to fade, and when she heard the Holy Chord of her forager sisters' wings turn for home, she joined them.

As Flora's feet touched the sun-warmed wood of the landing board, a heavy weariness overcame her. She gave her nectar to the ardently admiring receiver, too tired even to register her kin. Then she stood quietly as careful hands unpacked her pollen panniers and voices marvelled at the double load she had brought — and then she was free to rest.

It was all Flora could do to latch her wings then take herself to the canteen and eat whatever was put in front of her. She sat at the forager table and drew comfort from their presence, and now she understood why they did not speak, for it was not possible to do any more than eat, drink cool water to rehydrate her burning wings, and find a place to rest. The idea of going to the Nursery, and the energy required for her planned interaction with Sister Teasel, was unthinkable. Flora made her way to a dormitory and collapsed. It was almost too tiring to seal her antennae, but she did it lest she dream of her egg — and then her weary body sank down into sleep.

142

Many foragers died of exhaustion every night and in the morning sanitation workers carried out their bodies. The survivors stood by their berths until they had passed, singing the plainsong chant of farewell and respect:

Praise end your days, Sister. Praise end our days.

Flora's first thought on waking had been to go to the Nursery to pay her visit to Sister Teasel, but despite her intention, her feet took her to the canteen for fuel, then the landing board with all the other foragers. Her secret love for her egg glowed deep inside her, but once again, as soon as she stepped out into the dazzling warmth and unlatched her wings, the physical desire for flowers took over, and all she wanted to do was fly. The sun was bright and strong that day, and the more she gathered, the more she wanted. Each time she touched down on the landing board she remembered her egg, but her missions were already celebrated and the Dance Hall crowded to watch her dance, and there was no possible opportunity until the day was over.

Each successful mission improved Flora's skills and added to her knowledge, and on each one she went further and visited hundreds more flowers. She brought back dandelion nectar and the soft purple-black pollen from poppies; she knew the right time to visit the mallow when its nectar was just rising, and she stormed through a bank of ultraviolet ox-eye daisies, tasting which were tainted with road-wind and which were fresh to gather from. Her sense of smell enlarged so that the air-vector back to the hive was easy and fast to locate, and when she returned and disgorged her loads, her choreography became more detailed and roused more cheers.

She flew so many missions on her second day foraging that her sense of the hive stretched far and wide, for she saw and smelled her sisters at vast distances, and each of their bodies was a point of beloved familiar scent. She was near one over a deep swathe of pink rosebay willow-herb when she heard a strange rattling sound. Before Flora knew it, a beauty of dragonflies was upon them, mesmerising and terrible in their iridescent armour. Moving with astonishing speed and agility, the sublime monsters cut through the field taking bees out of the air — and then they were gone, high and distant before any could cry alarm.

On her return to the Dance Hall Flora left no detail un-danced. In graceful steps she told of the dragonflies and all the flowers that were safe to forage — and then her rhythm changed as she danced of the lost sisters from another hive. She had passed them on her return, their blind and dizzy flight striking pity in her heart as they cried out for their mother and home, the wet grey film weighing their wings and burning their minds. The bees stopped following as they recognised the stark message, and each one looked down at herself and her neighbour, to check she was clean. When Flora stopped there were no cheers, but slow applause for the valuable warning.

It was night again, and Flora still had not visited her egg. Her mind was filled with flowers and pollen and the stream and the hedge, and all the sights and sounds of her forage, but she forced them back. *Her egg.* She

144

felt its need for her. She wanted to get up and go to it, but her exhausted body would not move. *Tomorrow*.

The bees woke to rain, battering the hive wet and chilling the air. The floras came to take the dead to the morgue because the air was shut to flight, and despite the wear and tear in the field, many foragers groaned at the prospect of a day of enforced rest. Flora waited until the bodies were carried out, then dipped her antennae and followed her kin-sisters, eager to put her plan into action.

She clamped her antennae shut, folded her wings respectfully, and went into the Category One ward. Sister Teasel sat sobbing with her nurses at the station. They all looked up as Flora walked in, and she saw their tear-stained, frightened faces.

"What has happened?" Flora ran to them.

Sister Teasel could barely speak.

"A most terrible calamity." She burst out crying again. "It must have been a novitiate, her mind addled because she cannot get enough to eat!" She stared at Flora through her tears. "What are you doing here? I knew when I heard a flora had been promoted that it must be a bold thing like 717 — I said so! Oh, my poor babies, my poor, poor innocent nurses — now I must train these girls from scratch and no one for them to follow and learn from." She reached out her hands to the young nannies clustered round her, and Flora saw their fur was flat and damp and fresh from Arrivals. "If we go hungry, we cannot concentrate properly, and mistakes will be made! It is not my fault if the food supply runs short, it is yours: it is you foragers who should answer — and now look what has happened!" Sister Teasel burst out weeping again.

"Sister Teasel, please will you tell me!"

"Why are you even here? Have we not had our fill of grief and terror for one day without everyone coming to stare at us?"

"I came to see you." Flora fought down the impulse to run through the ward to search for her egg. "It is raining, we cannot fly so I thought —" She stopped, smelling the fertility police.

"Yes, they came." Sister Teasel shuddered. "How many more nurses must I lose to them? And even Lady Speedwell, dragged out of the Queen's chamber — oh, it was unspeakable!" She looked at Flora. "You know how they are. And one girl lost her mind in fear and said it was Her Majesty's doing — well, they tore her apart on the spot, right there where they found the egg." She pointed to the end of the ward. "There, in that last crib. I don't know how we will clean it, the blood went everywhere, and the child screamed and screamed for so long I will never forget —"

Flora's whole body went cold. "What child."

"A new-hatched drone. Oh, the most beautiful little boy he would have been, such a handsome face — but in the wrong crib! A new nurse must have put his egg into a worker cell, and of course the boys must always get more so no wonder he was starving by the time we found him. I said he was not yet stunted, I said there was still time to feed him up and move him, but the Sage hear everything. Next thing the police are here —

146

and then —" Sister Teasel gathered the new nurses to her and sobbed against their fur.

Flora stared at the crib where she had placed her egg. Sanitation workers scrubbed the floor around it, and a bee from Propolis repaired the broken edge.

"You said something about Lady Speedwell."

Sister Teasel wiped her eyes.

"Well, I had to tell the truth. She came into the ward late one night, so I thought I should mention it. I never intended them to — to do what they did. And in public, even while she screamed on Holy Mother's life she was innocent." Sister Teasel shuddered and waved the young nurses away. "But the police must do their job, else where would we be? Overrun with monsters and cripples. *Accept, Obey and Serve,* even when it hurts."

"Yes." Flora turned away, sick and heartbroken.

"Look around, if you want. The trouble is over, and this is still the holiest place in the hive." Sister Teasel shook her shabby old wings straight. "Holy Mother will make it right at Devotion. I don't mind telling you, I shall be first to breathe it today." Her smile was weak. "How well you've turned out, 717. I'd never have believed it. Is something wrong? Your antennae tremble so."

Flora clamped down on them so hard she gasped.

"Quite well, Sister. It is just — very sad news."

Sister Teasel groomed her own antennae straight and combed down her chest fur.

"One egg is nothing. Holy Mother will lay a thousand more this sun bell, and a thousand more every day. It is the nurses I grieve for. All that training wasted." Sister Teasel laid a light claw on Flora's arm and pulled her close. "I'll tell you what I really fear, 717. That it was not one of my poor nurses, but a vain and evil laying worker." She stared at her. "We must all be vigilant."

Flora wanted to strike Sister Teasel, or scream, or shout that it was her child, and beg she be torn apart to save her from her grief. Instead she bowed very gracefully.

"Yes," she said. "We must."

Flora walked out of Category One not knowing where she went, numb to the pulsing floor codes. She bumped into sisters and did not hear their words; she passed by others carrying food whose scent meant nothing. While she had obsessively gloried in her forage and fallen exhausted into sleep, her baby son — *her son* — had hatched and starved and died in agony. No flower on earth could heal her pain, but her steps still took her to the landing board.

Other foragers had the same idea, crowding the corridor until they could move forward and look out into the streaming grey. The close comfort of her sisters about her drew Flora's grief from her in a ragged gasp of anguish. A gentle hand touched her, and she turned to see an old and battered forager beside her, Madam Rosebay.

"Tell me," she said to Flora, "is it the headaches? We are all suffering them; no one will betray you. Do you feel it when you come in from the field and lie down? Because I feel your spirit so dull and sad within you."

Her kindness made Flora yearn to weep and tell her everything, but she forced her antennae tighter closed.

"I — I long to fly." That was all she could say.

Another bee, overhearing, smiled. Even in her grief, Flora could still see the forager's beauty through her age and the wounds to her face and shell. She was so old every trace of her kin had faded, and though it could not be, she reminded Flora of Lily 500.

"We will have our flowers again," the old forager said. "Have faith."

"We take Devotion at these times," said Madam Rosebay. "It helps."

They returned inside but Flora kept her distance from them, devastated at her failure to protect her child.

"Why the long face?" A leg missing its back hooks stuck out across her path. Sir Linden lounged in one of the forager rest chambers in the lobby near the Dance Hall. He indicated the vacant one beside it.

"You are a forager: when will this rain desist? It is dull beyond describing in our chambers, and I grow enraged hearing Poplar or Rowan or some other buffoon praising himself to the skies. As for the food — that is another reason I sit here, that I may overhear information about the latest deliveries to know if we are fairly fed, for there is never enough choice."

He groaned. "To think it has come to this: gossiping with a hairy maid in a public thoroughfare. Although you are a forager now, free to throw your earnest bulk wherever you may." He pulled a face. "Oh, come now — I do not mean to offend you, it is just my offensive nature: I cannot help it. Flowers must be quite something, if their loss for one day makes you so sad." Sir Linden crossed his middle legs and admired his hooks.

"By the way, since your bilious attack on my rival at Congregation, I find myself quite fond of you — is that not a strange thing to say? And probably to hear, but as you do not speak, I have no idea. So . . . I will leave you to contemplate this or that."

Flora straightened her wings and felt a new tear in the membrane. Until now she had not felt the wound, nor its throbbing pain. "So the princess did not see you."

"Aha! You speak to taunt. Of course she did not, or I would be reigning in kingly bliss far from this gloomy place. With special deliveries of hot-sucked spurge for my ever-so-slightly aberrant royal taste." He glanced at her. "*Euphorbia.* I shall use its polite name after my coronation. At any rate, Her Nubile Regality will find it charmingly adventurous, and let me corrupt her pure palate to share mine."

"Queenspeed to your desire."

"In fact, the next time you go out —"

"Spurge is not in season." Flora found his smell comforting.

"Pah — nothing is in its proper season any more. I believe this is supposed to be summer and the time of plenty, but you are confined by rain and I am starving." He sniffed at her. "But no wonder you're sagging there like you're waiting for the Kindness — not a molecule of Devotion in your scent. Here."

Without warning Sir Linden touched his antennae to Flora's and, despite the lock she had put on them, he pushed the Queen's Love straight into her brain. The divine fragrance had changed — or she had — for it no longer provoked ecstasy, but gradually it numbed the clawing feeling inside her. She shuddered in relief.

"Better?" Sir Linden smelled her again. "Must be something to it, though I don't know a single chap who rates it. We're Mother's favourites, so we don't need it — but the way you girls go in for it: life or death business!"

Flora's despair lifted. Holy Mother still loved her — she felt it in her heart.

"Thank you," she said to him. "The rain eases — I must go."

She ran to join the eager foragers crowding for the board. From this moment on she would be the hardest-working, most devout, dutiful and self-sacrificing daughter of the hive. *It was good her crime had died — it was good — danger would purge her —*

The sun broke the clouds, the foragers' engines roared and Flora leapt the air, in flight from her own desires.

CHAPTER
EIGHTEEN

The break in the weather did not last. A sharp east wind drove heavy rains over the hills and down across the valley and many sisters were lost that day. Heeding the early warning from Lily 500's barometric data, Flora made it back with a scant last load of willowherb pollen and, because there were no ready receivers, took it herself to Pollen & Patisserie. The desperate gratitude of the yellow-dusted sisters baking there made her determined to go out again, but on her return to the board the Thistle guards stood barring all further flights.

"You are too valuable to lose," one said, with her kin's awkward jocularity. Flora forced a smile and watched the air as the last few returning foragers managed to land in the rain. All were bedraggled with badly torn wings, others had broken antennae, and they crowded into the corridor to let the receivers salvage what they could from their sodden pollen panniers.

Then exhausted sisters went not to the Dance Hall but to find a berth for their final sleep. Other foragers touched them as they passed and murmured the salute, *Praise end your days, Sister*. The pain eased from the wounded sisters' faces and their beauty shone, for to die like this in honour and safety was every forager's hope.

Flora joined one of the many fanning details set about the hive due to the cold damp air. First she used her wing-power in the lobbies, moving when the shift changed to let exhausted house-bees rest their weaker bodies, and then when the emergency message flashed through the floor tiles, she went up to the Fanning Hall. A leak in the roof was letting in moisture and sisters rushed to make a chain of their bodies and pass beads of pre-softened propolis to seal it. Mould spores had been found on some of the highest honey vaults and every kin but the sanitation workers were called to the fanning rotas, even the Thistle. They came in from the landing board, for no predators attacked a wet hive, and they fanned hard and fast as if heating a wasp to death. Even drones came in to watch, admiring the sisters' agile antics and calling at frequent intervals for refreshments to be brought to them, as it was a tiring sight to behold.

By the end of the day the rain was still strong and the spirits of the sisters — the foragers most keenly — had grown weak. The smell of damp fur and high kin odours filled the hive; every sister's wings were limp and crumpled from the ceaseless running to and fro to fan or carry. All were desperate for a long ecstatic service of Devotion. When it came, the comb shivered and the fragrance poured forth, but the beating of the rain, or the pressure of the sky had affected the transmission, and the bees struggled to find their natural state of Oneness and Love.

By the second morning the foragers were irritable as they turned back from the drenched landing board, the sanitation workers smelled even stronger as they carried the night's dead to the morgue, and in the cold damp canteens the food had lost much savour. Devotions came and went, crowded, humid and silent as each sister concentrated on restoring her own spiritual harmony.

By the third day, the streaming bars of rain locked the hive into cabin fever. Bales of waste accumulated in the freight depot, and some frustrated foragers refused to accept the law and flew out to their deaths. The Thistle reinforced their presence in the approach corridor to stop further waste of worker resources.

"Selfish," other bees said when they heard. "More work for the rest."

After the fanning and the cleaning there was nothing to do but talk, and gossip bred like mould in the damp confinement. Nothing was off-limits as the sisters struggled to find occupation for their constant restless energy: every kin was discussed by every other, the décor of the hive and its state of repair, the food, the standard of hygiene — even the Queen's laying.

This last topic, which could have been the death warrant of any who spoke of it disparagingly, was always discussed in fulsome terms. Every bee knew a Nursery worker or had recently been one herself, and every bee had her own most personal relationship with Holy Mother. They compared their feelings during and after Devotion, and there was more than a little competition over who felt Her Love most strongly, for ecstasy was piety. The conversations always concluded with the acknowledgement that Her Majesty continued to lay at magnificent speed and volume, was more beautiful than ever, and as She was the mightiest force in the universe, this rain must be a sign of her displeasure, and so they must all work harder, *Accept, Obey and Serve*.

Flora said the words too, half devout and half ashamed. Her body surged with unused energy and despite the deepening tear in one wing-membrane she longed to fly to escape the tension of confinement, not only with her sisters but her own thoughts. Keeping her antennae shut at all times was a terrible strain, for it meant she could hardly rest at night lest she dream in scent of her egg. It was pointless to lie there in guilt, unable to sleep and occupying a premium rest chamber some more worthy sister might take, so like many other forager sisters who could not sleep because of their confinement, she got up and wandered the corridors.

On her way to the landing board to check conditions, Flora paused to peer into the Drones' Hall. It was a squalid sight. The long days of inactivity had made many drones corpulent, the floor was filthy and the sisters tending them did so with a disconsolate air, more interested in the falling crumbs than on praising Their Malenesses. The curling pungent pheromones of the males cut through the stifling smell of ten thousand damp sisters, and Flora went in to breathe a change of air. To her surprise many other sisters were there and she saw from their faces that they too breathed the drones' scent as some relief from the unventilated female fug of the dormitories.

A strange atmosphere hung in the large chamber. In their boredom and hunger some sisters took liberties with the drones' food and drink, and in return the drones with the sisters' bodies, touching them idly whilst speaking to each other of princesses they would seize when the rain ceased.

Flora withdrew, a strange feeling stirring in her body. Without realising it, her antennae channels had spread wide open and she drew deep breaths through all her spiracles. When she tried to draw them shut she found they were stuck, and a spasm shot through her whole body. Her belly swelled warm and tight and a tiny vibration flickered deep within her abdomen.

Flora hurried away from the Drones' Hall, renewed in terror and in joy that her crime would come again. In the empty lobby outside the Dance Hall she paused to scent the air from the landing board. The orchard was sweet and cool in the rising dawn, and the rain had almost stopped. The comb began to thrum as the hive awoke and a multitude of sisters began moving. From being desperate to be out on the wing, Flora no longer wanted to forage, only to be still and breathe sweet wax.

The egg in her belly glowed brighter inside her like a tiny sun. As the first foragers came down the main staircase Flora ran up a smaller one, to the mid-level. Soon she would lay, and in secret. In order to survive, her egg must have a pure wax crib — but she could not risk going to the Nursery.

156

Flora hesitated in the mid-level lobby, pretending to pore over the mosaic codes with the other sisters checking which area first required their services. She could smell the Nursery cribs from where she stood, only ever made of the purest new wax that came from the hallowed and restricted Chapel. To prevent the risk of accidental contamination, the entrance was always veiled from full public scent and impossible to find with the naked eye.

Checking there were no Sage priestesses or police in the vicinity, Flora unlocked her antennae to locate the Chapel. Immediately her love for her egg rushed upon her and she felt her kin-scent rising warm and strong. Someone must smell her, would seize her — but all Flora felt were the pulsing prayer tiles beneath her feet, for she was already on the path. A purifying scent shimmered across the plain wax doors ahead, and parted at her approach. The doors swung open.

CHAPTER
NINETEEN

"We are honoured, Madam Forager." An aged sister from Cyclamen held out her hands in greeting. Not since Lily 500 had Flora seen such a wise, beautiful sister.

"What gift can we give you?"

"I — I come to learn the skill of Wax."

When Sister Cyclamen smiled, Flora saw that she was completely blind.

"Not a skill, but a prayer of the body," she said. "And all are welcome to join with us. Come." The doors closed behind them and Flora felt a great sense of peace and safety. The whole Chapel was made of new wax, pure white and sweetly scented.

"It is like being inside a crib." Flora breathed in the wonderful perfume.

"All are children while they pray. What was the flower of your emergence, my child? You smell young, yet I feel your risen fur."

"I have no flower. I — I am a flora."

"Do not be ashamed," said Sister Cyclamen. "This Chapel accepts all who enter. And when you pray, the Wax will come or it will not. Only you will know, and you may leave at any time."

She took Flora's hands and joined her into a circle of young bees standing a wing apart.

"It may take some time. Breathe, and be still."

Flora stood between two young sisters, their fur barely risen. She clenched her belly to keep the egg from travelling down. Gradually she became aware of the very soft humming around her. It came from the wax itself, made by the bodies of the bees, themselves made by Holy Mother.

Flora's egg quickened and she clamped her antennae shut.

"Now touch them to the floor, so that you may truly feel it." Sister Cyclamen's voice was beside her, and her kind hands guided Flora's head down so that the tips of her antennae rested on the comb. Immediately the image of a beautiful drone baby glowed in her mind.

"This place is holy. I should not be here."

"You are a child of Our Mother. She makes nothing that is not holy."

Sister Cyclamen repositioned her, and the two young bees either side of her moved close enough so their wings just touched. The hum began again. Flora's body filled with a soothing glow, her head sank in relief and as she drew in the scent of pure new wax, all her clenched muscles relaxed. Her abdominal bands parted, and from them slowly seeped warm liquid wax.

"Bring it forward." Sister Cyclamen spoke quietly.

Flora reached down and stroked the liquid up in her hands. It became translucent and malleable as she touched it, and like the other sisters in the circle, she moulded it into a thin disc and laid it in the centre, building a light and fragile pile.

"How long may I do this?" Flora laid another down. She wanted to go now.

"As long as your spirit and body may unite in prayer."

"Thank you, Sister." Flora knelt and laid her antennae at Sister Cyclamen's feet. The beauty and trust of this old sister made her want to confess the treacherous crime she was about to commit for the second time — but instead, part of her brain was storing up the exact vibration of the Holy Chord, and the timing, and the sacred knowledge, to use to build a crib.

Devotion was in progress when Flora emerged, but she did not want it. While the Prayer of Wax was still fresh in her body and she knew she could draw more out, she wanted to find seclusion. This second egg made Flora's senses as keen as if she were foraging, and she could locate Holy Mother herself, far down on the opposite side of the hive. She was resting, her scent was calm and steady, but as Flora breathed it in, one thought burned in her mind: *Only the Queen may breed —*

And only the most foul and polluting daughter, who deserved to be torn head from thorax from abdomen and given to the wasps, would ever contemplate this evil act of pride. Every sister she walked past, spoke to, fed or flew with, she betrayed by her selfish crime. What if she carried a maggot, a ball of sin and sickness, a heretic's abomination?

160

A screaming bleeding child, pushed into her arms and clinging to her in terror. A baby, devoured alive by the fertility police.

Outside the Chapel of Wax Flora pulled some of the purifying veil of scent from around the doors and wrapped it round herself. She re-sealed her antennae, but she could not draw in her abdomen for her egg grew larger all the time. She loved the feeling of the life inside her, and she did not care if it was a crime: she wanted this child — and must find a place to hide.

A place of seclusion . . . quiet, with three doors.

Sister Sage had taken her to one such place, immediately after her emergence. Flora thought of that small room where she had first met Sister Teasel. It was behind the Nursery, on this floor. To reach it, she would have to cross the lobby now, while Devotion was still in progress. If she waited, she would give birth in public.

While the Holy Chord continued and everyone was preoccupied in prayer and unity was the best time to move — but as soon as the Queen's Love began to shimmer down from a psychic trance to a fragrance, the sisters would wake and some vigilant bee would find her out.

Flora edged into the transcendent crowd. The signal of Devotion in the comb made it hard to locate the exact route she sought, and the egg pulsed at her harder, demanding she lie down. There was no time to lose. Flora moved to where the scent of different kin was strong and varied, then she opened up her antennae and searched for the exact location.

161

Following Sister Sage . . . The big central mosaic . . . and then —

The Queen's Love.

Sister Sage had given her the Queen's Love. If she took some now, in Devotion — she would find the way.

Flora opened her spiracles, pressed her feet into the comb and drew in as much of the divine fragrance as she possibly could.

Dull gold tiles then blank white tiles not cleaned just blank.

There it was — underfoot the same pattern led away through the lobby.

"Where do you go, before the service is ended?" Sister Sage stood before Flora, tremors of Devotion still flying up her rigid antennae.

Frantic to hide her thoughts, Flora pulsed out a chunk of Lily 500's data.

The azimuth of the sun never lies, unlike the wasps and every creature of the Myriad but the Spiders.

Sister Sage recoiled. "You mention such things at Devotion?"

"Forgive me, Sister. It is the long confinement." Despite the pain it caused her, Flora pulsed another surge of Lily's data at Sister Sage.

When confronted with soiled blooms and evidence of bluebottles —

"Enough! Incontinent, impatient foragers — while the rains last, you will consider your sisters!" Disgusted at the rude interruption to her prayers, Sister Sage pushed her way through the shuddering crowd.

Flora picked up the trail of the golden tiles again. At the service corridor behind Pollen & Patisserie and the Category Two ward they became blank, but she recognised them from her time in Sanitation, because it was here nannies and nurses left their waste for collection. Here was the gutter she had swept and sluiced so many times, and there, at the end of the corridor, a blank wall. If there was no door, she would go into labour in front of thousands of sisters and die with her egg.

The Holy Chord faded, the vibration of sixty thousand feet resumed, and Flora ran down to the end to check, her belly swelling with every step.

Invisible until she stood directly before it was a small carved doorway and a tiny panel marked with a crown. Flora touched it and the door swung open. To her relief, she stood in the little empty room she recognised, with the three doors.

She closed the one door she had entered from. Another one led to the Nursery, and the third . . . was where the worn tiles ended. Flora went to listen at it. All was silent behind, and she opened it. She found herself on the landing of a staircase, tall and steep. From beneath rose the scent of the fresh air of the landing board, and from above, the scent of honey. Immediately Flora knew where she was. This was the staircase she had used when she fled from Sir Linden, when the greedy drones had invaded the Fanning Hall. The air was still, as if it had been unused for some time. She began to climb.

★　★　★

The staircase ended at a little landing with one door. Beyond it, Flora could sense the corridor and the vibrations of sisters' feet. She gasped at the pounding of her belly — the egg was coming. Warm wax began seeping from between her bands and flowed over her hands as she struggled to hold it back — to waste such a precious substance, to strive so hard to protect her egg, to think she could hide it — Flora beat her head against the wall in grief at her failure.

Very slowly, a section of wall swung round and Flora stood facing a dark open space. The egg began pushing its way out of Flora's body and she managed to get inside and push the wall closed behind her. She sank down onto the ground and breathed the old still air in the chamber. Despite the pain, two scents instantly registered.

The first was the strong smell of honey, carried on vibrations from one of the walls. Flora opened her antennae to read them — and knew they were the movements of sisters working in the Treasury beyond. The second scent was much fainter, old and dry and undisturbed by any living vibration.

Her egg trembled inside her and halted its passage. Feeling its fear, Flora turned to face whatever threat was there. Her distended abdomen left no space to slide her dagger, but she raised her claws and circled against the strange force in the chamber. The scent clarified into an infinitesimally small signal in the air. It was not trying to repel her — it was calling her.

Clenching her egg tight in her body, Flora followed it to its source. She stopped in shock. There against the

164

wall was a sight so extraordinary that for a few seconds she felt no pain. Three tall cocoons stood anchored on a thick wax plinth, each one a long and faceted oval, intricately decorated. All bore little round holes in the lower section, but one also had a jagged rip across the top.

Flora drew in their scent, and screamed as the egg pulsed hard in response. Each cocoon was a coffin, and each held a long-dead Sage.

Flora's egg began travelling down her body again, fast and violent. She fell to the ground before the three sarcophagi, twisting in silence as her abdomen was forced apart. The egg slid from her body and the roaring air calmed. She could feel it, warm and alive and huge, resting against the tip of her body. She curled round to hold it and her heart filled with love.

This egg glowed golden and smelled sweeter than Devotion. Flora felt her body wet with liquid wax, and quick and grateful she brought it forth handful by handful, building up the roughest crib of sweet white wax, directly in front of the three cocoons. Then she knelt and held her egg close, thrilling to its living vibration. Though slightly larger, it was the same shape as before — and Flora vowed that this time she would feed her little son everything he needed to grow strong — and discover what she must do to seal him for Holy Time.

My beloved egg — my wicked blessed sin I love —

Never again would she forget herself in the field. She placed the egg tenderly in the rough crib.

"In three days," she whispered to it, "I will hold you and feed you."

Fearless by the power of birth, Flora rose to examine the strange cocoons. They reminded her of the grand decorated cells in the Drones' Arrivals Hall — but these were much larger and bore no hint of male smell. Each one showed three or four of the small holes, positioned over where the occupant's abdomen would be, and when she sniffed at them, Flora's own sting pulsed at the faintest trace of old dry venom — but they were all long dead. She climbed onto the plinth so she could see into the one with the hole at the top.

The barely formed face of a young Sage female stared back, dead before she was born. She would have been as big as the Queen herself, and almost as beautiful. One of her hands was raised, a fragment of wax caught in her juvenile claw. Flora climbed down. It was the living Sage she must worry about. She washed herself very carefully and let the tip of her abdomen fully contract. Then she slipped out the way she had come, ready to rejoin the life of the hive.

Inside the chamber, under the sightless gaze of dead priestesses, her egg began to grow.

CHAPTER
TWENTY

Flora stepped out on the lowest storey of the hive to freezing-cold air blowing in from the landing board, and the battering of hail against the wooden hive. Thistle guards ran to push back the boulders of ice rolling in, and Flora joined the sisters running to help them. She felt completely disoriented, as if she had slept for a long time and missed the news of the hive, for by the rush of house-bees towards the Dance Hall, a meeting had been called.

The scent of Sage priestesses came from within, and Flora pressed herself against other sanitation workers in the crush to share their kin-scent and mask any smell of her egg. In the centre of the Dance Hall the massed choir of Sage priestesses hummed the Holy Chord, until the vast harmonic drowned out the sound of the hail. Then they sent their silent will through the comb, in the voice of the Hive Mind.

In obedience, the bees formed themselves into concentric circles, as if this were the Fanning Hall. Then the priestesses were lifted up by their own kin so that all could see them. Their wings were unlatched, their scent shimmered stronger and their eyes were

167

luminous. They spoke in their beautiful low choral voice so that every sister heard them above the hail.

"We are the holy Melissae, born of the Queen's kin, and guardian of the Hive Mind. The season is dark, the flowers have turned against us, and the Air to Flood and Ice. Spores of evil growth enter on the damp wind and blight our chalices of nectar, and our Treasury shrinks faster than we can fill it. Holy Mother's sacred work is halted, and the sins of Apathy, Despair and Inertia settle on us like flies."

The scent of the Sage rose stronger and the foragers stirred uneasily, for beneath it crept the heavy masking odour of the fertility police. Flora immediately sealed her antennae and drew her breathing spiracles tight to withstand its domineering influence. Her instinct was to run, but that would be fatal and if she died so would her —

She forced the secret thought back down and looked around her. Every sister's antennae stood in fear, even the foragers. They could not all be guilty — she must remain calm.

The priestesses scanned the chamber. Extending their elegant antennae to their full length, they absorbed information flaring from every fear-struck sister. Frightened little buzzes came from different areas of the crowd as the thick scent of the fertility police crept low and tight around their legs and feet to hold them fast. Flora did not resist it, despite the waves of panic that ran through the chamber from thousands of sisters. If they found her, then it was Holy Mother's will she must die.

168

Holy Mother ... To even think of the Queen was painful. Her kindness, her beauty, the way her loving touch had taken away Flora's shame at her kin —

"We, the hive, are guilty of Sacrilege and Waste," resumed the choral voice of the Sage priestesses. "Nectar in Fanning has been drunk without permission, foragers lost on the wing, and even mistakes made in the Nursery" — there was a gasp of shock at this — "because of errors in this very chamber." The priestesses shimmered their wings to spread their scent.

"The Queen's Love is carried by the Rule of Law, and we show our loyalty to Holy Mother through our trust in Her priestesses, the Melissae. The season has grown hostile and bloom after bloom we have called it aberration, and waited for change. And now it comes in this rain of ice, and the meaning is clear: it is a judgement on our hive and a call to penance!"

The dark bees wove in from the edges, driving the crowd tighter.

"We have consulted the ancient codes in our Holy Mother's Library," continued the priestesses in their several voices, harsher now but still beautiful. "The Queen has reassured us of Her Love, and we are permitted to celebrate our sisterhood with the Rite of Expiation."

The silent bees stared back.

Expiation ... Flora tried to think where she had heard that word before. Then it came to her — the fourth panel of the Queen's Library. She wanted fresh air, she wanted to leave this chamber, but the choral voice of the Sage continued.

169

"The sacred Act calls upon the sacrifice of love, one bee for her sisters, her Mother, her hive. Who here is old and near the end of her use? Who hides a weakness that may be illness, or has in any way sinned? To save your sisters and free our hive from this suffering, give yourselves now."

No bee moved or spoke but kin-scents streaked with terror spiralled in the air. Flora saw the serene blind face of Sister Cyclamen, who had been so kind to her in the Chapel of Wax. *Expiation*. The old sister began to lift her hand.

"I will do it!" Flora called out loudly. "I will atone!"

The crowd turned and the focus of every Sage priestess locked onto her as she walked forward. Sisters shrank back, awed and frightened. Flora unlocked her antennae and felt a rush of relief. *Only the Queen may breed* — that was the truth, and to acknowledge it reunited her soul with her sisters. Gladly would she give her life for them, and win back honour with her death.

"I am Flora 717 and I —"

"And I will too!" called out another voice in the crowd.

"And I," shouted another.

"I will die for Holy Mother."

"I am of the spring, my time draws near, take me!"

One after another they called out.

"Let me —"

"I cling to life but I am old —"

"I am greedy —"

"I am weak —"

Sister after sister walked forward after Flora. The priestesses directed them all to stand in a group in the centre. One walked around dividing them.

"Young, old. Old. Old. Old." She stopped at Flora. "But you are very young." She raked a claw through Flora's fur. "Barely risen."

Flora looked down at herself and saw it was true — her fur was thick and lustrous as if she were still just a young nurse. The priestess drew a slow claw under Flora's abdomen and brought it out. A curled filament of wax hung from it. She smelled it. Flora waited for the blow, for none of her kin were permitted to work with this sacred substance.

"You still make Wax — of course we cannot spare you. A noble gesture, but stand aside." The priestess passed on, inspecting the volunteer bees.

Flora could not believe it — surely the priestess had smelled her guilt. Then she felt her antennae sealed tight again. She had done it unconsciously, and she knew why. Deep in her mind, her tiny egg shone pure and bright. It did not want to die, it did not want its mother to die — and they were still connected. Joy rushed through Flora's body and she looked down at herself. It was true, she did look young again. Her fur rose thick and lustrous, her cuticle gleamed, her joints were supple. Very quietly she opened her wing-latches and sent her consciousness running down the four membranes. Each one was strong and supple and whole, with no trace of damage. The deep tear she knew had been there had healed.

Holy Mother's youth restored with every egg. And she, a flora from Sanitation, was stealing the gift of life and youth and power from Holy Mother herself, bringing destruction and death on her hive.

"Do not spare me!" Flora shouted. "Let me die, destroy my sins!"

"Religious mania, 717." In the group of the old selected volunteers, Sister Teasel stood watching her. "But I know you spoke first, and it was brave." She plucked at her bald thorax as if the fur still grew. "It should have been me — it is up to the higher kin to set the standard." She twisted her hands. "I shall do it in death though. Now hush, and let us pray in peace."

The Sage priestesses bowed and addressed the ragged old group.

"Daughters of Our Holy Mother, servants of our hive: do you willingly give your bodies and souls in the Rite of Expiation?"

The old bees nodded and held each other.

"We do," some managed to say.

"Thank you, noble sisters. Then *Accept, Obey and Serve.*"

"*Accept, Obey and Serve,*" the old bees whispered.

The Sage priestesses brought the younger bees who had volunteered themselves to surround the older group.

"You shall lead the Rite."

The Sage priestesses recommenced the Holy Chord, and from the back of the Dance Hall the dark-slicked bees from the fertility police started driving the others forward. Then the chant began:

Blessed be the Sister

Who takes away my sin.
Blessed be the Sister . . .

The kin of Sage had initiated it, but each kin group took it up as a round until the whole chamber resonated with the words and the words blurred into a low surging sound as the crowd pushed forward.

Flora felt the weight of a thousand sisters against her back. All around them were gasps and cries as old sisters went down under the force of the crowd and the chant grew louder.

Blessed be the Sister — Her antennae roared with the overlapping words as her feet were forced forward. *Fertility is Life itself.* The thought made her stumble, but she dug her hooks into the wax and felt the strength powering down her six legs. *I am fertile.* Blood rushed into her wing-veins and she longed to spread them on the air. She must get back within three days to watch her egg hatch —

Her body slammed hard against one of the old bees — and she looked straight into the terrified face of Sister Teasel.

Blessed be the Sister
Who takes away my sin —

"Holy Mother, forgive my fear!" Sister Teasel clung to Flora and pressed her antennae tight against hers. Flora cried out in shock, but it was too late. The scent and the feel and the love she felt for her beautiful egg rushed into Sister Teasel's mind. The old sister recoiled.

"YOU! You are the laying worker!" Sister Teasel struggled for footing in the hardening crush. "Here!" she screamed out. "Here is the heretic —"

Flora kicked her legs out from under her but Sister Teasel only staggered. She clawed at Flora's face and pumped her alarm glands wildly.

"She sins again! Kill her egg!"

The waves of the chant rolled louder above them as Flora pushed Sister Teasel down onto the throbbing comb and broke her neck.

Blessed be the Sister

Who takes away our sin . . .

Flora stood up, her kin-scent pumping hard. All around the Dance Hall the sisters pushed forward, moving the dead into a pile of frail old bodies in the centre. Sister Teasel's body disappeared under others.

Blessed be the Sister . . . sang the beautiful chorus of the Sage.

Who takes away our sin.

Our Mother, who art in labour,

"*Hallowed be Thy Womb*," joined in all the other bees. As they spoke the ancient words of the Queen's Prayer together, the vibration in the comb changed, and the fragrance of Devotion began to flow.

Many bees wept at the sight of the old dead sisters, and kin comforted kin, but all kept breathing deeply of the Queen's Love, calming themselves with its purity and strength. Flora spoke the words and closed her antennae tight. They were bruised from Sister Teasel's attack, but she was alive, and so was her secret.

"*Amen*," she said, with all her sisters.

They stood in silence, the pressure eased. The only sound was a blackbird's song, far out in the orchard. The hail had stopped.

174

The Sage priestesses raised their arms in triumph and the bees wept in joy, their terror forgotten. With a fine fierce sound the foragers unlatched their wings and the house-bees cheered them on as they ran for the landing board, bright and steaming as the clouds released the sun.

CHAPTER
TWENTY-ONE

Shocked at her own act, Flora was among the first out. A rising front from the south wiped the last shred of grey from the sky and below her spread the wide plain of different greens, pushed together in crude four-sided shapes as if by some primitive insect ignorant of the beauty of the hexagon. In the distance where once had shone the field of golden rapeseed, two lumbering machines toiled away at the soil. Flora flexed a wing-tip and veered away from the smell.

She had offered herself up, but she had not been taken. For whatever reason, it had not been Holy Mother's will that she die — otherwise her confession would have been heard. Instead, a Sage priestess had passed her to the side of the living, and Sister Teasel to the dying.

Flora tucked her antennae sleek down her back as she advanced her speed. Never again would she leave her channels open in the hive, for any bee to grab and read. Sister Teasel was old and could no longer work efficiently — but Flora's wings beat with a new strength. She felt she could fly a hundred leagues to serve her hive, and the sky streamed with all the scents rising from the wet earth — including mesmerisingly delicious nectar. Flora locked onto it.

Fresh nectar, after days of stale, damp food in the hive — how her sisters would cheer and what a balm to her conscience, to see them feasting on her forage. Flora was ravenous, and she increased her wing-beats. With luck she might even be first to stand on the velvet lip of a petal as the day's nectar rose.

She sped along the stinking grey line of the road, towards the red- and grey-roofed town and the tiny green gardens that prised the houses apart. The tarmac veins multiplied, the dank monoxide wind billowed higher, but Flora rose above it, glorying in her extraordinary new power. Perhaps Holy Mother had spared her for this very purpose: to bring the finest forage for the hive, and fill its Treasury with wealth. By her efforts foraging and the value she brought to the hive, she would offset the crimes of her body.

Flora steadied herself on the high warm current and checked her position, logging all the visual markers into her antennae. The town was straight ahead, but if she veered to follow the rising land on one side, she could approach its tiny gardens from the back — and those flowers whose sweet mouths she could smell. She felt for the thermal flowing towards the slope of the land and rose up to catch it. But instead of the warm curl of air she expected to ride with ease, it spiralled and spun her into a big fast current streaming through the valley.

Get down! Lily 500's voice burned through her antennae. *Descend!*

So the old forager had travelled this way herself then. Flora struggled lower to clear her antennae from the strange sound in the wind that kept snagging her attention. The interference got worse. With a rattling snap, all but her visual data completely vanished.

Alarmed it might be from particles of that grey film of sickness, Flora flew towards a clump of trees on the hilltop. Her body felt strong and well, but a pressure was building in her head and the trees came in and out of focus.

One was larger than the rest and its dark-green branches barely moved. It was some sort of massive conifer, its leaves stiff and gleaming, its trunk covered in a strangely uniform-coloured brown bark. Some of its branches appeared to be made completely of metal and a dismal emanation transmitted from its core, like a prayer mumbled backwards. It had no smell and its energy was neither living nor dead.

The wind scattered on the hilltop and once again Flora tried to descend, but an alien force pumped at her brain and blocked out her senses. She found herself flying around the tree's dead shiny branches on which no insects crawled and no birds rested. Far below were four shining metal roots, ugly and symmetrical, dug deep into a stone platform on which were scattered many black dots. Their shape was familiar, for they were bees. Revolted, Flora tried to use her strength to break out of the prison circle in which she flew, but each effort merely increased her speed. A hideous power pulsed from the metal tree, sapping her strength.

A sharp pain shot through her head as a burst of Lily's data broke in again.

Do not look down. Follow —

Flora strained to draw more out but her antennae sagged like dead things. Follow what? She tried to focus on one spot beyond the tree and hurl herself out towards it, but her whirling momentum blurred everything to writhing green lines.

— the Myriad — the Myriad — the Myriad —

Now the old forager's data looped over and over, mixing with the dull moan of the tree's core until Flora wanted to tear her own antennae from her head to stop it. A high hissing sound cut in and as she was dragged round again she caught a lurid flash of black-and-yellow livery.

"Greetings, Cousin Apis," called the high, wicked voice of a wasp. It hung in the air watching her, completely unaffected by the shining tree. "Are we outwitted, so far from home?" It flew alongside Flora to show itself.

She was a young female, much smaller than the huge Lady Vespa who had tried to raid the hive and been cooked for her pains — but even in her dulled state Flora could see her malicious face and smell her ready sting. The wasp laughed again.

"Oh, we do like to see our cousins Apis in trouble . . . Even the Chosen People must sometimes struggle, no?" She floated closer to Flora. "None of you know this tree, do you? Until it is too late!" She made little backwards bounces without moving her wings, showing off. "We are not the Chosen People, but we are still superior, do you see, cousin? We make no honey, but we are more intelligent, more beautiful." The wasp smirked and pirouetted, and even in her battered state Flora longed to strike her to the ground.

"And, oh yes" — the wasp slid out her little dagger to show the bead of poison glistening at its tip — "so much better equipped!" She flexed it lasciviously then flew so close to Flora that her buzzing drowned out the moaning of the tree.

"Admit that we are better and curtsy to me," simpered the wasp, "and I might show you how to leave."

Follow — the Myriad — Lily 500's voice bit through Flora's heavy mind — *Because they are not affected* —

"I admit it!" Flora spread her knees in a clumsy curtsy and tipped in the air. The wasp shrieked with laughter then whirred her wings in her face.

"Follow me quick and close, stupid cousin, and do it now."

Flora lunged after the wasp and fell from the tree's hold. The ground spun towards her but she grabbed onto a dry brown stem. The wasp settled on the dead bush beside her and waited while Flora righted herself.

"So clumsy! How the flowers must hate your touch. Curtsy again."

"No." Nauseous and angry, Flora could barely speak.

"La la then I will leave you," sang the wasp, "and watch how long you take to die." She flew off a short distance and hovered. Flora gathered her strength to fly, but her body was weak and her fuel supplies low. As soon as she felt the air between her wing-beats, the moaning tree sucked her back towards it.

"Curtsy," sang the wasp, "and see your hive again. Up to you!"

Flora clutched the twig again and curtsied to the wasp.

"How the Chosen People grovel, when they must! With all your treasure and your fur, and your superior holy attitude that you make such a song and dance about. As if you are the only ones the flowers care for!"

"You are right, cousin. You are better. Now how may I leave here?"

"Ah well, first you should have kept to your side of the road," said the wasp.

"The air belongs to all. No wasp decrees our flight."

"Is that the royal We? Well, dear cousin, let me tell you: We, the Vespa, think that your royal Mother sickens. Indeed we do."

"You lie." Flora's sting flexed at the insult.

"Oh no, for we found a poor sister from your orchard, lost on the wing just like you." She made her small sizzling laugh. "We know your livery, of course we do. Even when sullied with nasty grey specks. Poor dying Apis, we carried her in to comfort her last moments, and how freely she spoke! How she called for her sisters — oh, we did not take offence, for she was very weak, but it was charming how she shared her news with us, of Lady Vespa's rude reception, and all about your holy Sage." The wasp put her head to one side. "And how Mother's odour grows weaker."

"*Holy* Mother! And Her Love stays strong." Flora's sting tingled to be used.

"Forgive me, cousin, you are right to mark my manners." The wasp giggled, then shot her a sly look. "Do you think we are inferior? An Apis cannot lie."

"Yes — but it is not your fault." Flora did not want to anger the wasp. "You are stronger than me, for you can withstand this tree."

"Not a tree, stupid cousin!" The wasp hovered and lifted one claw in time to a silent beat. "Can you not hear it? Boom, boom, boom — it never stops! And so loud and boring — but at least it cannot broadcast scent. That would be much harder to ignore."

Now the wasp had pointed it out, Flora could feel the heavy magnetic throb dragging on the air. Completely immune to the pulse of the cell-phone tower, the wasp wove about in the air in front of Flora, demonstrating different wing-beats.

"Subtler frequencies, you see. We set them to miss that dreary beat — because we are better fliers than you. Better at everything!"

"Indeed," Flora said sincerely. "You are very wise to understand this tree. And if I can return home, I will gladly tell my sisters of your skill."

"Of course you can. I will show you the kindness of wasps. How are your aerials?"

Flora's antennae were raw from the brutal pulsation of the shining tree and she could neither smell nor orient herself in any way, but she raised them to show good spirits.

The wasp smiled.

182

"Then follow me, and all will be well."

Senses blunted, Flora set her wing-beats to the wasp's strange frequency and flew in her slipstream. If her cousin had not left her there to perish, then she could be trusted.

CHAPTER
TWENTY-TWO

As they descended over the treetops Flora strained for any trace of scent of drones in case Congregation was near, but all she could pick up was a fragmented smell of an alien nectar. They flew low over the big grey road, its bitter stench soaking up into the air, and then across a small field of rye. That brash familiar scent pushed into Flora's brain and her senses began to revive. Vast grey-green fields swayed into the distance, but no fragrance of nectar or pollen drifted from ahead, only the dreary useless odour of fibrous crops and the strange tang of the earth beneath them.

The wasp hovered on lissom wings and watched Flora.

"So, that way lies your orchard, cousin — and as you see, it is a route to give you empty baskets." She sighed. "To think of all you poor cousins, your flowers rotted in the rain and no clue what to do."

"There will be more flowers."

"Not in our lifetime — do you not see the berries swell? All religions can read that sign. Many times we say at home how we would willingly share our bounty with our cousins, for we have so *much* — how sad the

Chosen People are too proud. Yet we Vespa long to forget the ancient feud . . ."

"You have pollen and honey?"

The wasp burst out laughing.

"Cousin, you work too hard! We have *sugar*, like hard dewdrops of nectar, but soft as larvae inside. Sweeter than honey, stronger than that scabbing tree blood you gather." She spat in disgust.

"Propolis. It has many uses." Flora tried not to be angry at her, for much might be gained from this friendship. She imagined herself on the landing board, unloading exotic treasure for her hive, insisting on the truth of its provenance.

"Whatever you like to call it, cousin. But you might feed your whole hive with just a few mouthfuls of what we have. Never mind — here I must leave you. Good foraging, cousin."

"Wait —" Flora flew after her. "You *truly* would share with us?"

The wasp dipped her wings demurely, and smiled.

Flora expected they would head for the maelstrom of scents coming from the town, but instead the wasp led her to a cluster of grey warehouses on its edge. Brown-belching vehicles laboured to and fro, and Flora noted them, to add to her homecoming choreography. There would be so much to dance about, and such a fervour of excitement — to think that the ancient feud with the Vespa might be over — that would be expiation indeed.

The wasp checked over her wings that Flora was still behind her, and then began her descent towards the warehouse buildings. Flora logged as much information as she could, though her antennae remained slow and sore. She had never seen a place with so few plants, their stunted flower-heads with barely enough strength to open. Sensing the presence of a honeybee, they mustered their energy and breathed a poor wisp of scent to her.

"Leave them," said the wasp. "They're pathetic —"

But where one plant stretched and pushed out its scent, so did all its neighbours and supplications and pleas came from every flower in every crack of concrete or breeze-block wall for Flora to come to them, to them, they called and begged her, they wanted to speak with her and feel her feet on their petals.

"Very quickly." Flora dropped down onto the soot-stained head of a buddleia, trembling for her touch. It sighed in gratitude as Flora secured her hold, then pushed her tongue deep into a floret. A dirty film of oil coated its petals and she released it in disgust, rearing into the air. The buddleia drooped in shame.

"Told you!" sang the wasp. "Come now, if you wish to feed your family. Or go home empty." She flew into the dark cavernous mouth of a warehouse.

Flora hovered outside. She was glad there was no one from her hive to have seen her try the weeds — for despite their nectar and warm welcome, surely that was what they were: low, coarse, desperate weeds. There had to be a good reason their forage was shunned — but she could not think of one. The words of the Catechism

186

came back to her: "*nor may she ever forage for she has no taste*".

The weeds had made a fool of her, and Flora was angry at herself for succumbing to their pleas. She whirred her wings louder to muffle their voices. The bees certainly did not know everything — if they did, they would not have lain dead at the foot of the murmuring tree in such numbers, while the wasp went free. Ignoring the cries of the weeds, Flora flew into the warehouse.

The cavern was dim, vast and vague, and a sharp peculiar scent hit Flora in the antennae as soon as she flew in, making them twitch in excitement and revulsion at the same time.

"Here," called the wasp, her voice deeper in the gloom, "this way, cousin."

Flora flew towards her under the crackling bars of fluorescent light that hung at intervals down the dark curved ceiling. The walls were made of stacked containers, and below her on the concrete ground, slow ungainly vehicles laboured to move them to and fro. They reminded Flora of sanitation workers rolling balls of drone wax, and she noted this little detail to further enhance her choreography on her return.

"Come." The wasp had returned to find her. Under the flickering lights Flora saw how young she was, her pointed black-and-yellow face completely smooth. A smile shone from her glossed black eyes, flatter than a bee's and with elegantly glittered edges. She pivoted in the air and a wisp of formic acid drifted from her. She whirred it away with a sudden thrum of her wings.

"Forgive my excitement," she whispered to Flora. "Come and taste the sugar." She flew to the wall and alighted on an irregularly shaped ledge, a glowing mosaic of rock in colours more lurid and vulgar than any petal could attempt. Flora's antennae lashed in repulsion at the blaring scent, but her tongue stretched out to taste it.

"Fill your crop, cousin," said the wasp. "Feel your hunger."

The sugar was solid like propolis, soft like wax, then it melted like nectar. It was the most extraordinary substance and the more she ate the more she wanted and the faster she chewed. As the taste raced through her brain, Flora abandoned decorum and gnawed at it as if she were breaking out of her arrival chamber. Each of the colours tasted slightly different, underlaid with a tang that almost made her want to retch, yet sharpened her appetite for more. She wanted to ask about it and where she might find it for herself, but she could not stop eating.

Far below on the ground, the vehicles whined and groaned.

"You like it, cousin?" The wasp chewed sugar nearby and watched Flora eating. She was generous, Flora thought, and she wanted to say so, but something in the coloured nectar-rock kept her gnawing faster and faster.

"Eat more," the wasp said, a peculiar smile on her face. "Eat your fill."

Suddenly self-conscious of her greed, Flora slowed down as she prised the last blue crystal out. There was a strange vibration at her feet as it came free, and Flora looked down and noticed what she stood on.

Extending either side of the gaily coloured ledge of sugar beneath her was a chewed grey mix of paper and clay. It curved out in an irregular shape, and finished some distance underneath, tight against the wall. It was a colossal wasps' nest, and the roof was made of sugar. The vibration she had heard did not come from the vehicles on the ground, but from inside the nest. It was the high-pitched whining of thousands and thousands of wasp larvae under her feet.

Flora did not move. Now she felt the presence of all the wasps hovering close by in the air behind her, their scent masked by the thick smell of sugar she had raised by her frantic chewing, and their sound by the machines on the ground. In the time it took Flora to realise, the sugar under her feet hardened like propolis and held her fast.

The wasp watched her. Flora did not turn. Instead, she bowed her antennae.

"Thank you for this feast, cousin," she said, as calmly as she could. "You are so beautiful, with your tiny waist and sharp smooth stripes. Will you spin so I can admire you?"

The young wasp could not resist. She pirouetted on the air.

"Please," Flora said humbly, and curtsied low, "that was so rare a sight, I have only seen it done faster once before."

"Faster?" the wasp retorted. "That was nothing: watch this." And she spun again. Deep in her curtsy,

Flora saw the massed horde of wasps hanging in the dim air of the cavern behind her. Quickly she bit her feet free of the sugar.

"Are we not superior?" called the wasp within her spinning. "Admit it!"

"You are!" Flora cried, pulling her feet free. "Faster!" Then, roaring her thoracic engine like a rampant drone, she shot backwards as hard as she could into the ambush of wasps, scattering them in the air.

"*Apissss!*" they screamed, rearing up from their shock. "*Apisss die!*"

They came at her from all sides, shrieking their fury and filling the air with the scent of their wet-drawn daggers. Flora plunged and swerved while inside the nest the larvae whined a thin sick note of hatred through the paper walls, and their captives screamed for mercy in all the languages of the Air.

At the obscene intimate brush of wasp wings against her own, Flora lost her axis and fell. She tumbled in a sickening mist of sugar and formic acid and righted herself just before she hit the ground.

The mouth of the cavern was bright but as Flora threw herself towards it, one of the big lumbering vehicles drew across it and blocked the entrance. In a desperate swerve she dived through the tiny aperture into the driver's cab and the torrent of wasps poured in after her.

The driver yelled in fright and thrashed his hairy forearm around his head, knocking Flora to the ground and maddening the wasps. As they stung him from all sides, Flora crawled into a groove of dirt and hid. He screamed and pressed on the horn so that the vehicle itself bellowed like a wounded bull then he wrenched open the door and staggered out. At the touch of air on her wings Flora dragged herself over the metal step and fell to the concrete floor. While the wasps descended on the writhing man she crawled towards the light and air. The weeds pulsed their scent to help her and she used it to pull herself forward until she felt the sky above.

The clouds were violet-grey and the cold air trembled in bursts and stops. Fighting off the numbing fog of the formic acid, Flora struggled for altitude, her wing-joints burning. Below her she could still hear the enraged buzz of the wasps and the shouts of the men running to drive them from their screaming victim.

Flora climbed higher, trying to pick up the azimuth of the sun with her sugar-jangled antennae. She thought she had filled her crop with sugar, but it was light and empty.

Ashamed at her failure to forage and sick from her own greed, the only thing Flora now wanted was the scent of home. She turned again and again, but nothing registered except the racing pulse of the sugar.

Flora cursed her pride — she of all kin should have listened to the weeds. If she lived to see another sunrise she would kiss every one of their mouths. She flew in a circle, then in a figure of eight, trying to pick up the scent of the orchard, of the great road, of Congregation, of anything familiar, but huge waves of wind collided and she had to flatten her antennae and tighten her wings lest they be ripped from her body. A colossal cold swell threw her sideways and a warm front flung her back. With a tearing flash of light, the storm broke.

A water bomb hit Flora on her right side, and she felt her wing-latch breaking between the front and rear membranes. Clenching her thoracic muscles to hold her wing panels together, she aimed herself into the racing air current streaming towards the tree-line. Pelting rain bombs knocked her lower and lower, and with a lurch of strength she flung herself into the nearest canopy of leaves. She tumbled down the dripping green slides trying to grab hold of anything, but her claws slipped and she fell to the earth.

Directly ahead under the drumming leaves was a place of shelter. To reach it she must crawl across a shining track left by some unknown creature, but if she did not move the rain bombs would take away all choice and she would lie drowning with broken wings. Nothing was in sight so Flora stepped quickly across it. She was almost at the dry sanctuary of twigs when a sound made her look around.

It did not see her for it had no eyes, but, its orange frill rippling as it moved, a fat brown slug pulled its way back towards her along the silvery mucus trail. It was nothing but a rhythmically convulsing sack of muscle, then it raised its gaping drooling mouth, and made a sound between a grunt and a moan. Two flaccid horns engorged and lifted, and only then did its tiny eyes bulge out from their tips. It moaned again as its slime spread behind it.

A forager's suicide from the water bombs was better than cowering on the ground waiting to be engulfed by the slug. Soaked and battered, Flora fought her way higher until a snarl of air caught her up and sucked her tiny body into the roaring mouth of the storm.

CHAPTER
TWENTY-THREE

Flora's body hit something solid. She could move neither wing nor limb of her waterlogged body but tumbled down through the leaves and bounced against hard branches until some spongy lichen slowed her fall. Her claw caught and she hung there in the rain. Gradually she managed to dig more hooks in, and found that none of her limbs were broken. She hauled herself the right way up, and pushed her cuticle bands apart. Water drained out. Very carefully, she crept towards the bole of the tree and pressed herself into a dry crevice.

It was an old tree and true, after the vile pretence of the metal one. She could feel its strength drawing deep into the earth as it stretched its countless arms wide, welcoming the storm passing through. It was a beech; she recognised the leaf pattern from one of the trees at Congregation, and for a wild moment she hoped that when the rain stopped she would see drones of her home livery emerging from their hiding places, and they would all shake themselves out and fly home together.

The rain slowed, then stopped. The tiny bright eyes of cars moved slow across the dark plain of the fields, and far beyond that shone the lights of the town. Flora tried to lift her antennae to read even one scent, but storm-racked and sugar-rushed, they told her she was still in flight. She checked her numb wings. On both sides the latches were smashed and the membranes showed tears in many places.

Flora began to shiver uncontrollably. Not for her the dramatic oblivion in the storm, with the Queen's Prayer coursing through her body so that death would find her in a state of grace, nor even a forager's Kindness, meted out with respect and a strong merciful bite. This death would take time. How bitterly now did Flora crave the sweet dark warmth of home and the comfort of her family around her, like those noble sisters who went to their final rest in their own berths with peace in their hearts. *Praise end your days, Sister.*

Flora wept in shame. She had been reckless and proud in trying to forage in the town without following any bee's dance — then tricked by the wasp who had promised her safety and sugar. It hurt too much to try to open the inner channels of her antennae, but she already knew that Lily 500's knowledge was destroyed. She clutched herself as if to feel a sister's touch, searching her body for any last remnant of the Queen's Love. There was not one molecule left, only the racking physical need for her lost home and family. At the thought of her second child, her little drone son who would now starve to death, Flora howled out her heartbreak, knowing she had done this to herself.

A rabble of crows cawed across the darkening sky. By primal reaction her alarm glands fired and she

195

instinctively scented for any answering flare of support — but there were no sisters and nothing changed but the sun, sinking at that precise moment behind a bank of cloud. *The azimuth!* If she had felt it shift, all was not lost. As the birds grew louder Flora blocked her fear, searching deep inside her body for that magnetic sensor that could show her the way home — but the flickering awareness had vanished.

Acrid waves of air came blowing towards her, then the raucous mob of birds came clattering and shoving down through the leaves. They snapped their blue-black beaks and swore at each other as they grabbed for better perches, they clacked and clambered about the branches, stabbing at crawling insects, and their fire-rimmed eyes roved the branches for more. Flora kept very still.

More crows came down from the air and filled the branches, then with a heavy flapping they all shook themselves dry. A long black feather came spinning down past Flora then jarred against the trunk, its bone-white point stuck in the bark. Behind it stretched a long deep shadow, leading into the trunk itself.

Flora waited until the crows were once again swearing and arguing before daring to move. She drank fresh rain from the bark to wash away the sickly taste of the wasps' sugar, then crawled and slid down the slippery trunk towards the feather. Her war-gland automatically blasted alarm at its flesh-feeding smell, but she forced herself to go closer.

Its point was wedged in an old split in the bark. Behind it was a hole. Flora stood on the edge behind the feather and raised up her throbbing antennae. She could not sense any movement inside, nor smell anything but the living beech. She edged deeper into the cavity and scanned the space: hollow, dry and empty. Near the entrance was a pocket in the bark almost the same size as a rest hole in the hive, but to fit it she would have to close her wing-latches. As she brought the torn panels together she could not help buzzing loudly in pain.

With a rustle of feathers, a jagged black shadow jumped down from a high branch. Flora held herself completely still as the crow clambered down to search for the interesting sound. Its red gaze zig-zagged over the trunk towards her hiding place, and when it could not see her, it pecked hard at the bark to try to flush her out. When she still did not move, it made some low croaks deep in its throat, shook out its feathers, and settled down to watch.

Its smell was strong and bitter, from the old sweat between its feathers, and the red mites that ran across them. Only when the crow lowered its head into its chest did Flora clamp her wing-latches shut, and press herself into the tight gap in the bark. The sense of enclosure was some comfort, and with the crow sleeping a few branches above her, Flora settled herself to watch the darkening sky and wait for death.

The beech leaves surged and shimmered in the wind. Far below a vixen paused to stare up then melted away. Stars burned tiny holes in the twilight and then a pale moon traced a slow silver arc through the sky. Its beauty made Flora's heart burst with love for her lost egg, and only the shadow of the crow above stopped her sobs. To die without holding it again, or breathing its tender scent — and then when he hatched . . .

Her cheeks pulsed and her mouth moistened with royal jelly. She swallowed the sweetness down, for there was no more sin to commit, nor sister to rebuke her. Alone in the dark, cut off from the Queen's Love, Flora swallowed another mouthful of the precious liquid, wasting it on herself and willing death forward.

She gazed out into the darkness, waiting. Somewhere across the scented night was her lost orchard home. She imagined it under a bright blue sky, the sweet bouquet spreading in welcome as she drew near, sun on her wings and her body loaded with nectar and pollen. She imagined her ten thousand sisters dancing for joy, Holy Mother wrapping her in love — and somewhere, hidden deep inside all that she loved, the secret that could be no crime, for its memory filled her with bliss.

In her mind's eye Flora saw her rough white crib under the shadow of those three tall cocoons, and in it, her precious egg, pulsing strong with the golden glow of life. She imagined its fragrance, and something inside her broke.

My child, my sisters, my mother, my home.

Love filled her heart and Flora wept with joy, for she could pray again.

Morning light leaked over the ridge. The leaves turned from cool silver to glowing green and a warm woody fragrance rose through the bark of the trees. Flora woke at the smell. She scanned around her in shock. No sister could survive a night outside the hive — yet here she was, alive and lying in a crevice in the bark. A warm slant of light fell through the hole across her body. She was sore, but her legs were unbroken and her wing-latches had knitted back together. She straightened her antennae and winced at the pain — but data pulsed through again.

. . . the flight, the storm, the wasps . . .

Flora crawled to the edge of the hole into the sunshine. The crows had gone, and this old sheltering beech was one of many, high up on the hills and overlooking the fields and the distant town. Bright specks of insects wove across the air, and on the moist earth below two blackbirds stretched a worm to a wet brown thread.

Flora groomed herself and made a detailed inventory of her injuries. Under the bruising and windburn, her antennae slowly restored their function. There . . . was the place of the murmuring tree . . . and the wasp's warehouse.

And there — Flora shouted for joy — there was the faintest scent of the hive. To reach it, she would pass through that scent of foreign flowers she had tried to find before. The sweet thread came stronger as some petals opened in the still dawn air.

Flora touched her antennae in gratitude to the beech that had sheltered her. She would not go home empty, she would complete her mission and redeem herself. She would find forage for her sisters, she would dance, *and then she would go to her egg.*

★　★　★

The little gardens were already crowded when she arrived. Bees from hives unknown moved purposefully from bloom to bloom, along with ants tending their aphid flocks on the roses and flies that stank of putrefaction. Honeybee sisters, no matter from what hive, united in barging every fly out of their way, whether they wanted a flower or not. For their part, the flies took pleasure in advancing so close to a sister that she was forced to either touch the unclean creature, or leave her flower to its filthy embrace.

Flora watched from above, trying to decide which bloom to visit first. Some were dewy and plump from the rain, thrusting their faces at any who wished to touch them, whilst others dipped shy heads and could only be approached with skill from below. Flora chose a newly opened dog rose with pure sheeny petals and thick golden clusters of pollen. She drank the nectar for the instant energy transfusion then worked her way over the rambling bush until her panniers were packed full. Then she went to investigate other gardens.

Many were neat paved deserts dotted with garish tubs of flowers neither scented nor nourishing, but in one small overgrown plot, a buzzing crowd of insects could not restrain their excitement at the thrilling foreign smell.

Towering spiked echium plants, tall as sapling trees, made an ultraviolet forest of treasure. Silver hairs along their slender green trunks and tapering branches illuminated their silhouettes and the multitudes of insects whirring for joy at the bounteous harvest. Each of the countless purple florets showed a fluorescent line pointing to the nectar, and bees, hoverflies, hornets, flies of every kind, white butterflies, meadow browns, red admirals and fritillaries greeted each other and gorged together. The big furry bottoms of Bombini bees bounced white, yellow and red as they rummaged, and Flora waited for a gap between them before diving into the sweet abundance. She filled her crop and panniers to maximum capacity, and then set off for home.

With each wing-beat her excitement at seeing her sisters grew stronger, until despite her heavy bounty she was racing at full speed. Her antennae found the scent vector to lead her in, but as she neared the orchard she smelled the change.

The bouquet of the hive was drenched in the smell of its own honey and coiling with smoke. Thousands of her sisters swirled above the hive and in the trees, choking in the dazing smoke.

"The Visitation!" some screamed. "The end of the world!"

"Thief!" shrieked others, alarm glands flaring uselessly. "Thief!"

Dagger at the ready and determined to defend her home, Flora tried to keep to her homecoming path, but the rising smoke forced her back up into the orbit of her raging, helpless sisters, foragers and house-bees alike.

The smell of honey rose stronger — and the cause was obscene.

CHAPTER
TWENTY-FOUR

The roof of the hive lay upside down on the grass so that the top storey was totally exposed to the air. The smoke came from a spouted canister, held by an old man in a red dressing-gown and bare feet. He crooned to the bees as he waved it, sending them higher into a smoke-dazed gyre. Slow and stiff, he lifted out an entire wall of the Treasury, dripping golden wealth from its broken vaults, and slid it into a white plastic bag.

Unable to come down through the powerful smoke, sisters glimpsed the atrocity and roared in disbelief. The air was filled with the rich golden fragrance of their stolen wealth, and smoke, and their helpless panic.

"The Visitation!" they cried out to each other. "It is all true — the Visitation!"

At this word Flora reeled back in the air. *The Visitation* — the third panel in the Queen's Library. Now the smells and symbols fitted together in a fearful shape — the ugly gaping hole in the top storey, brutal damage to the beautiful labour of generations of sisters. *The honey and the smoke.*

The old man bent to pick up the angled wooden roof. It was heavy and he staggered as if he would fall — then with painful effort he replaced it over the exposed hive. Then he stooped for his smoker and the white plastic bag, and shuffled barefoot back through the orchard.

The Sage took charge. Many sisters were set to lay home-coming markers on the landing board and scouts were sent to bring in house-bees still whirling in fear at the furthest reaches of the orchard. More Thistle guards were stationed in full public view, to repel any of the Myriad that might be drawn by the uproar and smell of honey. Inside the hive all scent-gates were cancelled to allow sanitation workers access to the desecrated top floor and bring down the dead and wounded, crushed as the Treasury walls reared into the open sky.

Her crop still distended with her full load of nectar, and her panniers with pollen, Flora waited for a receiver. None came, for the smoke had provoked a deep atavistic urge for the bees to gorge on whatever food they could find, and now their crops were full. Returning drones thumped down onto the board and barged past their sisters, appalled at the disorder and eager to be safely inside.

No peace was to be found there either, for somewhere during the trauma of the Visitation the Queen had disappeared, and now every sister ran through the hive searching for her and craving Devotion. The comb echoed with their piteous cries of *Mother! Mother!* and the exhausted Flora dragged herself into her ravaged home to join the search.

She could not smell a single molecule, and by the rising wail in the air, nor could any other sister, for the raw ugly void on the top storey had affected the entire scent balance of the hive. Everything was in disorder, from the coded floor tiles to the air itself that screeched a maelstrom of signals. Then the comb shook.

Find the Queen!

The voice of the Hive Mind stopped each sister's wailing and united in a systematic search to find Holy Mother. Flora moved up to the mid-level, where a strong fragrance of new wax floated on the air. It was so pure and beautiful that, despite their mission, soul-hungry sisters paused together in the lobby to breathe it like Devotion.

It was exactly that, for the veil of scent parted to reveal the doors to the Chapel of Wax, from whence the Queen herself walked out, her ladies behind her. She was clothed in a mantle of pure white waxen lace, so light it flowed like air around her. Her divine fragrance was now blended with the wild air that had blown through the broken and ravaged hive, and when she smiled on her daughters, bright and steady waves of love and reassurance flowed through the air.

All over the hive the bees cheered and cheered, their fear turned to triumph. Here was Holy Mother, and what was wealth without Her? They could make more honey — they *would* make more! The Queen was never more radiant, and all the sisters marvelled at the fresh mantilla of wax lace she wore, and sighed in admiration at the new royal style.

Holy Mother stood in the mid-level lobby for a long time, allowing every sister of the hive to pass through and draw on her scent, a once-in-a-lifetime privilege for the thousands who had never seen her or ever dreamed of such holy proximity. As the massive pilgrimage of sisters continued through the lobby, the chemical atmosphere of the hive stabilised and the vibration of the Holy Chord restored power to the Hive Mind.

Flora stood at the back of the lobby watching the endless procession of sisters pass through, their faces glowing and exalted from contact with the Queen. Feeling the intensity of Flora's attention, the Queen looked across and called with her eyes. Flora ran and knelt, her heart surging.

"We missed our story-telling child; we sent word to bring her back. But she did not come."

The Queen's scent filled Flora's soul.

"Mother, I have sinned — forgive me —" She could not go on.

"I do, beloved. And I always will, because you are my child."

"I do not deserve it —" At the Queen's soft touch, Flora began to weep.

"Enough. Holy Mother must not tire her strength." Ladies-in-waiting ushered Her Majesty away, and the crowd dispersed from the lobby.

Flora rose to her feet again. Her soul longed to be with her egg and see how it had grown — but her panniers and crop were still full, and all around were her starving, traumatised sisters. A forager's first duty was to the hive — and to share her news would not take long.

Normal etiquette of the Dance Hall was suspended following the Visitation, so foragers took the floor wherever there was a space, keeping their choreography rapid and brief. Thistle guards were in attendance to keep the crowd moving.

"Everyone up to the Treasury," they kept calling out, "no tasting down here, everyone up to the Treasury to mend the vaults."

Flora stumbled in her dance. The Treasury, its broken walls streaming gold. And hidden behind them, *her egg*. Knocking sisters aside, she ran.

The movements she could feel were a receiver's hands, unpacking bundles of pollen from her panniers, and the smell was her kin of Poppy. The strange acoustics were the many voices and sounds of building work, taking place in a large high space. Dazed, Flora came to her senses standing in front of a half-full chalice of echium nectar in the Fanning Hall, now a construction site.

She looked around. The broken Treasury walls above still bled honey, while hundreds of bees worked to save it and re-cap the cells. Hundreds more worked in living chains, passing blocks and panels and shards of wax in from the doors and up to more sisters hanging high on the walls, hooked foot to arm to foot so they could reach the roof. They were rebuilding the vaults with whatever wax they could summon — fragments from the Arrivals Hall, piles of fresh white discs commandeered from the Chapel, and even bundles of

206

yellow scraps reclaimed from the freight depot. On the ground, hundreds more sisters sent freshly chewed propolis to seal the gaps.

The young Poppy followed Flora's stunned gaze.

"I know! Two whole walls of wealth completely stolen, and a third one damaged. But, Mother be praised, the other three still intact. And look at the Sage working with us — have you ever seen that? So elegant, even as they crawl!"

Flora stared at the priestesses moving along the high vaults.

"I must dance," she said. "I must go to the Dance Hall —"

"Madam, you *did* dance, do you not remember? And so well that many have already returned with that new nectar, and it smells most delicious." The Poppy looked anxious. "Do you feel better now? Would you like me to stay longer?"

"What do you mean?"

The Poppy looked around, then lowered her voice.

"Madam — your collapse. The foragers said it was the terrors of your flight upon you. When you ran in and saw the destruction, oh how piteously you took it — striking out as if every sister was a foe, wailing for our lost walls. We cannot bring them back, sister, but we can rebuild them."

"The walls. Yes." Flora stared across the raw new space. "I saw it."

Those wet golden walls of wealth disappearing into that white bag. Her egg had drowned in honey. Her egg was gone. She felt the Poppy clutching at her hand, and knew the little thing wept.

"I saw it too, Madam — and how will we forget? How can we? Our home torn apart, so many lost — I can never forget!"

"Hush." Flora gazed across at where her crib had been. The outer wall of the secret chamber remained, built strong and old of a different-coloured wax from the rest of the hive. Numb and cold inside, she comforted the Poppy. "Hush," she said, again and again, to both of them. "Hush."

A wave of masking scent rolled into the Fanning Hall at the arrival of a police squad. Every sister working there looked up in disapproval, for despite the vigorous activity it was still a sacred place. Flora recognised the particularly harsh scent of Sister Inspector and watched her speaking quietly with Sister Sage. Very slowly she averted her antennae, lest her notice rouse their attention. The priestess turned.

"Immediately on completion of repairs," Sister Sage announced, "the Treasury will be re-consecrated." She scanned the workers. "But the theft of our wealth has revealed a greater evil. We are no longer in any doubt: a laying worker hides amongst us. From now on there will be spot checks throughout the hive, day and night. Any sister who resists an officer will be deemed guilty. Is that clear?"

"*Accept, Obey and Serve*," the bees murmured their accord. When the police left, they returned to work, but now in total silence. The Poppy receiver moved on to a new arrival in the hall, and Flora bent her head and pumped the last of her crop of echium nectar into the chalice. Sisters joined her and began to fan their wings to cure it. Gradually the water from the nectar evaporated as silver mist and the Holy Chord began to rise. All over the broken, desecrated Fanning Hall, the working bees joined with it, a hymn of courage for their labours. The sound filled the emptiness in Flora's heart. She would not weep, she would work. As her nectar cured, brave and industrious Flora 717 stood amidst her sisters, her mind's eye gazing deep into the dark sky of her body, searching for a new star.

CHAPTER
TWENTY-FIVE

The hive resumed its normal life. Flora did not. Since the loss of her second egg she kept her antennae sealed, making loneliness her constant inner state. Her sensual pleasure in food vanished, the busy gossipy canteens alienated her and though she still attended Devotion, it was more a way to kill the time between flight and sleep, and had little effect.

The challenge of the forage was the only thing that kept Flora's grief at bay, and efficiency on the wing her only satisfaction. She flew harder and longer missions than any other bee, and felt herself becoming grim and intent as she returned to the landing board. It was as if she observed herself in the body of some strange sister who neither spoke nor smiled, intimidating to the nervous young receivers who unloaded her panniers and took her nectar. Though she felt kindly towards them she did not show it, for to give or receive a loving touch might break her open.

Summer waned. The flowers pulled on their last strength to shine and breathe their sweetness on the air and Flora skimmed the roadside to harvest one final flush of purple-black pollen from the dusty orange poppies even as their tired petals fell. The cornflowers finished, then the lady's mantle, the rosebay willowherb, and the scant cow parsley that was Flora's favourite flower.

Careful of the rank unkempt ponds where frogs and dragonflies lurked, she made the long trip to the town gardens. All the echium had been cut down, and the remaining flowers were time-wasting potted ornamentals. There was still some comfort in the thin wild borders of the fields, where the flowering weeds clung together and raised their scent, then one day the harvesting machines tore the fields edge to edge and the birds screeched above.

She had just that morning danced exact directions and confirmed them safe — but now crows endangered any foraging bee who used them. Far more important than filling her own panniers was the need to protect her sisters, and Flora sped back to give warning. Running into the Dance Hall, she stopped short at the sight of the fertility police moving through the foragers, forcing them into their long-discarded kin-groups.

"Keep dancing," one of the police rasped to a Calluna who stumbled in her steps. "Continue as normal."

"Sister Officer," Flora called out. "I must dance at once, for the crows are now on the field and my sisters must not go."

The officer looked up at her, then beckoned. Flora walked to the centre, where the Calluna very gratefully gave up her place.

The officer stood too close while Flora danced her news, including her new signature choreography, details of the air currents she had used. These subtle steps

211

helped any who followed to save on fuel, but the presence of the police inhibited the audience and few danced behind her. As Flora continued she saw the young and tender sisters standing at the edge. They had come to watch and learn, but the fertility police bore down on them with questions and they stood dazed and stupid with fear.

"This is a place of freedom!" Flora called out as she danced, not caring that all eyes fixed on her. She repeated her steps to warn of the birds in the field, then looked directly at the officers. "How can anyone dance freely or give of her best, if the air smells of terror? Respect this place or leave!"

"You dare direct the police?" An officer grabbed at Flora, but her reflexes were faster and she whirled her abdomen round to buzz the location of the last flowers she had found, a stand of dog roses climbing up a metal fence, south-facing and still in bloom. Emboldened, other foragers fell in behind her and picked up the steps. Ignoring the rising scent of the fertility police and remembering her own youthful joy in Lily 500's dance, Flora took her steps nearer to the young and frightened bees by the walls.

She danced the falling poppies and the naked fields, she ran figure eights to teach them direction and azimuth, and as she turned she felt the answering rhythm in the comb floor as more bees joined in and danced behind her.

She danced the ivy that crawled along the town fences, and its buds that would soon bloom, she danced the empty dahlias, and the last dragonflies hiding in the ponds. And then she danced of her hunger for weeds.

"*Enough!*" Sister Sage stepped forward and Flora stopped. "Are you falling prey to the madness of the field? Or is it pride?" The priestess signalled an officer. "Measure her."

A ripple of dismay ran through the crowd.

"Yes!" Sister Sage said to them all. "Even foragers may be measured, for no sister is exempt from the Holy Law. Eggs blight in the Nursery — which means she who curses this hive still runs free, and seeks to pass her evil spawn as the pure issue of Holy Mother." A frightening tone entered her voice. "What is our highest law?"

"*Only the Queen may breed.*"

"Again!" Sister Sage's voice seemed to come from all around the Dance Hall and the bees repeated the phrase over and over, staring at the humiliation of the famous forager.

Flora stood completely still while two officers ran their callipers over her. They were rough and pried at her intimately; they went over her antennae again and again with their burning scanners until the smell of her heating cuticle rose into the chamber and the bees wept at her pain, but Flora was strong from her forage and withstood it all.

"She smells, Sister," said one of the police, her jaws ready to bite.

"And her belly is swollen," said another, her hooks gleaming.

"That scent is my kin. I am a flora and a forager, and I stretch this belly with nectar from a thousand flowers

213

a day if I can find them, to bring home to our hive. *Accept, Obey and Serve.*"

"*Accept, Obey and Serve,*" shouted the bees, as if a Sage priestess had said it.

"Silence!" The inspecting officer cuffed Flora's head. For a moment her anger caused her antennae lock to shift.

"She hides something!" cried the officer. "She locks her antennae from us!"

"Open them." Sister Sage walked close to Flora. "*Open them.*"

Flora resisted until Sister Sage was using all her psychic force to break her mind apart — and then she released her seals.

High roaring air currents — the murmuring tree — the wasps in the warehouse, gathering for attack —

"How dare you!" Sister Sage stepped back and Flora resealed her antennae and stood quietly. For the first time in many days, she became aware of the weak and distant pulse of Devotion in the comb. Then she saw the numbers of sanitation workers clustered around the edge of the room. Some of them twisted their faces in grimacing smiles at her and she knew that, despite the unspoken rule against their presence here, they had all come to watch her dance.

Sister Sage turned to the foragers.

"Ego is the great peril of your occupation. You begin to believe what the flowers tell you, instead of the Holy Law. Only Queen and Colony matter." She turned back to Flora. "For the rest of the day you will return to Sanitation and all will command your labour.

214

Tomorrow you will go out at dawn, and if by the noon azimuth you have not returned with a whole cropful of nectar, you are exiled."

The foragers crowded forward, not waiting for permission to speak.

"None of us could do that — it is not to be found — the flowers come to their end — any of us would die trying!"

Sister Sage stared at them, her antennae crackling. "In the Air, you may think for yourselves. Here, the Hive Mind takes that care from you. Do not reject it."

Flora stepped forward.

"I accept the task." She looked across at the sanitation workers. "I will try my best, for the honour of my kin."

"Then you will fail, for the honour of your kin is found in dirt and in service. To teach otherwise is to wound them with confusion." The scent of Devotion rose stronger through the comb, and the priestess raised her antennae.

"*Our Mother, who art in labour, Hallowed be Thy Womb.*"

All the bees took it up, releasing their tension into the formal beauty of the Queen's Prayer until the Dance Hall echoed with their voices. Flora spoke it too, her heart stirred back to life by the confrontation. The air grew warm and soft around her as many sister bees came to stand wing to wing with her, protecting her and sharing their strength. They hummed the words of the Queen's Prayer but they did not speak, for they were floras.

CHAPTER
TWENTY-SIX

The next dawn was cold and bright. High and sweet the birds sang their territories in the soft green light of the orchard — but standing on the board Flora felt a change. She unlatched her wings but did not start her engine. All was calm and still, except for the dazzling skein of light floating between the trees. It drifted until it caught on a twig. The next moment it shuddered taut as a spider sailed down it, another line unspooling behind her. Deftly she fastened it to the same twig, then ran back up the double line on her eight scrambling legs.

"I heard the Sage speaking of it yesterday." It was another forager, Madam Dogwood. "When the spiders come, winter soon follows."

Flora looked out at the gossamer webs shining in the trees, exquisite traps set across the flight corridor.

"So they knew."

More foragers emerged onto the landing board but when they saw Flora, they stopped. Knowing her impossible task, they made room to give her first departure. The Thistle guards saluted her.

"Queenspeed, Sister," some said.

"Mother be with you," said others.

The sun was shifting. Flora bowed to her hive, set her engine to hard ascent and leapt the board.

After the harvests, the fields were brown deserts menaced with birds, and the narrow green sanctuaries at their edges all gone, now piled with broken stalks and clods of earth. The roadside flowers hung their dusty heads, empty and exhausted of anything a bee might want. Flora went to check the dog roses she had danced, and found their scent faded and their simple beauty wrinkled and spent. When she did not alight, their petals fell in sorrow.

In the town there was very little to be had; the gardens were nearly empty of friendly flowers, though many provocatively dressed foreign ones stood bold and bright, flaunting their sterile sexes. The foxgloves and the snap-dragons, whose particular tricks of access Flora had delighted in perfecting, were long gone, the echium had fallen, but there were still some fuchsia, whose hanging bells required skill to plunder. Flora took all she could find, but it was paltry. She was about to leave the gardens and their reeking black waste bins buzzing with flies, when she smelled a thistle in bloom.

Even for the most orthodox bees of Flora's hive, this plant transcended its weed status by the strength of its nectar and the skill of the forage. She located it behind the stench of the bins and went closer. The thistle was so strong it had forced its way through the tarmac, then the dark space between the bins, straining its sharp purple crown up to the light. At Flora's approach it pushed its scent harder, and at the touch of her feet its prickly petals shivered in gratitude.

She drank it dry then searched the town for more of its kind, or dandelions, scrubby red dock bloom, or anything at all that might give nectar, for her crop was not even half full. The smell of sugar rose from litter blowing on the ground, but it reminded Flora of the wasps, and she went on. The azimuth of the sun shifted closer to noon. Her crop was only half full, but to keep searching would be to use what she had gathered as fuel. There was nothing more to find, and nowhere to go but home.

The midday light all but blanked out the webs and Flora almost forgot them until she heard the warning yells of the foragers on the board. She veered steeply up above the apple trees and made a vertical descent to the landing board, feeling her fuel level drop at the expensive manoeuvre. By the tense faces of the other foragers, they too had been forced to do the same. Guards approached Flora.

"My sisters Thistle. I have only a half-crop of nectar, but call a receiver and I will go out again and keep searching —"

"Forgive us, Madam Forager, we have our orders. It must be a full crop, and before the noon azimuth, or we must deny you entry. The Sage will it."

Flora breathed in the deep warm smell of the hive.

"But I have good nectar, even from your own kin-flower: smell! The kitchen will surely want it —"

The guards' faces showed the pain of their order, even as they blocked Flora's way.

"Forgive us, Sister."

"But this is my home, you are my family — where else can I go? Give me the Kindness, for I cannot leave here while I can still serve —"

"Without a full crop, the Sage forbid you entry."

"She has it." The forager Madam Dogwood's voice was hoarse and her sides heaved from her hard flight. She went up to Flora. "Show them," she said to her. "They will see."

As soon as Flora opened her mouth to answer, Madam Dogwood bent hers to it, triggered her own crop and transferred every drop of nectar she could. Before Flora could respond, other foragers quickly did the same, sharing their own loads until her crop was full. The sun shifted.

"There," said Madam Dogwood to the Thistle guards. "The azimuth only now rises noon, and she brings a full crop to the board. You will admit her."

"Admit her!" shouted the foragers.

"Gladly." The guards bowed.

Flora knelt low in gratitude to her forager sisters.

"*Praise end your days, sisters.*"

"Such sentiment!" The voice was oily and malignant and it came from a spider, hanging soft and wicked in the nearest web, listening to all that passed.

"Do not waste your old and useless, trade them here!"

The Thistle straightened their abdomens in threat. "Do not insult us, foul things. Every sister is useful."

"Not she who first gave her nectar. She . . . is old."

The spider trained her four hard little eyes on Madam Dogwood, who flared her venom gland in defiance. Flora stood by her comrade's side, anger rising.

"Yes, that one is weak," the spider said to others. "Soon they will fight amongst themselves."

As the webs shimmered again, the bees saw that some held long white lumps.

"Never!" The Thistle guards held up their arms to the spiders. "You lie!"

"Oh, come come," said the spider, "you know we must tell the truth — that is why your Sage trade with us."

Flora's anger lifted her off her feet and her chest roared.

"They would not! You are the Myriad and you are evil!"

"The Sage do not mind." The spider smirked. "They pay for knowledge."

Flora forced herself back down to the board.

"Is it true?" she asked the guards. "Do the Sage trade with them?"

The Thistle guards looked down and did not answer.

"How? Spiders do not eat honey or pollen —" Then Flora turned again to the white shapes hanging in the webs. They were shrouds, wrapped tight around the bodies of sisters.

"That's right!" called out the spider. "Spend your old, your weak, your clumsy and your stupid: buy knowledge of winter to keep your hive alive!" It pointed a claw at Madam Dogwood. "That one's time is nearly up, I can smell it. Send her!"

"How would it happen?" Madam Dogwood stared out.

"No!" Flora held her back.

The spider inhaled deeply and her soft moist body pulsed with excitement.

"A quick bite." Her whisper crawled through air and Madam Dogwood took a step forward. "A moment of pain —"

"Silence, foul thing." One of the Thistle buzzed a blast of her war-gland towards the web. "Attend your own affairs and gorge on flies."

"My name is Arachnae. And you bees . . . are my business."

A second spider stepped across her own web with rippling feet.

"It is just a plea for simple economics, which you of all people must admire. You are many, with much treasure. All we have are answers, to questions you dare not ask . . . But when someone has a question . . . we want to help."

"Turn around! Do not look at them!"

Every bee on the landing board wanted to heed the Thistle's words and turn her wings on the spiders, but their webs were of hypnotic craft and beauty.

"Look closer, sisters," whispered the spider. "Read your poor hive's destiny . . ."

"We are not your sisters!" Flora forced herself to look away. "And our hive is strong — we need no tricks from you!"

"Knowledge is power," said the spider, plucking a silvery chord from her web. Every other spider did the same until the orchard chimed in dissonance.

"The length of the season, the number of suns before the honeyflow comes again, who will be the next to die . . ." The spider dropped on her thread so that she hung in the air. "With winter coming, your hive could budget to the last sip of honey, the last grain of pollen. With knowledge, you could save yourselves . . . One bee, one answer. One bee . . . one answer." She began to revolve, her white belly shining and disappearing, shining and disappearing.

"One bee . . . one answer . . ." Other spiders dropped down from their webs, slowly twirling pendants beneath the leaves. Brown and white. Brown and white.

"Look away!" Flora pushed back the foragers who had walked to the edge of the board. Then she saw Madam Dogwood at the far end, unlatching her wings.

"*Praise end your days,*" she cried to Flora. Before anyone could stop her, she leapt from the board and flew towards the trees. A silver web bounced as she hit it and her whirring wings slowed and stuck. The bees cried out in horror as the spider ran to greet their sister, her fangs bared.

"Here." The spider climbed on Madam Dogwood's back. "Something to calm you." She bit the forager between her head and thorax and held her until she stopped moving. Then she rolled her in sticky netting, quelling the last of her cries with a clot of silk in her mouth. She ran back to the centre of her web.

"So. Now I owe you an answer." Malice twinkled in the spider's four eyes. "What about . . . how to defend your hive? *Oh, the Visitation, help us, Holy Mother, all our honey is being stolen!*" Her laugh made liquid move in her body so that her loose brown skin bulged. "Tame things forget how to fight. Arachnae can remind you." The spider smiled. "And what of starvation?" She ran back to Madam Dogwood and crouched over her. "Your Treasury is not as full as it could be, is it? Who knows if it can last the winter?" She bared her fangs above Madam Dogwood. "Blood and nectar — my favourite."

With a thoracic roar of rage, Flora aimed herself for the centre of the web and stopped just short in the air, whirring to try to drive the spider away.

"Tell us then. How can we survive the winter?"

"Just a moment." The spider's face took on a look of absent concentration, then she reached behind herself and pulled forward a fresh skein of silk. She showed it to Flora then licked it. "My new ropes taste of nectar and pollen. Now, come a little closer, my dear, I haven't seen one like you before. Not pretty, so you must be nutritious. That's always a good rule." The spider winked two of her four eyes at Flora. "You have a secret as well as a question, I can smell it. We'll chat after I've had a bite to eat. Drink, I should say. Before she dries out."

"Answer me!" Flora drew her sting, but the spider just smiled.

"But which question? The one about your hive? Or that secret desire deep inside you?" The spider sank her fangs into Madam Dogwood's abdomen and sucked noisily, then looked up. "Surely it is a relief I know . . ."

As the spider drank again, Flora felt her wings tiring, and heard the distant cries of her sisters on the landing board, calling her back. The spider paused in her drinking.

"I will whisper, so they do not hear: *You will have one more egg.*"

Flora reeled in the air.

"I did not ask that!"

"Call it a gift." The spider looked at Flora slyly. "But why not stay with me now, and sacrifice yourself for your hive? I will credit your sisters three lives, because I really think you will taste quite special." She indicated Madam Dogwood's body. "It would not be like this; we could talk for a long time. Think about it."

Flora hung in the air as she had seen the wasps do. "I asked about my hive. You gave me an answer I did not want."

"You did want it!" hissed the spider. "You long to sin again!"

"You have your payment, Arachnae, and you owe my hive. Now answer my question: how may we survive winter?"

"You try to trick a spider?" She spat Madam Dogwood's blood at Flora. "*Winter comes twice.* That is all I will tell you, and may your hive suffer!"

Though it was a short distance, the malice of the spiders reached up for Flora as she passed above their webs, blurring her sight and willing her down towards

224

their clutches. She collapsed on the landing board, and foragers touched her gently in support.

"What did Arachnae say?" Sister Sage stood on the board, the sun in her wings. "Your private parley was so long, we thought that you would stay."

"I will tell you, Sister, but let me first deliver my crop. I have fulfilled the task you set." Flora beckoned to a young Daisy receiver and gave her the golden load.

Sister Sage observed without praise. She looked out into the orchard.

"Kindly repeat the spider's words."

Flora sealed her antennae before she answered. "Winter comes twice."

"Strange." Sister Sage's antennae gave rapid pulses. "Anything else?"

"They wish our hive to suffer."

"Do they indeed? The loathsome traders."

Sister Sage drew herself up to her full majestic height, extended her antennae and pointed them into the orchard. In the trees the webs flashed taut in response and, though there was no wind, the leaves shivered. The priestess turned back to Flora.

"I hear Madam Dogwood gave her life for yours. Endeavour to deserve it."

"I will, Sister."

Flora ran inside, her heart tight with guilt and joy.

CHAPTER
TWENTY-SEVEN

The summer was ending, but no egg came. Day by day Flora scanned her body for a signal of another egg, but nothing changed except the shortening days, and the growing hunger of the bees. Rather than return home empty, many dispirited foragers chose to give their tired bodies to the spiders in the hope the hive would profit. Then a priestess would fly out to the shroud and speak with the spider.

The first time she witnessed this strange conversation, Flora watched in dread from the landing board. When the priestess looked back at the hive and nodded, Flora's antennae searched for the approach of the police, convinced the spider had revealed her secret. But the priestess landed on the board with a sombre face, and hurried into the hive. The Thistle guards and all the bees on the board looked at each other at this discomposure — but none dared speak of it.

The orchard shrouds became a terrible, and then a normal, fact of life. The diminishing band of foragers grew used to avoiding the webs but each night many died of exhaustion, and each day fewer returned than set out on their missions, for the smallest miscalculation of route could be fatal if their fuel was low.

Flora kept going, managing to gather what little there was. She discovered golden ragwort growing on the mounds of rubble behind the industrial estate, and though the bread it made was coarse and tough, it provided a day's food for the hive. Wasps also frequented this area, leaving smeary scent-trails in the air. Refusing to let fear prevent her forage, Flora took to revving her engine drone-deep and battle-loud as she approached, daring any creature to stop her. The wasps watched her from a distance.

"Proud cousin Apis," one called out, and her voice was as drunken and slurred as her wing-beats, "we owe your hive a visit. After winter, when we have slept . . ." She reeled away in the air without finishing her words, her sisters with her.

In the Dance Hall Flora relayed what the wasp had said. Her sisters buzzed uneasily, for everyone knew that wasps were full of threats, but none had ever heard of them sleeping. The casual quality of "After winter" was also disturbing, as if the wasps had no anxiety at all about their survival — whereas the dwindling rations in the canteens made all the orchard bees food-obsessed, and secretly convinced there was not enough to go round.

All the bees in the Dance Hall began talking and speculating, their voices growing louder and louder — and then every sister halted, her mind transfixed by a strange new signal in the comb.

It was a vibration, almost imperceptible, yet it carried a pheromone more powerful than the strongest Thistle's war-gland. It was definitely not Devotion, but it demanded their complete attention. As the sisters set their feet to read it more clearly, disturbing waves of energy pulsed into their bodies. The sensation was the opposite of the blissful reassurance of the Queen's Love; they felt apprehensive and pent-up, as if they were about to defend their hive — and yet there was no call to arms. Antennae poised and ready, the bees waited.

Sisters! The voice of the Hive Mind was low and intimate. *To celebrate the new Age of Austerity, we shall perform the Obeisance to the Males. Go each of you and find them all. Allow no delays, but bring them to the Dance Hall.*

The sisters ran to obey. Many of the drones were in their hall across the lobby, but it was with much grumbling and resistance that they were roused to go the short distance, for the smaller rations had provoked their gluttony, and staff shortages their laziness. Gradually they were cajoled out with pleading and flattery, and Flora felt a jab of irritation at their musty smell. Many of them had stale food in their fur and one, Sir Poplar, refused to go another step without being groomed. The comb pulsed harder underfoot.

By any means. Bring every drone to the Dance Hall.

"Bloody Queen needs to know," Sir Poplar muttered as they coaxed him into the Dance Hall. "Always Her fault, when it comes down to it." The sisters looked at him in shock.

"Welcome to Your Malenesses," spoke the beautiful wall of Sage priestesses, their wings unlatched and shimmering to heighten their kin-scent.

"Bah!" said Sir Poplar loudly. He looked around the crowded chamber and wiggled himself closer to Flora. "So this is where you old girls rattle and shake, is it?" She drew away from him, disturbed by the new vibration in the comb and the alien smell of so many drones in the feminine preserve of the Dance Hall.

"We have performed our Treasury Audit." Sister Sage came forward. "Before we make the Obeisance to the Males, we shall read out the roll of honour. Sir Quercus: Gone to glory!"

All the sisters applauded fervently, the drones less so.

"Sir Whitebeam: Gone to glory."

The sisters applauded again, but slower.

"Sir Alder —"

"Here," his voice came, from deep in the crowd of sisters.

"Sir Chequer —"

"Here."

As Sister Sage went on, the roll-call of answering drones sounded increasingly sulky.

"Sir Poplar —"

He yawned loudly.

"What? Oh . . . Here . . ."

"Sir Linden —" Sister Sage waited. "Missing in passion. Honour to him."

"Honour to him," responded the sisters.

"Clever little git, good riddance." Sir Poplar pressed closer to Flora. "Very touching though, how you sisters get these crushes. Even when you know nothing can ever happen." He fumbled intimately with her wing-joint. "The way you followed him all the way to

Congreg —" He gasped in pain as Flora squeezed her wing-latch shut and trapped his hand. "Holy Mother, where's your sense of humour?"

"Attention!" Sister Sage commanded the chamber. The new vibration came more strongly through the comb and Flora let Sir Poplar retrieve his hand. He glared.

"All our brother drones are now accounted. Every sister kneel, then rise for the Obeisance to the Males."

"Yes" — Sir Poplar shoved Flora down — "back in your place."

As the sisters all knelt to the drones, the vibration surged deep into their bodies.

"Now lay your antennae at their feet," continued the choral voice of the Sage. As every sister obeyed, the vibration went straight into their brains.

"Hah!" Sir Poplar's voice was small and distant and the sound made Flora want to sting him.

"All rise." The Sage priestesses came forward to stand in a line of beauty and power. They touched their wings together.

"Beloved daughters of One Mother," Sister Sage addressed them, "Sisters of the hive, the turning season draws our prayer —"

"I've had it with that canting old hag." Sir Poplar tried to get past Flora.

She broadened her thorax to block him. Anger curled inside her and she felt the urge to hit him.

"You will stay."

"Surely you are mad." He shook his head. "You need the Kindness —"

230

"We will now observe the ancient ritual," continued Sister Sage, "given by Our Mother in the Time before Time. In the Great Obeisance to the Males, every sister shall play her part in the dance, and her body will know the steps. Accept, Obey and Serve."

"*Accept, Obey and Serve,*" the sisters repeated, their voices low and strange.

"Enough of this drivel, out of my way." Sir Poplar tried to shove past Flora, but his path was blocked by a close ring of sisters. "Are you all mad? Move!"

The vibration amplified into a low hum, coming from every sister. As Sir Poplar looked at their faces, his own changed. "Obey at once, before I report you all."

"Report us . . ." More than one of the sisters said it, and some of them crooned it, dancing seductively in front of him. "Report us . . . Your Maleness . . ."

"Stop that!" Sir Poplar's voice was high and strained, and all around the Dance Hall other drones were similarly protesting.

The sisters' hum grew louder.

"*We praise Your Malenesses . . .*" As Sister Sage began the oblation, each of the circles of sisters started moving around their drone in formal steps, pushing him back to the centre when he tried to break free.

We give thanks for Your power and grace
And Your glory on the wing —

The dancing sisters changed direction, singing louder over the complaints of the drones.

We have lived to serve You,
Your time has come, Your time has come.

Led by the choir of the Sage priestesses, the sister bees sang it in overlapping rounds, their dancing circles changing direction then flowing in criss-crossing lines moving through the Dance Hall, imprisoning the bewildered drones between them.

We give thanks for your bodies and your lives, sang the Sage choir, and the sisters danced faster, their words over-lapping over the protests of the drones.

Your lusts and sloth,

And your idleness we now repay.

Louder and louder they sang to each drone as they passed him, and in flagrant contradiction of all etiquette, each sister defiantly let her kin-scent rise in his face.

We now repay —

The drones scrabbled round, trying to break through the singing, chanting chains of sisters, panicking at the new smell rising up through the comb. As the driving rhythm of the dance carried their bodies forward, all the sisters inhaled the thrilling scent of their own long-held anger, now released into their brains.

Our labour, our hive.

The sisters danced around the drones, faster and faster in a swirling pattern. Some hummed with a high strange note, others let out little yelps of excitement.

Forgive us, Your Malenesses, Sister Sage's voice led them.

Before we cast you out!

Many drones shouted it back at them, fear in their voices.

"Cast us out?"

232

"What are you talking about?"

"How dare you speak to Our Maleness in that way!"

"Right, you filthy servant, move." Sir Poplar shoved Flora hard. She did not flinch. He stared at her in astonishment. "Did you hear me?"

"Yes." With one blow she struck him off his feet. He looked up at her, stunned.

"She hit me!" he yelled as he struggled to rise. "Someone tell Holy Mother —"

"Why don't you?" A meek little Cornflower kicked his feet out again. "Tell Her how you blame Her for everything! Isn't that what you said?" At this, all the sisters began kicking and biting at the drones.

"You should have found your princess, shouldn't you?"

"Then you would not be here —"

"All your bragging of sex and love —"

"There, I have it, brothers!" yelled Sir Hornbeam. "They are mad with jealousy! We must flood them with our scent to make them docile!" He pumped his glands so that his male pheromone poured into the air. Others did the same and some tried to start their engines to fan it harder.

Sisters made strange cries as they breathed it in and sank their heads low, swinging them from side to side to breathe it more deeply. Others shrieked as they smelled it.

"Yes!" cried Sir Sycamore. "They need our dronewood, they crave it for themselves —" He grabbed a sister from Woodbine and held her close as if to mount her. "Shall I make you a princess, sister?"

She screamed in rage as she twisted from his grip. "He mocks our virgin state!" She sliced at his face with her claws and he leapt back as she lunged at him — and then a command in the comb held every sister still.

Like every other sister in the packed Dance Hall, Flora paused and felt the tremors running up and down her antennae. She loved the feeling of venom swelling her sac, and her sting flexed strong and supple within her, longing to slide forth. Every sister in the hall slowly raised her claws, waiting for the signal in the comb.

The drones sought each other's eyes and nodded in common purpose. They widened their thoraxes and raised their fur. Sir Poplar gave the signal.

"Now!"

As the drones ran roaring at the sisters to barge past and escape, the comb fired its own chemical trigger. Shrieking and whirling, the sisters joined themselves together in chains of dancers three strong and corralled all the males into a circle. Some threw back their heads and splayed their antennae, while others dipped theirs and swung them from side to side with guttural sounds.

Isolated in their spinning rings of sisters, still shouting in protest, the drones could not hide the scent of their fear. The smell made Flora's abdomen contract hard with pleasure, and at the thrill of her sisters' flaring war-glands she screamed with excitement.

Blessings on our brothers, called out the choir of Sage as the bees danced.

Blessings on their flesh —

"Sisters!" shouted a drone into the dense swirling motion of the dance. "We beg you, cease your madness!"

Blessings on His Maleness! cried the Sage priestess. *At the moment of his death —*

She fell upon him with her jaws and before he could scream his kin-scent burst bright and fatal on the heated air. The Dance Hall erupted into a frenzy of motion as the drones fought to escape and the sisters dragged them back.

Sir Poplar roared and started his engine as his body was lifted up in the air by teeming sisters, but they broke his wings from his back and threw him down.

"You insult Holy Mother —"

"Squander our food —"

"Pretend you would mate us as if we were queens — how dare you!"

It was the sister from Woodbine whom he had so insulted. She stood where he could see her face. "*Only the Queen may breed!*" She ripped his abdomen open down to his genitals, then tore out his penis and ate it. Sisters screamed in excitement as his blood splashed on their faces.

"*Only the Queen may breed!*" Flora screamed it again and again with all her strength, as if to purge herself of her guilt and shame, and as the drones screamed and tried to fly above the crazed females, she too leapt to catch them and drag them back down into the savage mass.

Drones screamed as they were ripped apart or bitten to death, and sisters' feet slid on the blooded pulsing comb. Filled with consecrated anger at every insult and humiliation, wasted forage and sullied passageway, they avenged themselves on the wastrel favourites, the sacred sons that did nothing for their keep but brag and eat and show their sex to those who must only labour for them, and never be loved.

Flora and her sisters dragged one drone after another out into the corridor, and all throughout the hive was screaming and pleading and the high thick smell of blood as every single sister took active part and every drone fled for his life towards the landing board. Males who fell were dragged struggling out into the dazing sun, and there they were dispatched, down into the grass where the Myriad crawled to eat them alive, or tossed out upon the air they once ruled, flying towards death on torn and bloody wings.

CHAPTER
TWENTY-EIGHT

The pulsing in the comb subsided and the throbbing air fell still. Throughout the hive every sister paused in her action as her senses returned to normal.

Crouched in the receiving area connecting the Dance Hall and the landing board, Flora heard the loud rasp of her own breath. Something large, warm and motionless was beneath her, gripped between her legs. The drone's head was pressed into the wax and her abdomen was curved hard and tight against him, her sting buried deep in his bands. He did not move as she pulled her dagger out. She backed away in horror. It was not possible — yet blood soaked her fur black.

All around her the comb showed dark wet swathes where bloody bodies had been dragged to the landing board. Other sisters rose to their feet, surrounded by shattered, torn and decapitated drones. They stood panting and ashamed, not daring to meet each others' eyes.

A dense unnatural silence emanated from the Dance Hall, reaching out to touch the bees and compel them to return.

A sickening spectacle hit them. Amber and brown slicks of blood, yellow intestine spilling half-digested pollen and honey, segments of antennae, shattered eye-lenses, clawed and bitten plates of armour, and gore-clogged plumes littered the comb. The highest concentrations were in the favoured places where foragers danced, and every sister wailed in shame.

Bloodstained sisters from other parts of the hive came staggering in, called by the same signal. Some were having convulsions, and one knocked into Flora and held on to her. She was a receiver, and the sight of her open gasping mouth triggered a reflex in Flora's body. Suddenly her crop felt distended and heavy as if she had just returned from a long forage — but it was not nectar that was rising. Flora choked in horror as blood gushed from her mouth and splashed across the comb.

Other foragers yelped and screamed as they too voided the terrible contents of their crops, and some almost tore their pollen baskets apart trying to empty them of any foul matter. The Dance Hall echoed to the wails and sobs of their shame, but many more sisters were locked mute with terror and could only stare.

The fragrance of Devotion mingled with the smell of the drones' blood. As it grew stronger, those who were sobbing ceased, and those who were stricken felt released. A physical surge swept through the chaos of the Dance Hall bringing every sister to her feet, then a great cry of joy rang out for the Queen stood in their midst.

"Rest, my weary daughters," she said, and her voice was soft as petals. "Lie down and let me heal you with your Mother's Love."

238

The Queen let her mantle open so that the scent of Devotion flowed stronger, and the bees sank to their knees in gratitude. A soft vibration rose up through the comb, a smooth rhythmic wave travelling back and forth across the Dance Hall, lifting and rocking them as if Holy Mother carried them all in her arms. She walked among them with her wings spread wide, and each sister felt the blanket of forgiveness settle upon her as she breathed in her Mother's Love. As each sister began to weep, the bitter essence of vengeance drained from her body in her tears.

Flora lay on the smooth worn comb where so many times she had danced. The blood-scent of the drones rose up into the Queen's Love and strengthened its fragrance. She could see the endless gold and brown carpet of her sisters lying wing to wing, and the pale shimmer of movement as the soothing frequency rolled through the comb beneath them. She wanted to sit up and look upon the beauty of the Queen, but as the wave travelled towards her and she inhaled the divine fragrance, she entered its rhythm and joined the shared trance.

The Queen spread her wings and every bee sighed in bliss.

"Give me your shame and your sins, my daughters," she said, "and I will wash them away with my love. Give me all your grief, your guilt, your secrets and I will tell you a story to lift your wings and fill your heart with joy." The atrium filled with a soft low hum, and the Hive Mind joined every sister with the Queen. Held in sound and scent, the bees lay perfectly still as their minds travelled.

In the Time before Time in this very hive, a young princess paced in her chambers. She had slain all her rivals and cleaned her crown of blood, but her triumph felt empty and her soul hungered for adventure. But each time she tried to leave her chambers her ladies blocked her with curtsies and sweet words until the princess grew to hate her rich robes, her food lost its savour and she was vexed beyond imagining.

One day her strength rose. When her ladies came with nectar and ointments the princess burst past them and ran through the hive towards the wild air she yearned for. Down and down the hive she fled — but instead of trying to stop her, her ladies ran behind cheering in excitement, for the day had come.

The princess reached the landing board and stopped in shock, for no one had warned her of the sky and the sun. She wanted to run back in to safety and return another day, but now her ladies blocked her way, forcing her on towards the edge.

At this behaviour the princess grew so angry she spread her wings, and a humming roar filled her chest. In an instant she was high in the air, her home far beneath her and her body made of light and air. Her ladies sped behind her on their own, cheering and singing in praise.

The princess did not know where she went but a strange new scent called her on. She was fearless and a joyous power filled her body. Her ladies could not keep up and she heard their cries as birds dived at them but she did not stop. The huge tossing green heads of the trees were close ahead and at that place the smell was strong and rich and thick.

And then the princess saw them, the host of handsome gallants that thronged the air, calling her praise and showing their strength and valour. Some begged for her choice and those she ignored, but others came rushing to claim her. She tested their speed against her own, whirling above them in pride and freedom until the fleetest sprang upon her from above, where she had not seen him. At his clasp, the princess knew this was the sport she had hungered for.

Together they rode the wind until she felt his essence in her body. Keeping his dronewood tight within her, she cried out and released him, and the gallant's body tumbled down towards the earth. But her sport was not over. Again and again she chose a noble drone to capture her, on the wing, and again and again she sent his body spinning down to earth, empty of dronesong and missing that part she kept.

At last her body was filled by the finest males in the air, and her hunger sated. Then she turned her wings for home, and never had her palace smelled so sweet. Her ladies licked every trace of dronesong from her body and fought to share the last male organ lodged within her, a testament of each drone's love. And all the bees in the hive rejoiced in triumph, for with her marriage flight their princess was crowned Queen, and mother of generations to come.

In her trance, Flora felt the presence of the Queen close beside her, and she wanted to reach out and touch her, but her body was not hers to move. The Queen spread her wings again, and the beautiful scent renewed itself across her sleeping daughters.

"And as you slew my sons your brothers, in sacrifice to winter, so did I slay your several fathers, in sacrifice to spring. Each one's life I took for love, and each year

241

I tell this tale. When you wake you will forget, every word of it. By my love, you shall be cleansed of sin and whole again."

Flora sighed as the Queen touched her with a wing-tip, then walked amongst all her daughters, covering them with the mantle of her scent.

"Wake, beloved daughters," she said. "Attend your sister and wash her, every one of you healed and reborn in your Mother's Love."

The sisters roused themselves and obeyed. The air was pure and sweet again and Flora washed every sister near her, combing and grooming clotted fur until it was smooth as thistle-silk. Not since she had been taken into the Queen's private chambers by the ladies-in-waiting had she felt any kind and gentle hands on her, and her heart filled with love and gratitude to all her sisters. Only when she felt the delightful feathering touch of her antennae being groomed did she understand the wonderful feeling. They were wide open, and she could not close them.

"Thank you, sister." Flora pulled away. She scanned about her — every bee's antennae were the same — wide open to absorb every molecule of the Queen's Love, and enraptured by the story trance. The relief was exquisite, and with it came the beauty of the hive, rushing upon her after so long held at bay by her narrowed senses. Now she saw it all again — the curved vaulted ceiling of the Dance Hall with its frescoes of flowers and leaves carved into the ancient wax panels, and her sisters — her beautiful beloved sisters, with their warm clean smell.

Flora tried again to close her antennae. All it would take was for one bee, as Sister Teasel had done, to grasp them, and her secrets would pour out. She did not know when the spider's prophecy would come true, but her egg might be forming at this exact moment and any bee might scent it. *One more egg* —

At this thought, Flora's antennae opened to their full extent. To her joy and terror, the radiant scent-memory of her last egg began to form in her mind, then in her body. She began to smell it and feel it as if she cradled it in her arms, and its fragrance seemed to drift around her, mingling with the Queen's Love.

Possessed by the ghosting memory, Flora could not move one step, though all around her the different kinscents began to rise as the sisters returned to work. As she smelled the distinctive tang of the fertility police, Flora felt someone watching her. Fear released her and she spun round, expecting to be confronted by a masked sister. But the beam of attention came from a huddle of sanitation workers. Realising she had seen them, they dropped their eyes and antennae and busied themselves with grooming each other. Flora went to them.

"Honour to you, sisters," she said. "You work for the police now?"

The first worker shook her head in horror, and the others bobbed their antennae to emphasise that they did not. They gazed at her with bright intelligent black eyes.

Flora could not look away — and the image of her last egg returned sharp and clear in her mind's eye, the

243

memory of its fragrance pouring strong from her antennae.

My beloved egg, my lost child —

She waited for them to screech the alarm, but instead they shuffled closer to her. Then they lifted their kin-scent stronger and joined it around her. With a shock of gratitude, Flora knew they used it to shield her from discovery. They knew she was the laying worker, and they did not reveal it. The wall of scent thickened as strong steps approached. At the astringent scent of this particular Sister Sage, Flora's antennae sprang shut, and their roots throbbed in warning.

"Overwhelmed with love for your kin, I see. You no longer shun them?"

Flora curtsied. "No, Sister. *Accept, Obey and Serve.*" She felt Sister Sage's penetrating attention examining her antennae, taking particular note of the fine line of the seal.

"Always diligent, 717. In all you do." The priestess studied her. "Now that you have found your way back to Sanitation, you will remain until further notice — is that clear?"

"Yes, Sister."

Sister Sage indicated the Dance Hall. The Queen had gone.

"You and your kin will restore this chamber to its immaculate state." With an elegant foot, the priestess pushed aside a drone's broken torso. "You will transfer all debris to the morgue, which you will then clean from top to bottom, and in all corners. You will

244

completely empty that chamber, and permit nothing to interrupt this task. Do you understand?"

"Yes, Sister." As the calmed crowd of sisters filed out of the Dance Hall, Flora signalled to the sanitation workers to wait for her.

"I see they recognise your authority." Sister Sage scanned Flora again. "Do not close your mind to us, 717. Soon it will be time for the Winter Cluster. Do you know what that means?"

"No, Sister."

"Life, for those who join it." Sister Sage looked at the sanitation workers, who were already sweeping and scrubbing the Dance Hall clean. "But not all sisters can. When the last task is completed, send that detail to the spiders."

"The *spiders*? Sister, why? They are fit and strong —"

"Silence! Winter is merciless, your kin is legion, and their few lives traded will help the hive." Sister Sage paused. "The Melissae care for every kin, 717, even yours. I assure you their sacrifice has value, and their end will be quick." The priestess walked away.

Flora stared at her kin-sisters as they swept and cleaned. She picked up a broom and went to join them. Feeling her sadness, they touched her in concern. This time, their kindness hurt.

CHAPTER
TWENTY-NINE

Flora divided the sanitation workers into two details. One ferried drone remains directly from the Dance Hall to the landing board, while the other started from the morgue. It was full since Flora's last visit, the storage racks near the front tight with compacted dry bodies of old sisters, crushed together for maximum efficiency. The older dead were stored further back in the long chamber, from whence came a strong odour of propolis disinfectant. To Flora's surprise, all her workers crowded away from it, little jabs of fear bursting from them.

Heartsick at their imminent betrayal, Flora did not force them deeper but went herself. It was usual to treat the storage racks with propolis, and the large numbers of dead sisters were unsurprising, for all were old and from the early summer — but as she walked further between the racks, she felt the difference in the air. A stillness . . . a secret. Beneath the bright antiseptic top note of the propolis, there were clots of decay. The bustling sounds of the workers faded and the blackness thickened.

Flora stopped. Stored bodies in the morgue were always dry — but here the comb underfoot was wet.

246

The seepage came from a soft and shapeless pile in the corner. Forcing down her instinctive revulsion, Flora extended her antennae to decipher the material. She stepped back in horror.

The pile was made of brood of all ages, from collapsed eggs, to decomposing larvae, to perfect fully formed young sisters, their limbs compressed as if their emergence chamber still held them safe.

Sister Sage could not possibly know about this, for no bee would tolerate such decay and concealment, and Flora's time in the Nursery had taught her that dead brood were always promptly removed. Tightening her spiracles against the polluting smell, she touched her antennae to the freshest-looking corpse. It could not be — she moved her antennae to scan the kin-scent of other heads protruding from the pile. All were Sage.

"Do not tarry, 717." The priestess's voice came towards her down the corridor. "Simply arrange a rota to carry the debris a safe distance from the hive. Then clean every cell of this place." Sister Sage appeared at the doorway.

"Sister, something terrible —"

The priestess examined the detailing of the morgue doorway.

"This needs attention too. And when every last hexagon is cleaned, complete your orders. You alone will remain behind. Your strength will be needed."

"But, Sister, the dead Sage brood —"

The priestess stared at her.

"You are mistaken."

"No, Sister —" Flora staggered as the Hive Mind roared in her brain.

Do not question the Melissae! Accept, Obey and Serve!

"Accept, Obey and Serve —" Flora managed to repeat, over and over, until the pain subsided. When she could focus again, the priestess had gone, and the corps of sanitation workers stood in silence in the corridor, waiting for more orders. Their eyes were bright and steady, an urgent question in their gaze.

Flora could not bear to trick them.

"Winter comes, and to help the hive survive the Sage have bought knowledge from the spiders. The price — is the life of every flora who steps into this chamber to work." She looked into their trusting eyes. "If I could spare you, if I could go in your place —"

The floras came closer to her and touched their heads against her abdomen. Even though her antennae were sealed, the image of her egg shone bright in her mind. They knew. The floras stepped back and waited for her to speak, but she could not. The Holy Chord for Devotion began to vibrate through the comb floor.

"Go," Flora whispered. "Those who would spare themselves, find another task and do not return. I will finish the work and go in your place."

The sanitation workers bobbed their strange curtsy to her then ran to receive the sacrament. Flora watched them go, stunned at their knowledge. It must have happened in the Queen's Dream, when all antennae were opened. That was why they had shielded her with their kin-scent.

248

She sat down. She had been ordered to send them to their deaths, but she could not do it. She betrayed her hive in every way. The vibration of Devotion rose around her and she knew she had only to walk down the passageway to receive more, but she craved stillness.

The memory of her egg shone again, perfect beauty in a raw wax crib. Flora clutched her empty belly and wept for her lost motherhood, richer than any Queen's blessing. A thought hit her.

The crib, in the shadow of those three huge cocoons, each one with their unborn Sage priestess. Half-formed, like the largest in that pile behind her.

She got up to look at them again — and screamed in horror, for the mound of dead was moving. A foul odour stirred and Flora readied her claws to start killing a tide of parasites — and then with a violent retching sound the centre of the pile shifted, and from it appeared the slimed body of Sir Linden.

"Kill me," he gasped, "for I would rather die than hide in here another moment." He scraped at the repulsive matter that covered him. "A coward to the end, I should have stood by my brothers and died with them." He fell on his knees in front of Flora and bared the join of his head and thorax. "I heard all that passed today."

"Your name was called." Flora could not look at him. "You were presumed missing in passion."

"Passion to eliminate — I could not wait. When I returned I heard the screaming — at first I thought the wasps came, then when I saw I could not believe it . . . I still cannot."

"Nor I."

They were silent. The vibrations of Devotion began to fade. Linden reached up with stiff arms and tried to pull his sodden ruff right, then abandoned the effort.

"It is not strange to me, really, that you should turn on us at last. I know how vast we lived, with what ease, at every sister's expense. Not one grain of pollen or drop of water, let alone nectar, did we ever bring in. Nor one stroke of work — but very quick with our demands. Clean my hooks, lick my groin. Admire me, attend me, and you may eat my crumbs. And all the food we wasted . . . Forgive me."

He knelt forward and bared his join again.

"There is nowhere left for me, I understand. I ask but one thing: spare me the police and kill me yourself."

Flora turned away. "Ask some other sister. I am weary of death."

He looked up.

"You are merciful?"

Flora could not speak, for the image of the egg was bright in her mind. She curled her abdomen in and held herself, searching for the feeling. The emptiness was pain.

"You wept," he said. "I heard you. Are you sick?"

"For love," Flora said.

"Ah, all you sisters fall in love with flowers, it is your only release. That, and your adoration of the Queen."

"Not with a flower, not with the Queen."

Sir Linden wiped gore from his face and puffed his thorax a little.

250

"Anyone I might know?"

"No. And lost some time ago."

The comb rattled with the returning steps of the sanitation workers and Flora shook her memories away. Linden looked at her in alarm.

"I have not seen you." She went to the door to meet her workforce. Every one of them glowed strong and beautiful from Devotion, and all stood tall.

"Work fast, my sisters," Flora said to them. "Save it for the end."

The sanitation workers nodded. Fearless now, they went to work on every section of the morgue, cleaning and scrubbing and carrying out bodies until the floor was spotless and every mortal remnant was gone and the whole chamber was empty.

Sir Linden was nowhere to be seen.

Then the sanitation workers bowed to Flora and drew their kin-scent strong about them to hold in the last of the Devotion in their bodies. Six by six, they walked in silent procession out to the landing board, Flora with them.

They shivered as they stepped out into the light. Then they opened their spiracles to release one last saved breath of the Queen's Love, and drew in the divine healing scent.

"*Praise end your days, sisters,*" Flora said to them. They twisted their little faces in their grimacing smiles, then one by one they set their engines. When all were ready, they leapt the board together.

Their aim was good and their force strong as they hit the webs, and the orchard chimed with the Holy

Chord. Flora forced herself to watch as the spiders ran to meet the bees, and she cried out as her own sisters' kin-scent burst bright on the air. The priestess had told the truth: their end was quick.

But she had also lied, for Flora knew that decomposing pile of bodies at the back of the morgue held no other kin than Sage — yet the priestess had flatly denied it.

Nothing made sense. The sanitation workers were strong and healthy and seemed only ever to die of old age — yet they were frequently sacrificed. Exhausted and empty, Flora walked back inside. She tried to remember which scripture ordained the Sage the power of life and death. It was not in the Catechism, nor the prayer tiles, nor could she recall it from the Queen's Library — but it must surely exist, for their rule was Law.

CHAPTER
THIRTY

Within two days the hive had adjusted its bouquet and it was as if the drones had never existed. When word came from the Nursery that the Queen no longer laid male eggs, the news spread fast. The austere meals served in every canteen, the slowing of foraging, and now this signal from Holy Mother — winter was near.

Many house-bees died in their sleep each night, and foragers in the day, courageous sisters dropping in the chill air as their strength gave out far from home. Some made it to a flower but could not rise again; even the best and strongest of them only ever returned to the board with half-full panniers and near-empty crops. The receivers no longer applauded.

Feeling responsible for the growing hunger in the hive, Flora stretched her endurance further, scouring the fields and town gardens for the smallest sip of astringent nectar. She found a patch of waste ground tumbled with garbage, lent grace by a bank of purple-and-yellow Michaelmas daisies. Their petals spread wide to offer their coarse ready pollen, and she fell upon them. By nightfall every forager with wit to find it and strength to return had added Michaelmas pollen to the coffers of the Treasury and the joy of the table — but by morning the sanitation workers were using the freight area overflow for the newly dead, for the morgue was full and high winds had closed the landing board.

Foragers crowded the corridor to peer out at the racing grey sky, and hear the orchard creak from its roots. When it was Flora's turn, she stuck all six hooks into the wax of the corridor and leaned out into the gale. Leaves whirled in the air and the branches rattled. To her fierce satisfaction, the spiders' webs had gone.

Later that day the Sage reappeared in the hive en masse, walking in groups of six. Deep in prayer and chanting an unknown mantra, they were more beautiful than Flora had ever seen them, and she and many other bees stopped to watch their passage through the lobbies. Their long elegant wings were unlatched so that their strong kin-scent flowed behind them, and Flora's antennae twitched as she felt some hidden code within it. The priestesses did not speak, but when they had passed, every sister looked down at her feet in surprise. The comb had stopped transmitting.

Completely unnerved, sisters collected around the big central mosaics in each lobby. They tapped their feet on all the codes and hushed each other while they tried to detect with their antennae the strange change in the air, but they could see no priestesses to ask and the mystery frightened them.

The evening was more disconcerting than the day, for the priestesses appeared in the canteens to serve their meal. This was so unprecedented that the sisters were speechless, forgot their kin places and sat

254

wherever they could best stare at the extraordinary sight. The Sage had turned the edges of their wing-mantles to show their fine gold stripe, their cuticles were polished to a bronze lustre, and their fur stood soft and scented. Below their eyes each had made a subtle mark of gold so that as they turned their faces on each sister they served, the effect was one of almost queenly radiance.

Flora thought she was dreaming as a priestess placed a golden cup of honey before her. Every sister at the table looked up in amazement as the same was done for her, for never in their lives had they eaten like this. Each was scared to start in case she was mistaken, for even in the Drones' Hall this luxury would have been excessive. But the priestesses were genial and encouraged the sisters to eat.

A thousand flowers' sweetness burst upon the bees' tongues, and euphoria flooded the air as they fed and felt their strength return. The honey made them sing with boldness and joy: the Sage were good, the priestesses cared for them and would never let them starve, every bee loved her sisters, they loved the hive, the wind might blow and the frost might bite, but Holy Mother kept them safe and the Sage were her beloved envoys!

As the bees licked the last honey from their cups and wiped them clean with the last crumbs of pollen cakes, the Sage moved amongst them, chanting softly in words unknown, until the Hive Mind filled the mind of each sister.

We share the Last Feast, before the Cluster.

Winter comes, and we join in the Cluster.

The priestesses began to hum the Holy Chord and signalled all rise. The sisters gathered their voices as one, feeling the delicious heaviness of honey and pollen in their bodies give new timbre to the sound. Then the priestesses led them out and the corridors filled with honey-scented bees, singing in a great procession. Flora expected that they would go down to the Dance Hall for Devotion, but instead the Sage led them up to the Treasury.

The bees gasped as they went in. Two towering walls still showed empty vaults, but before they could feel any fear at the gaping lack of honey, they were smitten by the heavenly scent of the Queen. All the chalices of the Fanning Hall had been cleared away, and Her Majesty stood in the centre of the atrium with her ladies, her scent billowing strong and pure. Her smile was so beautiful that each bee knew her Holy Mother saw her and loved her, and they hummed softly in wellbeing.

"Blessings on you, my daughters," said the Queen. "May we meet again."

"We will now form the Cluster." The Sage priestesses spoke with one voice, and began to guide the bees into formation.

Starting with the highest kin groups, they encircled the royal party, hooking themselves together in elegant tessellation, kin after kin, reaching down and pulling each other up, supporting each other as they climbed around the mass that hid the Queen from sight at the centre, careful always to leave the correct space for air.

256

Kin after kin they climbed and clung, climbed and clung, until every bee had her place and the Cluster filled the Treasury to the very top, where it was anchored to the comb by the strong kin of Thistle, and where open honey cells mingled their perfume with the Queen's scent. The exquisite fragrance reached all the way down to the sanitation workers who formed the outer layer of the Cluster, so that even the lowest of the low were held by the Queen's Love and reassurance.

As a forager, Flora had the right to go in deeper, but she chose to stay with her kin-sisters, calming them and making sure they were correctly hooked together before she joined them. Then from the centre of the Cluster, the Hive Mind spoke:

Accept, Obey and Serve.

"Accept, Obey and Serve," responded every bee, and as each one spoke her nervous system joined with that of her sisters, and she released her antennae. Flora spoke the words too, but she pressed her antennae seal tight. Nine thousand bees slowed their breathing, and their individual kin-scents quieted as they breathed as one, drawing in the combined bouquet of the Queen, the Sage, and the honey.

Without the sisters' bodies in constant motion, the hive cooled rapidly. The sanitation workers on the outer edge felt faint warmth emanating from the central mass, but their wings and backs remained cold as they synchronised their breathing and set their antennae to rest position. Flora listened as they all sank into sleep.

Still wide awake, she inhaled the Queen's Love again, feeling its delivery slowing as Holy Mother

257

herself slept — but her own metabolism would not attune. Instead, she heard the distant rattle of the orchard branches, and the wind sweeping the sky. Under the cold press of night, a lichen of frost bloomed on the wooden hive. Deep inside, on the rim of the dark ball of bees, Flora heard its structure creak, and the quiet breathing of her sisters. She re-focused her attention on the Queen's slow pulsing scent.

The wind roared below the stars and Flora listened for any other sisters who might still be awake too. Her mouth was dry and the base of her tongue felt tight. She wanted a shining drop of water from the cool green groove of a leaf. She wanted the soft velvet slide of petals on her body, not the cold clutch of her sisters' claws.

She could not sleep and she could not fly and her wings were locked cold down her back. If she completely relaxed her antennae she might be able to sleep, but to do that might release dreams of her egg. Flora jerked her legs at the thought of it and sanitation workers on both sides mumbled and moaned in their sleep.

Was it so cold outside she would die? That might be better than this — she would die of boredom and frustration if she failed to sleep. Flora now desperately wanted to call out to the other foragers — surely they would be struggling as well, for foragers only rested for short periods, and already the Cluster felt like an eternity.

Flora concentrated on calming herself, trying to synchronise her nervous system with her sisters' — but her mind streamed with memories of the Air, and her travels, and the life she had lived before. Her tongue twitched to unroll into the sticky little mouth of a mallow, or roll amidst the fat creamy grains of poppy pollen. She could almost feel the capsules weighting her fur, and smell their savoury aroma as she combed them into her panniers. She wanted to draw in the cool herbal tension of plant stems under her feet, not the dust from some sister's back. But more than anything, she wanted dew.

She must have slept, for she woke because the Cluster was stirring, rotating its layer so that all bees moved up towards the top where they would eventually be fed, then revolving back down. In this way the Cluster would travel the walls of the Treasury, opening honey cells as it went, and always would the Queen be fed first.

The smell of honey percolated through the layers as a new kin group was fed, and Flora's appetite returned with a burst. She looked around for the source of the food, but after several hours, the Cluster had already re-formed and the sanitation workers had barely moved. As she scanned up the dense ball of her colony, Flora knew it would be many days before they ate.

She carefully extricated herself and joined the two workers together to seal the gap she left, then picked her way across the surface, treading lightly on her sisters' thousand backs so as not to disturb them. At last she smelled a faint trace of sky and found the ragged wing-tips and toughened thorax of another forager.

"Madam Rosebay," Flora whispered, for she saw the other stirred restlessly. "Can you sleep? I cannot."

"No, for I cannot bear this confinement, and do not tell me about the Last Feast for my belly eats itself! How long before our layer moves in for feeding?" Madam Rosebay's voice was hoarse with anxiety. "Foragers should not have to wait, foragers do not need to Cluster — why are we even here?"

Other bees shushed them from all directions.

"House-bee prisoners," she retorted. "I will not hold a sister's hand for the rest of my life — I have spent my life on the air, I will find food for us now."

"Sister —" Flora could hear the wind moaning in the night. "Not now!"

"Yes, now! I go wild with this confinement."

Madam Rosebay broke the link with the two house-bees either side of her, and climbed unsteadily onto the surface of the Cluster to stand with Flora.

"Sister, please — it would be better in the morning —"

"I cannot bear another azimuth here." Madam Rosebay unlatched her wings. Flora saw they were withered on her back. At her look of horror, Madam Rosebay pulled one round and gasped. "My wings! What has happened? Help me close them, Sister. It must be the cold — they will come straight again." She tugged at them and they tore. "These are not my wings," she whispered to Flora. "My wings are whole and strong. They must be underneath. I must shake these free outside."

Madam Rosebay ran down the Cluster, waking many bees. She jumped for the Treasury wall but could not hold on. Scrabbling and clawing, she fell to the bottom of the chamber, crying out in pain.

"Forager sister!" she called out to Flora from the black depths of the Fanning Hall floor below the Treasury walls. "Help me to the landing board. My flowers are waiting for me; they will not open until I reach them — please, you must help me!"

Flora ran to the edge of the Cluster and jumped onto a Treasury wall. She climbed down over its sealed vaults all the way to the bottom, where many sisters' bodies lay dead upon the ground. Madam Rosebay stood among them, struggling to spread her withered wings. Her legs gave way and she reached out for Flora.

"My flowers," she whispered. "They are waiting. You must go."

"Yes, Sister." Flora sat down beside her and stroked her antennae. "Tell me of your flowers, so I shall know them."

"Willowherb," said the broken forager, "has the best nectar. Remember that."

Flora waited until Madam Rosebay was still, then laid her with the other bodies.

"You are very kind," said a familiar voice.

CHAPTER
THIRTY-ONE

It took a moment for Flora to see Sir Linden, sitting hunched and small at the foot of a broken Treasury wall. The sight of him made her glad.

"I could have shown myself at any time before this," he said, "and met a quick end. Now I must die of starvation, like the coward I am." He looked up. "Unless I call out for someone to come and finish me off."

"Do not disturb their rest. Where did you hide?"

"In plain scent — I joined your work party. Look —" And Sir Linden pulled his antennae in short and blunt, hunched his back and dropped his head. Even his wings seemed lower-set. He scuttled from side to side, his gait quick and anxious like a sanitation worker. "I think they smelled the difference, but of course none could speak it. Or perhaps . . . fool that I am . . . I thought them kind enough to allow it."

They both looked up at the Cluster. Flora hesitated.

"There is room up there, amongst us. At least you would be warm."

"Oh yes, one's own blood flowing freely from one's wounds is very warming, for a short while anyway. Do you think me crazy?"

"The blood-lust is past. No one will hurt you now." Flora began to climb back up the Treasury walls.

"Wait." Linden followed her, his movements weak. "Could it work? Why would you do this for me? You are unnatural. Though that is not news." As he drew level with her he tried to puff his thorax. "Yes, thank you, I agree to your plan," he whispered, "but surely my noble groin will draw much interest? Some sister will long to groom it —"

"You will be quite safe."

"Good," he whispered back, "for my popularity fatigued me in the Season, you know. Very greatly."

The sanitation workers hung silent in their latticed sleep. Flora signalled Sir Linden wait while she gently unhooked a couple of sisters, then she beckoned to him. They murmured and stirred as she joined him between them. He grimaced as he sniffed them, then entwined his arms and legs.

"Still quite a strong-scented bunch, aren't you?"

"Be glad of it." Flora let a wave of her own scent cover him. "And be quiet." She trod on him as she climbed up one level of hanging sisters.

"But where are you going?"

"You talk too much." After her journey to the Treasury floor, Flora was glad of her sisters' warmth. Carefully she squeezed herself back into position and the scent of the Queen stole up through the slow-breathing Cluster. She waited until she was sure her sisters' scent covered that of the drone, then a weary peace soaked through her body, and at last she slept.

★   ★   ★

263

The Cluster moved very slowly as the whole hanging ball of thousands of bees revolved in on itself to travel the Treasury walls. Honey vaults were cracked open one at a time and those whose turn had come could cling to the bitten edge to take a few sweet sustaining sips of energy. Then they moved on, down along the outer edge of the Cluster, and the mass revolution continued so that all would be fed.

The only bee whose position never altered was the Queen, for the sisters kept her close to the honey source and huddled in the warmth of their bodies. Her divine fragrance flowed slow and steady as each honey vault in the wall was emptied, and the Cluster made systematic progress around the walls ensuring no honey was missed.

The sisters did not wake as their dense mass revolved, only stirred in their sleep as they shifted their grip on legs and hands, rising or sinking as the Cluster turned. When the great ball shifted again, the smell of honey spiked hunger in Flora's belly, strong as when she emerged from her arrival chamber. Her whole body felt empty and trembling — and when she saw how far she was from her turn to feed, she wanted to wail in despair. There were maybe another thousand mouths to feed before the turn of the sanitation workers — if they had strength to wait.

Her limbs ached from the long holding position, but all around her the other floras slept on, as did the strange new sister she had joined into them. Flora did not want to wake them, but nor could she bear to remain like this. She drew in her consciousness and tried to pull shreds of the divine fragrance around her antennae to soothe her impatience, but there was not enough to be had, and the effort only exacerbated her need for food, or action, or anything but this dark, crowded confinement. Other foragers were also awake — she could feel their frustration pulsing through the Cluster. She pushed more energy into her senses — the air had changed and the wood of the hive smelled different. It was drier, and the wind had subsided. Very softly, Flora unhooked herself.

The view from the landing board was a shock. The orchard raked black branches against a white sky and, beyond it, raw brown fields stretched to the high and distant tree-line. Several foragers tested their cramped limbs and looked at each other. All were ravenous. They shivered as they raised their antennae and scented the cold air. There was no wind or rain, and a pale haze in the cloud showed the sun still lived. One by one they started their engines. The sound was loud and unnervingly different in the winter air. There were no Thistle guards to do it, so each of the foragers laid down her own homecoming marker to guide them all back in. Flora watched them. A Calluna forager nodded to her in approval.

"You have the right." Her voice was cracked and dry, and Flora could hear how empty her belly was. "And your kin-scent is so strong —"

"— none of us could ever miss it!"

"Do it, Sister."

For the first time in her life, Flora laid her kin-scent down on the landing board, proclaiming her kin could forage. The homecoming marker immediately absorbed the new chemical signature, and rose up more strongly.

Flora's wings were weak from their long time folded, the cold air shocked her and she struggled for altitude. Every scent and air current had changed, and the smell of the warehouses was stronger. Her antennae suddenly flashed with an incoming message — and to her delight she recognised the unique frequency of Lily 500's data running in her brain. A foraging location, with coordinates over the town.

Cage of glass, cage of glass, were the only words attached. Flora had no idea what it meant, but the coordinates were so insistent that she began her descent over the houses and their dirty green patchwork of the gardens.

The wind grew stronger, and with it, the cold. Each pump of blood to her wings took more fuel than before, and a lightness in her crop signalled danger. Her pride again, insisting she would find forage in the hardest conditions, in the furthest fields. Now she would have to chase the sun's dropping azimuth home without refuelling —

Cage of glass! insisted Lily's data in her brain. *Cage of glass!*

"Be quiet! Be quiet!" Flora whirled in the air, her energy level sending a warning to her brain. If she touched cold ground now it would suck the last of it from her body and she would never rise again.

She caught a trace of sweetness — bright and young and pure. A flower — a young, beautiful flower. Flora locked onto it. Fragrant beyond buddleia, iris or even honey-suckle, a thread of scent curled from a cube of light against the side of the building. Flora veered away from her reflection before she crashed into the huge window.

The cage of glass was a conservatory and inside were plants, some bright and luscious of petal, some tiny and white. The sweet scent she followed was inside, coming from a flower calling to her, imploring any bee, any pollinator to come in — but Flora did not know how to enter. The wind dragged her along the glass wall and she caught the scent more strongly. It came from a little gap halfway down.

The air in the conservatory was warm and humid and the plants did not grow out of the earth but from brightly coloured pots on stands and on ledges along the walls. A metal dish of mashed meat was on the ground and several flies fed from it, but more lay dead or dying on the windowsills and on the floor. Flora ignored everything but the beautiful plant calling to her with its pure sweet scent, open and untouched, and longing for a bee.

First she had to avoid the drunken bluebottles contaminating all the bigger flowers. Many alighted on the heavy orange lily heads still waiting to open, drawn by the thick bead of nectar showing at the ruched tip of the petals. Other flowers also waited, and Flora did not know if they were ready or not, for their petals were fleshy and green like pea-pods, their pursed and meaty red lips edged with strange white tendrils like fangs. Feeling her wing-beats, they murmured lasciviously to her and pushed their murky perfume across her path, but they did not appeal.

Amidst their lewd clamour rose the one true scent that called to Flora, the virgin bloom of a little orange tree, a tortured miniature graft of three different plants. Its tiny ultraviolet florets shone in the dull winter air, and she felt its desire for her straining from its roots.

"Hush, hush." Flora pushed her own scent through her feet as she settled on the dark glossy leaves. The plant's citrus sweetness immediately brightened her senses and the fatigue of her journey fell away. There was not one other bee in the glass room, and Flora's panniers opened in readiness for the haul of pollen and nectar she would surely be able to take back to the hive from this marvellous place. She climbed up and positioned herself over one of the creamy white florets, and the contact of her feet on the flower's virginal petal made them both tremble. Flora held it softly then sank her tongue into its depths. The exquisite taste sparkled through her mind and body like sun on water, and she drank until each floret was empty.

Behind her, the green-fleshed flowers waited their turn. As Flora combed the minute gold pollen beads of the neroli into her panniers, she felt their patient desire. When she looked again, their green lips had parted to show a glimpse of inner red, and their white fringing had a more festive look. Their thick coarse nectar could not compare with the near-divine bouquet of the neroli, but it was plentiful, and the way it rose to her attention was very flattering.

Despite herself, Flora's own scent pulsed more strongly from her body. So strong was their desire for her that they actually moved towards her, their inner petals moistening under her gaze. She hovered, mesmerised by their lust.

"Come to me instead," crooned a high voice. Flora looked up to see a big black Minerva spider sitting in her hazy cobweb. "What a sweet servant. Come, let me hold you."

"I have seen your kind," Flora called back. "No thank you."

Her wings beat harder with the adrenaline of spider-danger, exciting more thick perfume to rise from the green flowers. Perhaps they were a type of weed. In these conditions, sisters would drink spurge if they could find it, and it would be a fine thing to go back with a cropful of fresh nectar, no matter its provenance.

The fleshy blooms gaped wider, encouraging her decision. Who knew when the weather would permit another forage? Perhaps she could drink the neroli herself, and then bring back this more plentiful nectar. Flora opened up her antennae channel a little more in case Lily 500 had some comment, but there was no signal.

The green flowers suddenly pumped their scent, flooding Flora's brain and forcing her attention back to them. Their red mouths gaped wider, and on each inner lip stood three long white filaments like pistils or anthers, except they bore no pollen. The only nectar was a viscous slick at the join of the petals — crude but plentiful.

At the cloying smell, Flora hesitated. Shamelessly, the vulgar flowers begged for her touch, swelling even more nectar so that the thought rose in Flora's mind that here was enough to feed the whole Cluster.

Before she could decide which bloom to choose, the conservatory swarmed with flies driven wild by the same scent. Flora swerved out of the way as they buzzed crazily around the green flowers. The bluebottles shouted crude compliments, they kicked at the white fringes with filthy feet to tease them, they swooped and swirled until the air twisted with the heavy perfume of the flowers and the carrion and excrement on the flies' bodies. Some of them crashed into the bright glass and fell to the ground, stunned and buzzing. Irritated by their antics but mindful of the Minerva in the corner, Flora rose higher. The spider peered out between her sticky curtains.

"Bee with secrets," it whispered. "I can smell them from here."

Flora moved away but a jet of alarm gland escaped her, and the spider laughed. "We will have some entertainment today, I think. First, watch the fools."

The flies taunted the green flowers, zooming close so that the petals gaped red, then screeching past without touching them. But the largest of the strange blooms had not forgotten Flora, and forced its fragrance up to her where she hovered.

"They always want you!" a bluebottle screamed at Flora as he tore past, demented by the flowers' smell.

"But we are as good! Our very name tells you our skill: fly! Watch me!" His body was a metallic turquoise and he scrawled lines of obscene poetry in the air behind him. Flora felt dizzy watching him and his smell made her sick, but his companions roared their approval.

The young fly sped between Flora and the lusting green flower. He kicked along its white fringe with a filth-encrusted foot, and to Flora it looked as if the petal moved to touch him.

"You must beg me!" he called to the flower as he spun loops in the air.

"Oh, oh, sit with me and tell me your tales! Come here!" Excited by the bluebottle's ravings, the Minerva clutched convulsively at the edge of her web.

"We are as good as you!" he cried, racing around Flora, chasing his own slipstream, "though you despise us and call us Myriad — yet here we are, feeding at the same flowers!"

"Bee, honeybee," the Minerva called to Flora, "drive the little shit-feeder up to me; he can tell his tales here . . ."

"Nectar!" screamed the bluebottle. "Only nectar now!"

He landed on a dull fat leaf near the green flowers. With his faeces-encrusted feet and the remnants of some gory meal dried to his face, he looked pitiful and poor beside it. Beneath his clutching feet, the plant began to tighten in its own skin, filling and pumping its sap higher. The musk became dizzying and Flora settled on a ledge.

271

"You make honey so you think you're better," he said to Flora, climbing higher towards the green and red flower, which slowly turned its petals to meet him. "But flowers love us too, and I have sucked so well from one that I learned its true name, *Euphorbia*. Do you believe me? It is true, no matter what you think."

The fly's craving for respect made Flora angry. She understood why the Sage despised her own kin — because they were ashamed of themselves.

"Stop cringing," she said. "If you are a fly, you are a fly! Some of my people love spurge too — and I am the lowest of my kind, I clean waste —"

"Ha!" called the spider. "What do you expect, with your filthy foreign blood?"

Flora fired her war-gland at the spider. "I am queen-born and hive-hatched!"

"Fool, I meant your *father*. One of those fierce black wanderers from the far south." The spider opened her mouth and picked at her fangs. "I'll warrant no one steals *their* honey!" Her little eyes grew soft. "Your blood will be perfectly spiced . . ."

"Ignore her." The fly waved to distract Flora. "She can only get you if you let her." He looked admiringly at Flora. "Do your people really eat spurge, like ours?"

"I know one." Flora could not help smiling. "But my hive frowns on it." She felt the intent gaze of the spider raking her wings, but she focused on the fly.

"Thank you." He bowed to her. Under their crust of filth, his legs were slim and well-turned and his thorax was iridescent blue-black and beautiful. "You are the

272

first of your kind ever to speak to me." He turned and walked up the stem to the green bloom.

"Wait!" Flora cried out. "That plant — I do not know its name —"

"Nor do I, but I am thirsty, and it wants me."

"Yes, wait, boy!" A huge male bluebottle missing his wings ran along the window ledge. "I've told you —"

"And every time, I live to drink again." The young fly stepped onto the red inner skin of the flower and stood between the long white filaments. "Stop worrying — I dance between them, I tickle them — look! They love it!"

He tapped one of the white strands, then his shiny back reflected red as he ran to drink the nectar at the petals' join. He buzzed in pleasure at the taste, and stood up, his face sticky and wet.

"Delicious. No danger, so long as you don't touch two."

"Danger behind you!" the spider screeched. "Quickly!"

The young bluebottle jumped back in alarm, knocking against another long white sword. The second touch triggered the trap. Flora just glimpsed his shocked face as the white-fringed petals bit together. He screamed and buzzed frantically, his hands clawing wildly through the gaps as the sound of fluid rose up inside the bloated bud.

"Fooled him!" The spider shook with laughter, as his screams turned to gurgles, then silence. "Serves that greedy flower right too. It was really after *you*, but I will take that prize." The spider held out her claws, checking their edges.

Flora clung to the wall and forced herself to look away. The smell of the fly's liquefying body seeped from the green flower's swollen lips and hung low in the air. Unable to locate the open window by scent, Flora searched the vast plane of shining glass for a visual clue. All she could see was the conservatory reflected back at her. High on the wall above, something black moved.

Flora sprang from the wall, buzzing and whirring her wings in panic as she hovered. The spider crawled from her web and hung upside down from its thick elastic.

"Treacherous little egg layer — challenging the Queen, if you please! But I suppose it must be time . . . How old is she now? Three winters, four? I forget. But the fuss to change her — dear me!"

"Holy Mother is immortal — no one *changes* her." Flora's voice was strained, and the spider tutted.

"Calm, my dear — terror ruins the taste. I only mean to help, by saving you from more blood on your hands." Very slowly, the spider began creeping down the wall, closer to Flora. "If you go home you will cause madness . . . and sister to turn on sister . . ." Her voice crawled low and insidious. "You will bring disaster on your hive . . . with unimaginable horrors . . ."

"*You lie!*" Before she knew it, Flora was whirling in the narrow space of the conservatory, churning the terrible smell of the green flowers into the air. Unable to see or think, she crashed into the bright glass again and again. As she reeled in the air, the spider dropped heavily to the floor and ran about beneath her, waiting for her to fall.

274

Flora caught hold of a nail sticking out of the wall and clung there.

"Good!" the spider called. "Wait there! I come to take you to a cradle of silk."

"Shut up, you ugly sodden bag. You have no silk." The huge wingless fly crawled along the window ledge and called across to Flora. "Bee! You spoke fairly to one of mine. Come to me now and I will show you the way out."

"How dare you? She is mine!" The huge spider ran about on the tiles in rage. Flora stared down, paralysed.

"Trust me," the old bluebottle shouted at her, "if you would save yourself!"

Flora tore her eyes away from the monster, then whirred her wings. Still stunned from all the collisions, she struggled to land on the windowsill near the fly. On the ground below, the spider searched for a place to start climbing towards them.

"Here — you must go past me." The fly steadied Flora and pushed her forward to a thin vertical strut of metal running up the glass. "Lick your feet before you climb," he said, "or you will fall."

Flora could smell the cold air coming from a gap in the glass above, and the oily stench of the spider rising from below. Then two huge hairy black legs crept up over the white windowsill and clutched for a hold — then two more. The spider reared up behind them, hissing in excitement.

Flora lashed her tongue across her dirty feet and scrambled up the slippery metal until she could claw herself onto the flat base of the tiny open window. The cold free air stirred her wings and she looked down to thank the fly.

Buzzing defiance, he stood his ground before the black spider towering above him.

"Go!" he yelled.

Flora tumbled in the freezing cold until her engine roared to life. The sky was almost dark as she flew back across the gardens, searching for any familiar scent. She flew by instinct and the few remaining landmarks she could detect — the diesel trail of the road, the bitter tang of warehouse drains — and then to her joy and relief she smelled the thin bright marker beacons. She hurled herself towards them, through the black tracery of the orchard branches, down to the hive and the scents of her forager sisters.

Flora touched down on the landing board and ran into her beloved home with her quarter-crop of nectar, and her life, and her burden of secrets.

CHAPTER
THIRTY-TWO

The hive was unnervingly quiet, as if she were the last bee alive. The pain of her freezing flight home bit into her body. Her wings throbbed as they thawed and her brittle shell burned as it began to soften. Flora's gasp of pain echoed in the silent corridor. She could hear no other foragers, nor any motion through the hive. What if the spider's words were true, and her very presence brought disaster to her home? The silence pressed against her brain.

Then she felt it — the faintest vibration of wings, coming from the top storey. The Cluster lived. And there — as Flora ran up the eerily still comb — there was the sweet filament of honey-scent, carried on the warmth of her sisters' bodies. They were all still alive! Desperate to press herself back into the embrace of her family, Flora burst into the Treasury.

The sanitation workers had hardly moved. Intending to go straight to the Queen with her nectar, Flora climbed onto their trembling backs and found them all awake, and breathing in the scent of honey from the top.

"It moves so slowly," whispered Sir Linden from the darkness nearby. His smell was entwined with that of the workers, and he supported one on each side. "It will be days before we eat — if we can last."

Too cold to speak, Flora immediately gave the nearest worker a drop of the neroli nectar. Despite her ravenous hunger, the little bee took the smallest sip before passing the larger portion into her neighbour's mouth. She too drank most modestly, then passed it on. To Flora's surprise, Sir Linden did not lunge for a greedy share, nor even ask for any.

Remembering the drones' incapacity for feeding themselves, Flora fed him a tiny shot as if he were a newly emerged sister in Arrivals. His antennae shuddered in relief. Then he pressed his body close against hers and whirred his wings to warm her. The little worker on Flora's other side did the same, and then many others. Flora felt her body thaw, and breathed the comforting scent of her own kin, mingled with the scent of Linden.

"The Queen," Flora whispered, when she could speak. "I must find her."

The Cluster was dense and slow to traverse. Bees yelped if Flora stepped on their sleeping antennae; some woke at the smell of the nectar she carried, and from the depths irritable foragers called out to know its provenance, for many others had also ventured out, but few returned, and they found nothing. Without comb to efficiently transmit choreography, Flora tried to pass on the location of the cage of glass, but she dreaded their fate if they found it.

278

Even in the Cluster, the Sage priestesses were alert to all that went on. They sent an escort of the Queen's ladies-in-waiting to safeguard Flora's progress with her precious nectar. She smelled the honey on their mouths and it reminded her of her days in the Nursery, when she was left the dregs and crumbs. Now that she bore nectar in time of hardship, all these beautiful well-fed sisters from Fragaria, Broom, Foxglove spoke softly and prettily to her, and made way to let her through to the warm sweet enclosure of silken wings protecting Her Majesty.

The Cluster closed around them and Flora felt the Queen's body against hers. The divine fragrance was fainter in the cold, or because the Queen was half asleep. Flora triggered her crop so that the tiny precious quantity of neroli nectar rose up in her mouth, and at that sweet bright scent, the Queen stirred. Her fragrance pulsed stronger, warming and restoring Flora's cold exhausted body. Her Majesty dipped her long proboscis and drank deeply. Almost immediately Flora felt the energy surge glow from the Queen's body, and then pulse out in a bright wave of the divine fragrance. It rippled through the Cluster and eight thousand dreaming bees murmured in relief.

The Queen touched Flora's antennae with her own.

"My child is cold. My child suffers . . . I feel it."

A surge of anguish rose in Flora's body at the memory of the spider's words.

"Hush . . ." The Queen held her. "Mother is here. Do you sicken?"

279

Before Flora could answer, one of the police pushed into the winged enclosure.

"Who sickens? I will take her —"

"Holy Mother —" Flora dropped to her knees before the Queen, daring the officer to stop her. "You sent a message for me before but I did not receive it. But I am here now and I will do whatever you ask."

"Oh . . ." The Queen's voice trembled. "I wished to recall a story . . . from my Library. The fifth one . . ."

A Sage priestess pushed her way in.

"No, Majesty, please!" She prostrated her antennae to the Queen. "Holy Mother, we must not speak of such things in the Cluster. If Your Majesty grew distressed in any way, your children would feel it."

"Our own child advises us?" The Queen turned her gaze on the priestess. "Our own daughter sends police, to regulate Our conduct?" As the Queen's scent began to change, the whole Cluster pulsed in stress. The priestess waved the officer away and bowed low, her antennae trembling.

"Forgive me, Your Majesty. The Sage have only the common good in mind and will sometimes err for caution. But if Holy Mother grows excited she will tire, and the Cluster will suffer."

The Queen nodded.

"Truly." She folded her long shining antennae, and began to sink into a deep trance.

The priestess signalled and the enclosure of silken wings parted to allow her to escort Flora out. Then the wings closed again to guard the Queen and keep her warm.

280

"Take this to your kin and bid them be patient." The priestess gave Flora a large drop of honey. "Next time you bring nectar for Her Majesty, we will deliver it. Nothing must disturb Holy Mother, even though She asks it." The priestess scanned her. "You are distressed, yet you have just breathed the Queen's Love."

"Fearful things on my forage. If I could dance them I would release them."

"And spread nightmare to every sister. You must bear your burden alone."

"Yes, Sister." Flora returned to her own kind.

The next day a thick coat of snow muffled the hive. The Cluster had moved across the Treasury ceiling and wall, leaving large patches of empty honey cells behind, and now at last it was the turn of the sanitation workers to feed. The Sage uncapped a different kind of honey for them, thinner and coarser. Ravenous, they did not complain. Masked with their scent, Sir Linden stayed hidden deep in their midst, and Flora shared her ration with him as they moved along the wall and back down towards their allotted level.

Freezing winds tugged the hive so hard the bees feared it would fall, and outside in the orchard branches cracked and fell. The sky howled and there was no more foraging. Flora joined the small first-aid corps of bees who checked the Cluster for those whose hooks were slipping, and helped secure them. The strong encouraged the weak and assisted them, but as the daily casualties mounted, the Sage took the decision to break open emergency rations for those in dire need, then use vital energy to summon the Holy Chord and take the Hive Mind itself into trance.

The bees stilled their bodies as if in death, and the faint molecules of the Queen's Love still rising from the heart of the Cluster joined them together as one being. Freed from their bodies, each bee felt herself travelling the hive, exploring its vastness and its details, both ancient and new, so that she loved its every cell and understood its whole construction, from the landing board to the Treasury walls they clung to.

The Hive Mind travelled back to the entrancement of Holy Time, when every sister floated in knowledge and bliss, slowly accreting wisdom into the cells of her transforming body until it surged with the power of incarnation and she woke within her emergence chamber. Each bee dreamed herself in the Chapel of Wax, her hands stroking up soft translucent discs from her abdomen, standing alongside sisters from the Time before Time, moulding the very fabric of their home together.

They dreamed their way through the bright physical delight of Construction, and each intricate exquisite coded tile was a triumph of all they knew and loved, laid down in the lobby floors for all to share. The blissful aromas of Pollen & Patisserie drifted through their shared dream, and the entire Cluster murmured in delight as they saw the plenty on the tables. The touch of cold wings around them became the warm gossipy camaraderie of standing together moulding sweets for the Queen and bread for the sisters, and

282

when the foragers' trance grew vivid, the whole Cluster sighed in its sleep at the wonder of their knowledge.

The Hive Mind lifted their dream up into the blue and blazing summer air, where the foragers swooped in daring and elegant flight. It took the bees down to the flowers in a kaleidoscope of beauty and wonder as if the foragers shared their skills, dreaming how to pack a pannier with rapid economy, how to tickle a flower to yield the sweetest nectar — and how to watch where the hoverflies gathered to tell that air was safe from the Myriad.

The Thistle guards' dreams unravelled the complex etiquette of the landing board, and the minutiae of its many signals, and then, in the powerful anonymity of the Hive Mind, the bees shared their fear and loyalty to the Holy Law, their long-repressed terror of the Visitation and the warning smell of the smoke that preceded it. The Cluster buzzed as it released its anxiety, and then every kin relaxed their minds and their knowledge poured out with joyful abandon, and sharing detail after detail of their beloved communal life.

The Hive Mind absorbed it all, and enlarged.

Far down below the Queen and the Sage, Flora dreamed as well — she could not help herself. She dreamed she cradled a warm golden egg in her arms, translucent and beautiful as a drop of honey. From its heart shimmered a tiny golden bee, flying closer and closer to her mind's eye. The Holy Chord resonated from its fragrant body, and its tiny face came into focus, beautiful and fierce. Harder and harder it beat its wings, until the hum became a harsh scratching sound.

All at once Flora was awake. The scratching was real and it came through the wood of the hive with an alien heavy vibration. Her cold limbs cramped in agony as she pulled herself free of Sir Linden.

"Sisters, wake up!" She ran across the backs of the sleeping sisters, stamping out her alarm and firing her war-glands to wake the whole Cluster.

"Intruder! Intruder in the hive!"

CHAPTER
THIRTY-THREE

The comb juddered with the predator's powerful bites. It was somewhere below them on the middle floor, near the Nursery. The sisters paused, counting the pattern of its feet — not eight so not a spider, not six so not an insect — four! A quadruped, with warm blood and dirty fur. Quick and silent, the party of Thistle guards and the strongest sisters from every kin moved towards the vibrations.

The gnawing stopped, as if the creature also took stock of the bees' advance. Then the smell of its urine rolled down the corridor towards them and they heard the cracking of wax as it resumed its attack on their precious walls. As the sisters crept forward their venom sacs filled and their daggers slid ready.

In the lobby by the Drones' Arrivals Hall the intruder reared up before them. Its long grey head towered over them and its red eyes stared blindly into the darkness. Hundreds of thick trembling whiskers drew in scent and its hairless clawed feet gouged marks in the floor mosaic as it moved. The air was musty from its fur, and when it opened its mouth and panted, the bees saw the long yellow incisors and smelled its rank breath.

The mouse paused, confused. Its long scaly tail twitched, spreading traces of its urine across the floor tiles.

One of the Thistle guards at the front buzzed angrily and fired her war-glands, and every sister did the same.

Protect the Queen!

The mouse scrabbled round to face their sound and the bees stepped forward slowly, buzzing low and staccato to drive it out. The mouse backed away and the sisters pressed forward, increasing the warning note in their buzz. With a sharp exclamation of revulsion, the first Thistle guard stepped into the trail of its urine. The mouse screeched too, twisting in panic. Its lashing tail knocked some bees off their feet and the others rushed forward, buzzing in rage and nipping at its flank.

It screeched again and turned to run, crashing down the main staircase to the bottom storey and only stopping when it knocked its head on the propolis-carved doorway of the Drones' Hall. Squealing in pain, it bared its long yellow teeth, so close they smelled the woodlice on its breath. Then it turned and ran towards the landing board but the collision had stunned it and it missed the corridor to the free air and struggled instead towards the back of the hive. Flora felt a through-draught of air — it must have gnawed a hole in the wood somewhere else.

As one, the sisters knew they must drive it out. They buzzed and pressed forward in angry feints, but the mouse could not run any longer. It fell on its side and lay staring at them, its breath coming fast and shallow.

286

They bit at it and flashed their daggers, but it was old and weak, and its eyes stopped moving.

Hundreds of sisters were mobilised to bring propolis from other parts of the hive. For hours the bees chewed and carried, chewed and carried until their long-unused jaws throbbed in pain, but finally the ice-hard propolis grew soft enough to mould. Little by little, under the direction of the Sage, the bees embalmed the dead intruder until not a hair nor whisker could be seen or smelled.

Most of the bees were sent back to the Cluster, but Flora stayed in the last work detail, making sure that not the smallest airspace remained between the mouse and the floor. The pungent smell of propolis masked the approach of a priestess, and Flora jumped when she saw one. The identicality of the Sage unnerved her more than anything, for as she never knew which had beaten her or which been kind, so she feared every one of them. She tried to close her antennae — but could not feel them.

"So diligent in all things, Flora 717." By her rich voice, it was Sister Sage from the Nursery. She stood near Flora but checked the join of another bee's work. "And still so strong and young."

"I am honoured at your notice, Sister." Flora tried again to close her antennae, but the smell of the propolis slowed her reflexes. The priestess was faster, using her own chemical signal as a lever to prise them open.

"Do not shield your thoughts." Sister Sage probed more deeply into Flora's mind. Touching on the memory of the black Minerva spider, she shuddered in horror, but pressed her awareness harder into Flora's consciousness. "We must know, 717, what troubles you. We know you have a secret . . ."

Flora's abdomen twisted and, for a second, the image of her egg shone in her mind. In desperation, she thought of the Queen clutching her arm, long ago in her boudoir. She remembered the flicker of pain on Holy Mother's face.

I promised Her my silence!

"Holy Mother was sick in her chamber," Flora whispered. "That is my secret."

Sister Sage withdrew her pressure, and when she spoke her voice was gentle.

"Her Majesty is sick?"

Flora stared at the resin sarcophagus, then nodded. Her beloved Mother had begged her not to speak of it, and she had promised not to tell another soul. Now she had betrayed the Queen in every conceivable way. But even as she despised herself, Flora felt her control returning — and locked her antennae tight.

"That was long ago," she said. "But just now in the Cluster, when I gave Her Majesty nectar, She was strong." Flora stared at the priestess. She had cleared the morgue herself and seen the Sage bodies. She had touched those three strange tombs in the secret chamber behind the Treasury, and knew that they too held Sage.

"Is there sickness in our hive?" she asked.

"Of course not." Sister Sage groomed her own antennae, as if from soiling contact. "But the Cluster permits nightmares, as a way of cleansing our minds. And, as foragers must withstand more sights than most, you might well have fearsome fantasies." The priestess let her scent flow smooth. "If Holy Mother has been unwell, it is crucial you tell us. For the good of the colony."

Light footsteps sounded in the corridor, and five identical priestesses entered. Sister Sage made an almost imperceptible motion to them, and they stood silent.

"Return to the Cluster," she said to Flora. "The Melissae must confer."

The living orb of sisters still pulsed with gossip of the mouse when Flora got back. To her astonishment, she heard the sanitation workers talking in low voices. She took her place and looked at them. They were smiling.

"In the Dreaming," one whispered, "we took back our tongues."

Then the scent of the kin of Sage flowed towards them as the priestesses returned. All the bees stopped talking and parted to let them disappear deep within the Cluster, near the Queen. Then the Holy Chord began to vibrate, and the Hive Mind spoke.

The danger is passed. We now resume our trance.
Accept, Obey and Serve.

The bees murmured in response and settled their antennae for rest. Threads of the Queen's Love drifted to the outer layers where her daughters clung in the cold, but the beautiful fragrance gave Flora no comfort.

CHAPTER
THIRTY-FOUR

Freezing fog crawled down on the hive, its clammy touch probing every unsealed gap. In the dense chilled clump of life within, there was no more energy for dreaming, and the only message pulsing slowly through the Cluster was that every sister's warmth was vital, and none might leave. In the rare few hours of runted sun, Flora and other foragers raised their antennae in hope, but it was still too cold to fly.

Three-quarters of the Treasury walls were empty when the first signs came. The sisters did not stir, for even to think of spring would cost them psychic energy — but secretly each of them began to register a change.

The wooden walls creaked as they dried. The air thinned, and new scents stirred. Was that the soil they smelled?

Sisters began to shift their grip but kept their antennae connected to the trance, fearful of the agonising disappointment if they were wrong. Flora unsealed both of hers, then raised her head in excitement. The air pressure was definitely changing — high above the Treasury ceiling the skies were opening. Since her desperate frozen flight back from the cage of glass, she had not been out or smelled any green and living thing; but now as the first seeds split deep within the earth, a primal scent began to rise.

One day the sun shone warmer and in the orchard the first bird sang. Deep in the Cluster the Queen stirred. Her fragrance pulsed stronger and stronger through her daughters' dreams, rocking their senses back to life — until with a shimmering burst the bees awoke to the change in the air, and joy at the coming of spring.

Euphoric with relief, Flora untangled herself and stretched her cramped limbs. She looked immediately for Linden, to acknowledge his survival, but he had already disappeared into the shifting landscape of the Cluster's disintegration.

A brown-and-gold tide of bees streamed down the Treasury walls and a thousand scent instructions and affirmations wove the air. Comb tingled underfoot as thousands of feet reactivated the dormant scent codes.

"Make all ready! Make all ready!" the sisters called ahead, and everyone pressed back in thrilled excitement as the Queen herself came rushing through on a cloud of fragrance.

"Attend, attend!" she called, and the smell of her rising fertility trailed behind her sweeter than nectar. Then came her ladies-in-waiting running behind, all their pretty fur in disarray, antennae waving dishevelled at their sudden return to duty.

"Attend, attend!" they cried as they ran, and all the bees cheered in joyous relief and sang the Queen's Prayer to spread the good news: Holy Mother was preparing to lay again, and winter was finally over.

★ ★ ★

It was wonderful and strange to be at liberty in the hive again. Sisters from Propolis immediately got to work repairing the damage the monstrous mouse had wreaked with its gnawing and crashing around, and sanitation workers set about cleaning the dirt it had brought with it. Foragers rushed past Flora towards the landing board, but a phalanx of priestesses stood in the mid-level lobby surveying the damage and repairs. Flora could not help herself. She sealed her antennae and went up to one.

"Sister, may I be permitted to ask a question?"

"Speak."

"Did the spiders in the orchard speak truly?"

The priestess's antennae pulsed hard and high for a second, then she drew them down.

"Why do you ask?"

"They spoke of two winters. But now it is spring."

"A strange memory, to hold all through the Cluster. Would you rather the spiders spoke true, or false?"

Flora was silent. *Winter comes twice; one more egg.*

"False, Sister, for they wish us no good."

"Then why bring their malice to mind?"

"So many lives were sold in payment for what they said, that if they lied —"

The priestess groomed her antennae, and when they rose again, Flora knew she had sealed them, as if she too had something to hide.

"The Cluster survived, did it not?" The priestess let her kin-scent flow. "Fly while you can, old forager. Bring us food!"

"*Accept, Obey and Serve.*" Flora bowed, and ran for the board. The priestess had not answered her question. There was still hope.

It was a joy to see the Thistle guards standing at arms on the board again, and when Flora laid her own kin-scent along with all the other homecoming markers, they saluted her as any other forager. She shivered her engine back to life and stretched her long cramped wings. They hurt as the sun roused blood through the silver membranes, and her joints felt stiff. She was ageing, there was no doubt — and so were other foragers who showed yet more wear and tear. But as they streamed high into the sparkling air, the sound of their engines was joyous and strong.

Flora leapt to join them. If anything, the long confinement had made her faster and more agile than before, and the very thought of a cold sister clinging onto her body sent her racing in pursuit of the wonderful smell of pollen.

It came from a straggly line of willows edging a field, their leaves still furled in sleep but their acid-yellow catkins just opening. There was no nectar, for all the trees were male, but after her long fast Flora craved the thick carbohydrate of pollen. She ran up and down the golden pendants triggering the precious dust to shower all over her body, then as she combed it off and packed it hard and tight into expert bundles, she ate until her strength was restored. The taste and the freedom made her hum for joy, and when bees from other hives joined her in the branches they greeted each

293

other in the most beautiful word of their tongue: *Spring!*

Each returning forager was met with a storm of applause as she touched down with her load, but none had such a haul as Flora. She danced her directions to a packed and enthusiastic crowd in the Dance Hall, and many did not even wait for her to finish before they rushed off to find the catkins themselves.

All the foragers did well that day, only stopping as the sun sank early in the afternoon and the chill evening forced them back. Some had found bright orange pollen from crocus, some early daffodils with their rough vivid taste, and the mood in the canteens was buoyant.

More good news came as they finished their meals. Two young Teasel nurses burst in, their faces bright with excitement.

"Sisters! Holy Mother's eggs flow strong again," cried one, "worker after worker!"

"And for every hundred of us, a male! Their Malenesses are coming, sisters! Truly it is spring, tell everyone!"

Like the memory of summer, the massacre of the males had vanished with the Cluster, and so their joy and excitement was fresh and pure. All the bees remembered was the thrill of Devotion, once again travelling through the wax comb to reassure the colony of Holy Mother's health, and her ongoing love for them. Spring was here, and all fear was gone.

But Flora remembered everything, and that night as she lay in her berth, listening to the happy gossip and chatter of her sisters, she carefully scanned her body.

There were nicks and tears along the edges of her wings, and their joints ached from her first long flight since the Cluster — but there was nothing else of note. Though she knew she aged, she was healthy and strong — except for the emptiness in her heart and the void in her belly. There was nothing to hide, and nothing to fear. The spiders feigned power with cruel empty taunts, and there would be no third egg.

The next day a Calluna forager rushed back to the hive dancing wildly of a blazing forsythia bush on the edge of the town, and all the foragers sped to find it. It was better than they hoped, wild and untrimmed so that its thousands of golden florets yielded nectar at the slightest touch, and so many bees visited it that it hummed with the Holy Chord.

All the foragers from the orchard hive visited it for hours, enraptured at the constantly twining threads of scent and the sudden bursts of glittery pollen showering onto their backs. At last even the most vigorous foragers were finally ready to stop, and with loaded panniers and well-filled crops they flew home together. This was a comforting strategy they only permitted themselves when the sky was clear of the scent of the Myriad, otherwise the scent and sound of so many richly laden bees would be irresistible.

The cold spring breeze was in their favour and as the sisters sped back towards the hive, they hummed in bright anticipation of the praise that would meet them as they thumped down onto the landing board.

It was not to be. Approaching the orchard, Flora saw that the foragers who had left the forsythia bush before

295

them were still hovering fully loaded in the air, held back by a cordon of Thistle guards. They were demanding to land, and complaining of the extra fuel it was costing to keep them waiting.

"Forgive us, Madam Foragers," shouted back the Thistle, "but the Sage decree you wait, for Special Purpose."

"What Special Purpose? What could possibly be more important than bringing in forage?" It was an Ivy, a late-born forager with plenty of strength. "I cannot believe you turn us away — shame on your kin!"

"Please, Madam!" The Thistle closest to the Ivy buzzed in distress. "We cannot — we are instructed by the priestesses. *Accept, Obey and Serve!*"

Black dots of sisters appeared on the landing board, and Flora smelled her kin-sisters, the sanitation workers. All the elimination flights had been performed, so it was unusual for them to appear on the board. They wept and each carried a little burden. One by one, they lurched off the board and flew away, far past the place of elimination. When the last had disappeared, the Thistle moved back for the incoming foragers.

"Forgive us, sisters," they said.

On the landing board, Flora smelled the traces of her kin-sisters' feet, and the peculiar and unpleasant load they had carried. She stood waiting to see if the floras came back, but there was no sound or scent of them.

"What did they take?" she asked the little Clover receiving her forsythia nectar. "What were the floras carrying?"

The Clover shook her head and hurried back into the hive. Flora followed and grabbed her.

"Tell me what happened to my kin!"

The Clover started to cry.

"I am forbidden. *Accept, Obey* —"

Before she could finish Flora pressed her own antennae round the Clover's and held her firmly so that she could not run. The Clover did not know how to seal them, and her panic spilled into Flora's mind, tumbled with images of the Nursery.

"They say the brood is plagued." She leaned against Flora and wept. Flora pulled some pollen from her pannier and stuffed it in her hands.

"Hush. Tidy that and stop weeping, or the police will smell your distress —"

The Clover looked around in terror. "Are they here?"

"Not yet, so tell me quickly — what do you mean, 'plagued'?"

"The babies turn to slime in their cribs, still begging for food even as their flesh falls apart. No one may speak of it on pain of the Kindness, and now I have disobeyed —"

Flora pushed more pollen into her hands.

"You have done nothing wrong. Who forbids it?"

The Clover looked at her in terror.

"The priestesses. They are angry." She fled.

Flora went on to the Dance Hall, looking for any sanitation worker on the way. There were none to be seen and the hive was immaculate. The scent of the Queen's Love hung fresh and plentiful in the lobby, and the atmosphere was so calm that Flora wondered for a moment if the little Clover had been in her right mind.

Watching her forager comrades dancing their joyful day's adventures pushed the strange incident to the back of her thoughts. Despite the peculiar cordon of Thistle guards outside the hive, and the sight of her sanitation kin-sisters with their little bundles, a strange calm settled in Flora's brain, not at all unpleasant, but quite alien to the vivid alertness of the foraging state.

She looked around her. Her fellow foragers also seemed unusually calm, with none of their characteristic acerbity of expression. The smell of Sage was strong and constant, as if markers had been laid around the chamber, but even as Flora noticed it, she felt too tired to think of such trivia.

When it was her turn to dance, she added her steps to the vast choreography laid down in the floor, of alder catkins, and daffodils, crocus and aconites. Dancing sharpened her mind, and she focused on conveying very precise information — the exact azimuth of the sun to catch a warm air current, the roundabout to avoid where all the flowers were now smog-tainted, and last, the route to the blazing forsythia bush. At this, the bees finally roused themselves to applause.

"Bravo!" called some male voices from the back.

The sisters spun round and gasped in excitement, for a party of newly emerged drones had come to watch. Their smell was pungent and thrilling and even those older foragers who had seen males before were unprepared for the virile magnificence of these new specimens. Every sister in the Dance Hall gazed at the males, each with his massive powerful thorax, bobbing plume and dazzling armour — then they rushed to greet them.

Flora stood alone, her dance now forgotten.

"Honour to Your Malenesses! Oh, Your glorious Malenesses!" came the infatuated cries of the young sisters, and the drones laughed and let them stroke and polish them. One of them swaggered over to Flora.

"I'll take a bit of that stuff you're giving out," he said, and held out his hand. He was a brightly striped fellow, broad of thorax and blunt of face, with a high proud plume. Pastry crumbs were in his fur and Flora knew his kin was Poplar.

"Don't take all day," he drawled. "We've the Honour of the Hive to perform, we need all the sustenance we can get."

"It is late. You will not be flying today."

He stared at her in amazement, then turned to his fellows.

"Why, this old crone keeps our schedule of love, brothers!" He stuck his hand into one of Flora's panniers and groped for pollen. "And titbits for herself!" Flora gripped his arm and removed it. The young drone shook her off.

"Insolence! Send her for the Kindness!" He looked for support.

"Oh leave the old husk alone."

The drone that spoke was small, his fur twisted with propolis wax into outlandish dandified patterns. Flora smiled.

"Linden. I looked for you —"

Sir Linden straightened his ruff. "That is my kin, but I have never seen you before."

"How can you say that?"

Sir Linden turned to the young Sir Poplar. "I warned you we should not come here — it is full of addled females." He gestured at Flora. "And by the state of that one, she's not long for this world — so we shall pardon her."

The young drone glared at Flora. "She shall kneel and beg forgiveness, or I will strike her down myself."

Linden shoved him so hard he fell over, then stood above him.

"Ha! Brother, you must work on your balance if you are to seize a princess." He gave the fallen drone his hand and hauled him up. "A goblet of nectar will fix it, and I know where the best is to be had." Avoiding Flora's eyes, Sir Linden led the younger drone away. She watched them go, then felt all her sisters' eyes on her.

"Who else has heard of sickness in the Nursery?" The words came from Flora's mouth without warning, but as she spoke them she felt her anger rising. "Is that why my kin-sisters have been sacrificed yet again? There is sickness, but we may not speak of it? We must let it spread unchecked, until there is not one sanitation worker left to carry out the bodies?"

She looked to the foragers for support, but none of them would meet her eyes. Instead, all the bees began hurrying out of the Dance Hall.

"Sisters!" Flora cried. "Why do you go? Hear me!"

Alone in the great chamber, Flora felt their abandonment as keenly as a physical wound. To fly alone was one thing, but to be isolated within the hive, to be shunned and denied —

The terrible taunts of the Minerva spider ran through Flora's mind. *Madness. Sister against sister. Disaster.* Her antennae throbbed as if they would burst, and to comfort them she pressed her head into the old wax floor to breathe the smell of home. As she drew in the thousand strands of its bouquet, a new scent fled between them. Any other kin would have missed it, but Flora was a forager from Sanitation. Fast as thought she read its molecules — and knew it for what it was.

A fatal sickness lurked in the hive, sheltered in the body of a single sister.

CHAPTER
THIRTY-FIVE

Outside the Dance Hall hundreds of bees bustled across the coded mosaic of the lobby. Motionless, all her senses trained on locating it again, Flora stood in their midst searching for the odour of sickness — but it had vanished into the scent-tapestry of the hive. Using all her skills from foraging, she summoned back a trace of its elusive molecular structure.

It aped a flower, with a top note sweet like petals, but its disguise lacked definition. Foragers would not pursue it for it had no smell of food — and sanitation workers would ignore it, for its superficial sweetness held it apart from the smells of hive waste.

The sound of incoming foragers' engines broke Flora's concentration, then a group of young receivers ran past towards the landing board, kin-scents streaming in excitement. By the time their wake had cleared, so had every last atom of the scent, as if it had its own intelligence and was evading capture.

Frustrated, Flora ran up to the mid-storey of the hive. At this time of day the worker dormitories would be unused and there, in relative stillness, she could try to revive the data before its essential nature faded. To her surprise, as soon as she entered the main lobby, the scent revealed itself again. Its thin twisting core was the same, but under its superficial floral disguise, it was changing. It was beginning to copy the scent of the comb itself — and when it succeeded, it would become undetectable.

Heedless of the risk to her own safety, Flora sucked the odour into her spiracles as hard as she could. Every instinct told her this was the foulest kind of impurity, rapidly gathering strength as it adapted itself to the bouquet of the hive. Soon its faint twisting core of corruption would diffuse so completely that every sister would naturally breathe it — and her body become host to its foul purpose.

Flora concentrated all her strength on the hidden core structure. It was the merest thread of corruption, as if she flew high above some long-dead creature — but it grew stronger as she approached the dormitory. Ready to encounter some wretched sister festering in a corner, Flora burst through the doors and ran between the rows of berths searching for her — but all were empty and clean.

The trail of scent had vanished again — except for a few molecules clinging to the blank wax of a dormitory wall. Flora raised her antennae and felt all over for hidden panels and entry tiles, but the walls were plain and true, laced only with the kin-scent of honest sisters' bodies.

Flora ran back out into the lobby. She stood between Pollen & Patisserie, the Chapel of Wax, and the entrance to the Drones' Arrivals Hall, now completely repaired and smelling strongly of the new propolis carvings. Inside was the usual fuss as a new drone was helped from his emergence chamber, and she sealed her spiracles against the cloudy pheromones before they could distract her. Ahead were the big double doors of the Category Two Nursery, and a faint peculiar odour hung about them, but it was stale and not the live and wily scent she hunted.

Like the humblest sanitation worker searching for the next load to clear, Flora knelt and touched her antennae to the gutter. The voices of her sisters and the pulsing in the floor codes fell away. One faint scent remained — the sickness. If she tried to grab it with her conscious brain it slipped away, but if she breathed it in softly, she could advance on it. As if turning for home at the end of a distant forage, Flora switched all instinct to her inner compass, and began to walk.

She did not know where she went, nor did she rouse herself from the semi-trance she moved in. She was only dimly aware of her sisters' exclamations as they swerved away, or that her antennae twitched in pain as she burst through every scent-gate in her path. She walked on, closing on the foul scent that ate its way through one more beautiful.

Something struck against Flora's chest and stopped her. Six identical Sage priestesses blocked her way, each dressed in high ceremonial robes. A dark group of police stood behind them.

"What is your business?" the priestesses asked, in their choral voice.

"I — am from Sanitation. I search for the source of sickness."

304

They gazed at Flora, fast tremors running up their antennae as their minds conferred.

"So it is true." The single voice of the priestesses was full of sadness. "And we can wait no longer."

The words struck at Flora's heart, for now she recognised where she was, a place she had not seen since her eviction by Lady Burnet's jealous will. She stood at the beautiful carved doors to the Queen's chambers again — and pressing against them from within, like a demonic cloud, was the odour she tracked.

"No!" she screamed. "Not Holy Mother!"

The priestesses pulled her back. The police raised a harsh veil of their own scent before them, and smashed open the Queen's doors.

Every bee stopped on the threshold. The fertility police buzzed their alarms but did not move. The priestesses uttered one cry. Flora's antennae stood rigid as the full horror drove into her brain.

Spilled goblets and broken cakes lay scattered on the comb and Her Majesty the Queen sat amidst them, her lace mantle of wings spread all around, covering her body. Her face was as beautiful as ever but her scent had changed. Coiling through the divine fragrance of Her Love, air-worms of the malign odour grew stronger with every pulse of her heart.

Dishevelled and wide-eyed with fear, the Queen's ladies-in-waiting reached out to the fertility police. Their wings curled shrivelled on their backs like dead half-eaten things and when they tried to speak no sound came out, for their tongues had turned to slime.

"Who comes to Us so rudely?" The Queen lifted her head and scanned the chamber. "Who would disturb Us in Our labours?" As she rearranged her mantle they all saw the dead baby cradled in her arms.

"No, Mother!"

Flora wanted to run to her but the fertility police held her firm. The Queen turned her sightless eyes in her direction.

"Let my daughter come."

"Forgive us, Your Majesty, but it is you who must now come to your daughters." The priestesses knelt.

"But We are nursing Our child."

Through the foul odour, a trace of pure Devotion rose from the Queen's body, and carried on the beauty of her voice. Every bee in the chamber yearned towards it.

"Forgive me, Mother," Flora sobbed.

The Queen turned her blind head.

"Darling child," she said, "hush your tears." She beckoned to where her ladies lay, and one of them crawled towards her, her kin-scent devoured by her sickness. "Take Our new son," said the Queen, "take him back to the Nursery." As she handed over the dead baby it fell apart, and the lady-in-waiting moaned in horror.

"Come, Majesty," said the Sage priestesses, "we must go at once." They threw out a cordon of their powerful astringent scent, and the Queen rose and walked through it towards the big carved doors. Her ladies

306

began to crawl after her, but the fertility police blocked them.

"Forgive us." They twisted each one's head from her thorax. Then they turned to Flora. "Come."

Every task was halted as the Hive Mind summoned all sisters. The passageways were filled with silent bees hurrying to the Dance Hall, crystals of propolis, flakes of fresh wax or half-chewed pollen dough clinging to their fur. Marching within her escort of fertility police, Flora saw some of her own kin throw her agonised looks of fear.

As they went into the Dance Hall the bees coughed at the wall of masking scent in the centre of the floor, then fell silent at the sight of the Queen behind it. Her mantle glowed bright through the strange energy waves coiling around her, and pure threads of her divine fragrance still rose above it all. She smiled at them, and even through their fear, each bee felt her Mother's Love embrace her. Then the Hive Mind spoke:

Behold the Sacred Rule of Law.

A whole fresh leaf was carried in by more of the fertility police, and on it was a thick gold layer of forsythia pollen. By the sheen of each grain, it was clear that it had been prepared the day before, and the foragers sought each other's eyes in silent question, for none had been part of this.

Flora alone recognised it. *The Golden Leaf.* The fifth story in the Queen's Library. The flickering fear in her belly hardened into a tight knot as, from the back of the chamber, the Sage priestesses walked forward.

At their approach the Queen lifted her wings and the bees murmured in relief and awe, for at first they shone bright — but then ragged spots of darkness appeared in them as the sickness crawled upon her. As the Queen's wings began to disappear, the Sage priestesses made a crescent around her and the bees began to weep.

She raised her blind head.

"By what power am I called hither?" Her beautiful voice was unchanged. "I would know by what authority, I mean lawful."

Then the Hive Mind spoke.

THE QUEEN SICKENS.

All the priestesses knelt, and all the bees in the chamber and listening motionless throughout the hive now did the same. The Queen alone stood firm.

"But Our Love still shines —"

"Holy Mother, Sovereign of our hive, forgive us," intoned one priestess, her voice transmitting through every cell of comb, "for it is our most grave and sombre duty to announce your reign has ended."

"*Ended?*" The Queen laughed, and held her belly. "How can that be, when I hold the future of Our hive? Within me are eggs for countless generations."

"And each one tainted by the sickness you bear, which spreads affliction through our home. We have found it out: it is confirmed. Let the witness be called."

Police officers pushed Flora forward. The Queen drew in her scent.

"My reading daughter . . . Are we in my Library?"

"Forgive me, Mother," Flora sobbed. "I have betrayed you —"

308

"Ah . . ." The Queen turned her antennae towards the pollen-coated leaf. "Now I remember . . . we come to the fifth story. And I to death, for I know how it ends." Then her face shone and light glowed back into her magnificent wings. "Let all my children come to me —"

"No. It is time." The Sage spoke together.

"But I wish to bless my daughters — I am Immortal Holy Mother —"

"You were." The Sage signalled and the fertility police seized the Queen and forced her to her knees. "Your reign has ended."

Every sister felt a terrible pain inside her, yet could not look away as the police dragged the Queen's mantle from her body. She did not protest, even at the long high ripping sound of the beautiful membranes tearing. Sister Inspector stepped forward, her huge claw ready.

"Not you." The Queen's voice carried on the still air. "Let it be a noble Thistle."

All eyes in the chamber went to the priestesses. They did not move. Then Sister Sage beckoned back Sister Inspector. She pointed to a large Thistle at the front.

"You."

Stricken, the Thistle shook her head.

"I — I cannot. I cannot!"

The Queen nodded.

"Bravely now, daughter," she said. "If ever you have loved Us."

The Thistle stepped forward, and every sister's body clenched in terror at her task. The Queen stretched out her ragged wings and bent her head.

"I forgive you. Quick, belov —"

With one blow, the Thistle struck the Queen's head from her body. It rolled on the comb and lay still. Its beautiful blind eyes gazed up at the vaulted ceiling, and blood seeped from her severed thorax. The Thistle stepped back, unable to believe what she had done. Flora's belly drew so tight she could not breathe.

The silence in the Dance Hall choked the bees as the scent of the Queen's blood rose up around them. Then as one they shrieked and wailed their agony and rent their wings.

What have we done? sobbed the Hive Mind. *We have murdered Mother! What have we done!*

They rushed to the Queen's body and beat their antennae on the comb in their anguish, and many tore their own fur out in clumps. Alarm glands flooded across the thundering comb, the air throbbed with the Queen's Love and the scent of her blood, and every priestess was surrounded by a wall of convulsing bees.

Flora too ran through the crowd screaming her agony, for each bee had watched the act without resistance, and each of them felt guilty. Only the Thistle executioner stood rigid in shock — and the fertility police, standing behind the patient priestesses.

Gradually the comb stopped drumming, and the Hive Mind sank dazed and exhausted back into the bodies of the bees. Flora raised her antennae. The odour of sickness was gone. Other bees began to know it too, standing to scent the changed air. It was clean, and filled with kinscent of the Sage. A priestess stepped forward.

310

"Our hive is freed from sickness. And as the Queen's body failed, the holy power of fertility passed to the Melissae, her priestesses. All assembled, hear now in public that we exercise our Divine Right to raise a princess from pure Sage stock — for we are the kin of queens. In three days' time, a new Queen shall rise, and usher in a new golden age of summer and of plenty."

The comb began to tremble and the Hive Mind spoke.

BY TRADITION, BY KIN, BY DIVINE RIGHT: ONLY THE SAGE MAY RULE.

Faces shining, open wings radiant with light, the Sage priestesses looked out over the crowd. The Hive Mind repeated the words, so that no bee held any other thought.

BY DIVINE RIGHT, ONLY THE SAGE MAY RULE!

"Merciful sisters!" The Thistle executioner's loud cry broke the spell. The bees turned to see her on her knees in the Queen's blood. "Kill me," she begged. "I cannot live with my sin — I must die!" She held up her blood-wet hands.

"Behold," called out Sister Sage. "Behold the suffering of our noble sister Thistle. Blessed be the sister who takes away Our sin." She signalled, and Sister Inspector stepped up behind the Thistle, then twisted her head round so that the crack echoed in the air of the Dance Hall.

"And so are we absolved." Sister Sage raised her wings, and six Sage priestesses walked forward with the pollen-coated leaf and laid it down beside the dead queen.

"A queen cannot rise in three days!" cried out another voice. "How long have you planned this?" It was a Teasel, standing in the centre of a group of her kin.

Every priestess turned her antennae on the group — but the Teasel kept theirs high in defiance. A bright channel of air crackled between them.

"Our Sisters Teasel, of the Nursery." Sister Sage nodded slowly. "It is right and proper you should ask, for matters of hive health and security have ever been our kin's gravest concern. Long have we dreaded this dark day." She raised her wings higher and addressed the furthest reaches of the Dance Hall. "The Teasel say we have prepared, and they are right. A queenless hive is a prize for the Myriad, and to raise a princess is the state secret and holy burden we have borne in silence, until now." Sister Sage raised her wings proudly.

"Know you, all sisters gathered here, that we the Melissae, keepers of the Holy Law, protect you with our foresight, for to save our hive from queenless peril, we have made ready a princess for this moment." Then the priestess bowed low to the group of Teasel. "We thank our sisters Teasel for acknowledging our sacred responsibility. We ask no more of them."

Then the comb trembled and the Hive Mind spoke again.

In three days' time a new queen will rise.
ACCEPT, OBEY AND SERVE.

With solemn ceremony, the six priestesses lifted the Queen's head then her body onto the bier. The Holy Chord rose from the wax comb up into the bees' bodies, and the sisters wept again as the pall-bearers carried their royal burden through. Some sisters rushed behind them out of the Dance Hall, while others staggered, and yet more stood paralysed with the horror, their eyes fixed where the Queen had fallen. All the Thistle remained, beating their antennae on the comb in shame. The Teasel watched it all, then left together.

Flora stood gasping for breath, antennae pulsing from the horror she had witnessed and the Minerva spider's words echoing in her mind.

Unimaginable horrors . . .

If she had died in the cage of glass, she would not have traced the sickness to the Queen, who would still be alive. But then — the sickness would have spread to every sister. The pain in Flora's belly twisted harder, but even as she sank to her knees and wept, a part of her mind took her back to the Queen's Library, where there was still one more panel to be told.

CHAPTER
THIRTY-SIX

By the next morning many bees had not the heart to rise from their berths, while others had lost their minds, and ran in circles buzzing and babbling or beating their antennae against the comb until they broke. The fertility police took all of them away. The rest, almost nine thousand motherless daughters, wandered desolately through the hive, unable to settle to anything, for without the Queen's Love no task had meaning.

Pollen dough dried on patisserie tables, chalices of nectar stood unfanned, Sisters in the Chapel of Wax could not pray, and in the Nursery, the nannies could not comfort those ceaselessly crying infants who had survived the purge of foulbrood.

Most frightening of all was the plight of the foragers. Again and again they went to the landing board, but despite the good weather not one could start her engine, for that required joy and courage.

"Tomorrow," they said to each other. "Tomorrow, in good heart," for to fly in sadness was to make mistakes and die — and the hive could spare no more losses.

At midday the canteens were closed, and at each a Sage priestess stood with a police guard.

314

"Two days of fasting," the holy sisters told the bees, "in purification before our princess comes." And they smiled, and let their Sage kin-scent rise strong. *"Accept, Obey and Serve."*

"Accept, Obey and Serve," responded the bees, breathing in its new opiate element. The smell of the Sage was calming and dulled their fear, and as they walked away from the canteens, they told each other a fast was good, and would cleanse them. It also weakened them, so to conserve their energy for flight, most foragers sought solace in sleep.

Flora was lying in her berth at the back of the sanitation workers' section when she heard a dim murmur of voices, and smelled the kin of Teasel. A group of them had gathered, concealed behind the strong scent of the sanitation workers. Flora lay back again. She did not care what they were doing there, nor had she the slightest intention of reporting them to Sister Sage, as she had once promised to do should she see them in conclave. All she could think about was the Queen's Library, and what came next after *The Golden Leaf*.

There was a sixth story . . . she had walked right up to it and then . . . but the more Flora concentrated, the more tired she felt, until all she could hear were the murmurs of the Teasel, whispering like wind in the trees.

Morning brought sharp cold air and a rime of frost on the landing board. The hungry house-bees hurried into the lobbies to start fanning their wings for warmth, but their strength was low from fasting and the temperature did not change. Foragers ran to the landing board and shivered as they looked out at a low white sky. Yesterday it had been warm and blue, and they had wasted it.

"But we have Clustered!" someone cried. "Winter is over!"

"Tell the sky," said another. "Tell the new buds, who surely die."

Flora looked out. *Winter comes twice.* Her hands went to her belly, and in immediate answer, the pulse of life beat hard against them. She gasped in joy. *One. More. Egg.*

"Excuse me, sister." A Daisy forager unlatched her wings and stepped out around Flora and onto the board. "Enough talk of death!" She forced a smile. "Tomorrow comes the new queen — so today I will fetch nectar, to welcome her."

"And I," many foragers shouted. They set their engines high and took off over the apple trees, but within a few seconds the cold seized their engines and they lost altitude. On the landing board the bees watched their little dark shapes whirl helplessly in the freezing wind. Flecks of snow blew into the hive, and the Thistle guards closed the landing board.

Energised by joy and fear, Flora ran back inside. Her grief and apathy had gone and she needed to move her body. If it were not possible to fly, then she would work with her kin-sisters, sheltered by their warmth and kindness — and their very strong scent.

"It will not last," said the Sage priestesses in cheerful voices as they went about the hive swinging their censers filled with a strange fragrance. "By the time the new queen arrives, the sun herself will come to greet her."

"Tomorrow," was all the bees dared whisper to each other, breathing in the new scent. Scrubbing the mid-lobby floor with her kin-sisters, this new smell made Flora feel sick. Glazed with a top note of honey and bound by the complex scent-structure of the Melissae, it referenced every kin except flora, and its message was simple and clear: *Strength in Sage*. Some of the bees even murmured it without knowing, and as they passed, the priestesses smiled.

The scent forced its way into Flora's spiracles, and then her bloodstream. It made her head hurt, and sent shooting pains through her belly. Nauseous, she excused herself and ran down to the bottom storey, intending to flush her body with cold fresh air near the landing board.

She got as far as the lobby outside the Dance Hall before the egg within her began to pulse. Sage priestesses were within, and Flora hurried away. Footsteps and voices came from all sides and now she did not know where to go. This egg had grown so quickly and given no warning — and now with frightening force it pushed at her body, telling her it was coming. She could smell the cold rain falling outside on the landing board and she longed to breathe more fresh air, but she had not a second to lose for her body was opening to lay.

She could not go up to the busy mid-storey, nor into the Dance Hall, so in desperation Flora ran down the dark corridor that smelled of propolis disinfectant. It was marked out of bounds since the Cluster because it was where the dead mouse lay embalmed, but the swelling egg left no time for choice. Covered in the scent of propolis, Flora dropped to the raw wax floor as the egg pressed her body apart. It came so fast and the pain was so startling that she could not even cry out — and then it was done. Gasping, Flora turned around.

Like her two other eggs before, this third one had a pearly skin, and in its depths held a tiny point of light. Unlike them, it did not lie on its side, but balanced on its narrower tip, as if supported by some invisible force. It was also very large. Flora moved her body to block it from the corridor entrance, then feathered its skin in wonder. She could feel its radiant life force warming her as she touched it.

Madness and disaster.

Flora raised her claw over her egg, as if the Minerva spider scuttled in the darkness — but all was still. Above her loomed the vast propolis tomb of the mouse, and the only thing that moved was a cold curl of air, coming from behind it. Flora raised her antennae. The hive creaked in the wind, and the air moved with it.

She knew what had happened — in their Cluster-dulled state, the defending bees had completely sealed the mouse to the hive floor — but when it was done they forgot the gap it had gnawed in the hive wall. Flora listened for footsteps. If the fertility police were

318

coming, she would fight them to the death to protect this egg.

There was no sound, and she put her claw down. She breathed deeply, realising the thick propolis veils would cover the scent of an egg even better than that of her own kin-sisters.

Flora flushed cold fresh air through her spiracles to rid herself of the controlling scent of Sage. Her brain cleared. It was cold in here, and her egg needed protection. In one more day the new queen would come, and start laying. Surely in all the excitement there would be opportunity to smuggle one new egg into the Nursery. Until then, she must protect it.

Flora bent herself forward to examine her wax mirrors. She stared at her dry abdominal bands, harder and older since she had last looked. There was no trace of those soft sliding glands that would give her wax, and she knew that since the Queen's death, her prayers were as dry as her belly was now. She concentrated — but there was not one single synapse of response. The strong smell of propolis made it hard to think what she should do. *Propolis.*

Flora looked at the sarcophagus of the mouse, hurriedly built with lumps and crags sticking out of it. It was not wax but, made from the blood of a thousand trees, it had its own ancient purity. A sister with the strength and endurance to work it could mould it as she chose.

It was night before Flora had finished her task. The hive was silent, and her jaws ached from chewing, but the amber walls of the crib glowed with the spark of life within. Flora's tongue was numb from prolonged contact with propolis, and no pulse of Flow lit her cheeks. Her time in the Nursery was distant and she struggled to remember how many days before an egg hatched. *Three sun bells chimed —*

Three days — Flora was sure of it. And then the pearly skin would moult to reveal her baby, beautiful and hungry for Flow. She cleaned the crumbs of propolis off her fur in preparation for returning to her dormitory. The new queen was coming tomorrow, the anxious fast would be over. In the time of celebrations she would let herself feed and love her baby, then she would smuggle him into the Nursery — and this time, put him in the right section. She would make no more mistakes.

Not until she was lying safe and quiet in her dormitory berth, surrounded by the reassuring kin-scent of her sleeping sisters, did Flora become aware that her heartbeat had an echo, as if a tiny second heart pumped inside it. She hugged herself in silent joy, for even though she was one floor above, and on the other side of the hive, she knew that it was her connection to her living egg, growing stronger with every pulse of her blood.

CHAPTER
THIRTY-SEVEN

On the morning of the third day, the bees sprang from their beds and rushed to make all ready for the coming of the new Queen. Foragers ran to the landing board to check the weather, and kept their spirits high despite the Thistle still blocking their exit, for the rain fell thick and cold. No Sage priestess appeared to announce the period of fasting over, nor did the Hive Mind speak, but the hungry bees milled around outside the canteens waiting for some signal, some smell of the upcoming feast.

There was none. By afternoon, every sister's belly was clutching at itself, and even the most devout had no more energy for pacing in prayer. They were ready to welcome the new princess, they were ready to eat, they were ready to cheer to the skies for the return of order and security.

It was almost evening before the Sage appeared, and then en masse in every lobby and canteen. They all wore mantles, the style of dress favoured by the Queen and her ladies. The Sage were decorated — the day had come at last! Whirring in joyous excitement, the sisters rushed to be close to their priestesses — but at their sombre expressions, they fell silent.

"Due to the inclement weather" — the Sage used their choral voice — "the arrival of the new Queen has been delayed. The period of fasting is over, but the Interregnum is extended."

The bees burst out with questions but the Sage held up their mantles.

"There will be no questions. *Accept, Obey and Serve.*"

There was the briefest pause before the bees responded.

"*Accept, Obey and Serve.*" They watched the priestesses go, a cordon of police around them.

As soon as they were out of sight, a ravenous hunger seized the bees. They ran into the canteens and pulled whatever rations they could from the stores. With some difficulty, they forced themselves to pass and share. Nobody wanted to be the first to speak. Flora ate what she could, but she knew it was not enough. She felt her cheeks. If the princess was late, then her egg would hatch and need feeding before the Nursery was fully operational again. Her baby would need Flow — and if there were no nurses it would die.

Starvation. Someone had said the word in the canteen, and the long-repressed fear burst in the air above all the bees. Before they knew it, every sister was asking about food or speculating on its lack or demanding to know from the foragers when the weather would lift and they could start working again, for the fasting had sharpened their appetite for Devotion — but the Queen did not come! *She did not come, and they had been promised!*

Their voices became a din, with some sisters shouting for silence, others for answers, and arguments broke out over a crust of pollen bread. Flora's brain jammed with her panic for her child, and she felt a scream building in her chest.

"Sisters! Hear yourselves!" It was the booming voice of a Thistle guard. She stood up and banged her plate down amidst the squabbling bees. "Take mine! Would you be like the wasps?"

Every other Thistle in the room put her own plate down for others, and the noble gesture silenced the bees.

"We will wait," said the first Thistle. "The Queen will come."

"The Queen will come," repeated the bees. The words gave them strength. "The Queen will come!"

By the next morning, there was still no sign of the Sage, but the skies had cleared and the air was warm again. Bees gathered to applaud and shout Queenspeed to the foragers as they ran for the board, for the sisters longed for order and security. If they could not have it in the form of Devotion to and from a new queen, then the next best thing would be to refill the Treasury and make the canteen tables groan with food.

The drones had no such patience. The new queen was late, and they did not care if the sisters ate little — they wanted more. Working themselves up to a high hormonal display of temper and resentment, they joined together and marched up to the Treasury to protest to the Sage priestesses gathered there. Frightened and fascinated, sisters rushed after them to witness it.

When the Sage priestesses simply listened, the drones grew angrier.

"You hear our complaints, and do nothing?"

Sister Sage inclined her head politely. "We have more pressing matters."

The drones looked at each other in astonishment.

"Than *our* comfort?"

"Brothers, if they think so little of us —"

"We shall find a better home!"

With that, and despite the wailing protests of the sisters, the drones stormed down to the landing board in a rage, and took to the air.

Returning with a scant crop of viburnum nectar, Flora passed them in the air and felt their turbulence. Sisters wept on the landing board, crying for the males to come back, but Flora pushed past them to give her load to a waiting receiver. All she wanted to do was quickly pass on the directions in the Dance Hall, then find a way to get to her egg without being seen.

She ran into the atrium and stopped. Foragers were standing waiting, but there was no atmosphere of joy or anticipation, and though many dutifully followed her steps, she knew it was without enthusiasm. Flora wanted to rouse them — but all her energy was focused on going to her child, and she left with a guilty heart.

Outside in the lobby she paused. Since she had danced it had become crowded with many sisters, but instead of passing through on their business, they stood talking in little clusters of kin groups. Most numerous were the Teasel. Some huddled together, but others moved around the gathered sisters, murmuring earnestly.

No bees loitered near the entrance to the prohibited corridor, for the propolis disinfectant smell was overpowering, but as the lobby kept filling up, more and more sisters collected near it. Every defensive urge sparked within Flora — she wanted to run down the corridor and protect her vulnerable egg — but to go now was to invite discovery. She forced herself to remain where she was. The tiny second heartbeat within her own had grown stronger.

Flora's cheeks prickled, then a faint sweetness filled her mouth. She swallowed quickly, her heart thudding. *Flow.* It could only be the sign that her egg was hatching — at any moment her baby would emerge, and cry for food.

She looked around in desperation. The only way she could reach her baby was to ask the noble kins of Violet and Speedwell to move aside — a breach of hive etiquette guaranteed to focus attention on her. If she could only see her own kin-sisters there, she could join them — but mindful of the general distaste for their presence, all the sanitation workers had withdrawn.

Flora swallowed down a mouthful of Flow. If she saw anyone going down towards her egg, she knew she would run and fight to protect it — but until then, the best thing she could do was pass unnoticed, and move when the crowd dispersed.

"The Queen will come," intoned a Thistle's voice from the centre of a sombre-faced group of her own kin. "The Queen will come," her sisters repeated, but their tone lacked conviction.

"But not from the Sage!" a young Teasel shouted from the centre of her own group.

All the bees in the lobby turned to stare at this reckless sister with the brindled fur.

"Because they are sick," she continued, her eyes wild. "Why else have they not produced their princess?" She looked around the lobby. "If even Holy Mother could sicken, then why not her priestesses?"

Before she could say another word, a group of police burst the gathered Teasel kin apart and dragged her out. One of them beat her hard against the side of her head, another kicked her legs out from under her.

"Blasphemy!" said one of the officers.

"The Kindness is too good —" said another, raising her hooked gauntlet.

The brindled Teasel tried to claw her way up through their bodies. "Sisters!" she screamed from under the heavy blows. "This is what happens when you speak the truth —"

The bees heard her shell cracking.

"Stop at once!" The group of Thistle guards rushed to pull off the fertility police. "What is the meaning of this outrage, *Officer*?" The most senior Thistle guard used her claw to hold Sister Inspector between her head and her thorax. "This lobby is a place of gathering and talk — what laws do you enforce here?" She released Sister Inspector, who stared at her with hate.

"The Law of Treason!" She spat the word at the Thistle, and her officers held their claws ready, pointed at the group of Teasel. The young Teasel on the ground stood up, and all the bees could see she was wounded, but she turned to face her attackers again.

"Without our Queen," she said loudly, "how can there be treason?"

The truth of this silenced every bee. Then Sister Inspector hissed in rage, "Treason against the Sage!"

"The Sage are a kin like any other," cried the young Teasel, her hand to her wounded thorax, "but they think they are all queens —"

The bees gasped to hear this and Sister Inspector raised her claw. Before she could strike the Teasel again, the large Thistle guard stepped between them.

"What dark days are these?"

"Indeed, when the kin of Thistle seeks to advance itself!" Sister Inspector's voice was harsh and ugly. "But all the hive knows who killed the Queen."

The Thistle guard bowed her head.

"To our eternal sorrow." Then she looked at Sister Inspector and raised her own antennae thick and strong. "All sisters may gather here and speak freely. Remove yourselves."

Remove yourselves. The thrilling words rippled through the bees like the Hive Mind, but the comb had not spoken — only one brave Thistle guard. The sisters gathered behind her, a silent show of strength.

Sister Inspector looked murderous — then called off her officers and left. The bees began to applaud, but the Thistle guard who had spoken so bravely rounded on all of them. She pointed to the group of Teasel.

"The Queen will come! And until then, do not provoke the police."

"No, Sister. Thank you." Many of the Teasel bowed to the Thistle guard, but she was not looking. Her antennae were turned to the corridor to the landing board. Flora smelled it at the same time.

A wasp approached.

Every bee in the lobby flexed their dagger and ran towards the landing board, the Thistle at the vanguard. Flora and other foragers squeezed themselves to the front and joined the line of Thistle guards scanning the orchard.

There, at the perimeter of the hive scent markers, one lone wasp cruised. She was long and gleaming, and her legs were bright yellow. At the sight of the bees on the board she came closer, and they saw the two white dots painted above each eye. She hovered above the hive — then with a flash of her stripes she was gone.

Sisters cheered, and congratulated each other in high tense voices. Their show of strength had driven her off; how dare a wasp come prowling in the orchard? They had shown her; look, even the sisters Teasel from the Nursery came to fight!

The foragers did not join in, nor the Thistle, still scanning the air. The wasp was of a kind none had seen before, and they did not like it.

More sisters came pouring down to the Dance Hall lobby, for news of the stand-off between the Thistle and the police had spread through the hive, and they wanted to talk about the mad and reckless Teasel, and the way everyone had driven off the wasp.

In the mass of gossip and grooming and anxious talk, Flora slipped away.

328

CHAPTER
THIRTY-EIGHT

The tomb of the mouse loomed over Flora, reminding her how far she was from the sanctity of the Category One Nursery — but never in her life had she seen a more beautiful baby. He had hatched perfectly, he was pure pearl, big and firm and glowing with a soft light — and even through the smell of the propolis, the sweetness of his breath made Flora catch hers.

She settled herself to feed her child in her arms and he nestled so sweetly against her that when he opened his little mouth, her cheeks tingled as the Flow rose from its secret source, and soothed her like Devotion. The child ate until he was sated, then curled in his mother's arms and slept. A missing worker was only ever presumed dead and never sought out, so Flora made herself comfortable, and gave herself the luxury of falling asleep holding her child.

By morning he had grown to fill her arms and was hungry again. The sounds in the Dance Hall lobby beyond told Flora the hive was long awake, and she felt her own body light with hunger. Until she ate, there would be no more Flow to feed him. Flora settled her baby as well as she could, soothing him with soft loving words and a covering of her own scent. He closed his eyes, and she gazed down at him, her heart bursting with love. Then she slipped out of the corridor and went in search of food.

With her first few steps on the lobby comb, she knew something was wrong. The tiled floor codes, normally so fluent and reassuring in their familiar messages, stuttered and jerked underfoot so that every bee walking them winced at the gibberish going into their brains. Flora hurried across to the big central mosaic, where many foragers were gathered — and, unusually for their kind, talking most animatedly.

The problem came from the Dance Hall itself, they told each other — the comb interrupted all their steps, it threw the phrases back in jumbled order — no one could dance and pass on knowledge — how could they forage effectively if they could not communicate? Every forager stopped talking as a group of Sage priestesses emerged from within the Dance Hall, and walked towards them.

Flora clenched her antennae shut, a split second too late. One of the priestesses looked at her.

"We are glad that some sisters at least are happy. Can you share the source?"

Flora pushed her kin-scent out of her spiracles as strongly as she could, praying she did not smell of Flow.

"I humbly beg I might lead a cleaning party." She made her tongue thick and ungainly in her mouth. "Were we to clean the floor again . . ."

"Yes." Another priestess spoke. "That must be the cause — there must still be traces. Purge the hall one more time."

Flora bobbed her head like the humblest sanitation worker, and the priestesses swept away. The foragers watched them go, then turned back to the Dance Hall. The doors stood wide open, but it was completely empty. In the centre, a dark patch still showed on the old wax floor.

"She is right." An Ivy forager spoke. "Always I smell the bl —"

"Do not!" Another forager, Madam Coltsfoot, turned away. "I wish only to forget." She looked at Flora. "So you *willingly* choose to be a house-bee again?"

Her words stung, but Flora kept her eyes on the corridor to her child. She nodded. Madam Coltsfoot shook her head in disbelief. "Then let me tell you this: I will never dance in there again, unless it is clean."

"I will do my best." Flora watched them go down the corridor to the landing board. At the sound of their engines rising up into the sky, she felt a huge pull in her own body, and her wings longed to spread above the currents. But even as she felt it, that faint pulse within her own thrummed harder, and she knew her child hungered.

She ran to the nearest canteen — and found it crowded with arguing sisters, for the malfunctioning floor codes had told several different shifts to arrive together. The food was scanty pollen bread of poor quality, but Flora fell upon it and it was gone in seconds. She heard someone talking to her — and turned to see an old sister from Teasel clinging to a table, food in her fur and antennae disordered.

"Manners are wasted on your kin." The old Teasel shook her head. "You were the one in the Nursery, weren't you? Still alive . . ." She pushed her plate of crusts at Flora. "Greedy thing, take mine. I know I die today."

"Thank you." Flora ate them, too hungry for pride. She felt her raging body calm, and knew her Flow would come again. "Thank you, Sister."

The old Teasel surveyed the canteen. "Category One is ruined now." She plucked at the table. "Look at this crib, the wax is filthy! We can't expect Her Majesty to lay in this, can we?" She waved an arm at the bees around them. "And all these foreigners, how am I supposed to train them?"

"Sister, this is the canteen, and they all are from our own hive —"

"Foreigners!" shouted the Teasel, her breath starting to rattle in her thorax. "Go away! Where are my lovely nurses?"

Flora settled the old sister's disordered antennae and leaned close.

"Right here, Sister," she said. "But I have forgotten where to take the babies for Holy Time."

The old Teasel gripped her arm. "All that matters is it must be clean."

"Yes, Sister, but *where*?"

The Teasel bent her head close, and stopped. Flora waited for her to continue, but the old sister did not move again. Flora finished every morsel of food on both their plates, then lifted the Teasel into her mouth and took her down to the morgue. Then she went to the

Dance Hall to start cleaning up the Queen's blood. To her surprise, she found her kin-sisters scrubbing at the last of it, without any supervising sister.

"Who told you to come? The comb?"

The sanitation workers looked around, as if to make sure no one could hear.

"You did," said one of them. "Did you not mean it? We heard you tell the priestesses you would clean the floor."

"But how — I did not see you."

"Madam — you signalled. We read your wishes in scent."

Only now did Flora notice how minutely their antennae quivered. Just like the Sage, they preferred chemicals to words. As they smiled at her, a commotion in the lobby took all their attention.

A group of Teasel carried the broken body of one of their own aloft, and stopped on the central mosaic.

"Left for dead in a corridor!" yelled one of them. No bee had ever heard such war-like tones from that kin. "A warning to us!" shouted another. "Murdered by the police, for speaking out!" The Teasel sisters looked around at the shocked bees. "That will be *your* body, sisters, if you dare to ask where their princess is!" They laid the broken Teasel down, and all who could see shuddered at the sight of the young brindled Teasel who had addressed them all the day before. Her lower jaw had been ripped from her head, her tongue with it.

"No Devotion," shouted another Teasel. "No answers — we want the truth!"

"The truth?" Sister Sage stood in their midst, radiant and serene. She looked down at the dead Teasel and shook her head. "You lack the stomach for it."

"Tell us!" The Teasel sisters were raw with grief. "What truth keeps you in power, yet you cannot give us a queen?"

"Divine Right." Sister Sage was calm, and as other priestesses entered the lobby, their strong opiate scent began to rise. As Flora closed her spiracles, she sensed the other sanitation workers do the same.

"The right to murder?" A mature Teasel in her prime shouted it out. "Is that what you mean? The Sage are corrupt and wicked!"

"Dear Sister Teasel." Sister Sage held out her hands and walked across the lobby to her. "Uncertainty is very troubling to weaker kin, the Melissae do understand that."

"And the Teasel understand the Sage cling to power at any cost!" Sister Teasel kept her voice strong, but her body hunched in fear at the approach of the priestess.

Sister Sage stopped, her hands still outstretched.

"Touch me, Sister Teasel. Divinity flows through me. Feel for yourself, before you further wound our hive by voicing such cruel doubts. Open your mind, and make your own decision."

Sister Teasel stared at the other priestesses around the lobby.

"It is a trick. You will join together and hurt me."

"Any harm that comes to you can only be from your own soul."

334

"Then I am not afraid." Yet Sister Teasel hesitated to clasp Sister Sage's hands. "Our kin are loyal servants of the hive, and we deserve respect!"

"Then keep no secrets." Sister Sage stepped forward and gripped her hands. Sister Teasel started, then stood rigid and still. All the bees stared at the joined pair, but only the closest could see the shuddering at the base of Sister Teasel's antennae. All the Teasel gasped as her legs collapsed and her body sagged. Then the priestess turned Sister Teasel's lifeless body to face them. Her eyes were covered with a white film, and the base of both antennae was cracked and seeping.

"Spiritual pollution destroys the bearer." Sister Sage let Sister Teasel's body fall to the ground, beside her dead kin-sister, then she wiped her hands.

Madness. Sister against sister. Disaster.

As if Flora had spoken aloud, Sister Sage turned to focus on her part of the crowd, her powerful antennae scanning. Flora felt the burning sensation in her own antennae, but stood motionless. Then the priestess returned her attention to the silent assembly.

"The wicked secret that just killed Sister Teasel is that her kin raise their own princess in secret, and now think of themselves as royalty."

"We have as much right as you!" shouted another Teasel. "Your kin sicken so that you cannot make a healthy princess, but we are the kin of the Nursery and we know how to do it! There *is* no Divine Right; food means destiny! That is the truth and you know it: every girl child is born a worker but it is how we *feed* her that makes her Queen!"

At this, the bees broke into uproar. Something ignited in Flora's brain. The Nursery rotas. That was why no one must see them, or learn to count. That was why the Sage had tried to destroy her brain when she left — in case she knew. Deep tremors began racking through the comb below their feet.

SILENCE! came the voice of the Hive Mind. At the mouths of the corridors joining the lobby, dark clusters of police had gathered.

"NO!" shouted back the Teasel. "Three days for a worker, four for a drone!"

Sister Sage signalled, and the police began pushing through the crowd towards the Teasel. Bees scattered in terror as she tried to take cover behind them.

"And five days makes a Queen — Flow is the secret!" she screamed as the police surrounded her. "Any female could —" The police unleashed their rage on her body and the smell of her blood filled the air. An officer held up a wet red mass on her claw.

"The traitor made more eggs." She ate them. "And was rich in Flow."

Before the bees could scream, the priestesses drove their scent hard through the crowd, so that their brains were seized and the sound of terror died within them. The comb jerked beneath their feet.

Our M-Mother — came the voice of the Hive Mind.

Who art — Our Mother — from Death comes — Our Mother —

At the stuttering of the Queen's Prayer, the bees began to moan in fear. The comb hummed higher and higher until a terrible frequency went through the bees' brains — then abruptly ceased. The air felt sucked dead.

Sister Sage held up her hand. "Hush." She smiled at the bees. "Do not be afraid; the Hive Mind tires of conflict and must rest." She turned to the chief Thistle guard. "Brave Sister Guards, surely you see the damage of discord? Stand not in martial judgement, but join your strength with our own officers, for the greater good."

"How?" The Thistle's face gave nothing away.

"Search the hive for queen cells. Those not guarded by our trusted police or a priestess, destroy. Leave nothing inside them alive."

"We have never seen queen cells, Sister. How will we know them?"

Sister Sage permitted herself a grim smile.

"They will be unlike any you have ever seen. *Leave nothing inside them alive.* That is all you need to know."

Sickened, the Thistle nodded. The Sage withdrew, their scent-lock slowly releasing the bees' bodies. Confused and panicking sisters collided as they tried to pick up instructions from the floor codes, but the comb transmitted no information. Only the sanitation workers remained calm and industrious. Flora looked around — the Thistle guards were already conferring with the fertility police, standing in groups at the head of each corridor to the lobby, so that every bee must pass between them to leave. Her mouth filled with the sweetness of Flow and spilled out onto her fur. She swallowed, but more came and it would be impossible to hide. Any moment someone would smell it and kill her — and then her baby would die.

She would not let that happen. As yet no Thistle guards had returned to the landing board, and no police stood at the entrance corridor. Foragers were only just moving across the lobby to return to the air, and Flora ran to join them, pushing past to get out before anyone could challenge her scent. Unless she went now, she would never be able to get to her baby in time.

The sun shone on the board and the skies were clear. Flora did not wait to lay a marker signal, but roared her engine as hard and loud as she could to signal she was going a great distance, then made an almost vertical take-off. She rose up high above the hive and orchard and then circled round behind it and dropped down onto its sloping roof.

Keeping her scent glands tight to avoid any sisters on the wing from smelling her, Flora began walking down the side of the hive. Every insect that crawled there had left a trace, as well as the bird droppings that seared her brain, and the film of dirt deposited by the wind — but there at the bottom was the ragged black gap. Even after the winter, the gnawed edges held the rank scent of the mouse, but beyond it came one much sweeter. Flora crawled inside.

High above the orchard, a wasp watched with interest.

CHAPTER
THIRTY-NINE

The mouse's embalmed body almost blocked the space, but there was a gap between its jagged propolis tomb and the wooden wall of the hive. As Flora squeezed through, her baby squealed in excitement at her smell and wriggled towards her. He had grown since she had left him and was ravenous again. Flora lifted him into her arms and he opened his mouth. Her cheeks pulsed in relief as the shining Flow poured out.

Her baby drank and drank, until his whole body glowed. She kissed him and cleaned his face, then held him up to the propolis wall of his crib, so that the ancient tree sap glowed amber and bronze with his light.

"One would almost say you loved the maggot." Sister Sage crouched on top of the sarcophagus. She had seen it all.

Flora clutched her baby to her and raised a claw.

"Extraordinary that you should still be able to make Flow." Sister Sage climbed halfway down the side of the mouse's tomb, the better to watch. "Bold and resourceful beyond our wildest imaginings, Flora 717." The priestess raised her antennae and pulsed her kin-scent. "Tell me, how many times have you laid?"

Flora's heart slammed in her body and her sting slid ready for use, but her child nestled against her and she spoke calmly for his sake. "This is the third," she answered. "It came upon my body without my will."

"You know there is no mercy for you." Sister Sage smiled. "But one must admire your brazen spirit — to stand there in the lobby, reeking of Flow, while a Teasel was torn apart for the same crime? Strong nerves, 717. The only reason I let you go was to find your foul issue myself. One of the Thistle guards had reported the smell of freshly worked propolis near the board, and I did wonder why — but I must say I did not expect to find a crib! That is indeed a marvel — and as we speak the police are on their way to admire it."

Flora looked towards the mouse hole.

"Flee if you wish," said Sister Sage. "Death is certain either way."

"I will not." Flora held her baby close one last time. "But I beg you, Sister, now the males have deserted us, let him go to the Nursery. I will recant before the whole hive, you may tear me wing from limb, devise any death — but let him live."

"*Him?*" Sister Sage dropped to the comb floor. "Do you try to fool a priestess? Your evil spawn is female."

"*Female?*" Flora looked into her child's little face. "A daughter?"

"A monster." Sister Sage raised her antennae. "And your crime is the death sentence for every one of your kin. Bring the foul thing into the passageway — it is impossible to signal through its stench." She flicked her antennae again and again. "A wasp or ant has more

340

honour than you — after your first crime, why did you not offer yourself for death?"

"When I was with Holy Mother in her chamber, she gave me her love. And then when I laid — I felt it for my own eggs. And I changed."

"*Changed*, 717? From an ugly monstrous deviant that should have been killed on emergence? What, pray, do you think you changed into?"

"A loving mother."

Sister Sage burst out laughing.

"No, Sister, I promise you — it is the most wonderful thing and stronger even than Devotion!"

"Can that really be true?" Sister Sage studied Flora. "It is the highest sacrament, more precious than any wealth we can make — yet *you* claim to feel it?"

Flora held her child close, and nodded.

"So when you look at your — child — do you feel it now?"

Flora gazed down into her baby girl's face, and the air shimmered with her joy. Too late she realised what was happening. Her antennae were wide open and in an instant Sister Sage had driven her own force deep into Flora's mind.

"So you thought yourself Queen," she hissed. "The spiders warned you — oh yes, I know all about that. Do you think they would keep your secret? How many lives did it cost me to find *that* out, but I did —"

Flora tried to move, but the priestess drove her own will deeper, paralysing her. Flora's baby began to wail, and she felt her being pulled from her helpless arms.

"*Love?*" Sister Sage had the little girl in her claws, and held her up in front of her mother's face. "That is what the flowers are for — foragers may lust to their heart and body's content for them — but the sacrament of birth is beyond you!" Flora's baby screamed and writhed in her grip and she struck it across its face.

No lock or bonds could hold back Flora's rage. She tore her child from the priestess's grasp and before Sister Sage could utter another word, with a mighty blow she knocked her off her feet. The priestess twisted her long abdomen up in all directions, stabbing at Flora so that the air filled with a cloud of venom — but Flora had fought a wasp. She tore off the priestess's pounding antennae then she slid her dagger between the glossy bands, waiting until she felt the pulse of Sister Sage's beating heart. Only then did she pump her venom, strong and steady, until the priestess lay still.

Flora's baby lay crying against her crib, trying to find a way to escape the terrifying odours. Flora held her close and wrapped her in her kin-scent, rocking her until she stopped her sobs, all the while listening for the pounding feet of the police. Her antennae were in agony from the priestess's lock, and the air was thick with Sage blood, strong enough to permeate the smell of propolis, and give them away. She had to get rid of the body — but it was already stiff and swollen from the poison of Flora's sting, too big to drag down the narrow space to the mouse hole.

Flora gripped the head of the priestess in her own powerful jaws and, with a swift flicking motion, broke it from her thorax. Then she lifted her daughter off the

342

venom-slicked floor and placed her back in the crib. The little girl watched her mother's work in silence.

Revolted by what she had to do and glad of her thick powerful tongue, Flora seized the joined thorax and abdomen of Sister Sage and dragged it through its own spilled venom, so that it soaked into the fur. Then she pulled it out of the mouse hole and tossed it into the long grass.

Getting rid of the head was harder. Though the antennae were gone, the dead lenses of Sister Sage's eyes were still potent with data, and Flora could feel it streaming into her tongue as she carried it out towards the mouse hole. As she shifted the shell of the head for better purchase, the wet heavy brain dislodged and dropped into Flora's mouth. Spasms of prayer code and images of violence pulsed in her mind at the contact, and Flora hurled the head as far as she could. She spat out the remains of the brain, then stared in horror. Sister Sage's head had caught on a spike of grass.

She flew down and tried to pull it free but every movement released more of the scent of Sage blood. Any forager would raise the alarm, any wasp would know the hive was stricken. Flora felt someone watching her and looked around in terror.

"Our priestess appears unwell."

Sir Linden sat shivering on the hive roof, no longer dapper and groomed, but dishevelled and travel-soiled. Thoracic engine sputtering, he flew down beside her.

The sight of him flooded Flora with relief — and every nerve in her body streaked with pain. She could not speak, only point down at the grass.

"Sister prefers the discretion of the dock leaves?"

Flora managed to nod. Sir Linden clasped Sister Sage's head from above as if he were mounting it. His engine sputtered dangerously as he struggled — and then he pulled the head from the stalk and dropped it down into the leaves.

"What a terrible accident befell her. How careless they can be." He settled beside Flora. She could not speak. He raised his drooping antennae.

"And what dismal air hangs over our old home — the chaps did hope for more."

Flora looked up and saw more drones clinging to the hive roof, all bravado gone. Sir Linden pulled at his ruff and she saw how he had aged.

"Would no other hive admit you?" The Sage lock still seared her tongue, so that it hurt to speak.

"Oh, we found too many. Some dead or abandoned, some with such moaning and foul smell within as makes this one fragrant as spurge — to me at any rate." Sir Linden looked at her. "Strange to say, I missed my family."

"We have missed you too — all of you." Flora gazed beyond the orchard, where bright machines moved across the nearest field and the crows wheeled above. She shook out her wings. "I — have more work to do."

"May I help?" Linden held her eyes.

Flora nodded. "If you would raise good cheer, and strong scent — for a short while . . ."

"Madam, I am ever at your service." He started his engine and flew up to his ragged cohort. "As I promised, brothers, they have missed us! Let us grace

344

them with Our Maleness once more, let us be fed and warm and wanted again!"

Cheering, he led the drones down to the landing board. Flora heard the high excited voices of sisters running out to meet them. She listened a moment, then slipped back inside to her daughter.

CHAPTER
FORTY

In the time it had taken to dispose of Sister Sage's body, Flora's baby daughter had grown again, and was now pressing against the sides of her propolis crib. Shifting her to try to make her more comfortable, Flora felt the new weight in her child's body and saw the change in her beautiful pearly skin. It had a new iridescence, and felt less fragile. She could not help herself — she lifted her up into her arms and gazed in awe at the beauty of her sleeping face — and at the way her features grew more adult and feminine even as she watched.

Flora froze at the vibration of footsteps running past the mouth of the corridor and the loud voices — and then she heard the shouts and guffaws of the drones coming in from the landing board, and the cheers and welcoming cries of the sisters. A crowd of them were gathering in the lobby, and their laughter had a hysterical edge. Flora stood with her daughter in her arms, listening carefully.

The sisters were falling over themselves to welcome the drones back. Desperate to keep them, they told them how well they were and how soon the queen was coming — and the drones were equally eager to be wanted, laughing and joking with booming bravado, telling tales of adventures in golden palaces that somehow could not compare to the pleasures of home.

Flora listened to them all thundering up the staircases to the mid-level, laughing and talking and heading for the canteens, which would surely be thrown open to welcome them back. The footsteps died away, but still she listened, wary of a trap.

Her daughter felt heavier in her arms — and when Flora looked down she gasped. She had grown larger, and her beautiful face had changed again. A slow and steady frequency travelled in waves through her child's body, and all at once Flora understood. This was not sleep, it was a trance. Her daughter was entering Holy Time.

Flora could not think what to do. It should not come this quickly — surely there were more days of feeding — but she could not remember. She could not think how many days' Flow she had given her, or what she should do now. Holy Time was sacred, there were prayers, there was ceremony — she must be covered, and at once — but now she was far too big for the propolis crib, and to seal her against the dead mouse was an abhorrent thought.

The pressure of the silence grew and Flora pulled at her antennae in desperation. Her daughter would die if she were left uncovered, and die if she were discovered. She had lost one egg to the fertility police, one to the Visitation, and now she had killed a priestess to save this child.

Flora's daughter murmured and shifted as her trance deepened. Her smell was exquisite, and Flora bent her head and breathed it in, watching in wonder as two tiny points of light appeared on the child's head where her antennae would be. The change was happening before her eyes — and Flora's every instinct told her she needed to protect her child, to cover her safely for Holy Time.

Where in the hive did it happen? She cursed herself for not finding out before. Surely she must have seen it — perhaps she had not noticed. Trying to keep calm, Flora thought of everywhere she had ever been in the hive, but she had never known of a place for Holy Time. All she knew was that when the babies were ready for it, they were moved from Category Two . . . to some unknown place, and then to Arrivals, where everyone hatched out.

It must be clean. That was what the old Teasel in the canteen had said.

Flora held her daughter tighter as she thought it through. The sanitation workers spent a large part of their time in the Arrivals Hall, cleaning out the vacated cells. For what? *Preparing them for re-use.*

All those long rows of chambers, the near ones busy with hatching, the middle ones being cleaned, and the distant ones, sealed and quiet. As every sanitation worker knew after a few days' labour, their use was rotated. Now Flora understood what the dying Teasel in the canteen had meant. There *was* no special place for Holy Time; the children simply went into a trance in Category Two, then were moved by their nurses to the

Arrivals Hall and sealed into clean chambers. The very place the fertility police would now be ripping apart in search of rogue eggs.

Flora heard the stamping of feet above, and felt the dim vibration of singing from the mid-level lobby. The drones were taking their mission of celebration seriously. Once she had saved Linden's life, and now perhaps he had saved not only hers, which she held to no account, but her beloved child's. She blessed him with all her heart, and the feeling of gratitude brought tears to her eyes. She bent to kiss her sleeping daughter's face, and to her joy, the words of the Queen's Prayer came unbidden to her mind.

If there was anything holy left in this world, Flora knew it was this love for her child, and for the Queen, her beautiful mother who had loved her, and told her not to be ashamed. While the drones and the sisters rejoiced on the floor above, Flora said the words of the Queen's Prayer in her mind, until it took over her soul.

From Death comes Life Eternal . . .

She looked up. The only other place a sister might lie undisturbed was behind this wall. It was not a dormitory, nor the Arrivals Hall. It was the morgue, and only her kin-sisters went there. While the drones still roistered above, there was time.

Flora raised her kin-scent as thick as she could, and waited behind the propolis scent-veils until the lobby was quiet. Then with her daughter still and white in her arms, she hurried out. A few bees looked at her in surprise, but she swung her head wildly and waved them away, making herself stumble.

349

"Sickness, sickness," she slurred and they shrank back in fear and ran.

The morgue was empty but for a couple of sanitation workers who nodded at her but did not speak. Flora laid her precious burden down in a shadowed corner and waited until they had gone. Her daughter was growing and changing as she watched — there was no time to lose. With all the strength of her kin and skill of her age, Flora bit through the division between two storage areas to make one large one, then used the broken wax to make a lid to cover her child. As she worked she repeated the Queen's Prayer silently in her mind until her body was warm with the labour, and her mouth sweet with Flow. Flora leaned over her entranced daughter and let the last drops fall around her face, in a glow of light. No words could hold the love she felt.

Then she sealed her.

CHAPTER
FORTY-ONE

The return of the drones lifted the hive spirits for one day, but the underlying tension between the Sage and the Teasel could not be repressed any longer. The hive became polarised, with both Sage and Teasel demanding that every kin group choose its loyalty. A priestess had gone missing — but so, shouted the Teasel loudly, had several of their senior sisters — and the lobbies filled with shouting and argument. Only the sanitation workers were ignored, for neither the Teasel nor the Sage cared about them except to make sure they cleaned properly. Flora remained with her kin-sisters despite the good foraging weather, for not only did she have a reason to visit the morgue, but she was extremely tired. For the first time in her life, she felt no desire to fly. It saddened her to see the scuffles between kin, and the deterioration of the hive condition. The beautiful central mosaics in the lobbies no longer glowed and pulsed with energy, and without the resonant frequency of the Hive Mind, the comb lost its beauty. The waiting made the bees both angry and despairing, for they had been intimidated into supporting one side or the other — but each one longed for Devotion, and heard her own mind whisper fearfully,

I will worship any Queen.

By nightfall, the bees were frantic. The dormitories were full of arguing, many bees complained they could not sleep, or did not want to sleep in proximity to sisters loyal to Teasel, or loyal to Sage, and the air was rancid with discord. Some lay in their berths wailing for Devotion, while others berated them for reminding them of the precious thing they tried to forget.

"We must be patient!" someone shouted near Flora.

"We are damned," spat someone else. "This hive is plagued —"

Uproar broke out and both the Thistle guards and the fertility police stormed in, each demanding to know who had started it. The bees cowered in silence. The guards and the police gestured to each other with extravagant and dangerous courtesy, to allow the other to be the first to leave. The Thistle allowed themselves to be the first to go, and as the police followed, they looked back into the dark dormitory, and sent a blast of their frightening scent across the bees loyal to Teasel.

No one dared speak. Gradually, the dormitory fell silent, except for those berths where some sister could not stop crying.

In the morning, many refused to rise.

"Without a queen," said one, and turned her face to the wall, "I have no will."

"No children born," said another, "no life to work for."

Flora shook a sister. "But we have each other —"

"We did." A Rosebay forager rocked herself. "Until we madden with fighting. To see such bitterness between us — I will die of heartbreak before a new queen comes."

Flora held her.

"Please, sister, do not. If the house-bees see the foragers stop flying —"

The Rosebay pushed her off.

"*You* have given up! You were one of our best — but now you cling in fear to your dustpan, too scared to fly. Your heart is broken too."

"It is not!" Flora stood up. "It is full of love, I swear it."

"Then forage!" cried a Cornflower, her wings dishevelled and dry.

"If my sisters ask me." Flora unlatched her wings. "If they will fly beside me."

The Rosebay forager sat up. She got to her feet.

"I care for my sisters. Not for politics."

The Cornflower stood too. "And I for flowers. And our hive."

"Our hive." All over the dormitory, wing-latches clicked open as other foragers rose from their berths.

On the landing board the sun shone hot and hard, and waves of sweetness poured through the air. The foragers looked at each other in amazement. In their despairing queenless state, they had almost missed the start of the spring honeyflow. Now they stood on the warming wooden ledge of the landing board, they felt the life force pull the green blades up through the soft earth, and swell the buds on the branches. Corms burst below the soil and high above it eddies of golden pollen carried on the wind.

The foragers laughed as they woke from their sorrow. The world was come to life again, and at the glorious sound of their engines starting, more sisters came running out onto the landing board. At first they too were dazed, for the grim power struggle within the hive had sapped them all of strength — but at the sight of their brave forager sisters rising up once more into a blazing blue sky, they began to cheer.

The tiredness in Flora's body was a benediction of her skill, for even as she felt her joints stiffen and her engine straining, she used all her knowledge and experience to effortlessly guide her through the currents and track the finest scents. She delighted when she discovered the first narcissus in bloom, the flower every bee longed to find for its exquisite fragrance — the somewhat bland pollen being an afterthought. Its scent filled Flora's soul with such flower-joy that she no longer felt any pain or weakness in her body — and then she foraged, with all her skill and power. She found crocus and daffodil and then pale-green hebe flowers, their startling pink pollen grains plump and moist like tiny berries. She filled up her panniers, she filled her crop, and a thousand fluorescent petals and patterns returned to her mind. She was deep in the apple blossom with the Holy Chord all round her, when she felt the jolt in her body.

That slow steady frequency, hidden in her own pulse so long she had ceased to notice it, abruptly stopped. She whirled around as if the hive had called her.

Her daughter had woken.

CHAPTER
FORTY-TWO

There were no Thistle on the landing board nor bees in the lobby, but the signal of alarm came thick from the top of the staircases. Wings unlatched, not caring who saw her, Flora ran straight into the morgue.

She could smell her daughter's strong scent, even as her brain registered that it had changed. Big jagged shards of wax littered the floor but there was no blood, nor trace of either fertility police or Thistle guards. A surge of raised voices came through the comb from above, and with it the vibration of thousands of sisters' feet, running across the mid-level lobby. Then came a savage sharp piping sound, travelling through the comb as if carried on the Hive Mind. A few seconds later, an answering burst of piping fired its own frequency through the comb, and the two sound waves clashing in dissonance made bees all over the hive cry out in fear.

So frightened for her child she could barely breathe, Flora ran up the main staircase. The scent of battle grew thicker the higher she went, blocking out every scent but that of the Teasel war-gland, against Sage.

Terrified sisters clung to each other in the corridors to the mid-level lobby and the scent of venom filled the air. Flora pushed her way through their shuddering bodies towards the dense wall of bees surrounding the central space. She pressed forward, squeezing her way through the wings and bodies, the only thought in her mind to stand by her daughter's side to the death —

Thistle guards grabbed her to stop her going further.

In front of her in the centre of the lobby, two huge princesses crouched opposite each other. Each was twice the size of every other sister, and behind them stood a dense wall of their own kin: the Sage and the Teasel. Every bee in the chamber was silent — except for the low hissing of the Teasel princess.

She was yellow-furred, her face flat and brindled and her bands bright brown. Flora could see the shining wet tip of her dagger as she slowly moved her abdomen from side to side and sank down lower, gathering her power. A snarl built in her throat, a low echo coming from the throats of her supporters.

The Sage princess began to draw herself up from her own crouch, until she stood at her full towering height. She rasped her wings down her back so the sound filled the air, then she slowly swayed her long pointed face from side to side, her eyes sending sparks of hate at the wall of Teasel supporters. As she began to hiss, the Teasel princess gathered herself to spring.

With a lightning motion, the Sage princess leapt to the ceiling and crumbs of wax fell down where her sharp powerful claws dug in. The startled Teasel princess looked up, her poise broken. The Sage princess picked her way across the ceiling, her venom spraying down.

The Teasel princess moved faster, and watched as the wax sizzled where she had stood. She drew her huge claws.

"She flees!" Her voice was hoarse and loud. Then she drew her dagger, longer and thicker than any Flora had ever seen, with four lines of barbs instead of two. "A coward may not be Queen," she called up to her rival.

"Nor may a fool —" The Sage princess dropped from the ceiling onto the Teasel's back, biting at her wings. The Teasel twisted round and threw her off, but the Sage princess's claw had caught, and the bees heard the ripping wound. Too fast to give her rival a chance to leap for the ceiling again, the Teasel princess clamped her wings tight to her back and attacked so hard the bees heard their shells clash and smelled their poisons mingling as they hissed and struggled against each other on the comb floor. Their abdomens curved hard as their daggers stabbed at the other's body and the two princesses thrashed in a blur of rage — then there was a harsh scream and the struggle slowed.

The bees stared as the two princesses lay still. With the sound of cracking limbs the Sage princess broke free of the dying embrace of her foe. Her dagger dripped venom, and the Teasel convulsed on the ground before her, stung through the belly.

Even now the Sage supporters did not move or make a sound, but the Teasel gasped as their mortally wounded princess struggled to rise. The Sage princess bent low and ripped the wings from her back. She held them up, then threw them on the ground.

358

"Behold the fate of pretenders!" She turned back to her foe. The Teasel princess tried to pull herself along the comb towards her stricken supporters. The Sage princess walked in front of her. She climbed upon her rival's twitching body and held her fast, before flexing her abdomen high so all the bees could see her shining dagger. Then she slid it between the Teasel princess's head and thorax, and stung her again.

Only now did the Sage raise their voices, in a strange humming ululation that pierced the bees' brains and made their stings pulse in terror.

"*Behold the Queen!*" The Sage priestesses surrounded their champion.

"*The Queen is dead — long live the Queen!*"

Flora stood transfixed. All around her she felt the gathering tension in her sisters, as if they would spring or scream or turn on each other.

"*The Queen is dead!*" repeated the Sage in their choral voice. "*Long live the Queen!*"

At these words the Sage princess raised her wings and spread them, and her face was beautiful and terrible. At her gaze, many bees sank to their knees, shaking in fear.

"We have others . . ." A weeping Teasel crouched by the body of her dead princess. "We have more princesses, we will bring them out as fast as they are born —"

The Sage princess hissed and drew her sting again.

"And I will kill them as I killed my own royal sisters, cowering unready in their queen cells. Divine Right to the first-born — death to the rest. I am your Queen and you will worship —"

A single piercing note tore the air. The Sage princess and every other bee spun round to face the source of the sound. Then the Sage princess piped back in outrage and lashed her antennae, but there was no answering sound. The bees froze in fear and listened. The sound had come from the long corridor that led to the worker dormitories and the Queen's chambers, but now there was complete silence.

"Come out!" screamed the Sage princess. "You foul Teasel pretender, come out and die like your sister here!" She piped again and again, until the lobby echoed and the bees shrank together in terror. "You are a coward! Come out!"

"I am here."

Then every bee's glands flared in fright, for from the dark dormitory corridor walked a huge black princess with russet fur, long quivering antennae, a tiny waist, and the strong hooks and limbs of her mother, Flora 717.

"I am the last princess." Her low voice carried. "And I have already wet my dagger with the blood of all others. But one."

The Sage princess slowly twisted her head from side to side, and began to hiss again.

"What foul thing are you?"

"She is my daughter." Flora stepped forward, her heart thundering in her body. "And I raised her as a princess, fed on Flow, like you."

The Sage princess stared, then she laughed in great hisses. "Kneel," she said. "Bare your neck for a merciful death."

360

When Flora's daughter did not answer, the Sage princess piped her rage.

"Answer your Queen!"

"No queen until mated!" Flora called it loudly. Behind her, the floras gathered together, and their dark faces gleamed bronze as they let their scent rise up.

"How dare you —" As the Sage turned to Flora the dark princess ran at her. Fleet and vicious, her pale rival spun round with a slicing claw, but Flora's daughter parried with her own massive hooks. Lacking the strength to fend off the blows, the Sage princess ran up the lobby wall again to attack from above — but Flora's daughter followed her, her massive hooks tearing tendrils of wax from the walls, dagger gleaming. With a shriek of rage the Sage princess flew down into the midst of the watching bees, making them scream in terror and crush each other as they struggled to get out of her way — and then she ran through them into the empty Category Two ward.

The fertility police beat the sanitation workers to the ground in front of their champion so that she would have to trample them to reach her foe — but the dark princess leapt at the wall and ran sideways above them, so that her wing brushed across the officers' faces and made them cry out in fear.

When she ran into the big dark Category Two ward there was no sight or sound of the Sage princess, but the air was misted with her venom. For a moment there was silence — and then with a terrible shriek she dropped from the ceiling above and stabbed at the dark princess with the full length of her sting, so that the two huge princesses hurled their joined body in rage against the cribs and the wax cracked and split around them.

Terrified at the combat and desperate to see its end, the bees followed, climbing over each other to escape the two roiling princesses as they slashed and bit and half-flew, half-staggered between the rows of cribs, neither one willing to release her hold. As the dark princess reached out to swing a shield of wax against her rival's head, the Sage princess let herself fall, so that her heavier foe lost her balance. With lightning speed she twisted and leapt on top of Flora's daughter, seizing her antennae and piping her screaming war-note directly into them to destroy her brain. The high harsh sound paralysed every bee but the Sage, and thousands screamed out in pain. The dark princess jerked her head in agony but could not release herself.

"*Submit and save them!*" the Sage princess piped louder, and bees screamed for mercy. "*You make them suffer —*"

A huge roar tore the air, its force blocking out the piping agony and sending a hard vibration through the comb. It came from the engine of the dark princess as she beat her wings against her rival and threw her back. Before the stunned Sage princess could rise, Flora's daughter was upon her, crushing her under her weight. Then she reared up, her dagger poised for the coup de grâce — but did not strike. Instead, her antennae pointed high.

In the sudden silence, every bee smelled the foreign scent. Their fur stood high with fear and their antennae pulsed. Wasps were in the hive.

362

The Sage princess sprang free, a gaping wound in her thorax. The priestesses dragged her to safety behind their bodies.

"She lives!" they shouted. "Behold the true queen; kill the pretender!"

"First the wasps!" roared the Thistle and the bees cried out for action, for by the high formic tang in the air, their enemy had entered in large numbers.

"First the true Queen!" shouted another of the priestesses. "Declare the rightful Queen then we shall win —"

"No! Defend the Treasury!"

"Fight the wasps!"

Panic streamed in the air and all was chaos. The Sage gathered their princess into their midst and ran through into the Category One ward. Bees milled in all directions, not knowing what to do. The Teasel stood helplessly, stunned at the ruins of the Nursery. Flora ran to her daughter and pulled her by her wet fur.

"Come —" she said to her. "Food — then you will strengthen — please, daughter —"

The smell of the wasps grew stronger — they were coming from the bottom storey, their numbers swelling. Flora grabbed a Thistle guard.

"Help me," she cried. "The princess needs food to lead us — break open the Treasury and I will bring her —"

The sibilant voices of the wasps were coming up the stairs. Soon they would be in the mid-level. The Thistle nodded. She signalled her sister guards, and then, readying their big claws, they ran quietly to reach the Treasury before the invaders.

"For the sake of your hive, come with me." Flora pulled her daughter by the wing and they ran. Terrified bees followed them, crying and weeping as they smelled the wasps pillaging the bottom level of the hive, their foul jests echoing in the Dance Hall. Her own mouth dry with fear, Flora dragged her daughter into the Treasury. She knew what they must do but she could not speak.

Rip them all open — and drink. It was the Hive Mind, and the bees heard. They climbed the walls and clawed and gouged open all the newly sealed honey vaults. At the scent, Flora's daughter ran to drink and immediately her scent flowed more strongly. She raised her head, then pressed her abdomen into the comb, and buzzed against it. The sound reverberated through the Treasury and ran through the wax. In the mid-storey below, the wasps shrieked in recognition of their prey above, and ran to find them.

"Let the honey flow!" Flora shouted. "Let it pour across the comb — everyone into the corridor — there is a way!" She ran into the corridor, searching for the hidden staircase that led to the morgue. Behind her the Thistle yelled as they ripped open the vaults, the precious liquid wealth beginning to seep down the walls and onto the floor.

"Holy Mother forgive us —" cried the guards as they broke open more vaults, and the air filled with the cured fragrance of a million flowers.

364

"More!" cried Flora. "Use it all —" She pulled her daughter behind her as the thick golden tide of honey flowed over the wax and into the surge of wasps rushing up to meet it. They hissed and screamed as they were caught in their hearts' desire, and were trampled by the greed of the coming horde behind. They screamed as their wings stuck and their legs broke, but their sisters did not care as they ran over their drowning bodies, screeching for joy that they had breached the bees' Treasury.

Flora's daughter ran behind her down the steep dark staircase, a weight of bees behind them. Every few steps she buzzed her abdomen hard against the comb walls as if she would break them. Flora feared she was mad but then knew it for a rallying call, for as they emerged through the morgue the bottom storey of the hive was packed with thousands of sisters fighting the intruding force of wasps.

With a roaring battle cry, Flora's daughter threw herself into the fray, slashing forward, tearing heads from bodies and killing all she could so that the wasps began screaming in fear and retreating. Behind her the bees roared in rage and triumph, breathing in her scent for courage and pushing forward to rout the wasps until none were left alive inside the hive and those few who survived fled the landing board.

Stunned by the vastness of the orchard world, Flora's daughter staggered in the dazzling bright air. She lost control of her antennae and her panic streamed. She tried to push her way back inside from the landing

365

board, but it was too crowded, for she had rallied all the bees who would come to follow her.

"The Sage have led the victory!" A priestess ran out onto the board, her wings ripped, one antenna broken. "Our princess lives — come back to crown her. And as for your kin —" she spat at Flora and her daughter. "Death is your fate. The one true Queen survives!"

Looking out beyond the orchard, Flora did not answer. In the distance, a huge dark veil rose and fell in the blue air. The high whine of the wasp army grew louder, and the black veil drew together, building its power as it approached.

"They have joined many colonies together." Feeling her daughter's fear beside her, Flora forced her voice to stay strong as she spoke to the priestess. "We cannot fight them, we must save ourselves —"

"Flee like cowards?" The priestess's eyes were wild. "The Sage will triumph — with Divine Right!"

Flora grabbed the priestess and shook her. "Do you not understand yet? Our hive is lost and all who stay will perish! It is too late!"

"You address the Melissae, invincible kin of queens!" The priestess shook herself free and ran back inside. "Strength in Sage!" she screamed. "Come now, the devout, and stand together!"

"You call them to their deaths!" Flora shouted after her. But when she turned to her daughter, and the massed kins crowding out onto the landing board, her heart failed her. The black cloud spread wider across the sky and the buzzing of the wasps filled their minds.

The pressure of bees fleeing from within the hive forced more and more of them out onto the landing board, and those nearest the edge were pushed off so that they whirled in terror above the hive. Too hoarse to speak, Flora tried to bite and push her daughter off the edge, but she was too strong and paralysed by the height of the sky and the oncoming wasps.

Some of the drones came crashing out of the hive, battered and bloody, some burned with wasp venom on their feet. Flora grabbed her daughter's antennae and twined them with her own. As Lily 500 had once done to her, with an intense burst of concentration she forced all her knowledge into her daughter's mind.

LEAD YOUR PEOPLE! she thought to her, with all her strength. She felt her daughter's antennae pulsing in pain but she did not let go. *SAVE THEM NOW!*

"How?" her daughter cried out. "I do not know —" But even as she spoke her engine thundered to life, its sound ripping the sky and tearing aside the sound of the oncoming army. Her massive copper wings hummed to power and her scent streamed behind her like a cloak. Roaring their engines, the orchard bees launched themselves up behind her, a soaring army rising into the air, blood and honey on their feet, war on their wings.

Flora hurled herself up beside her daughter, guiding her higher and higher up to the colder air where the wasps would not fly. The huge buzzing army passed beneath them, and the bees could smell the sugar they had fed on, which drove the rage of their attack.

You will bring disaster on your hive.

Flora watched in horror as the black cloud descended on the queenless hive, sweet with honey and defended only by the prayers of the remaining Sage.

CHAPTER
FORTY-THREE

The dark swirling cloud of fleeing orchard bees lifted in the wind, blank arable fields spinning below them. Flora saw that their mass grew thinner and they spread wider across the sky, for without a dance to follow, none of the foragers had a clear destination and so reverted to what they knew — scouting for the best scent of nectar. Behind them the loosening cloud of house-bees struggled to stay close to Flora's daughter, but some began to break away to follow leading foragers, others began to lag behind, and the whole swarm threatened to disperse. If they flew on directionless they would tire, the birds would take them, they would scatter and all would be lost. Flora fought her way into the wind and mass of wing-beats to find her daughter's scent.

She was a most majestic young creature, her dark bands sparkling, russet fur lit up and her broad face strange and terrifying. Flora tried to signal to her to go lower, but the princess was carried higher on the current she had found. Flora smelled what she followed — it was hyacinth, and it came from the town.

"No — we must not go there!" cried Flora in alarm. "There is no shelter —"

But the fragrance grew stronger, and other bees smelled it too. All at once the swarm was possessed by hunger; their crops were empty and light and their minds dizzy. There was nothing Flora could do but fly with her daughter. As the swarm began its descent, she located the flowers in the middle of a shopping plaza busy with people. Uniformed gardeners pulled the hyacinth plants from the soil of big concrete tubs, and threw them into the back of a truck.

People began screaming as the swarm came down from the sky. They ran for safety as the bees spread out and searched the half-dead flowers, but their scent was empty promise, for they were bred for show not pollen. Angry and disappointed, the bees buzzed helplessly above the truck.

"You must stop," Flora begged her daughter. "If you settle, so will they, and then we can think. Darling child, I beg you."

The dark princess slowed her wing-beats and fell behind her mother. Not knowing what else to do, Flora landed on some warm metal that smelled benign. Her daughter fluttered down beside her and clung to her, shaking with adrenaline.

Even in this exposure and fear, it was bliss to press her child close to her, this huge princess who held their lives in hers. The air shimmered with wings as eight thousand sisters gathered together as they had done in the Cluster, many drones amongst them too, for without their sisters they would die. Hanging from the hand of the statue, like a dark sack of treasure, the colony pulled close together around their princess.

Once more Flora pressed her antennae close to her daughter's.

"If we stay here, we will die."

Her daughter looked at her with huge innocent eyes, and Flora knew that she was stunned from her fight, and her emergence. She could not lead, she was too young.

"Madam, can we help?" Sanitation workers squeezed beside them, their eyes bright and antennae high. "Tell us how."

"I do not know." Flora tried not to cry.

Madness. Sister against sister. Disaster.

"Madam Forager, you must." One of them leaned forward to her. "You have fought wasps, and served the Queen. You have laid an egg for our kin, and spent the night outside the hive without dying!"

It was true. Flora's antennae surged with memories. The tree in the forest. The Queen's Library. *The last panel, the comet from the cradle.* Not a star in the sky, but a swarm from the hive — the hive was the cradle, and the swarm its one true child that she must nurse to safety.

"Quickly," she said to them. "Who is strong? Who can dance?"

Two came forward, their gaze dark and direct.

"All of us, Madam. We learned, in the Cluster."

"Then follow." Flora began to dance on the back of the mass of bees, as if they were the comb floor of the Dance Hall. "You must learn this exact direction if you would save us." She checked the position of the sun, then began dancing out the steps to the hollow tree, and the line of hills, and its scent of *beech, hollow beech*, until she felt the rhythm repeated back by the two flora dancers, exact and precise. Bees below them shifted and cried out in agitation, but Flora's pupils danced on, using their feet to spread the rhythm and the information to every bee they touched. Only when Flora felt the rhythm catch in other parts of the swarm did she go back to her daughter.

The dark princess's face had changed again. It was older, more beautiful, and more knowing.

"I am not a queen," she said to her mother, "until I mate."

"First we must find safety," Flora said. "I know where we must go." She could feel vibrations going through the hanging swarm, stronger and wider as hundreds then thousands of bees were stirring to the news. She wanted to ask the foragers to keep the swarm contained — but it was hard to look away from her daughter. Then she smelled Linden close by.

"Ever at your service, Madam." He stood by her side, old and ragged and beloved to her eyes.

Flora's heart fell from the sky. "I did not call you."

"No." The dark princess looked at him. "*I* did."

Linden stared at her. Then his whole face and body changed. Before Flora's eyes he grew young and handsome, and his scent flushed strong.

"Choose another . . ." Flora whispered to her daughter. "Please, there are others —"

"But he is best," her daughter said. "That is why you love him." She started her engine, and with thunderous roaring of the Holy Chord, the dark comet of the swarm lifted into the air, the true child of the hive.

Up it went, over the grey and red blocks of the town and its tiny patchwork of gardens. No longer dull and dark inside the hive, the gleaming bronze floras had spread the message fast, for many knew the way and flew as outriders, keeping the swarm tight to contain it. Flora kept up beside her daughter, the wind streaming fast and loud around them so that she could not beg again that her old friend be spared.

Linden flew close by them, and she looked at him one last time. Intent in readiness to fulfil his life's sole purpose, Linden's gaze was locked on her beautiful daughter and he saw nothing else. He let his scent flow strong and high, and other drones smelled it too, and raised their own pheromones in banners of lust. Excitement spread through the swarm, and the sound of its passage grew loud above the fields. Flora gazed on her dazzling daughter, her face no longer strange, but a new epitome of beauty.

They were over the fields and the hills were in sight. Flora's body was tiring, but they were nearly there. Then her daughter glanced around, and looked directly at Linden. A sweet musk spread behind her, and with a burst of speed she broke through to the front of the swarm. Flora heard the sharp rise in the high timbre of Linden's thoracic engine as he raced in pursuit of her daughter, a cloud of his scent blowing over her. The princess rose up above the swarm where all could see her, and circled to spread her scent and let every drone smell it.

Her cuticle glittered blue-black in the sun, her russet fur glowed bright red, and her wings beat bronze and gold sparks from the air. Flora drew on all her power to keep up and watch, admiring her daughter's strong young legs folded tight beneath her, and her elegant thorax. She could not see Linden — and then her daughter roared in surprise as he came upon her from above, seizing her with a new strength.

At his intimate grasp the princess soared higher above the swarm, his body fused tight against her for all to see.

The swarm chased below them, as faster and faster the princess fled the drone on her back, until with a cry of ecstasy he flung himself away from her.

"It is done!" Flora cried out. "*It is done* —" She watched the tiny speck of Linden's body spinning down towards the fields. She tore her eyes away and back to her daughter, whirling high to spread her mated scent across the air. The bees breathed it and cheered as a cordon of flora ladies-in-waiting rose up to escort their princess back down to the safety of the swarm, Linden's organ hanging as proof from her body.

She is mated!

The princess is mated!

The Queen is mated!

The joyful cries gathered the swarm together, tightening all the sisters as they rushed to breathe the stunning sexual perfume of their powerful new Queen. Other drones raced to try to catch her too, but the new

Queen was not to be caught again without consent, and she sped ahead, the swarm behind her.

Flora drew on all her strength to keep up with her mated daughter, but the swarm was young and fast, and she could only hold on to the tail of it as they flew.

The blank fields fell back and the forest came closer. She could no longer feel her body, and used all her strength to remember the destination.

The hollow tree. The forest.

A ragged silver-winged forager emerged from the air and flew beside her.

"You danced well. You have served your hive." Lily 500 smiled at Flora. *Praise end your days.*

Praise end your days, Flora thought back to her, and the words were sweet.

Her wing-beats slowed and the swarm moved on without her. She saw them enter the forest on the edge of the Weald. She smelled the warming earth, and the deep fragrance of the trees, and it was easy to follow the swarm by the musk of the mated Queen's scent, and the Holy Chord rising from the forest. Below her on the ground tiny blue speedwell flowers opened their little mouths as they felt the bees passing, and the air was laced with fragrance.

Flora's vision sharpened. Her body slowed and weakened, yet still she watched in eagerness as the swarm searched through the trees. She heard the sanitation workers calling out to each other, repeating her coordinates as they drew closer and closer — and then there was a shout and huge cheering, for they had found the hollow beech.

Oh, my daughter, my fierce beloved daughter . . .

The dark and glorious new queen flew down and settled on a branch. While scouts went in to check the tree, thousands of bees hovered around her as they waited, humming the Holy Chord. Some settled beside her and began to lick the sperm from her body, and the strong scent of the kin of Flora mingled with the sweetness of the kin of Linden and floated up through the leaves of the forest.

The scouts re-emerged, and began to lay their homecoming marker on the lip of the hole in the tree. The bees cried out in joy, to the forest and the sky, *Long live the Queen! Long live the Queen!* Again and again they cheered, and Flora wanted to join with it but all she could do was gaze on the newly crowned Queen, her heart filled with love. She watched the new flora ladies-in-waiting kiss and lick her, and then they escorted her into her new home.

A new Devotion drifted through the forest, the scent of a wild dark young Queen, strong and fertile. The sound of sisters rejoicing stirred the leaves and drew nectar from the flowers. Bees streamed down from the bright air into the dark fissure in the beech tree.

Flora could no longer move, but she smelled speedwell, and bluebells, and cyclamen, and felt the cool smooth leaves of aconite holding her body. She wrapped herself in the rich perfume of the forest floor and watched until the last bee flew into the tree. Then she rested.

Epilogue

The apple trees were in full bloom as the man, his wife and their two teenage children came through the orchard. They paused near the old hive. The man let a long coil of black ribbon unspool from his hand.

"So, this is a condition of Grandpa's will. It's from the olden days, when people thought the bees needed to be told important family news. Births, deaths and marriages." The man unfolded a piece of paper. "He even wrote it all out."

Then he stepped forward to the hive and tied the black ribbon around it, before knocking on it softly, three times.

"It is my sad duty to inform you," he read, "that your beekeeper, my father, has died. He will no longer be taking care of you, and he asks you to be patient with your new custodian."

The tone in his voice made his wife put her arms round him. He held her as he folded the paper back in his pocket, then addressed the hive again.

"And I have something else to say, for myself. I am very sorry that I have sold this orchard, and — I ask your forgiveness for what will happen." He wiped his eyes.

"Dad." His daughter crouched down and put her ear against the hive. "Listen . . ."

"Careful!" But he too crouched down and put his ear to the wood. They looked at each other. Then he moved round and looked into the hole on the landing board. His wife drew back.

"Please, both of you —"

"I can't hear a thing," he said. "I cannot see a single bee."

His son smiled. "Dad! They went with him!"

The family looked up into the bright and empty sky.

Acknowledgements

For making it happen: my agents Simon Trewin in London and Dorian Karchmar in New York — thank you both so much.

For making it better: my editor Lee Boudreaux — an education and a pleasure to work with you; my thanks also to Clare Reihill for her insight, and to Iris Tupholme for her support.

My thanks to all the teams at Ecco, 4th Estate and HarperCollins Canada, and to my foreign rights agent at WME, Annemarie Blumenhagen. For the two superb covers: Steve Attardo and Alison Saltzman for Ecco, and Jo Walker for 4th Estate.

For good fellowship: Richard Skinner and the Faber group of 2012, with honorable mention to the most generous polymath that is Cal Moriarty.

For sharing her knowledge and guiding my research, Dr Margaret Couvillon; I am also indebted to the work of biologists Dr Francis Ratnieks, Dr Thomas Seeley, and Bert Holldobler & E.O. Wilson. All mistakes are my own.

For support in many forms: Isabelle Grey, Heidi Berry, Kate Duthie, Sasha Slorer, Debs Shuter,

Deborah Gonzalez, Maggie Doherty, Linda King, Emmy Minton, Megan and Danis Dauksta, Janet Lyon, Emerald-Jane Turner, Sarah Kowitz; and for his words "dronewood" and "dronesong", Sean Borodale.

For lighting my path: Professor Julia Briggs and beekeeper Angie Biltcliffe.

Love and thanks to my family, including early reader Gordon Paull; early listener Rider Peacock (who advised more violence); Jackson Peacock (for his sketch of the hive) and most of all to my daughter India Rose, for all the ways in which she has enabled me to write this book.

Finally, my love and gratitude to my husband Adrian Peacock: for everything.

Other titles published by Ulverscroft:

THE DEATH'S HEAD CHESS CLUB

John Donoghue

SS-Obersturmfuhrer Paul Meissner arrives at Auschwitz fresh from fighting on the Russian Front. After being badly wounded, he is fit only for administrative duty, his first and most pressing task being to improve flagging camp morale among the officers and enlisted men. So he sets up a chess club, which thrives as under-the-table bets are made on the results of the games. Meissner learns that chess is also played by the prisoners and is intrigued by the rumour of a Jewish watchmaker, Emil Clement, who is "unbeatable". When Meissner's superiors demand that he demonstrate German superiority by pitting this undefeated Jew against the best Nazi players, an unusual friendship is formed. And as more and more games are played, the stakes rise, and the two men find their fates deeply entwined.

THE ROOM

Jonas Karlsson and Neil Smith

The Authority looks favourably upon meticulousness, efficiency and ambition. Bjorn has all of this in spades, but it's only in the room that he can really shine. And it's only in the room that he finds harmony, an escape from the triviality of the workplace. Unfortunately, his colleagues see things differently. In fact, they don't appear to see the room at all — eventually leaving Bjorn convinced that they are conducting some sort of psychological warfare against him. But who is right? Is the room a figment of an overactive imagination, the spectre of a mental illness? Or is there something more mysterious going on?

LOVE, LOVE ME DO

Mark Haysom

1963. The year the Beatles first top the charts. The year Martin Luther King has a dream. The year Truman Bird moves his family from their home in Brighton to a dilapidated caravan in the Ashdown Forest — then disappears.

Truman's a charmer, a chancer, a liar. He's always got away with it, too. But now he's gone a dangerous step too far and only has one day to put things right. For Truman's wife, Christie, life has not turned out the way she'd imagined. How has she, that young girl of not that many years ago, ended up like this? In a caravan. With three children. And an absent husband.

Even though life has a habit of getting in the way of dreams, people find their own extraordinary ways of bouncing back.

CROOKED HEART

Lissa Evans

When Noel Bostock — aged ten, no family — is evacuated from London to escape the Blitz, he ends up living in St Albans with Vera Sedge — thirty-six and drowning in debts and dependants. Always desperate for money, she's unscrupulous about how she gets it. The war's thrown up new opportunities for this, but what Vee needs (and what she's never had) is a cool head and the ability to make a plan. On her own, she's a disaster. With Noel, she's a team. Together they cook up an idea. Criss-crossing the bombed suburbs of London, Vee starts to make a profit, and Noel begins to regain his interest in life. But there are plenty of other people making money out of the war, and some of them are dangerous . . .

EVERYTHING I NEVER TOLD YOU

Celeste NG

Lydia was the favourite child of Marilyn and James Lee. Her parents had been determined that she would fulfil the dreams they were unable to pursue themselves, though she had also been under pressures that had nothing to do with growing up. Her father is an American born of first-generation Chinese immigrants, which makes him and his children conspicuous in any setting, especially in 1970s small-town Ohio. When Lydia's body is found in the local lake, James is consumed by guilt, while Marilyn is determined to make someone accountable, no matter what the cost. Lydia's older brother, Nathan, is convinced that local bad boy Jack is somehow involved. But it's the youngest in the family, Hannah, who observes far more than anyone realises, and who may be the only one who knows what really happened . . .

INDIAN SUMMER

Marcia Willett

For renowned actor Mungo, his quiet home village in Devon provides the perfect retreat. Close by are his brother and his wife, and the rural location makes his home the ideal getaway for his old friends in London. Among those is Kit, who comes to stay for the summer, bringing with her a letter from her first and only love, Jake, as well as a heart in turmoil. Years have passed since Kit and Jake last saw each other, and now he has written to Kit asking to meet again. As the summer unfolds, secrets are uncovered that will shatter the sleepy community, and even tear a family apart. But those involved soon realize that the only way to move forward might be to confront the past . . .